P9-AGV-050

The Legacy of

Linden Press/Simon & Schuster · New York · 1986

LADYSMITH

A NOVEL BY

JOHN KENNY CRANE

...es, characters, places, and incidents either ...gination or are used fictitiously. Any resemblance to actual events or locales or persons, living or dead, is entirely coincidental.

Published by Linden Press/Simon & Schuster
A division of Simon & Schuster, Inc.
Simon & Schuster Building
Rockefeller Center
1230 Avenue of the Americas
New York, New York 10020
LINDEN PRESS/SIMON & SCHUSTER and colophon are trademarks of
Simon & Schuster, Inc.
Designed by Eve Metz
Manufactured in the United States of America

10 9 8 7 6 5 4 3 2 1

Library of Congress Cataloging-in-Publication Data
Crane, John Kenny, date
The legacy of Ladysmith.

1. South African War, 1899–1902—Fiction.
2. Ladysmith (South Africa)—Siege, 1899—Fiction.
I. Title.
PS3553.R272L4 1986 813'.54 85-23180
ISBN: 0-671-60586-0

. . . In a short while
the generations of living creatures
are changed
and like runners
relay the torch of life.
—Lucretius

To My Parents
JOHN and DOROTHY
Who Passed That Torch to Me

and

To My Sons
KENNETH and SCOTT
To Whom I Have Passed It

Contents

PREFACE

In the interest of a unified South Africa, and also with an eye on its huge mineral wealth, Great Britain in 1877 annexed the Transvaal, till then an independent nation of Dutch-French farmers called Boers. Resentful of this appropriation of their homeland, the Boers rebelled and defeated the British forces in 1881 at the Battle of Majuba Hill, and so ended, for the time being, the British presence. For nearly two decades to come, then, what we know today as the Republic of South Africa was divided into four parts: two British colonies (the Cape Colony and Natal) and two independent Boer states (the Orange Free State and the Transvaal). It was well known, however, that because of the diamonds and gold they contained, the Boer nations were the prizes of the region, and the desire to incorporate them into the British Empire never died.

In the early 1890s, when Cecil Rhodes became Prime Minister of the Cape Colony, he began to develop the issue he felt the British could use to renew their endeavor to take control of the Transvaal and the Orange Free State. Because of the great amount of mining done in those two countries, particularly at the huge gold mine called the Witwatersrand (or, simply, the Rand) near Johannesburg, an enormous portion of the population consisted of European miners and engineers, called Uitlanders. Under policies of the Transvaal government of Paul Kruger, these outsiders had no voting rights despite their numbers, and Rhodes tried to fan their anger to the heat of open rebellion. In the last week of 1895, wrongly assuming that the Uitlanders would rebel against Kruger if given the opportunity, Rhodes sent a small force under the command of Leander Starr Jameson, a British soldier of fortune, to invade the Transvaal, draw off the defenses of Johannesburg, and allow the Uitlanders to take control. The Uitlanders did not respond, and the Jameson Raid went down as still another atrocity committed by the British against the Boers.

With German assistance, the Boers commenced to arm themselves for what they now saw as an inevitable conflict. Under the constant pressure of Alfred Milner, now Governor of the Cape Colony, and impelled by the greed of Cecil Rhodes, the British Government made repeated demands upon the Boers in the name of the British Uitlanders (whose ongoing allegiance to the Crown was faint at best). Cornered, the Boers invaded Natal on October 11, 1899, and thus began what history has called the Second South African War, known more familiarly as the Boer War. The British had sought this invasion as an excuse to retaliate and conquer the Transvaal and the Orange Free State, now in military alliance, once and for all.

But the British had miscalculated. They had forced the Boer invasion before they could transport sufficient numbers of fighting men to South Africa. Their grand plan for conquest thus had to be delayed for nearly six months while the troops who finally did arrive set themselves to relieve three British towns to which the Boers had laid siege: the great diamond town called Kimberley and the two small military installations at Mafeking and Ladysmith.

The Boer War, then, falls into four distinct stages. The first involved the relief of the three towns: Kimberley and Ladysmith by late February, 1900, and Mafeking in May. Then came the second, or "marching to Pretoria," phase, in which the British armies under Lords Roberts and Kitchener captured both Johannesburg and Pretoria by early June, 1900. At this point the war was presumed won, and Roberts returned to England, leaving the infamous Kitchener to mop up. And so began the third phase, in which the remaining Boer soldiers, actually just ununiformed farmers on horseback, turned from organized warfare to guerrilla activities, ripping up railways and communication lines and making sneak attacks against British military units. These forays continued unabated until well into 1901, at which point Kitchener devised the scheme that would ultimately bring the Boers to their knees. This plan, carried out as follows, was the essence of the fourth phase: All women and children of Boer families whose men continued to resist were incarcerated in concentration camps (where large numbers of them perished), their farms were burned, and the men themselves were rounded up and confined with the help of thousands of miles of barbed wire which Kitchener ordered strung through the Transvaal and the Free State. The barbed-wire lines were manned by soldiers who guarded them in blockhouses positioned, incredibly, one mile apart down the entire length of the longest fence ever constructed. The Boer spirit of resistance was finally broken, and the peace treaty signed at Vereeniging on May 31, 1902, officially ended the conflict. More than ten thousand British and Boer soldiers, plus uncounted civilians, had died to complete Milner and Rhodes's grand design.

The present story deals in part with the early event in the war now known as the Great Siege of Ladysmith. Outnumbered and insufficiently equipped for the war their leaders had sought, the British forces already in northern Natal, together with the British civilians who lived there, had fallen back on the garrison town of Ladysmith in flight from the Boer invasion of October, 1899. They got no farther, however, and on November 2, the Boer commandos surrounded the town, took possession of all the hilltops that ringed it, and laid siege for four months until General Buller's relief force finally broke through on February 28, 1900. During those 120 days, food ran short, water went bad, and disease set in, and before the siege was ended the death rate had reached thirty a day. In the distance the besieged could hear General Buller's guns pounding the Boer forces which refused to let him cross the Tugela River. By day they read his heliographic messages of encouragement, and by night they learned the next day's strategy by decoding his searchlight messages on the clouds above them.

Why did it take a large, well-equipped imperial army four months to batter through a thin line of Boer farmers with German rifles? Why did this same army ignominiously lose virtually every important battle it fought to relieve Ladysmith—Colenso in December, Spion Kop in January, Vaal Krantz in February—before breaking through at Pieter's Hill on February 27? Many have blamed General Buller and called him incompetent. Others have cited the dominance of Boer patriots over British mercenaries, of spirit over skill. Still others believe Buller was sabotaged, that somehow his plans were always known in advance. The correct answer is probably a fusion of all three opinions, though the last remains the most intriguing.

For the people trapped inside Ladysmith, there was little to do but wait. As the long summer days passed, they became more diseased, more angry, and more desperate by the hour. The

Scottish doctor with whom the present tale greatly concerns itself, however, used his time in a very different manner from almost everyone else.

Though a handful of characters who step on stage during the course of this story are real—specifically the Boer generals Louis Botha and Piet Cronje—this is a fictional tale. Neither Jason Glass nor Roberts Menzies ever existed, nor did anyone with whom they associate. Many Scotsmen have names such as Menzies or Macgregor or Oliphant, but all use of those names in this story is fictional, and no connection of these characters with real people similarly surnamed is implied or intended.

THE BOER WAR

October 11, 1899–May 31, 1902

A List of Significant Dates

1870	First Diamond Rush to Kimberley
February 27, 1881	Battle of Majuba Hill: Conclusion of the "First Boer War"
1886	First Gold Rush to Witwatersrand
December 29, 1895	Jameson Raid
October 11, 1899	Boer Invasion of Natal
October 20, 1899	Battle of Talana Hill, near Dundee
October 21, 1899	Battle of Elandslaagte, near Ladysmith
October 24, 1899	Battle of Rietfontein, near Ladysmith
October 30, 1899	Mournful Monday: British Loss in the Battle of Ladysmith
November 2, 1899	The Siege of Ladysmith Commences
November 15, 1899	The Armored-Train Incident between Frere and Chieveley
December 15, 1899	The Battle of Colenso: Botha Defeats Buller
December 18, 1899	Lord Roberts Appointed Commander-in-Chief over Buller
January 6, 1900	Boers Attack Ladysmith at Caesar's Camp and Wagon Hill
January 10, 1900	Lords Roberts and Kitchener land at Cape Town
January 24, 1900	The Battle of Spion Kop: Botha Defeats Buller
February 5–7, 1900	The Battle of Vaal Krantz: Botha Defeats Buller
February 15, 1900	General French Relieves Kimberley
February 27, 1900	Piet Cronje Surrenders to Lord Roberts at Paardeberg

February 28, 1900	The Relief of Ladysmith: Buller Defeats Botha
March 13, 1900	The Capture of Bloemfontein
May 17, 1900	The Relief of Mafeking
May 28, 1900	Annexation of the Orange Free State to the British Empire
May 31, 1900	The Capture of Johannesburg
June 5, 1900	The Capture of Pretoria
September 6, 1900	The Capture of Lydenburg
October 19, 1900	President Kruger Flees the Transvaal to France
October 25, 1900	Annexation of the Transvaal to the British Empire
November 29, 1900	Kitchener Succeeds Lord Roberts as Commander-in-Chief
April 10, 1901	Beginning of British Drives against Boer Guerrillas
December 23, 1901	Completion of the Kroonstad–Lindley Blockhouse Line
December 25, 1901	Christiaan De Wet Defeats the British at Tweefontein Farm
March 26, 1902	Death of Cecil Rhodes
May 11, 1902	Completion of British Drives against Boer Guerrillas
May 31, 1902	Peace Treaty Signed at Vereeniging between Kitchener and Botha

The Legacy of *LADYSMITH*

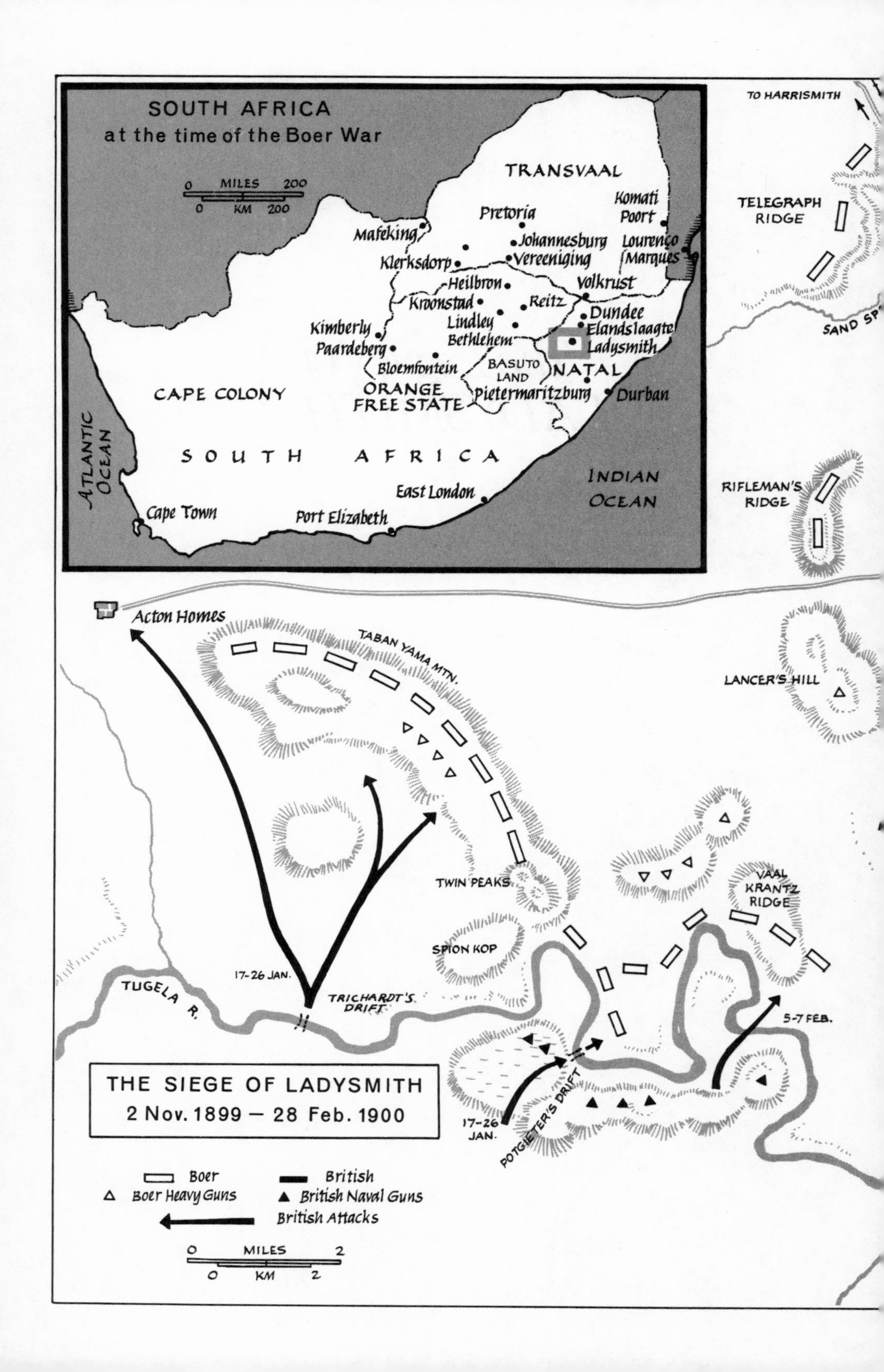

THE SIEGE OF LADYSMITH
2 Nov. 1899 — 28 Feb. 1900

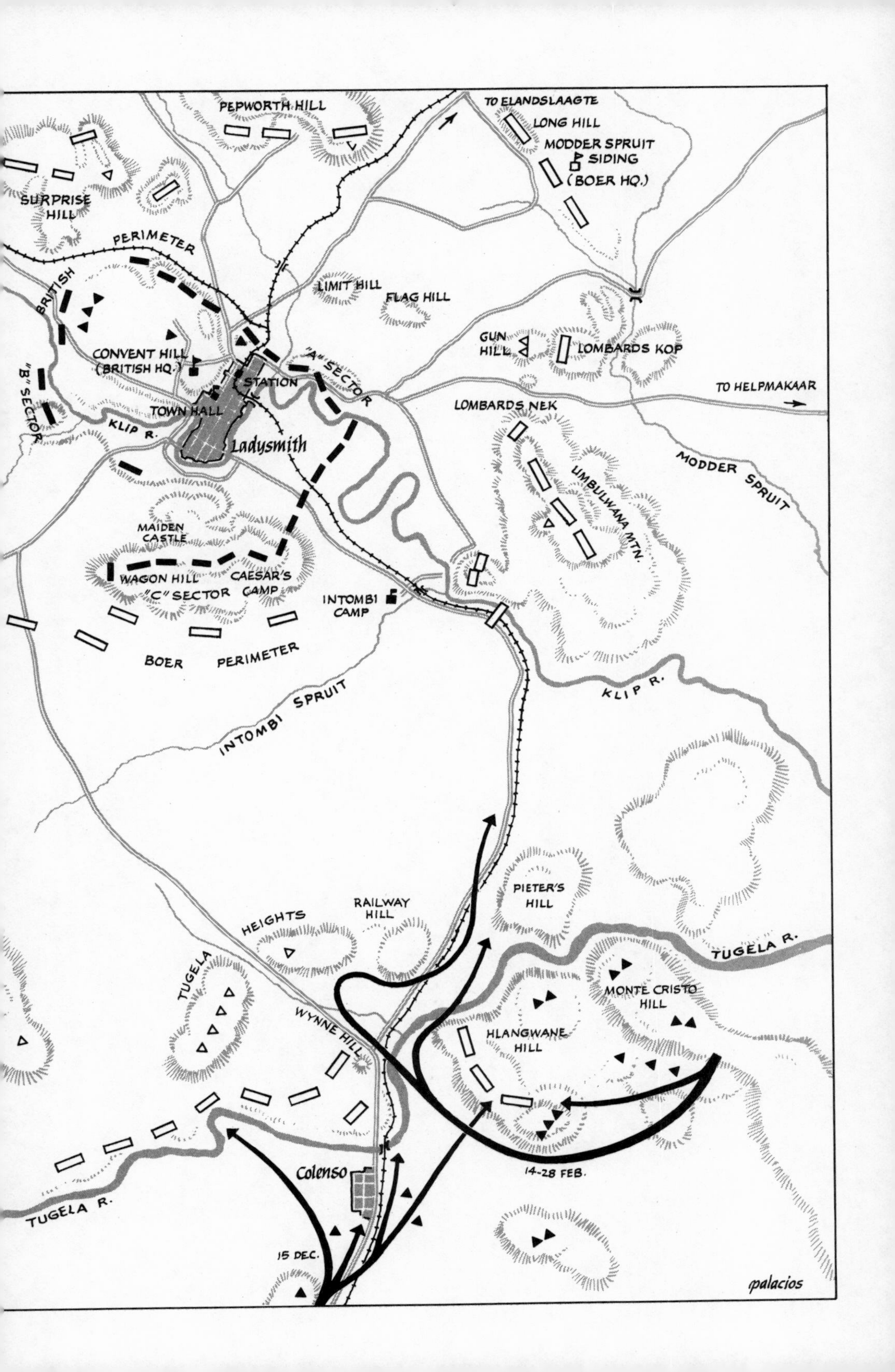
PEPWORTH HILL
TO ELANDSLAAGTE
LONG HILL
MODDER SPRUIT SIDING
(BOER HQ.)
SURPRISE HILL
PERIMETER
BRITISH
LIMIT HILL
FLAG HILL
GUN HILL
LOMBARDS KOP
CONVENT HILL
(BRITISH HQ.)
"B" SECTOR
STATION
"A" SECTOR
TO HELPMAKAAR
TOWN HALL
LOMBARDS NEK
KLIP R.
Ladysmith
MODDER SPRUIT
UMBULWANA MTN.
MAIDEN CASTLE
WAGON HILL
CAESAR'S CAMP
"C" SECTOR
INTOMBI CAMP
BOER
PERIMETER
KLIP R.
INTOMBI SPRUIT
PIETER'S HILL
RAILWAY HILL
HEIGHTS
TUGELA R.
TUGELA
MONTE CRISTO HILL
WYNNE HILL
HLANGWANE HILL
Colenso
14-28 FEB.
TUGELA R.
15 DEC.
palacios

Generations pass while some tree stands,
and old families last not three oaks.

—*Sir Thomas Browne,*
Urn Burial

Part One

TRUISMS

1 GRATUITOUS GLORY

WHEN JASON GLASS WAS INVITED TO SCOTLAND in the spring of 1975 to write a commissioned biography, he did not expect to have to kill someone to complete his work. Yet he had. Not that he had done so on purpose. He had witnesses—among them a police officer and a relative of the victim—to attest that his act had been justifiable homicide and not manslaughter or murder. The newspaper reporters who interviewed him afterward were convinced that Glass had had to do what he did, that he was guilty of no crime, and that he had not wanted to kill anyone; these reporters said so to their readers. In the end, Glass was found innocent without even the formality of a trial.

Yet they were all wrong about one thing: Jason Glass *had* wanted to kill his victim and was actually glad when it was over that he had done so. He would have preferred that someone else had done it, of course. He wished he had never heard of the victim in the first place, and thus would not have had to kill a fellow human being; he wished he had never come to Loch Killilan, and thus could not have killed the person he had; he wished ultimately, perhaps, that either he or his victim had never been born and so have had to endure the collision of destinies that compelled, it seemed, the elimination of one of them.

Dozing on *The Flying Scotsman* as it sped north from London to Edinburgh early that spring, Jason Glass could not have imagined that the troubles he was running from could possibly be superseded by anything he was drifting toward. Although he had just won the International Book Award for his biography entitled *Gratuitous Glory*, and despite the fact that he had earned a six-figure income for 1974 when his receipts for other years barely reached the five-figure bracket, he had become embroiled in a public scandal which had made him, to his own mind at least, *persona non grata* west of the Atlantic. So he had accepted a commission in Scotland to write a life story that looked straightforward enough at first, in exchange for what would probably amount to still another six-figure payoff when he was done. He could not have foreseen, of course, that he would quickly grow to detest the assignment and despise the money and would finally kill a human being in order to be done with both.

Jason Glass was a novelist by aspiration, a pamphlet writer by trade, and a "biographer" only by accident. He would have preferred to win the book award for one of the five novels he had heroically crafted, one a year since the age of twenty-seven, but none of them had ever been published. So at the age of thirty-two, dejected by his flops at fiction, he had begun, almost as a pastime, to delve into the papers of his ancestor Peter Daly, who had fought in the Civil War—or, as he found out later in contravention of family myth, at least *served* in it. Knowing of Glass's propensity to apply pen to paper, a great-aunt had willed him Daly's "papers," such as they were, and suggested, perhaps ordered, that the family hero's story be told for the world to read. The papers Glass received numbered only three: Daly's Army discharge certificate; a letter of recommendation written for his oldest daughter, Bridgit Ann, six years after Daly's death; and a diary this same daughter had kept since the age of ten. With clues provided by these sources, Glass had strung together a biography constructed from oral tradition, military records, newspaper accounts, and half a hundred other things that dealt with Peter Daly, except that before long Glass discovered to his dismay that the family hero was not Peter Daly at all but rather his daughter, Bridgit Ann, known familiarly as Annie.

Initially Glass had been chagrined by his discovery. This switch hardly seemed probable at first, especially after Glass had determined what the guarded language of the discharge certificate really meant. "To All Whom It May Concern," it had begun above the symbol of the American eagle:

> Know ye, That Peter Daly, a Private of Captain David L. Beckwerths [*sic*] Company (A) 22nd Regiment of U.S. Invalid Corps VOLUNTEERS who was enrolled on the Twenty-third day of October, one thousand eight hundred and sixty-two, to serve three years or during the war, is hereby DISCHARGED

from service of the United States, this twenty-third day of March, 1864, at Washington, D.C., by reason of [left blank]. (No objection to his being re-enlisted is known to exist.) [These last ten words, however, had been duly struck out and the following ten penciled in beside them:] He is physically unfit to re-enlist in the Invalid Corps. Said Peter Daly was born in Ireland in the state of [left blank], is forty-one years of age, five feet eight inches high, ruddy complexion, grey eyes, light hair, and by occupation, when enrolled, a mason. Given at Washington, D.C., this twenty-sixth day of March, 1864. [Signed] *Allan Rutherford*, Lieut. Col., 22nd Regt., U.S.I. Corps, Commanding the Reg't.

The reason Daly was no longer fit, this twenty-sixth day of March, 1864, to serve in the U.S. Invalid Corps, Glass's research had finally uncovered: he had had his right leg shot off—not wounded and later amputated, but shot off in the most literal sense—while removing Colonel Rutherford, himself wounded in the right leg, from the Chancellorsville battlefield only moments after dragging the Colonel's son Stephen from that same ill-fated plot of Virginia acreage. Moreover, before losing his leg, Peter Daly's record of battlefield courage and heroism read like a memorial plaque in a town park. There were the letters which those whom he had rescued had written to their relieved loved ones; there were the official reports filed by Rutherford and his predecessor to their immediate superiors; and there was the oral tradition of the Invalid Corps itself for decades afterward. All these sources glorified Peter Daly without restraint, and Glass at first felt he had found a real hero in his own bloodlines.

Gratuitous Glory was intended to be the town-park plaque that Daly never got. But then difficulties turned up. When Daly enlisted to go to the war, he had been thirty-nine years old. He had a sickly wife. He had eight children. He had no savings. He went, apparently, because he liked fighting—had, it seemed, done a good deal of it at a neighborhood tavern in the Bronx—and had wound up in the Invalid Corps only when the Army decided he was not physically fit to take part in the actual bloodshed. At the time he had his leg shot off, his wife was supporting the eight children by taking in sewing and laundry, despite crippling arthritis which made both activities gruesomely painful. When Daly came home from war, unfit to return to masonry, he received a pension of nine dollars a month to support his wife and eight children, who ranged in age from fifteen to two —which meant also that his wife had been pregnant at the time he quit his job and volunteered to go to war. Daly's ninth child, Paul, Glass discovered, had died in 1863 at the age of one while his father was at various Virginia battle sites. A daughter—Elizabeth—died in a fall from their roof during the first month the one-legged Daly was back in New York, and a son—Frank—drowned the following summer in the Kill Van Kull. And Peter Daly himself lived only until 1866, when he died of the gangrene that had infected his gouged leg stump on the battlefield. His comrades were treating others who because of Daly's efficiency had been removed first and were thus ahead of him in line.

The six remaining children did what their ages permitted for the sustenance of their family both before their father's death and after it. Daly's pension was cut when he died from nine dollars to six, and it was discontinued entirely when his wife died in 1872. In this year, then, the entire support of the hero's family fell upon the shoulders of Annie, now twenty-two, and John, nineteen, except that John was an epileptic and could not hold a job.

So if Peter Daly had been the hero through the first third of *Gratuitous Glory*, Annie Daly dominated the final two-thirds and ultimately the entire book. She had found employment in 1864 and by 1869 had advanced to the level of forewoman at the Golden Crest Perfumery division of Phalon & Son in New York. This job was to become the principal source of income for the support of her mother and siblings. And thus the second document in Peter Daly's papers: facing a permanent layoff because of the declining finances of Phalon & Son, she requested a letter of recommendation with which to apply for other employment. Dated 9 October, 1872, three months after her mother's death, the letter was issued by Phalon & Son's Broadway office and read as follows:

> This is to certify that Miss Annie Daly has been in our employ for the last eight years during which time she has proven herself to be an honest and faithful employe [*sic*] unceasingly devoted to the best interests of her employers. For the past three years, Miss Daly has been our forewoman, which position also she filled to our entire satisfaction, and, regretting that want of employment for her forces us to part, we should be pleased at any time to avail ourselves of her

services should we need them. Energetic, capable, trustworthy in the highest degree, we cheerfully recommend her to any party in want of her services.

[Signed] Phalon & Son.

Through a long parade of ill-paying, short-lived, and foul-dutied jobs of every conceivable sort, Annie Daly saw her brothers through for several years until Peter, Michael, and William, each in his turn, became a bricklayer like their father. All of this was meticulously and modestly documented in Annie Daly's private diary, which was the third and last of the papers Glass's aunt had bequeathed him. In the final chapter of his prizewinning book, he traced the Daly lineage into the 1970s and found there doctors and lawyers and bank officers and even one "writer"—himself—to replace the earlier bricklayers and forewomen and potwallopers and nursemaids. More than ninety percent of the current generation of Daly descendants held college degrees, and half of these held more than one. "A glorious recognition and celebration of a familial past," *The New York Times* had called *Gratuitous Glory*, "which insists upon the awareness we all must have of our individual heritage because of the debt we owe it." Though by this time only distantly related himself to Peter and Annie Daly, Jason Glass owed them his own international fame and his income for 1974.

But as he rode *The Flying Scotsman* north, intending to change at Edinburgh for another, slower train to Inverness and then again to still another pokechug string of cars for the last sixty miles to Loch Killilan, he knew he owed them other things as well, and all of these were bad. They had routed out of blissful oblivion Jason Glass's wife.

In every way but legally, Margot Glass was an ex-wife. She had disappeared six years before, taking with her almost everything that was not nailed down and some things that were—everything save their two daughters, Patricia and Elizabeth, whom she did not, for a while, need. Then, when *Gratuitous Glory* moved rapidly up the *Times* nonfiction best-seller list, she wrote him a chipper note, the first, chipper or otherwise, in five years, congratulating him and offering to "take the girls" for the following summer while Jason did a national publicity tour for the story of Annie Daly. Glad for them to renew acquaintance with their missing mother, Glass agreed, packed the girls off to Cape Cod, and spent the rest of the summer signing his name and showing his face in towns from Minneapolis to Miami to Modesto to Missoula to Moose Jaw, Saskatchewan. When he returned to Boston, he was not in town twenty-four hours before he was served with divorce papers, a custody suit, and a demand for $1,000-a-week alimony and $500-a-month child support. He fought it all in court, of course, and lost on everything but the alimony claim, which was ruled excessive. At which point Margot withdrew the divorce suit and altered her terms for child support, now called "maintenance," requesting that Jason pay $2,000 a month for the next nine years and $1,750 for two more after that. Then, when both girls had passed their eighteenth birthdays, Margot, Jason imagined, would be on with the alimony claim once again.

Would that that were all Jason had imagined. Unfortunately, he imagined an extended short story as well, which he published easily, despite his agent's best advice, in *True Adventure*, entitled "The Birth of the White Male Counterrevolution." In it, an embattled husband has his children stolen from him by his wife and his suits cut to ribbons by the psychologically warped little girls. Resigned at first to bearing his burden, he one day sees pictures of them on a Rhode Island beach in a guide to nudist swimming places, in the company of their mother and two uncircumcised men who would have been known a decade earlier as "hippies." In the ensuing pages he and a league of other abused husbands wage a vigilante war both on the Rhode Island beach and on women who remove their children from the protection of their homes and fathers in order to have them participate in "liberated activities" with lesbians, exhibitionists, and unclean beach bums. The story was luridly illustrated.

For this Jason Glass got sued, again by Margot. And again Jason Glass "won" when the suit was dismissed by the judge, who claimed that Glass had indeed written fiction and, besides, surely Mrs. Glass did not frequent such places with her daughters. He did, however, take pity on three damsels in distress, tied up all the royalties on *Gratuitous Glory*, and told Glass that they would not be paid to him until he agreed to make the maintenance payments willingly. Glass, in a show of courtroom theatrics, declared he would go to jail for life; but the judge had yawned and decided to smoke him out. For the last year, then, Glass had been virtually penniless and had been condemned as a "male chauvinist and an irresponsible father" in *The National Enquirer*, a "rank misogynist" in *Ms. Magazine*, and a "no-good son-of-a-bitch" in a casual aside made by a woman in the audience of the David Susskind show on a program dealing with incest and Electra complexes in preteenage girls.

It got so that Glass had to remind himself that less than a year before, he had been internationally celebrated for his preservation (at least in print) of family values and adulation (again in print) of feminine heroism. Women in supermarkets would not speak to him, Barbara Walters too eagerly wanted to interview him, and *Blue Boy* magazine openly solicited his next piece of "meaningful" fiction.

Then, at midwinter, just as he was thinking of getting out of town, the letter from Scotland had arrived. Now, two months later, he was out of the country, riding *The Flying Scotsman* north toward the Scottish Lochs—which insofar as he was concerned was north toward oblivion.

Across the aisle from Glass, from London to York, rode an extremely pretty dark-haired girl of about seventeen. Though she wore white bibbed painter's pants, she looked tidy in her white boots and blue-striped T-shirt. For the entire two hours the girl scribbled furiously in a diary that had a picture of Snoopy and Woodstock on the cover. She appeared to be transcribing information from a more beaten-up-looking diary that said MARY QUANT on the front and had a World Wildlife Fund sticker on the back. Glass, taken by her evident devotion to autobiography, wondered about the two versions of the same life. Was Mary Quant merely a collection of brief notes scribbled down in the heat of whatever hand-to-hand combat a seventeen-year-old British girl had with life, while Snoopy was a fuller rendition recollected in tranquillity? Was Mary Quant what *really* happened and Snoopy the version she left around for her mother to see? He wanted to ask but didn't. Then, an equally curious man sitting across from her looked up from his London *Times*.

"Is one of those your rough log and the other your proper one?" He smiled at her paternally over his glasses.

"No," she replied with a polite smile of her own. "I copy it to relive my days. They're always better the second time."

At Newcastle-on-Tyne the train from London entered the canopied station, picked up and discharged its passengers and mail, and then rolled back out the way it had come. Though somewhere in the first mile it must have changed tracks at a switch and headed north toward Edinburgh instead of back toward London, passengers who, like Glass, had hitherto ridden forward now rode backward for the last two hours. This affected Glass curiously. Riding forward in a train gives one the feeling of proceeding forthrightly into the future. Riding backward lends the sense of being dragged against one's will back into the past one had intended to leave. Unlike those of the girl beside him, *his* days were *not* likely to be better upon later reflection than they had been in actual experience.

The letter from Scotland had been written by an editor who worked for Farneswells publishing house in London. Though she made little reference to herself, Glass detected that she had some regular connection with the extreme northwest district of Scotland in which Loch Killilan—lake and town—were secreted. At any rate, she was the bridge between the people—an old Scottish family named Menzies—who wished to contract for Glass's services on a research and writing project and the destined publishers of the resultant book—Farneswells of London. She had begun her letter in the most interesting fashion:

> Dear Mr. Glass:
> I am authorized by the Clan Menzies of the Loch Killilan district of the Highlands of Scotland to establish contact with you and to offer you any fee within reason to carry out for them the writing of a book. Publication of this work is already guaranteed by Farneswells of London, my employers, and I have been appointed as your editor—if, as we hope, you will consent to take this on.

The writer of such a paragraph was surely familiar with Achilles' heels in the writing community, for "any fee within reason" and "publication . . . guaranteed" were two phrases that could, under normal circumstances, get a contract signed without further ado.

> When the current chief of the clan, Farquhar Menzies, encountered your admirable portrayal of the decency and heroism of uncelebrated members of your lineage, he could not help but make comparisons with a figure in his own family's past who—though his story is known and admired in the valleys immediately about Loch Killilan—has been generally unrecognized by the British nation despite the very titanic services he once rendered it.

The figure I speak of is Roberts Menzies, who was born just to the south of the town of Loch Killilan in 1872 and who died in the same castle in which he grew up in 1925. In 1897 he finished his medical studies at the University of Edinburgh and went to serve as a civilian doctor for the Scottish settlers in South Africa. He arrived in Durban on October 2nd, 1897, proceeded to northern Natal immediately, and established himself in the civilian hospital at Dundee, a town with a Scottish heritage as deep as its name. When war was declared two years later and the Boers invaded Natal on October 11th, 1899, Roberts Menzies placed himself in charge of evacuating the Dundee hospital to move the sick and injured to the safer quarters around Pietermaritzburg, some two hundred and fifty miles back to the south. Unfortunately, despite his gallant efforts, he was unable to get them there.

We do not know all the details of this we should, Mr. Glass—it would be your job among others to determine them. But, because of the terrible speed with which the Boer forces moved south into Natal, the British garrison at Ladysmith fell under siege on November 2nd, about two weeks after the capture of Dundee. This siege, which I am sure you have heard of since it is one of the most famous and most heroic in the history of the world, lasted until the final day of February, 1900, when General Buller's forces finally managed to relieve the town.

The relevance of these historical facts to Roberts Menzies is simply this: He had moved his sick and injured by ambulance wagons as far south as Ladysmith but was trapped therein with the rest of the citizens and thousands of British troops when the Boer vise finally closed upon that unfortunate town. During four terrible months, however, Roberts Menzies was able to save the lives of fully ninety percent of the patients he brought with him despite conditions in which the most healthy men and women, military and civilian, were dying at the rate of thirty a day from typhoid, malnutrition, and enteric fever.

I trust the parallels between Roberts Menzies and your own Peter Daly are immediately evident and that you will agree to contract with us to serve his memory as well as you have served Private Daly's. In our own century, when the human race continues to blunder on in ignorance of the lessons and examples of the past, it would seem to me that the highest service someone with your talent could perform would be to insist that the Peter Dalys and the Roberts Menzies be rescued from the obscurity of their inevitable graves.

Here the second page of her letter ended; only by her handwriting did he even know he was in communication with a woman, for he still had not reached the signature page. The third page entered immediately upon the pragmatic details of the assignment. Since the bulk of the materials existed in the Lochs, Glass was to write the book there, living in a small cottage in an area known as "The Gap." He would be provided with everything from food to typing paper to the "luxury" of a feather bed. She concluded with a stuffily polite final paragraph which reiterated her own and Farquhar Menzies' hopes that Glass would assume the project and again implied that his acceptance of it was a duty to the human race. She signed herself "Miss Ann Macgregor," by her approach certainly a spinsterish miss rather than a nubile one.

Now, as the train skirted the North Sea near the sugar-loaf rocks at Oxmellans, he began to doze. The farther north he got, the less he saw of the dirty factory towns that hunkered alongside the rail tracks to the south; people had, in fact, been replaced by sheep, who grazed up to within two feet of the line and took no notice of the train, moving at one hundred and twenty-five miles an hour now as it flung itself toward Edinburgh. The only evidence that man had ever even inhabited this land was occasional ruined and abandoned houses and castles and abbeys which punctuated the fields. Sheep grazed within them as well. Glass had heard that there were something like five times as many sheep as people in Scotland, and here there were at least a thousand times as many.

In Waverley Station passengers from the south must leave their trains and pass through the terminal, across the taxi loop, and onto other platforms if they wish to travel farther north than Edinburgh. An hour later, Glass's train to Inverness (where he would still have to catch another for the remaining sixty miles westward toward Kyle and the Lochs) pulled out five minutes late. This train was only four cars long and very empty. Though he could have had virtually any seat he wanted, Glass had stacked his luggage on the three seats surrounding him (to ward off loquacious or perhaps seedy second-class seatmates), so that he wound up riding backward again. He slept all the way to Inverness, and then all the way to Kyle of Lochalsh as well.

Jason Glass began dreaming as he slept; but he did not dream that before this biography of Roberts Menzies could be completed, he would wind up killing someone so that the story he was about to tell could possibly make sense.

2 *SYBIL AND CLYDE*

THE ONLY PUB IN LOCH KILLILAN proved to be The Angus Bull, so Glass had the driver who had brought him the ten miles from Kyle of Lochalsh station in an old school bus drop him there. He had no idea what his next move should be —it was approaching ten at night by now—but he was desperately hungry and particularly thirsty. He would get in out of the pouring rain, eat, then consider his options.

At first the girl behind the bar had refused him a warm meal —such could not be gotten after nine o'clock, she said, no matter what the sign above the counter announced to the contrary. But then Glass saw a burly fellow drinker seated at the other end of the bar say something that Glass could not hear. There was little noise in the room, indeed few customers, but the vast amount of cigarette smoke those few managed to generate seemed to cut audibility as well as visibility. In a moment the girl returned with a pad and pencil, now apparently prepared to cooperate.

"Sorry, sir. I had no idea who you were, actually." She pushed her hair back from her eyes, as if she were even ready to be pretty for him.

"And who am I?" Glass recognized the idiocy of the question even as he asked it.

"Why, Jason Glass!" She seemed to be telling him the way a fan spots a celebrity in a hotel lobby and signals a friend.

Glass was confused. "How did you know that?"

She nodded toward the burly man. "Chap over there said he'd seen your photo on the back of a book in Sciennes' Store." The man nodded toward Glass, as did virtually everyone else in the room. While they observed him with caution, they seemed tolerant of an outsider—or perhaps just of Jason Glass. "I'll go and call Clyde and Sybil for you, I will."

Glass had not heard these names before. "Actually, I'm looking for a Mr. Menzies. Farquhar Menzies. Do you know him?"

She looked at him as if he had asked her if she had ever heard of the queen. "Clyde and Sybil be his son and daughter-in-law. Sybil told me that they're to watch over you until tomorrow. They're to take you to your cottage in The Gap." She pivoted and within ten minutes was back with a rather tender-looking steak, chipped potatoes, peas, and beer. Glass consumed the entire pint before touching the food, and she refilled it before turning to the telephone. Glass noticed that the others continued to stare at him as he ate, diverting their eyes only when Glass engaged them with his.

Twenty minutes later, a woman in a soaked raincoat entered the room, spotted Glass immediately, and approached him. "Hello, Mr. Glass. I'm Sybil Menzies."

She seemed in her late twenties, not what is called pretty, though not unattractive. A generally British face with the vaguest traces of German features about the eyes. A bit pudgy, perhaps five to ten pounds heavier than she ought to be, not more than that. Her cheeks were red, flecked with raindrops, as was her light brown hair. She had leaned over close to Glass's ear to speak with him; she smelled slightly of liquor.

"Oh, yes, thank you for coming out. I would have stayed here for the night, really, but the girl at the bar—"

"She did absolutely as she was instructed. Now, if you'll get your things together, I'll take you to your cottage. It'll be a bit chill, I fear, for we did not know when you'd be arriving. But there's plenty of firewood, and you can come to town for food in the morning." She turned now and spoke quietly to the girl, then reached into her purse and extracted several pound notes.

The motor of Sybil Menzies' Mercedes had been left running, as had the wipers, and she spun away from the curb perhaps too quickly once Glass had shut the door to his left. She did not look in either direction before she made the U-turn—luckily there was no traffic; perhaps there never was. As they headed back down the road by which Glass had entered Loch Killilan, she drove about five miles an hour faster than the wet road surface and the tight curves suggested might be wise. But she was familiar with the road. Once the town was obscured behind them, Glass again apologized for having brought her out on so poor a night.

"If I hadn't come out, Mr. Glass, I'd be drunk by now, so I suppose coming out was the more constructive thing to do." Glass did not like the tone of this—it contained information one did not tell strangers. "My son's asleep and my husband has already drunk himself into a stupor, so I could either do the same or come pick you up." Glass rode in silence so as not to encourage any more talk.

After passing a small church and cemetery on the lochfront to their right, she slowed the car sharply and veered off the paved main road onto a gravel side road which quickly became dirt. The car lunged up a steep incline, the headlights continually illuminating trees and boulders directly in front of them that only Sybil's knowledge of the road allowed her to miss by an eyelash with each spin of the wheel. The wheels twirled half-productively in the mud, and she had to keep her speed up to climb the hill. Then they were at the top, and though it got no better, the road did at least straighten out and level off. In another mile they passed a dimly lit home on their left but did not slow down for it.

"Mine." She nodded across Glass out the window. Half a mile later they drove by two unlit buildings, one on either side of the road, then through a narrow pass formed by two giant boulders and around a bend, and finally spun off the road and up to the front door of a small cottage not fifteen feet back from the roadway. "Yours." She jerked on the emergency brake as the car rolled to within two feet of the front doorway.

To his surprise, she needed no key to enter the place. "I'll give you a key so you can lock up when you want to, Mr. Glass. Jason—do you mind if I call you that, Jason? Good." She began flipping electrical switches which had clearly been installed several centuries after the cottage was erected. "Actually you're depriving me of my home away from home, I'd like you to know." She was only half joking. "I used to pop over here many nights when Clyde got too much for me." Glass said nothing. He could not take the trouble to be polite. He was too tired.

Sybil gave him a quick tour of the cottage, a duty that clearly bored her. Built in the eighteenth century for shepherds who were cleared off their land in the mid-nineteenth, it had external walls of stone, its internal ones finely polished mahogany. Its floors were slate, with only discreetly placed red throw rugs to give them warmth. The ceilings were barely six feet high, and Glass actually had to duck to enter the winding staircase to the upper floor. Two bedrooms and a bathroom occupied all of it, the latter rude but properly equipped. One bedroom contained only a single bed and a chest of drawers; but the other was dominated by a canopied, camelbacked feather bed and an antique desk that would be, perhaps, too small for his purposes. Yet it intrigued him, for its very appointments—leather-inlaid top, desk lamp with a tasseled shade, quill pen and inkwell—drew him back into the past, the arena in which a biographer by definition struggled. Yet he was quickly returned to the present by the two typewriters which rested on smaller tables to either side of it, one a portable, the other a huge office-sized Olivetti with all the self-correcting features. They contrasted with each other the way the girl on the train's two diaries did: one for the rough version, the other for the proper one; one for the immediate, the other for the recollected; one, perhaps, for the unadulterated truth, the other, also perhaps, for the reconsidered fabrications; one for the humble, the other for the mighty.

"Jason, I've found some brandy in the cupboard. Why not get your cases out of the car and we'll drink it all up?" Not have a drink, but drink it all up.

He descended the steps wearily and passed out the front door, able to find his way to the car only by the dim lights in the front windows. It was raining very hard, and silent lightning illuminated the dark sky now and again. The bitter cold of the wind made the rain sting like sleet, the season seem like midwinter instead of early spring. He suspected he might not know summer this year.

When he got back inside he placed the dripping suitcase on a small throw rug near the door, then pulled off his raincoat, his knuckles scraping the ceiling as he fought himself free of it and laid it across the handle of the suitcase. Sybil had pulled two deep chairs over in front of the snapping fire and placed the decanter of brandy, full to the top, on a small wooden table between them. To drink this all up would take most of the night, and it was now eleven o'clock. Glass sat down and extended his damp feet toward the blaze, listening to the logs crackle and the rain tick on the nearest windowpane in counterpointed harmonies. He did not know what to say to this woman, for she seemed to have a prewritten script that she planned to prompt him on.

Perhaps this was why he did not like her. She took her brandy from the snifter in long drafts, as if to hurry its effects.

"You'll want to be sure your firewood is dry and at hand, Jason. The nights are always chilly here, even after hot days. You have no other heat source, you see." As if to underscore her words of caution, a sudden gust of wind rattled the window casing and finished itself with the metallic buzz of a cheap harmonica.

"Yes, I'll do that." He sipped his brandy. "A bit of this should warm at least the insides of me, however." An International Book Award winner should do better than that.

"I've read your book, Jason. Admirable, I must say, even though I don't understand all the exigencies of your so-called Civil War." Next Annie Daly would be his *so-called* heroine. "Do you think you can do as well for my father-in-law?"

"Well, I hope to. Actually I'll have to research the facts before I can know how well I can do with them." It was an earnest statement on his part, but she laughed too heartily, perhaps already a bit boozily.

"You'll need to reach farther than the facts to do much with the Roberts Menzies story, Jason. Our clan chief will not be satisfied with a book based on what little we know of him. 'Twould be a slim volume indeed, and even some of that he'd want out before you published it." Again she laughed, sardonically this time. This was a bad first Menzies to have to run into. "You'll have to expand on things a lot."

"Biographers can't *expand* beyond the facts, Mrs. Menzies. Once you do that you're writing fiction. I've not done well at that."

"Well, I suggest you give our clan chief a bit of instruction in literary modes before you start, then. I am not sure he shares your sense of the distinction. . . . And call me Sybil, will you? There have been so many Menzies around here that we have to insist on our first names to preserve our identities." She emptied the snifter and refilled it as she swallowed. She took a long opening drag on it. She *did* plan to drink it all up.

The conversation went on. All the leads were Sybil's. They became somewhat disjointed. The script seemed to have lost some of its pages and, with them, its transitions. Getting very sleepy from travel and alcohol, he tried to stay awake through her loose talk about her husband's drinking and indiscriminate wenching, her son's mental retardation, her father-in-law's egomania, her sister's prissiness, her mother's suicide, and a hundred other things he did not want to know about. He began to ask himself why he did not just throw her out—no, thank her first for the ride, the fire, and the brandy. But he knew why, even if he was ashamed to admit it to himself. As her tongue floated more freely in her mouth, she was more than implying that she would be open to an invitation to spend the night.

She reached across the table between them and gripped his left wrist. In so doing she knocked the half-full decanter of brandy off it onto the stone floor. It did not break, but he could hear it glugging its contents out of itself. He decided to let it, and she did not notice that she had done it.

"How can I get you to invite me to stay tonight? I come here other nights. It is hard for me to await your invitation." Her blue eyes cleared a bit in the firelight as she awaited his response.

"You won't get an invitation, Sybil. But you have my permission. Take whichever bedroom you like." To dispose of her seemed unfair—he was the guest, not she.

She giggled coyly at this, and some of her jadedness seemed to melt away. She was definitely not much short of thirty, but she seemed suddenly more girlish—as if her husband did not drink and wench; as if her mother had not committed suicide—or did she say her sister?—as if she had never heard of Farquhar Menzies. "I'll choose whichever bedroom you do."

For some reason he did not at this moment dislike her as he had for the two hours before. Perhaps it was the drink in her that had rinsed the brassy edges from her personality; perhaps it was the drink in him that colored his outlook; perhaps it was just the glow of a warm fire on a night in a tiny cottage in the Scottish Lochs where the howling wind outside made simple rainfall ricochet like bullets off the windows. Perhaps it was that Jason, for all his troubles with women, was still male.

She stood up from her chair and moved in front of him. More properly, he found her standing in front of him when he recovered from one of those brief dozes that one can't recall having begun. She had her hands on his shoulders, looking down at him, more a shadow than a person in the dim room, her silhouette illuminated at the edges by the firelight. He was aware of the outlines of a woman more than the full and present reality of one. He shook his head slightly to toss off his grogginess. She was saying something to him, though his ears could not register her meaning. He reached forward instinctively and ran his hands up and down the thighs of her close-fitting knitted dress. He could trace the muscles of her full thighs, like the rest of her just ever so slightly larger than they ideally should have been. But they were good enough. His wrists pushed the tight skirt up awkwardly, so she removed her hands from his shoulders and eased it up waist high for him. He could see the outlines of her rounded hips against the glow of the fire, see the flames themselves between her naked legs. He was woozy, neither his hands nor his eyes nor his ears fully alert to the situation in which he found himself. He acted automatically, half from instinct, half from memory of the last woman he had been with, though he could not remember who she was or when either. He ran his hands, doughy from beer and brandy and travel and weariness, to her hips and felt her panties so soft and smooth and glossy. He drew her to him and pressed his right cheek against her abdomen, the soft fleshy part against the front of her bikini panties, which he saw in the firelight to be rose pink; his cheekbone against the flesh of her stomach below the navel. Then without planning to he found himself hooking his fingers in the waistband and began pulling them down. He stopped, and she pulled them the rest of the way down and stepped out of them on the floor.

But then he must have dozed again, because he found himself in the hallway now, one hand on the railing of the steps, the other in her hand, she two steps ahead of him leading him upstairs. And then he heard her tell him to undress while she went into the bathroom and he did and climbed naked into bed, only vaguely aware of the iciness of the unheated bedroom, less aware still of the violent shrieking of the toilet in the next room. He crawled under the two quilts on the feather bed and was immersed in the mattress, sinking so far down that the two sides almost caved in around and above him. It was the softest bed he had ever been in, and he fell asleep for perhaps fifteen seconds before he felt her crawling in with him, still talking about something and trying to find him amidst the all-consuming mattress and then catching up with him, giggling. She still had the dress on, but she was pulling it up to her armpits under the covers. Then she unhooked her bra and brought Glass's left hand to her right breast. And then she began to fondle him strongly for thirty seconds and then she slowed down and finally stopped and began to breathe heavily. She held firmly to his penis, and he brought his hand downward and inserted it into the hair between her legs at the last second before he too was breathing heavily, rhythmically, perhaps even snoring.

How much later it was that he heard footsteps heavy on the rudimentary plank staircase he did not know. Perhaps two minutes, perhaps two hours. Both their hands remained in the same places, but somehow even their heads were under the heavy quilts, so deeply buried in the feather mattress that there must have been several pounds of the stuff separating their faces. His head was already pounding; his brain felt separated from its moorings within his skull. So much so that he did not panic or respond in any way to the footsteps. He remained buried. Then he heard the door to the room creak open, and he exposed just the corner of his right eye from the covers and mattress to see a burly outline—definitely male—against the unextinguished hall light. The figure carried a flashlight and came slowly but directly toward the bed. He pulled the covers on Sybil's side loose and tossed them over on Glass's, further burying the International Book Award winner and blocking his single peephole.

"Get your hands off me, you fucking bastard." Sybil seemed still to be asleep, seemed to be cursing by recollection, as if her dreams too were scripted.

"Get your bloody ass out of that bed, you bitch, and get home where you belong. How many nights am I going to have to come after yer?" The voice was rough, crude, but patiently suffering, demonstrating a right to be annoyed. Glass was now thoroughly awake and, thoroughly, scared.

"I said to get the fucking hell out of here, you prick." Sybil was awake too, and had reverted to Sybil as Glass had first met her. She began to squirm and bounce and struggle against the man's attempts to remove her from the bed. Glass's first clear thought was that as yet, this man—certainly her husband—did not know there were two in the bed. He must usually have found only one. Every time she bounced, Glass used the interval she was off the mattress to slide her dress down to where it should be. She had finally let go of him, though not as quickly as he would have hoped or liked.

With a lunge now the man jammed his still lit flashlight into his back pocket and scooped the woman out of the bed and actually slung her over his shoulder. He was a big man, cursing gruffly, she retaliating more shrilly with combinations of epithets Glass had never heard assembled before, even when he was in the Navy. Her rolling Scottish *r*'s and her female voice failed to lend them any dignity. They were thoroughly gross. But Glass had only one purpose—to remain very still. He could hear a picture kicked off the wall as the man lugged her out into the hallway, then what sounded like her head hitting the low ceiling as he moved toward the stairs. Now she was cursing the clan Menzies proper, starting as far back into the lineage as she could recall names for. Finally they were out the front door and Glass heard the crisp engine of Sybil's Mercedes turn over and the car depart swiftly down the roadway in the direction from which they had come.

Glass was panting heavily, even now only vaguely aware of the close call he had had, of the absolute bizarreness of the situation. Still he did not poke his head out into the night, almost as if he were instructing himself on how to behave from readings in eighteenth-century bedroom farces.

Then he was awakened again, though it was daylight now, by the sound of the phone downstairs—tuned to ear-shattering, head-shattering shrillness. As he struggled out of the feather bed, he scraped his forearm on an earring that had been left behind. He bore down to recall whose it was, did so, then emerged from the bed. Naked, he took the topmost quilt and wrapped it about himself and, head slung forward, descended the stairs gingerly, expecting to fall on each.

He crossed the parlor and wrenched the receiver off the hook, not so much to answer as to shut it up. The operator told him it was a "trunk call" from London, and asked him to hold while she completed the connection. Sick to his stomach now, he leaned forward, pulling the phone itself off the table and onto the floor, which it hit with a ringing clatter. He did not pick it up, but the call was still alive.

Staring dully at the floor between his bare feet, Glass recognized Sybil's rose-pink bikini panties, soiled now by the muddy bootprint of the angry man who had trodden on them in the dark on his way upstairs. As he waited for his call, he picked them up and stuffed them into the pocket of his raincoat. He did not like Sybil, but he would give them back to her the next time he saw her.

3 DUNCAN AND HENRIETTA

"MR. GLASS?"

"Yes, speaking."

"Hello. This is Ann Macgregor calling. From London." She paused while Glass forced his memory through the wall of his headache. "Your editor . . . for the Roberts Menzies project, you recall?" She laughed a bit now, as if she knew he was, first, hung over and, second, naked but for the quilt with which he protected himself.

"Oh, yes. Sorry it took me so long to make the connection. I just got up. I was traveling all day yesterday and the day before." Why was he summarizing the obvious at long-distance rates? "How did you know I had arrived?"

"I asked my brother-in-law to be on the lookout for you, actually. He phoned me around five this morning."

"Your brother-in-law? I haven't even met any men in town yet—just two, uh, women."

"Yes, but he knew you had arrived. Clyde Menzies?" She seemed to feel that Glass might be familiar with him.

"Clyde Menzies? No, I haven't met him . . . exactly. That means that your sister is . . . ?

"Sybil, yes. You've met her?"

"Yes, yes I have." He did not know what to say next. The voice on the other end was younger than he had expected, though just as polished, just as British. He attached a less severe face to it than he had in their correspondence, in fact a very good one now, more slender, generally better than Sybil's, which wasn't at all bad. He wondered if Ann had spoken to her sister as yet.

"Well, I must get to the point so I can get to King's Cross. Mr. Farquhar Menzies has asked me to come up today so that the three of us might dine together at eight this evening, at the castle. Can you be there?"

"Well, yes, I suppose. I haven't exactly gotten my sea legs here as yet, or my geographical bearings. How can I get there, though?"

"Ask Clyde to lend you his car. They have two." Glass knew that already. "Take the road back toward Dornie, about ten miles. You'll see the castle easily because it's situated on a small island just offshore in Loch Duich. Park along the roadway and cross the causeway to the main gate. The gatekeeper will be expecting you."

"To be truthful, Miss Macgregor, I'd be happier going in with you. My only contact with the Menzies has been through you. Clan chiefs and Scottish castles in the middle of lakes are a new thing for me."

She laughed. Very pleasantly. "I'd love to help you, Mr. Glass, but I'll just make it on time myself. You know how late the train arrives in Kyle, and that is on the far side of the castle from where you are, I'm afraid. Besides, Mr. Menzies has sought you rather than you him. You'll have no trouble whatsoever, I'm sure."

Glass assented to this, though he was reluctant nonetheless both to arrive alone and also to sashay up to Clyde to borrow his car. He wondered how much Clyde knew. He wondered how much Ann knew.

"I must hurry to catch a taxi, Mr. Glass. But please stock the cottage with whatever supplies you need. Have them placed on Mr. Farquhar Menzies' chit at Sciennes' Store in Loch Killilan." Glass again wanted to inquire about a means to transport the stuff, but he knew in advance what the answer would be. "If you need help with anything in getting yourself settled, ask my nephew, Duncan. Sybil's son. He will do anything for a coin—any denomination, as long as it's shiny." She bade adieu quickly and rang off with cab-and-train-chasing urgency.

Glass spent the next forty-five minutes getting his clothing and toiletries in order. It was nine o'clock before he had time to realize that he was hungry and, next, that there was not a crumb of bread in the house.

Without knowing in particular where he was headed to find food, he donned a light jacket and stepped out into a sunny, though rather chilly morning. But what struck him much more suddenly than the weather was the delicately unreal beauty of the surroundings in which he found himself. His instinctive inclination was to make this project take a long time.

He could see roughly two miles to both his left and his right. To the right, back in the direction of Loch Killilan, the so-called "Gap" broadened into fairly flat, though slightly rolling grassland. Though the predominant color that met his eye was light green, the ground was dotted, and frequently more than just dotted, with gray boulders that sprang up, large and small, both along the flatland and up the high steep cliffs that formed the boundaries of The Gap itself. This gray-green fusion was further colored by a wild and freely growing purplish flower which Glass presumed to be heather. But this grand view was tinged as well with blue and white—a quickly moving stream which passed his doorway some fifty yards down a grassy slope across the dirt roadway and found its way to a placid lake approximately a half-mile on, a lake too small and unsalted to be called an official "loch" but large enough to reflect silver in the morning sunshine and so dominate the scene to the south of him.

To his left, northward away from Loch Killilan, the white road ascended ever more steeply, weaving and crisscrossing the river so often on rock bridges that it was sometimes hard to tell which of the threads he viewed was the road and which the river. In this direction The Gap narrowed sharply to a point where the two sides were ultimately less than fifty yards apart. Sheer granite cliffs triangulated in upon each other, soaring to heights of at least five hundred feet above the road surface.

The scene was perfectly beautiful. He had the distinct impression that The Gap was all his—no other animal life seemed at first to inhabit it. But he recalled that Clyde and Sybil's house was somewhere around the bend in the road to his right, surely to this side of the lake, and that there were two ruined buildings midway between them, attesting to the fact that still others had at least once been here. And yet there was other life which now began to reveal itself. A bird circled high above him for a moment—a small bird, but Glass was not good on birds and could only guess it to be a swallow—and he could also see horned sheep that he had initially mistaken for boulders, chewing away at grass at all levels and locations of The Gap. And there was another house in view, a white one with what appeared to be a slate roof, quite small, higher up the northern end of The Gap, perched on the side of the hill just short of where the road reached its highest level and passed over the back and out of The Gap entirely. Since he was not particularly keen about hanging around Clyde and Sybil's, he resolved to visit the house before very long.

Then there was more life—a horseman appeared on the higher reaches of the road, galloping his mount down the winding course, spraying white dust from its hooves as it dug in to round the bends. As he approached Jason the rider reined his mount in hard, creating a swirl of dust that preceded it. Glass shut his eyes tightly until it had blown by him.

Surprisingly, the fast rider turned out to be a boy, not more than nine or ten, physically unattractive, yet almost saintly-looking despite the speed with which he had arrived. He stared at Glass for several moments, his mouth hung slightly open, as if he were deciding whether to spur his horse or proffer greeting. Seeming about to do the former, he did the latter instead.

"You're Mr. Glass." It was a statement, not a question. The *r*'s rolled in thickly Scottish fashion, yet there was something else in his speech as well.

"Yes, I am. And your name?" Glass tried to be wholesomely warm.

"I am Duncan," he said finally, as if Glass should have known this as clearly as he had known Glass. He formed his words separately as he spoke, as if there were no such thing as syntax to embrace them or a system of phonology by which they intoned and inflected one another. "My aunt . . said that I"—he seemed to stammer now—"might have a coin . . . from you if I . . . t-t-took you into town to . . . buy food."

Glass was not sure how a nine-year-old could "take" him into town, but Ann Macgregor had already indicated that the boy could be of some service. He decided to risk a coin on the issue. "That would be very helpful, Duncan." He reached into his pocket and brought forth a handful of change ranging from a fifty-pence piece through all six denominations down to a halfpenny. The boy pulled his horse closer so he could inspect the coins. He pushed all but two, a five-pence and a ten-pence coin, to the heel of Glass's hand and let his two favorites rest on the forefingers. He could not make up his mind, but they were surely the shiniest two of the lot.

"I have been riding up and down The Gap since . . . daybreak. My aunt . . . said you had no food . . . and I should be here . . . when you rose." Glass could see that the horse *was* lathered, despite the briskness of the morning.

"Well, all right, take them both. But this one big one back here is worth more than both of these together." The offer to take both was what the boy had hoped for, and he did so, ignoring totally the richer coin to the rear.

"You wait here, Mr. Glass. I . . . will be back shortly." He spurred the horse firmly, not roughly, and sped off at the same rate of speed at which he had arrived, downhill in the direction of his home.

In ten minutes Duncan returned, now in a small cart pulled by a pony. The animal was a hangdog creature made to look even more so by the thick blinders it wore, but it pranced around the bend, tugging its load behind it at a quite lively step.

"We'll take this into . . . town, Mr. Glass. We can carry your . . . food back in it." He swung open a small door at the rear and gestured to Glass to climb in. As soon as Glass had positioned himself diagonally opposite Duncan, the boy whipped the horse and spun the cart around in the clearing in front of the cottage. As he drove, his lower jaw hung open loosely and bobbed up and down in rhythm with the cart. A small stream of saliva drifted down the right side of his jaw, slanted backward slightly from the force of the wind on his face.

"I think we should just ride down as far as the main road, don't you, Duncan?" Glass was worried about, first, a nine-year-old-driver; second, one who seemed short a few of his brain cells; third, a rickety old vehicle on a road frequented by modern cars and heavy trucks; and, probably, being seen on his first day in Loch Killilan riding in a pony cart. "Why don't we walk the rest of the way from there? It's only a mile or so, isn't it?"

Duncan said nothing, just shook his head negatively as if this were, for any one of a number of reasons, simply unacceptable. But as he sped on toward the two empty houses, he began to rein the pony off to the right side of the road, then through the open space before the gutted stone house to the right, aiming now for a much narrower wagon track that veered off diagonally toward a slender opening in the wall of The Gap. As they passed by the house, Glass could tell that it had once been three different dwellings, all attached and, probably, built at different times. The end they passed first had a gaping hole in its stone facade, the size of a freight-dock door, where a regular domestic entryway ought to have been. The floor was littered with rubble of various sorts, including wood from the collapsed upper story and roofing; though the beams still stood at the top, the roof itself was virtually all gone. The middle section of the solid stone building was more nearly intact, its three windows and one door still in their proper form, as was the third and final section. These were divided off from each other by interior stone walls as thick as the outer ones, but any material that might have created rooms or floors within each unit was now either gone or in a heap on the bare ground of the lower floor. A pile of gravel lay unnaturally on the grass directly before the center unit, and the pony cart rocked rather violently as Duncan steered the right wheel across the base of this mound. They passed quickly out of sight of the ruin.

Then over a rise, out before them, about a hundred feet below, lay Loch Killilan, six miles long, a half-mile across, surrounded on every side by high, steep green grassy slopes which allowed space for no more than the highway and, at one point, a small town between them and the water. The Loch too was beautiful, though in a more traditionally real sense than The Gap had been. Its deep blue waters which, from their present height, reflected the mountains were sunlit at the end nearest to them but fog-enshrouded at the far shores to the east where the Loch opened into the salt waters of the Inner Sound.

Duncan took the pony cart down the winding wagon track as speedily as he could—he seemed to have some nine-year-old craving for speed—saying nothing, slack jaw bobbing with each rut or pothole in the road surface. They arrived behind a row of stores about a block to the east of The Angus Bull.

Duncan, being a Menzies, seemed to have the option of using the rear door to the store, or perhaps being a retarded Menzies had been condemned to the use of that one, so that was the way they entered. They surprised a blue-uniformed woman who was tearing down corrugated cartons. As if she had recognized Glass on sight, she spun on her heel and rushed toward the front of the store, where another uniformed woman operated one of two cash registers in a stubby checkout lane. The first woman spoke a line to the second; the second peered at Glass's face as he moved toward the front of the store, then reached over to a rack of paperback books which abutted the checkout lane. Glass recognized the book she removed from it to be the British edition of *Gratuitous Glory*, which he had seen in King's Cross Station—indeed, every book on the rack was the same, and the rack was no longer full.

"Hello, there, Mr. Glass. We've been told to be on the lookout for you. It is indeed a privilege for us here at Sciennes' to be able to serve someone so distinguished as yourself." Glass sensed that she had not read the book, in all likelihood had no more evidence of his importance or even authorship than his picture on the back cover. Even before he could think of anything meaningful to say, she was pulling a ball-point pen from her apron pocket and bringing him the book for a signature. Glass made modest small talk while he did it, promised to sign all she had left "on another occasion," then watched her write a sign advertising the future availability of "signed" copies for a mere one pound more than the list price.

The store was modeled after an American supermarket, though everything had been fractioned by eighths. The aisles were shorter and fewer, the selections of brands barely plural, the prices apparently cheaper, the carts smaller, the ceiling lower. Never could Glass establish the long gliding roll past unwanted sections as one did in America; rather, he idled a long time at each spot, since jelly and toilet paper, cereal and ketchup were all stocked relatively close to one another. In gawking at these shelves to try to discern some subtle ordering principle, he persistently rammed the cart of the same dark-haired fortyish woman who kept trying to shop despite him. Each time he said, "Pardon me," she, "Sorry," and then they proceeded on toward what was doomed to be a replay of the same encounter in each ensuing aisle. Finally he let Duncan take over, and in the last aisle Duncan rammed her.

"Sorry, Aunt Etta." When Glass heard Duncan say this, he began to understand that the woman had perhaps been placing herself in their way from the start, had wanted to speak with him but was reluctant to make an innocent opening.

"That's quite okay, Duncan; my fault actually." She looked at Glass carefully as she made no attempt to guard the question she now asked her nephew. "And who is your friend, may I ask?" She never looked at the boy, only at Glass.

"Mr. Glass. He . . . just came here . . . to live."

She cocked her head slightly, as if she felt foolish for not having known. "Yes, of course, Jason Glass, the author." She looked him up and down unselfconsciously. "Somehow the picture on the jacket of your book made you look older and wiser, perhaps shorter, than you are."

This was not exactly the opening line to put an International Book Award winner at his ease. He groped for a response. "I'm sorry if I disappoint you," he returned with a clumsy and strained attempt at friendliness.

"No, no, no, Mr. Glass. No disappointment. It's just that you reminded me strikingly of . . . someone I once knew. Actually a brother of mine who's been dead thirty years now. I felt I was seeing some sort of apparition." Now she laughed uneasily. "So you have arrived to get under way with . . ." She lost the train of her thought simply because she continued to stare at him in amazement, her mouth set in a subtle smile, her eyes sharply analytical and constantly roving about him.

"Yes, I am here to get to work on the projected book your family wants me to write about—"

"I know, about poor old Roberts. Well, have at it if you must, Mr. Glass, but please understand that you are working for Farquhar alone on this. The rest of us would have been just as happy if he had never gotten this idea and had left you in America where you belong." At least this time she had realized the excessive forthrightness of her own words and was quick to apologize. "Oh, please forgive me, Mr. Glass. Jason—may I call you that? I am Henrietta Menzies. Farquhar is my older brother. We have nothing against you—please don't misunderstand me. It's just that you are the third, no, fourth person he's tried to get to write this book in the last five years. We thought he had given up, but it turns out all he has done is to stop fussing around with students, hacks, and unemployed free-lancers and gotten himself an international prizewinner instead." She sighed. "Oh, well, I suppose he will get what he wants this time."

Glass was surprised to hear that there had been others. "What was wrong with what the others gave him? That might prove useful to know." They stood in front of a small but very odoriferous butcher counter.

"I am not clear on all that, really. I see Farquhar as infrequently as I can. The first chap wrote the whole thing up but the publisher rejected it because it was boring or something. The second got in some sort of argument with Farquhar and quit. The third—last year—was sacked. You see, Jason, this story must be told just so. Farquhar's way, no other."

Coupled with Sybil's statements, this assignment was beginning to have about it the odor of the meat counter. "Why doesn't he do it himself, then?"

She laughed slightly as she picked up a pound of bacon the butcher had been wrapping for her. "First of all, he can't even write a letter to his investment counselors or his attorney that makes the least bit of sense. Second, he feels that no one with the Menzies name should author this gem. Third, Farquhar never does anything he can pay someone else to do. How much *is* he paying you, by the way?"

"I don't really know. Certain rather generous guarantees were implied in the contact letter. How much was he paying my predecessors?"

"The first chap got a quid a page." She watched Glass flinch on this. "The next perhaps a bit more—maybe two. The last chap, the one he fired, must have been about the same. Farquhar felt he did not need the money badly enough, however, and was not working up to par,"

Glass leaped ahead of her. "Oh, so it was essential also that he have someone now who *needed* the money. Is that right?"

She smiled ironically now. It was the smile of an older woman who felt herself far ahead of a younger man who was also an outsider. "Well, yes, but not just *that*. He did need someone who could write as well. Perhaps someone who had other needs also—such as a female interest. So you see, he got lucky—came up with an award-winning biographer who had no woman in his life because he was in the midst of a dirty divorce and who needed the money because his wife had taken all his cash. You were perfect, Jason, and here you are, aren't you?"

About to say more, apparently, she desisted, ruffled Duncan's hair, then pivoted with a very cavalier wave of her hand and resumed her shopping. While there was clear disdain in her sudden termination of the conversation, Glass could tell it was directed more toward Farquhar, perhaps even Roberts, than it was toward him. In terms of the project he was about to undertake, he would have been more comfortable if it had been the other way around.

4 *THE WELCOME*

IT REQUIRED MOST OF THE HALF-HOUR he had allowed himself to reach the Castle Menzies on the next loch to the south, Loch Duich. As he rolled through the small town of Dornie, he could already see the towers rising up on the tiny island in the Loch beyond it. It was not a big castle as castles went, but it was set spectacularly against the backdrop of water and mountain and twilight sky. From the parking area at the edge of the Loch, a solid, triple-arched stone causeway crossed the narrow channel between the mainland and the island and led to a cobblestoned walk which wove around the outskirts of a series of outer walls to the main gate beyond them. The castle itself comprised three distinct buildings, and these were tied together by high stone walls which frequently dropped straight down to the water's edge with only the barest of shorelines to reveal that the castle did not find its very foundations at the bottom of the Loch.

The main building, solid rock and heavily chimneyed, was turreted itself and imposingly square. It was almost completely windowless. The place probably had been too small to garrison much of an army in more difficult days, but in modern times it could not have been more romantically constructed for someone who wished to live in a castle that exuded only the myths and the glories of the past and not its violence and bloodshed.

Glass climbed the cobblestone walk carefully—the surface was rough and irregular, the lighting almost nonexistent save for the small lamp above the portcullis ahead. To his chagrin, he found the gate securely locked. The massive oak doors, which must have been twelve feet high and ten wide, were themselves barriered behind a gate of wood and metal bars which more closely suggested a long-outdated prison than a castle. There was no bell or knocker or any other means of signaling someone within to open it. He must have been spotted from the lookout tower as he came up the causeway, however, because he could hear locks and latches being undone on the other side of the doors, then a chain drawn through its hasps, then the creaking of the hinges as the left door began to swing slowly aside.

At first he could not see the man who had opened it, but within a few seconds he could dimly discern a small figure about fifteen feet back of the gate working a hand crank which lifted the portcullis straight upward into the stonework.

"Just this way, please." It was definitely an ancient voice, and the stoop-framed figure now clicked on a flashlight and waved Glass to follow him. Immediately they were in the fog again, passing through the gateway into the interior courtyard of the castle. Glass could make out a few faint lights from what surrounding windows there were, but he had to guide himself entirely by the old figure's flashlight. As they advanced he could hear a steady electrical snapping sound from the nether reaches of the gatehouse they were leaving behind—the castle required its own power plant probably. Several paces later they attained an exterior staircase, stone with an iron railing on the right side. They reached a level walk up against the solid-rock side of the main building, then ascended another exterior staircase, with a stone railing this time, which eventually terminated in front of another, though smaller, oak doorway. A barely visible lantern light illuminated this entrance from above, but Glass could see brighter lights within through the small peephole window. The old man rapped three times on the door with his flashlight; then, with no further word to Glass, he started his treacherous descent back down the slippery staircase.

For more than a minute Glass stood alone. Just as he was about to assume that he should knock again—certainly not go back down to locate his escort—the door latch was lifted within, and a very proper English butler scraped the door open along the rock flooring.

"Mr. Glass?" he said with forced inquiry once the door had been shut. When Glass had acknowledged this, the butler said, "Follow me, please" and began to lead him up still another stairway, interior this time. The light here was very bad as well, though at least there was no fog now, and Glass had to watch each winding step very carefully lest he strike one at too narrow a spot and thus fall on what looked to be a very unforgiving surface.

Glass was led into the main room at the next level, which the butler referred to as "the banqueting hall," and asked what he would like to drink. With little British experience as yet, he chose a sherry, sure they must have this. Without suggesting that he be seated, the butler disappeared to fetch it.

The room in which he stood, awkward and alone, was truly magnificent. It was perhaps twelve feet high, its floor planked with white oak, its ceiling crisscrossed with massive dark oak beams which spanned the length and width of the room. The walls were the same gray stone as the exterior, decorated with paintings of earlier generations of Menzies, some seated together around tables, others in single portraits. Pieces of brass and flags of clan significance were also displayed, as well as plaster heraldry which seemed to grow from the rock surface itself. The wall opposite the doorway was dominated by a ten-foot-long fireplace, already ablaze, which was encased in white marble and decorated with shields and script mottos painted on its front. The furniture —tables, chairs, benches, bookcases, a standing clock, and a grand banquet table—was Sheraton and Chippendale.

The banquet table must have been twenty feet long. It was laid with bright silver cutlery on a white tablecloth, and set for only three—one place at each end and one in the middle facing the fireplace. Each setting had its own salt and pepper cellars, water pitcher, and hors d'oeuvre tray. Glass hoped sound carried well here, though as yet there was no means or reason to test it.

The room was overpoweringly impressive and, despite its size, warm—but Glass felt yet again that this was the residence of someone who appreciated the concept of castles far beyond their practical worth or historical function. Then, out of an arched alcove at the far end of the room, stepped a startlingly beautiful woman.

She was strawberry blond—even in the low light and at great distance he could tell that—and wearing a brilliant red floor-length evening dress which was fastened closely at her neck and decorated by a gold chain and medallion. She was tall, perhaps five feet nine or ten, made to look even taller by her slender build and long blond hair which fell to well below her shoulders. As she approached she smiled, perhaps even flushed a bit, and extended her long gloved arm to shake his hand. He was stunned by her, and she knew it and appreciated it.

"I am Ann Macgregor—from London?" She inquired as if he had not recalled their conversation that very morning, perhaps because his gaping mouth indicated some sort of mental derangement that she had not expected in him. Glass found it hard to believe, as he stared at her, that she could look so fresh, so neat, so beautiful after having traveled the very same interminable string of railroad track that he had just the day before.

"Of course, Miss Macgregor. But please call me Jason. If you don't, you'll be lingering behind various others in the district who already are. Your sister among them." He could see the facial resemblance between them, the pure British line with just a touch of something indefinably Germanic which, far from impairing it, rendered it even more beautiful. But whereas Sybil's face was marred by the fact that she was toying with unwanted weight, Ann's was marred by nothing.

Before they could say more, the butler appeared with Glass's sherry and something else, he could not tell what, for Ann. They chatted idly for a while and then Ann gave him a tour of the room, oddly seeming to know the background, history, and purpose of every relic and antique it contained. She explained the rarity of the cutlery vase that stood as a centerpiece to the banqueting table; the history and individual purposes of the cutlery pieces on the sideboard; the watches, seals, rings, and miniatures that were displayed in a glass case near the archway where she had entered. She pointed to two slits in the stonework, barely two inches wide apiece, through which soldiers had in former times observed the proceedings at banquets and so protected their clan chief from the treachery of Judas guests. Throughout her description, Glass noted the mellifluousness of her rounded British voice, which echoed ever so slightly into the distant corners of the room. Ten minutes after meeting her, Glass already felt a strong attraction to this beautiful and unexpected woman.

Then out of the staircase from which Glass himself had entered rang another voice. This one did not echo mellifluously. Rather it roared in hearty laughter, laughter so loud that it almost seemed to have been mustered for the occasion by an actor who, by the very act of stepping from the wings, changes his mood, his bearing, even his identity.

"Glass, Glass, Glass, glad to see you at last, old chap." It was a Falstaffian voice, almost a bellow, though it was not a liquored voice in any sense. Farquhar Menzies nearly ran to where Glass stood with Ann before the fireplace, his hand extended ready to pump. Somewhere in his memory Glass recalled having once been afraid that Menzies would make his first entrance wearing a kilt. This did not happen, though he did wear his clan tartan in the form of richly tailored dinner jacket with a tie and cummerbund to match. It was one of the most colorful Scots plaids that Glass had encountered; there was only a little of the traditional red in it, and the most dominant colors seemed to be green, black, orange, and yellow and various cross shades in between each two of those. The red was more to be found in his hair, which was cut full and draped toward his shoulders in a sort of pageboy, in his mustache, which was profuse, and in his face, which was something well beyond ruddy.

"At your service, Mr. Menzies"—Glass had rehearsed his proper opening line numerous times and for some reason had come up with this one. Perhaps, on the basis of what he had already been told, it would in the long run be the most accurate.

"And you, Ann dear. How was your trip? Marvelous of you to come on such short notice . . . and so far, as well. How long can you stay?" He kissed her just off the lips.

She narrowed her smile just slightly, tingeing it with a bit of real disappointment. "Only three days at the most this time, I fear, Farquhar. I will try to get back as frequently as I can—as often as Mr. Glass needs me, I suspect."

Glass suspected he might decide to need her quite frequently; even now he caught himself planning to take note of every possible difficulty this project might throw happily in his path.

"Well, good, then, Ann. Three days will be enough to get Glass here doing what we expect him to do, won't it?"

Glass did not like the way this was phrased. Authors did not like to think of themselves as doing what was "expected" of them, especially International Book Award winners.

"It will be enough time," Ann responded diplomatically, "to acquaint him with the materials and the backgrounds. From there it will be up to his talents—we hope his genius—to take over." Glass loved her for this and feared he showed it as he beamed at her. "If *we* could have told this story properly, we would not have needed to retain his services, now, would we?" If there was some reprimand in this, it was done so beautifully, almost so sexually, that Menzies detected only a bit of it. Though he *did* detect that bit, Glass could tell.

Within minutes they sat down to dinner, seemingly miles from each other at their positions along the enormous rectangular banqueting table. Menzies' voices was so enormous, so gruffly powerful, that Glass could hear what he said at the opposite end even more clearly than he could have heard an average person sitting directly beside him. Ann, who sat along the side between them, was clearly audible when she spoke to him directly, but her voice was less distinct when she turned in Menzies' direction.

Not surprisingly, Menzies did eighty-five percent of the talking. He allowed the conversation to wander hither and yon until the main course was brought—venison, served by six servants—but then he focused discussion on the subject that had obviously preoccupied him from the start: Roberts Menzies. He talked loudly, exuberantly. His delivery seemed almost theatrical, cast to the balcony and the stalls at once. He could not help himself.

"There are so many unrecognized heroes in all wars, Glass, that I had despaired of ever having my grandfather's feats at Ladysmith known. Until I caught sight of your book in the *TLS*—Ann here brought it to my attention, actually—and from that moment on I knew we must have you." Glass wondered to whom the "we" referred—certainly not any Menzies he had so far encountered. "So I called Ann in London—she is still a girl of the Lochs even if she has deserted us for the time being—and told her to offer you what you must have to research and tell this story for us." Again the plural. "By the way, I don't believe we've come to terms as yet, have we, as to what your fee shall be." He looked confidently toward Ann, though she appeared uneasy in return.

"Well, Mr. Menzies," Glass replied, "I suppose all any author hopes for is the standard terms—a reasonable advance and then ten percent of the gross on the book." He hesitated. "I was thinking, though, that my success with *Gratuitous Glory* might enable me to get twelve percent after a little bargaining with Farneswells."

Menzies roared in what was almost anger. "A *reasonable* advance! *Twelve* percent! That's robbery, sir!"

Glass flushed. Ann clenched her teeth on a piece of venison, did not look up from her plate. "I was led to believe that . . ." Glass had been led to believe just enough to get him to Scotland, apparently.

"You are performing a service for the Menzies family and for the world, Glass! You should get twenty percent! Thirty! Fifty! Who should have this money but the man who fashions the words? Miserable green-skinned booksellers who would have to have sunshine explained to them if they ever stepped out into it? Technicians who cut paper and sew it into covers? Nigger-black printers? Ann, tell me, Ann, can't we get Glass here fifty percent at least?"

Now Glass recognized why she was clenching. "Actually, Farquhar," she said carefully, swallowing her venison, "I've never heard of an author receiving more than fifteen percent on the board-cover sales. Were the book to go into soft-covers, he could negotiate fifty percent of that, I suppose, but—"

"Fifteen percent! Well, I *demand*, Ann, that Farneswells *start* there. Glass, I will have my solicitor look into this. We shall construct some graduated scale that they will have to accept or lose this gem to Macmillan." Ann looked dubious. "Now, until then you shall have all your expenses paid by me so long as you are here, and I shall give you a ten-thousand-pound flat payment that need not be repaid. How is that for a start? I understand your wife has left you a bit short of late."

"Mr. Menzies, I will accept the expenses, though I will try to keep them to a minimum. But I can't really accept an outright cash payment. It could look later as if I had been bribed to write the book *around* the truth rather than according to it. If reviewers learned of it, they would say I was simply your puppet, speaking the words you mouthed for me."

Menzies looked distinctly uncomfortable at this. He too stopped chewing, did not bother to swallow, spoke anyway. "Well, of course, Glass, you would surely not be our puppet. But"—now he swallowed while he thought—"we would certainly like to exercise some . . . shall we call them 'editorial privileges' . . . with respect to your work."

Ann leaped in to clarify another line that she knew Glass, if he had any authorial integrity at all, would balk at. "What Farquhar really means, Jason, is that he would want the right to review what you have written here and there to make sure that nothing has been omitted, that you have acknowledged all the source material available rather than overlooked or misunderstood some of it and possibly misrepresented some dimension of the story that someone closer, such as Farquhar, might better understand." Ann, if she was a good editor, should not have been so wordy. Glass spotted the dodge, but decided to let it lie for the moment.

"Mr. Menzies, I will of course be open to criticism or reminders, just so long as I am not asked to write anything counter to what the diary reveals, the War Office records document, and the like." He sipped his glass of wine slowly while he studied Farquhar's silent response. He could tell that neither his words nor Ann's had stated what Menzies had hoped to hear. Menzies wished more control than either had yet offered, but he too let the matter rest for the time being. Glass suspected there would be some collisions between them down the line. He shifted into another question which had been forming for some minutes. "Also, Mr. Menzies, I was under the impression that I was working just for you on this. You speak of 'we.' Could you tell me who else will be reviewing my work?"

Menzies seemed to be jarred out of his other thoughts by this. "Oh, no, Glass. My mistake. I was using the figurative 'we.' My sister, Henrietta, has no interest in this project—don't even bother to consult her for any information, actually. My son, Clyde, is rarely sober enough to care, and my mother is not well mentally. It will just be me. Forgive the 'we,' won't you? No, Ann is right. It is just that we—I—have waited so long to have my grandfather's story told that I don't wish anything omitted."

Glass knew Farquhar was still waffling. "Since you have selected me to write it, however, you must give me some license as to how it should be structured and incorporated. Otherwise, you might just as well publish the diary unedited, with pages of footnotes and endnotes attached which, also unedited, document the substance of the diary from military records and the like. If you want this story told so that anyone other than Boer War scholars will read it, you must rely on my instincts with regard to an audience."

"Yes, yes, Glass, we understand each other on all that clearly." They didn't—Menzies was not even listening. Rather he was signaling to two servants to clear away the plates—his own was empty, though Glass still had a third to go and Ann a half. Their plates were taken on cue anyway. Glass looked confused, Ann embarrassed though not surprised. Now Menzies leaped from the table and moved quickly across the room to a bookcase full of leather-bound volumes. He selected from it the only one that was not—a ring binder overflowing with ruffled sheets.

"Here, then, Glass, is the document." He set it carefully on the table, the way an acolyte would set a Mass book on an altar. The pages Glass could see were quite yellowed with age and, probably, dampness, and some edges shed fragments of themselves despite Menzies' care. "I've taken the liberty of putting some holes through the pages and circling them with reinforcer rings so that you might handle them more safely." He did not open the volume, as if, having read it so many times, he could recite by heart anything Glass wanted to know.

"How regularly kept was this diary?" Glass had had problems with sporadically kept records in the Annie Daly research.

"Irregularly, though there is plenty there, I assure you. More than enough to write the story correctly. It begins in 1897 when Roberts, then twenty-five, took his wife, Catherine, to South Africa to serve three years in the Dundee hospital in Natal. For that period it is regularly kept, though the contents would be of more interest to a surgeon than to you or me. It becomes considerably more interesting as the climate of war begins to be felt. Roberts meticulously documents his removal of a hundred patients from Dundee to Ladysmith in the week before the war began. They were the only civilians to get away before the Boers took the town, Glass! And they were all in ambulances drawn by oxen. Marvelous, don't you think?"

How was this done? was all that crossed Glass's mind. He presumed the pages would tell him that. Menzies continued: "Then, of course, he is quite thorough through the Siege itself. There are a number of Siege diaries available, you might know" —Glass did—"but this is the only one that was kept by a doctor and which can speak directly to the medical issues. You were told by Ann, I think, that Roberts brought ninety percent of the patients he took from Dundee alive through the Siege—this when the mortality rate for healthy civilians was thirty-three percent. You see why this story just *must* be told, now don't you?" Glass nodded, but, he thought, how was this done too? "After he delivered his patients to the hospital in Pietermaritzburg on March fourth, 1900, the diary is more sporadically kept. Less excitement then, I suppose." Or less chance for self-aggrandizement, perhaps?

Glass interrupted: "Now, since Roberts was a civilian doctor, and since he could not go back to his assignment in Dundee, he left the war zone once he was freed from Ladysmith?"

Menzies shook his head negatively, proudly. "Not at all. He remained behind and assisted the British field hospitals during the march to Johannesburg and Pretoria in April and May of 1900. Then, when those cities were taken, he accompanied General Buller's troops eastward in pursuit of the fleeing Transvaal commandos and the government officials trying to escape through Lourenço Marques."

"That was accomplished by September if I recall my reading. Then he came home?"

"No. He then had himself reassigned to the hospital on the western front where the pursuit of the guerrillas was taking place."

Again Glass's reading came forward. "The British hospital at Bloemfontein, in the Orange Free State?"

A cautious nod. A pause. "But only for a while in that hospital, Glass. Then he made the supreme sacrifice. He took over care of the sick Boer women and children at the concentration camp outside Bloemfontein, where the mortality rate was even worse than Ladysmith's. He actually took up residence there! What courage, don't you think, Glass? It must be told!" Glass had read of Kitchener's terrible late-war camps set up to "protect" enemy noncombatants. No sane man would willingly take up residence there. But perhaps the sort of nobility or charity Roberts demonstrated was, to the man normally dubbed sane, madness. "He stayed on till the end of the war, did not leave that camp till the last survivor had exited before him." This sounded now like myth.

"Was he able to do as well in the camp—mortalitywise, I mean—as he did at Ladysmith?"

Menzies had taken a deep breath, about to launch in some other direction, but then deflated when he heard the question. "Well, no, not actually. But you see, the Dundee patients he brought to Ladysmith were his all along. He had worked with them from the first. The women and children he found at the Bloemfontein camp were well along in enteric, typhoid, dysentery; some had never known proper sanitary arrangements and habits in the first place. He did well, though, quite well—awfully so, actually." He was convincing himself.

"So then he came home? With the end of the war in 1902?"

"No."

"Why not?" Glass noticed Ann stiffen for some reason now, as if she awaited something she wished she would not hear.

"Two reasons, Glass." This was too well prepared, as if he had thought of offering one at one moment, seven at another, and had settled on two. "First, Roberts was a peaceful man at heart. He was appalled by the war—you will see that in his diary. He was against all war after that. So he remained on to work with those Boer and British officials who were the most enlightened, those like Jan Smuts who were committed to ending the friction, even the differentiation, between Briton and Boer at the earliest moment. Smuts was one of the founders of the United Nations in later years—this was the sort of man Roberts admired and stayed on to work with for as long as he could."

"What could persuade him to ever go home, then?"

"Well, he was Angus Menzies'—the clan chief—he was his only son. Eventually he would have to return here, and did, to accept his own role as chief."

"And when did he become chief?"

Menzies looked on more comfortable ground now. "He never did, you see, for his own death antedated his father's by several months in 1925. So Roberts' only son, Bruce—who had been born at the height of the Siege in Ladysmith—became chief then."

"So Roberts left South Africa in . . . ?"

"In 1914. He went to war with a South African regiment as a medical officer."

"I thought he despised war. He would have been in his forties then, he would not have had to go."

"He was a man of medicine and a man of peace, Glass." Menzies seemed annoyed now. "He could not single-handedly stop the Great War, now, could he? He had realized his dream of unity between South Africa and Britain at least; now he went to care for both." His voice was pitching high. "And he did a damn good job of it. We have his medals—not just from our own government and from South Africa but from Canada and Australia and the United States! He healed them, Glass, just as he did in Ladysmith and Bloemfontein years earlier! How many medals did Peter Daly get? One! You said so yourself in your book! Roberts had a full score of them. He —"

Glass was taken aback. "I am sure, Mr. Menzies, that he did! I was not questioning that. I was just trying to see the story in its broadest outl—"

Ann spoke above both of them. "Gentlemen, please. Farquhar, Mr. Glass meant no offense. No one is challenging you." Something in her voice suggested he had been challenged before.

There was a silence while Farquhar calmed himself. His face was red, so red it turned his long hair bright orange by contrast. Glass picked up the slack. "Now, what was the other reason—besides the humane one—why he stayed on in South Africa between the two wars?"

"His wife. He lost his wife during the Siege. She died in childbirth, or shortly after it. He could not bear to leave her remains there nor to live in Scotland without her. She was a noble woman, a nurse who labored through her own pregnancy to save the sick and dying in Ladysmith." Menzies was much more quiet now, as if he were afraid someone would overhear this part of the conversation, as if it were an emotion to be ashamed of.

"And he never remarried?"

Now repulsion came over his face. He whispered even lower now, as if he could not bear to hear himself say the words. "Yes, he did. Right after the Great War in 1919. A German woman. The enemy. A fat horse of a woman. And he brought her here to replace his beloved Catherine as wife of the next clan chief. He took Catherine Clyde to South Africa and brought home his so-called Maria from Germany. He did not want to marry her. He had to."

"Had to? Pregnancy?"

"No, no, no, Glass. He could not exist alone, you see. He suffered curvature of the spine during Ladysmith and used a cane for the rest of his life. But during the Great War he lost both his left arm and his right eye. He was severely crippled, you see. He needed a wife. Only such as she would have married someone so battered as he. But she was smart. She had conspired to be a clan chief's wife, hadn't she?"

"But she never made it once Roberts died before his father?"

"Yes, although she died the same year as well, also before Angus. But after Roberts."

"Of what?"

"How the hell would I know, Glass? I was less than a year old. Of overweight probably. No one speaks of her. They all hated her." Another silence. Glass could not help noting that there were areas of this whole story that Farquhar Menzies did not like being led into. These would be the ones over which they would undoubtedly come into disagreement.

Now Ann broke the silence, as if to lead the conversation back in the direction in which Glass needed it to go, even though Menzies was now being too defensive to get it there. "We were speaking of the diary, Farquhar. You suggest that it is less regular after the end of the Boer War."

Menzies seemed as if he had been wakened from a dream. "Yes. Less regular after Ladysmith, in fact. There are some pages from the Bloemfontein camp. That's all. After that, only a scattering of pages from disconnected dates. Very little. Nothing at all after 1914."

Glass was perplexed at this. "Then how am I to write the later years of the story? Are there other—"

"Damn it, Glass. All I want is the Ladysmith episode! The great heroism there. The great medical skill that saved all those people. What comes later is not important."

"What about all the medals from World War One, then?"

"Oh, yes, I would like those in, in an appendix perhaps."

Glass now leaned back from the table, crossed his arms, and stared directly at Ann. "Miss Macgregor, I was under the impression that this book was to be molded much the same way *Gratuitous Glory* was—a study not of a man in isolation but of a man in relation to the times in which he lived, the effect he had on those times and the effect he had on the future. Perhaps I am wrong, but that seemed to me the most praised aspect of the Annie Daly legend. I don't—"

"Damn Annie Daly, Glass!" Farquhar stood up now, had pounded himself erect when his right fist hit the table. "I want Roberts developed as Peter Daly was, not his daughter. She was a bore. She took jobs and wiped her sisters' and brothers' noses and bums. Dreadful. I did not even finish the tawdry story of all that." He dashed to the bookcase and produced a hardback copy of Glass's prizewinning book. The front third was sprung and riffled; in the final two-thirds it was possible the pages had not even been cut. "Peter Daly saved people under fire. Peter Daly saved his regimental officer and his son!" He was virtually shrieking now. "Peter Daly's is a story of a man responding under pressure in such a way and to such a degree that it will now never be forgotten!"

"But he did all this at the utter expense of his family! If you'd read the rest of the—"

"Damn his family and their whining! He brought them glory! What else he did does not count a fart! Peter Daly was a great man. Roberts Menzies was a great man. Daly has been recognized now. Roberts Menzies has not!" He reached in his side jacket pocket and produced a thick roll of currency wrapped in a rubber band. He shoved it past Ann down the table. As it neared Glass, the rubber band broke and twenty-pound notes sprayed all over Glass's end of the table and onto the floor. "There is your money, Glass. Pick it up! Tell the world of Roberts Menzies. Go on now, pick it up—before your wife finds out about it and impounds it!"

Glass stared at him expressionlessly. "I won't pick it up."

Ann was frozen. Menzies glowered at him as if he had never been defied before. He breathed heavily, started several other lines, then ceased and calmed himself. "Bradford!" The butler appeared in the doorway behind him. "Pick up those notes for Mr. Glass, will you? Have them sealed in an envelope and brought back to the billeting room, to which we shall now retire. Have some whisky brought as well." The whole time he said this, he never took his eyes off Glass. He had expected him to pick the money up, and Glass had not.

And so what seemed as if it were to be a simple after-dinner drink, if anything orchestrated by Farquhar Menzies could dare be termed simple, turned into perhaps the most bizarre incident of the evening. His plaid coat open, his bow tie askew, his long hair mussed by effort, his face streaming perspiration, Menzies sat at a grand piano, pumping it like one in a music hall rather than one on a concert stage, belting out patriotic songs with which he hoped, apparently, to frame and underpin Glass's efforts. He sang "Marching to Pretoria" at the top of his lungs, well down into the fourth or fifth verse before he ran out of lyrics, all the while using eye and arm signals to encourage Ann and Glass to sing as well; but they knew no more than the chorus, and this they sang with reluctance and reserve, eying each other all the while, she with a plea for tolerance, he with simple embarrassed confusion. Then "The Road to Mandalay," a song of the utmost masculine gusto that Ann seemed to back down from but which Glass, as if unwillingly and unintentionally caught up in it, hammered out with something approaching the enthusiasm of Farquhar Menzies. It was a good song, one Glass had sung in bars during his college days. He could sing if he treated the billeting room of the Castle Menzies like some Whiffenpoof rathskeller, but "God Save the Queen" drew him back to his present predicament and he could not help thinking of the American words to the same tune and wish, Margot excepted, that he were back there. He had been dragged all these miles to bastardize a book for a madman, an obsessed monomaniac.

The evening finally ended, well after midnight. Glass helped Ann Macgregor into her light coat and edged out of Farquhar's interminable and repetitive farewells and encouragements, almost counting the steps to the car, which still seemed miles off in time if not in distance. Menzies had offered them both accommodations at the castle for the night, but both chose to return to their "homes"—Glass to his cottage, Ann to Henrietta's, where she apparently regularly resided when she was in the Lochs. But enough had not yet happened even as they were on the winding staircase toward the outer door, and so now it did.

In olden days it would have been candlelight shining down from above them, but now it was a flashlight. A woman appeared and stopped them in their tracks on the stairway. She simply gazed at them, superior because of her distance up the staircase, recognized immediately by Ann and Menzies. Her frail frame was encased in a spotless white nylon robe. She was an old woman in everything but her face—seventies perhaps, but her hair and eyes and cheeks were of a much younger woman. Blond rather than gray, whether by dye or nature it was hard to tell; the blue eyes sharp rather than puddled by age. She stared without expression, not at Ann or Menzies, but at Jason Glass. Finally Farquhar addressed her, nervously.

"Mother. What are you doing up and about at this hour? Go back to bed. It is chill here." Something about the tone of his voice suggested greater fear for something other than her health.

She smiled back at him, not maliciously, more ironically, then returned her eyes to Glass and spoke. "Beware of delving too deeply into these matters, Mr. Glass"—the voice was young as well; only the body was old, quite old. "You will be happier with yourself if you tell the tale Farquhar wishes told." She sounded utterly as if she had been a party to the entire evening rather than an intruder in the midst of its breakup. "The truth is not worth knowing, Mr. Glass. It is dangerous to know. It has driven two of us to our graves and the rest of us to instability. The real Roberts Menzies *can* be known, but if you know him you will be driven from your peace of mind; driven from what is left of your youth; driven, perhaps, as others were, from life."

"Mother, please stop this babbling." Whatever it was, it was hardly babble. Menzies moved up the stairs and took her by the left biceps. "I'll just see you off here, Glass, Ann. Cheerio, now. I'll be in touch by phone in a day or so." He waved and turned her gently toward the upper reaches of the castle.

She began sobbing as he took her, but she did not resist. What she said, despite her age and emotion, was clear to all below her. "Now we shall all have to die. The others were safe because they were stupid, Farquhar. *He* is not. Now we shall all have to die."

5 *THE FIRST LADYSMITH DIARY*

JASON GLASS WAS SO ENAMORED OF THE BEAUTY of The Gap that he quickly found himself a place along the lakeside where he could work outdoors on fine days: his "perfect place," where he could lean against one rock, write on a flat one to his right, and receive advice (soon, he hoped, when she returned again from London) from his editor, who could sit comfortably against another rock on the other side of the flat one. Since Jason was right-handed and Ann Macgregor left, this was very convenient indeed. Since both "leaning" rocks faced the lake, it was also convenient for Sybil to send Duncan and his sheepdog, Charlie, swimming any time she saw Glass working there. Normally Glass did not mind; but today, as he savagely peppered the crystalline Scottish air with the grossest multi-hyphenated obscenities, he hoped the boy was not, in his simple mind, recording them for unwitting future use.

What Farquhar Menzies had given him was proving a sham. Glass had arrived at the lakeside to apply the broad tests to Roberts' diary that he had learned to apply to Annie Daly's. He wanted to know, first of all, why Roberts had kept this document. Most diarists simply want to prove to themselves, if to no one else, that they not only exist but also count. They wish to see themselves as active rather than passive agents in a world dominated by that impersonal force called history. A diary is a sort of defense mechanism, therefore. It downplays "facts," plays up perceptions. It sets the chronicle of events, knowable to anyone, to the rear and brings personal experience to the fore. No matter what the "opening speech" that most great diarists provide goes on to claim, at bottom the writer feels little duty to the reader, and much to himself.

Essentially, as Glass had determined with the Daly diary, the diarist was trying to satisfy two needs. The first was innocent enough and was much the one the girl on the train had set out to accomplish—to relive one's days and revive one's memories. The second was less cleanly motivated and characterized the diaries of adults who had become aware that neither they nor life would prove to be all that they had expected. Here the diarist's instinct suddenly shifted, not so much to the rewriting of facts so that they seemed better than they actually were but rather to a reportrayal of one's own behavior so that the writer would seem better than he was. While some diarists undoubtedly did this for other readers who might happen upon their pitiful volumes after they had died, most seemed to do it for themselves, to establish some testament upon which to base a more tolerant interpretation of their own shortcomings. Only because Annie Daly had proved so good, so noble in the words of others had he been able to lay this caution aside as he worked with her diary.

Something Farquhar had said about Roberts' diary—that it was unmitigatedly dull as it recorded his early days at Dundee but had picked up interest as the Boer War approached—had suggested to Glass that there might have been a change of purpose in Roberts' mind for keeping the diary which went further than a simple shift of historical circumstances. A dull writer writes dully no matter what is going on around him. If Roberts' early pages supposedly demonstrated meticulous rendering of his daily medical routine, his Boer War pages would have done substantially the same, speaking only of more severe medical crises which would have become "more interesting" only to another medical person. Where a layman would have accepted Farquhar's promise of ultimate excitement in the diary at face value, Glass suspected a change of purpose, perhaps a change of ultimate readership, perhaps the onset of a reinterpretation of self and circumstances.

But he had been totally duped. The diary was a shambles in every sense of the word and hardly invited the sort of close textual analysis Glass had planned. First of all, whole pages had been removed, perhaps whole series of pages—it was impossible to tell at a given moment how many had been taken out. It had only been toward the end of this morning's reading that Glass had noted this, for the pages which dealt with Roberts' unexciting medical activities in his first two years in South Africa had not been tampered with. In fact, the first date that turned up missing must conveniently have occupied an entire page from top to bottom—no more, no less. Only by reckoning that it contained something very significant, must have, could Glass have determined that it was gone at all. The entry for October 22, 1899, could, of course, have never been written, but two factors discounted this. First, up until that time Roberts had been careful to make one virtually every day, if only to check in with his journal; second, this was the date on which Roberts removed his hundred patients from Dundee in the ambulances. In the entry for the 21st they were all nestled in their beds; in the entry for the 23rd, they were bouncing along the road for the five-day journey to Ladysmith. Why did Roberts not discuss their removal? Or rather, why did someone see fit to remove the page entirely? Glass suspected he could piece the events of that day together from a multitude of historical and War Office records that he had already been accumulating, but he knew this augured badly for what was ahead.

It did. Later pages had been removed as well, several dozen of them from the four-month Siege period itself, the one Farquhar Menzies wanted rendered so accurately and thoroughly. And these removals were not even well disguised. In the entry for December 9, 1899, Roberts nears the bottom on one page discussing an argument he was having with the Chief Medical Officer in Ladysmith over the rationing of iodoform, and at the top of the next is the description of a polo match held two days later on the 11th. Not only was the 10th missing altogether, but the entry for the 9th stopped at mid-sentence and did not conclude and the entry for the 11th picked up in the middle of a different day, event, and sentence entirely. This happened a number of times. Not that what was left was not interesting and graphic—it was. But it was incomplete, and what had been removed, Glass suspected, was even more interesting and graphic. And it did not take him long to figure out who had edited the volume so crudely, for after first suspecting it had been Roberts himself a half-century or more before, he later discovered loose gummed reinforcements still looped around the three metal rings where pages had been torn rather than unclipped from the binding. Farquhar was the editor here. In two places he had even scissored out portions of pages and left the remainder—in both cases material so complimentary to Roberts that he would not want it overlooked—in the binding.

Worse still, there were not one but four different handwriting styles in the diary. The sheer number caused it to look to the naked eye like a ship's log on a plague-ridden frigate. Two were acceptable; two were not. One, the most prevalent by far, was Roberts' own—tiny little British straight-up-and-down unconnected letters that Glass wound up reading with a magnifier.

The second was his wife's, who signed her own initials—*ccm*—every time she made an entry for him. All of these occurred in the entries for the first two years, before the threat of war came on. None of her entries came after the flight from Dundee in mid-October of 1899, and by the first of the new year she was, of course, dead from complications of enteric fever and childbirth. The entries for late April, 1899, even suggested that she might have written of her pregnancy in the journal before she told Roberts himself.

What these two different handwritings told Glass, however, was that for the first two years the diary was kept, it was intended to be a public record; after October, 1899, it had become private. At least, that made it easy to detect where Roberts' intentions for keeping it had switched.

The two other handwritings were foreign entirely. One was clearly an attempt to imitate Roberts' own penmanship, but it was very poor and even forgot itself entirely at various places in the pages. Each time this handwriting appeared, it lasted from the first word on the page to the last, indicating forthrightly that a page had been rewritten and replaced, again by someone else. And again Glass suspected Farquhar.

Glass had at first tried to be fair, assuming perhaps that the appearance of the handwriting was changed by the surface on which Roberts might have been working. But he could not stick with this theory, for he found several passages in which the real Roberts apologized to his diary for writing on barrelheads and stone faces, and the alteration of his script was hardly significant. There was fraud in this third handwriting.

The fourth one could hardly even be called fraudulent, for fraud suggests secrecy, something of clandestine activity. This handwriting was so raw and huge that the writer got only four words to a line and needed three lines of space vertically to cross his *t*'s and bottom out his *f*'s. It looked as if a child had been employed to write this part, a bored child, one who had no intention of trying hard. Interestingly enough, all this handwriting came after January, 1902. Once it began, none of the three other hands reappeared—it was as if Roberts had in fact died in January, 1902, and someone had picked up in his place, much as comic strips are sold by one artist to another without missing a day of publication. So Glass, mostly for cynical reasons, labeled his four writers Roberts, Lady Roberts, Fake Roberts, and Non-Roberts.

More maddening still was the hodgepodge that resulted from all this. The first two years were dreadfully dull; but when the action finally got started, details of the most crucial sort had been excised, rendering not only gaps in the narrative but also confusion about other details. For instance, while there was no apparent significance to the partial entry for January 27, 1900, whatever the excised part contained would have made interesting reading. The incident dealt with the interruption of electrical services in Ladysmith on that day. How did it happen? Boer sabotage? Sick electrician? Storm? The missing part was what *told* why. What remained only revealed that Roberts apparently had some incidental electrical ability, for it was he who rectified the difficulty and kept the Ladysmith generator working through the night while the corps of engineers made more permanent repairs. Very interesting stuff, but Glass would have to guess at too much to include the incident in his narrative. An admirable piece of Roberts would be lost.

Another curious reference was noted in the Non-Roberts handwriting during the period after the Boer War had ended. The entry for April 28, 1904, began on the last line of a page, but the next page had been removed. The only words present in the huge caveman scrawl were "Today we set out for St. Louis." What the hell did that mean? St. Louis? At first he assumed St. Louis, Missouri; but what would Roberts—or someone pretending badly to *be* Roberts—be doing there? He checked an old atlas he uncovered at the cottage and found the only other St. Louis of any size in the world to be a port town in Senegal in West Africa, so Glass considered this more likely, if equally unexplainable. The final diary pages that remained were a mess of such things. In fact, Glass could make no sense of anything in the huge handwriting *after* the entry for May 30, 1902, wherein Roberts—or at least the diarist—was anticipating the release of the women and children from the Bloemfontein concentration camp. After that, there was plenty more, apparently, but someone—probably Farquhar—had withheld almost all of it.

Jason Glass was furious.

In terms of the matters he had sought in his analysis, Glass was able to tell at least a few important things. The diary was begun as a public document but switched to a private one around mid-October, 1899. Roberts had done something naughty perhaps. In the early stages of the private diary, the tone was sheer self-aggrandizement on Roberts' part, in stark contrast to the utter tonelessness of what had come before. But then, two months later, the tone was self-justifying without discussing anything—in the pages Glass had, at least—that seemed to require *any* justification or explanation. But this was also a section of heavy excisions from the text. Roberts had done, was continuing to do, even more naughty things than what had inspired him to take his diary underground in October. Then, toward the end of the Siege, in February, the tone shifted almost to deviousness and cockiness, though again pages were missing which might have suggested what he was up to.

It was only noon this sunny day, but Jason Glass was as tired as if it were midnight. He wanted a nap, so he signaled Duncan—for whom he presumed himself responsible, since no other adult was in evidence—out of the lake and toward his clothing. Charlie splashed out also and, after waiting until Glass had positioned himself in a soft spot on the ground, slammed down next to him to sleep as well. Amidst the smell of Charlie's halitosis and wet hair, Glass went to sleep, though not until he had resolved to have it out this very evening with Farquhar Menzies. He wished Ann had not returned to London so quickly.

The nearer he got to the Castle Menzies, the angrier Glass felt himself becoming and the faster he drove. By the time he parked Sybil's car along the roadside at the end of the causeway, he was angry enough to run across it rather than just walk quickly. He did not know how much longer he would remain here; it had even crossed his mind that he might resign this very evening. He wished he were here in other circumstances, for even in his fury he was impressed by the twilit and misty beauty of Loch Duich behind the castle.

The old servant whom Glass had seen before opened a peephole in the gate to see who had been rapping, told Glass that Farquhar would see no one, then shut it without further explanation. Glass rapped furiously some more, shook the iron bars of the outer gates, cursed, kicked through the spaces in the gate and toed the oak door until his foot ached. The old man never reappeared. Glass was so angry he thought of plunging into the lake and swimming around to the unfenced back side of the islet, but instead he retraced his steps to Sybil's car and sped over to the small inn called The Sheepshead, which faced the castle on a promontory several hundred yards away. He phoned the castle, faked a British accent, identified himself as "someone from Farneswells," and—when Menzies answered—let him have both barrels.

"Menzies, this is Glass, Jason Glass. I quit. That diary you gave me is crap. I have your money with me. I've spent none of it. If you get that Walpolean horror to open the gate for a second I'll shove it through to him. I'm getting out of here. There are pages torn out of that thing. There are four different hands involved in it, one of which is trying to fake being Roberts' own. There is not even enough material left to write three chapters of credible and interesting stuff, much less a whole book."

"Glass, look," the voice on the other end came back, "I can't talk now. I'm on an extension phone in the powerhouse, and I can barely hear you." This was true, for Glass could hear the continual electrical snapping that he had heard so vividly the first night he had arrived at the castle. "Let us talk tomorrow. I will—"

"No tomorrow, Menzies," Glass shouted into the phone, to the disruption of the entire pub beyond the hall from which he was calling. The bargirl shut the door haughtily. "Insofar as you have given it to me, the whole story of Roberts boils down to this: He was a tedious physician doing tedious things in Dundee; got his patients out right after the Boer invasion; got them to Ladysmith, where they had an unexpected four-month vacation without food or drink and with such tropical niceties as mosquitoes, tsetse flies, vultures, and a full-scale sewer floating by their hospital windows. At night there were fireworks shows and in the day there were futile displays of military tactics on both sides. You listening, Menzies? He fought with the Chief Medical Officer continually—a guy named Exham—and got to inspect the caldrons in which they cooked their horsemeat. He lost his wife to enteric fever but somehow saved his son. The missing pages tell how he did that, but since they're missing, I can't very well put it in my book, now, can I? He became General White's personal physician because he was so good at keeping his own patients alive. When the Siege ended, he moved his patients *and* General White to Pietermaritzburg, then disappeared, later turned up treating Boer women and children in the Bloemfontein concentration camp. Later he went to Senegal for an unknown reason, or perhaps it was Missouri—I can't even tell which St. Louis it was. That's the whole story. Not even enough for a pamphlet, much less a book."

"Glass, I can't hear what—"

"Yes, you can, damn it! You don't want to listen. I have a few appendices I could add so we could jack up the price from twenty pence to three and a half pounds perhaps—medical staff records which attest to what a good doctor he was at Dundee, to how many lives he saved in Ladysmith, to apparently real heroism at the expense of an eye and a limb in World War I. Yes, all of that is provable."

"Glass, I insist we talk about . . ." Glass actually just wanted to hear himself ramble. He knew Menzies could not hear. Finally Menzies issued his *coup de grâce*: "I'll call Ann in London tomorrow and you can discuss this with her. Goodbye now." He hung up.

Glass slammed the receiver on the hook of the ancient hall phone and blasted his way through the swinging door into the pub, extracting a fifty-pence coin from his pocket as he advanced forthrightly to the bar and slapping it down with a resounding clack when he got there. Everyone in the room stopped talking and eyed him the way the patrons in old Westerns eyed some rough hombre they had never seen before. The bargirl brought him a beer at once, as if afraid he might climb the bar and get one for himself if she did not hurry. He drank it, fast, then left. No one had spoken while he was in the room, and all were relieved to see him depart.

6 *THE MENZIES FAMILY TRADITIONS*

THE NEXT MORNING GLASS GOT HIMSELF under control. Though he received a phone call from a secretary at Farneswells in London saying that Ann Macgregor would come up to the Lochs in two days to discuss the "difficulties" he was encountering—and Glass had instantly decided that even Farneswells knew that Ann Macgregor was more effective in person than on the phone—he had already decided to go on with the project, at least for a while. One reason for this was purely professional; the other, purely vindictive.

Professionally he chided himself for his authorial sloth. He had come to make an easy buck, he had realized, and was prepared to do to the Roberts Menzies diary exactly what he used to do to organizational recruiting propaganda: take ill-written and badly organized material and polish it up for presentation to the eager recipient. Such he could do in his sleep, and he had planned, he supposed now, to sleep through this as well. What he had discovered was simply that he could not. He would have to research the story from top to bottom. The documents in the case had not been bequeathed to him by a great-aunt he could trust, as had been the case with Annie Daly. This would be a greater challenge, for there was a full-scale cover-up on here to protect the image of one man at the expense of the truth. Woodward and Bernstein had discovered that most people hated to keep secrets, that there was some instinct toward the truth, however perverse, which in the long run could not be denied. There would be people in the Lochs who knew "something," and their somethings could be pieced together with official documents, with history books, and with oral tradition to uncover the truth. Roberts Menzies had done something before Ladysmith and something else during Ladysmith's four-month Siege and probably something more—maybe many things more—after he got out, things he, or someone else, was ashamed of. Things, perhaps, which had changed the shapes of other people's lives for the worse, just as Annie Daly had shaped them for the better. Such things were worth knowing about.

Particularly when knowing them could satisfy his vindictive purpose as well. He had come to dislike anyone named Menzies intensely. Not just Farquhar, who seemed at least to be fighting for his cause head on, even if he was prepared to use Jason Glass, Ann Macgregor, and anyone else to get what he wanted. He disliked Henrietta, who probably knew the whole story, wanted to tell it, and wouldn't. She would be the sort who would drop a vague hint anytime his interest waned, just enough to move him ahead again. And he disliked Sybil, who was taking advantage of his vulnerability to fill certain voids in her own marriage, and he disliked her husband—whom he had not yet even met—for being constantly drunk and unable to keep her out of Glass's bed. And this "mother" figure—known to everyone but Farquhar as "Aunt Elizabeth": what was she doing creeping around uttering statements of doom that had the ring of something taken from *Tales of the Crypt* comic books? The only one he liked was Duncan, and Duncan was a retarded child. When Jason Glass finished his book, he would autograph a copy for each of them with some pretentious statement about the power of truth that he would quote from Shakespeare or Matthew Arnold or somebody who seemed to have a hot line *to* the Truth, and he would never have to worry about poor Duncan's reading a word of it.

He hated himself for this attitude and resolved to fight it. It would be tough.

That afternoon he made his first lunge at the truth, and things got worse. Before coming to Scotland, he had found the name of the best known expert on Scottish clans, a professor at the University of Aberdeen. Shortly after lunch he placed a phone call to the man's home, reached him, and introduced himself.

"I was wondering, sir, if you could give me off the top of your head some general information about a clan in the Lochs. Their general history, their contributions to the nation, the skeletons in their closets. That sort of thing?"

"Dundonald?" His inflection suggested an interest in speaking of this clan.

"No, Menzies."

Silence. A long silence. Then: "Oh, yes, Menzies." Now an ironic laugh he tried to repress but only half-succeeded. "What was it you wanted to know?" He did not wish to speak of this clan, just as most people do not like to discuss what other people do in a bathroom.

"Well, I gather first of all that they do not necessarily command respect?"

"Not necessarily." He seemed to be stonewalling.

"Could you tell me why?"

"How much money would you like to invest in this phone call, Mr. Glass? Is this for a book you are writing?"

"Yes."

"Then I am not sure I wish to tell you anything. I am a Scotsman, Mr. Glass. The Menzies are not our best side."

Glass leaped to correct a misapprehension. "I am not writing a history of the Clan Menzies." He laughed nervously. "Just a biography of a more recent one."

"Which one?"

"A doctor who went to South Africa. Roberts Menzies. 1872 to 1925."

"Dear God." This was not exclaimed. In fact, it was almost swallowed.

"You've heard of him?"

"Mr. Glass, perhaps I am one of the few left who recall Roberts Menzies, but at one time he was rather prominent. Only time has allowed Roberts Menzies to remove his name from a rather graphic list of four-letter words, I'm afraid."

"But he was a hero! I don't understand this." Glass sounded to himself the way Farquhar Menzies had sounded the first night. "He saved many people during the Siege of Ladysmith! He was widely decorated during World War I. By four nations. Or was it five?"

"As far as I could ever determine, he was put on the medals list of virtually every Allied nation for simply being the only one-eyed, one-armed doctor hanging around the war zone. He could have done nothing but get in the way. He could not have operated, now, could he?"

"He could have given professional advice. Also, how far into the war was it that he *lost* his arm and eye? If it was late, he could have done much good before that." Glass could not understand his own motives in this conversation.

Still cynicism. "First of all, while I have not researched this whole matter thoroughly, of course, Dr. Menzies lost his eye and arm very early in the war, not later than the end of 1914. Check me on that, but I'm sure I'm right. Further, what advice could a man twenty years out of medical school, and apparently not practicing medicine most of those years, possibly give to highly trained surgeons with all the latest knowledge and equipment?"

Glass was somewhat annoyed by the man's attitude. It was professional annoyance. "Professor, you seem very closed-minded about this, almost as if you were predisposed to think ill of Roberts Menzies no matter what might turn up in his favor."

"Mr. Glass, you've done some work on the Boer War and the Siege of Ladysmith before coming to Scotland, surely?"

"Of course."

"You've heard of two rather obscure places called Colenso and Spion Kop, then?"

"Professor, please come to your point. Certainly I've heard of them. Two of the biggest battles of the war were fought there."

"Both resounding Boer victories as well, do you recall? Well, then, I'll get to my point and perhaps then I'll get off. If you've done much reading about both those battles, you will find that there is suspicion on both occasions that General Buller's battle plans were known to the Boers in advance. It seems the Boers may have laid their hands on the British codebooks and were able to interpret the heliographic and searchlight messages which were being sent among the divisions and even into Ladysmith and so position themselves correctly when the occasion of the fight came about.

"Now I will tell you, Mr. Glass, what I have against Dr. Roberts Menzies personally and perhaps tomorrow you could go to the nearest library and look up my volume on *The History of Scottish Clans Since Culloden Moor* to see what I have against them in general. I have evidence which suggests that sometime while he was supposedly under siege in Ladysmith—early in that siege, in fact—Dr. Menzies came into possession of a codebook which he sold to the Boers, for what price I have no idea. Now, I do not claim that he was the only saboteur about Ladysmith in those days—the town was apparently a nest of spies—but since he was General White's personal physician during the Siege, he would seem to have had the best access to such a document, don't you agree?"

"You have no proof of that."

"No, I don't, especially since his father made some arrangements with the British Government to expunge Roberts' name from its records of investigations into spying at Ladysmith. This was done in the midst of the euphoria at the end of World War I when Roberts suddenly turned up again in Britain after twenty years or so of absence, now a mutilated hero whose very appearance brought patriotic tears to the English eye. Dig, Mr. Glass. You will find out I am right. He was a Boer agent who seemed to be saving lives in the town but was really trading them for young soldiers' lives on the battlefields at Colenso and Spion Kop."

"Is all this in your book?"

"Not in its last edition because, as I said, I could not prove it. It will be in the next edition, however."

"Why is that?"

"Because by then your book will be out and you are too good not to prove it for me. But read the entry on the Clan Menzies anyway. It's chock-a-block full of things I have proved. Cheerio now." He rang off without further comment, leaving Glass feeling like an attorney for Judas Iscariot at a papal inquisition.

On the following Monday, Glass drove to Ullapool, some thirty miles farther north into the Lochs. He had had a call from Ann the night before in which he summarized what he had been told. She seemed earnestly to have no knowledge of those facts, though Glass suspected she could predict what he would find out at the library on the following day. When Glass arrived at the small library in Loch Killilan, he had found the professor's book quickly, a thick tome of more than two thousand pages which, unfortunately, was missing thirty of them between McCorquodale and Moncrieffe. So the librarian directed him to Ullapool, and in Ullapool the volume was intact around the name Menzies though ravaged around other, probably more local names.

The entry for "Menzies of Loch Killilan and Loch Duich," even without the afterword regarding Roberts Menzies that undoubtedly would appear in the next printing, was a catalogue of familial disgrace and horror which Jason Glass had only to scan to understand the professor's resentment of them. It began at Culloden Moor, and the last chapter apparently had still to be written; perhaps was to be written by, or maybe even about, Jason Glass himself. In the Jacobite uprising of 1745, the Menzies, like so many other Scotsmen, were supporters of the pretender to the English throne, Prince Charles Stuart—Bonnie Prince Charlie. In the decisive battle fought on April 16, 1746, at Culloden Moor, southeast of Inverness, Charles ordered the Menzies to occupy a position to the extreme left side of the fighting line and to employ their huge family cannon, one of the few such weapons the Scottish forces had that day to resist the Duke of Cumberland's army, against the British right. Simply and summarily put, the Menzies refused what they considered a tangential position, much like that allotted pawns or at best rooks on a chessboard, and insisted instead that they be allowed to fight to Prince Charlie's immediate right. This made no sense, since the position was already in the able and secure hands of the huge MacDonald clan. The Menzies wanted the MacDonalds repositioned that morning, and when Prince

Charles refused them, they refused him and dragged their cannon from the field, leaving him considerably weakened and vulnerable on the left side. Consequently, in the only military battle he ever won, Cumberland defeated Prince Charles, and the era of Bonnie Prince Charlie was over; Scotland, for good or ill, was doomed to be part of Great Britain until the present day. From the volume he read, Glass learned that the Menzies could definitely hear the battle as it was waged, and perhaps even smell the gunpowder, as they wound their way back to Inverness and on toward the Lochs. Not only had they taken themselves and their cannon; they had persuaded a good portion of the Oliphant clan of the Isle of Skye to go with them.

In the ensuing years there were barrages of internecine generational quarrels over property ownership, rights of succession, even intermarital conflicts and several incestuous affairs. At one point in the mid-1800s there was even a conflict over the cannon itself when the second-eldest son purloined it from its storage place at the castle and had it brought to the top of the mountains on the opposite side of Loch Duich, threatening to shell the place unless the lands in the vicinity of The Gap were titled free and clear to him. They were, the cannon was brought back down unfired, and to the present day the eldest brother of the chief has possessed The Gap as his individual domain. Since so many recent generations of the Menzies family had issued only one child, The Gap had more or less reverted to the chief's direct control. Glass mentally noted, however, that The Gap was where Farquhar had chosen to farm out his recalcitrant sister and intemperate son (and flunky scribe).

The Menzies' record through the nineteenth century continued to be dreadful in nonfamilial matters as well. They evidently had been willing and eager participants in the phenomenon that came to be known as the Highland Clearances. An increasing demand for meat and wool in the Commonwealth made the raising of cattle and sheep highly profitable businesses for families with money to invest. The Menzies were one such family. However, cattle and sheep required space—a lot of space in so generally small a place as Scotland—so the clan chiefs began enclosing lands in their domain which had theretofore been in common use for farming and animal breeding by smaller tenant farmers. As a result, a large portion of the Scottish population was dispossessed and forced to emigrate to such broad but distant places as the western United States, the Australian outback, Canada, and South Africa. Major portions of Scotland were resultantly barren of people and crowded with animals. Not all of the displaced persons had left Scotland, however, for a lucky (or perhaps unlucky) few were able to leave their rural environment for the swelling cities of Glasgow and Perth, where the cattle were slaughtered, the meat processed, and the wool converted into linen-and-wool cloth in dark and gloomy factories. The Menzies, according to the entry, had quadrupled their family fortune by 1850 as a result of the Clearances.

Page after page of lesser incidents bespattered the Menzies name, and finally Glass came to an episode that concerned Angus Menzies, Roberts' father, just after he had become clan chief at the age of twenty-three in 1871. The railways were slowly being extended into the outer reaches of Scotland at the time, and one spur was due in the western Lochs by the early 1870s. As it progressed west-northwest from Inverness through Garve and Achnasheen and Glencarron and Strathcarron, it dawned on Angus that the line was aiming eventually for the north side of Loch Killilan, with its terminal in the town of Loch Killilan, just two miles from the grazing lands in The Gap and surrounding hills. This would be twelve miles, however, from the Castle Menzies and would allow Angus' younger brother, Walter, to whom possession of The Gap had fallen by birthright, to get his herd to market with considerably less difficulty and expense than Angus could. Angus saw either his profits lessened or his bids too high or both and demanded that the line come to the south of Loch Killilan for eventual terminus at Kyle of Lochalsh. His argument was rather built on the more buyable proposition that Kyle was in a better position to serve the Isle of Skye, on which there were and to this day still would be no railroads. His argument was rejected, and rail crews showed up at Strathcarron in the spring of 1871 to continue on toward Loch Killilan, where they had been headed in the first place. However, Angus chose to appear at Strathcarron on the second day of work that spring. He had already brought his cannon up before dawn and backed it along the bed that was being prepared for the next round of track laying, spun it around, and pointed it toward the rail builders' handcars and work tents and tie piles. At sunup, as the laborers slogged through the mud to commence their picking and digging, they found themselves staring down the loaded barrel of the Culloden Cannon, which, still, had never fired a shot in any sort of combat. Nor would it this year either. Work was suspended for two weeks while the railroad officials debated the matter with Angus. On May 1, 1871, *The Times* of London published the story that the rail officials had reconsidered and decided to lay track to the south side of Loch Killilan rather than the north in order to service the Isle of Skye and that since Angus Menzies owned the lands there would be no trouble acquiring the right-of-way, and so the cannon (though this was not in the *Times* story) was removed. The next year, Walter Menzies walked off his lands in The Gap and emigrated to Australia himself.

There was one reference to Roberts Menzies in this entry which surprised Glass for its generosity:

> In 1894, after completing his first year of medical school at the University of Edinburgh, Roberts Menzies, Angus' only son, asked to be given title to The Gap, the lands which traditionally fell to the second son. Since there were no other children of the marriage of Angus Menzies and Margaret Gunn, Roberts suggested he might put the land to use until such time as he himself produced a second son to give it to. Angus for a time agreed, and Roberts bought a large flock of sheep and hired two shepherds to tend it. In 1895, Roberts returned in the summer, sold the entire flock, and prepared to convert a vacant stone dwelling into a small surgical hospital for the district, there being none whatsoever between Ullapool to the north, Inverness to the east, and Fort William to the south. He was prepared to run this hospital after he took his medical degree in 1897, to hire a nurse, and to employ the services as well of the local doctor, who was the only one for twenty-five miles in any direction and whom Roberts would replace when he retired after roughly another decade. Work had hardly begun when Roberts returned to school in the autumn, and at this point Angus had it stopped. His reasoning was, it seems, that if his ancestors had cleared off all the residents for the grazing of sheep and cattle, it hardly seemed logical to convert four square miles of land into a mere backdrop for eight hundred square feet of surgery. Arguments ensued between young Roberts and his father, arguments which may have suggested to Angus that his only child was not of proper mental frame to assume the chieftainship on his death. As a result of these incidents, Roberts married a nurse he met at Edinburgh named Catherine Clyde and signed papers with the government to serve in the hospital at Dundee, Natal, South Africa. During that time he was

> forced to remove himself from Dundee with the onset of the Boer War, fell under siege at Ladysmith in late 1899 and early 1900, lost his wife to enteric fever, but did manage to save his infant son and return him to Scotland. Because of the arguments with his father, however, and because of his father's distrust of his motivations, Roberts did not return to Scotland after the Boer War ended in 1902 and generally fell from view until he reappeared in the Great War in 1914 and was severely wounded early on. Roberts never became clan chief, but rather his son, Bruce, did when, after much rejection and animosity, both Roberts and Angus died within a year of each other in 1925 and 1926.

With this the list of Menzies offenses against humanity, decorum, history, and Scottish tradition was terminated with a brief discussion on Menzies customs of the present day, which Glass merely skimmed before slapping the book shut.

He was surprised to find himself still calm and rational during his drive back to Loch Killilan from Ullapool. As he skirted the ice-blue waters of Loch Broom, sprinkled with a few hearty early-season swimmers, and proceeded on into sparse Dundonnell Forest, he had to admit to himself he was confused. The surname of Menzies was indeed a dirty one—there seemed to be something in the bloodstream which compelled each generation, no matter how good its initial intentions, to foul the earth and foul it badly before it gave way to the next. Roberts was an archetypal case in point: the beautiful instinct to return the cleared land to humanitarian purposes that had been stripped from it a half-century before him had given way, if the Aberdeen professor was correct (and he seemed sure he was), to high treason in the name of personal profit. And whatever his heroism in World War I had amounted to (and Glass frankly doubted it was the sort of nominal bootlicking the professor had claimed it was), this episode seemed to Glass to be tarnished by the fact that, if Roberts did not return to the Lochs for more than twenty years, he in fact deserted his son, whom he had sent out of Ladysmith, whether during or after the Siege, as an infant. According to Glass's research in Ullapool, the boy had been brought up by his grandparents, and no one, including the bitter Bruce it seemed, even knew (or maybe cared either) just where in the devil Roberts was all that time. Could he have been living a soft life somewhere—in Monte Carlo perhaps—with the cash he must have collected from the Boers for first rights to the British codebooks, volumes that had probably prolonged the Siege and cost the lives of hundreds of British soldiers no matter how many Roberts' own skillful hands had saved within the Ladysmith perimeter? This was an odd group. Roberts had been selected for the family encomium on no other evidence, apparently, than that he had, for one brief period in his life, done something useful that the rest of the Menzies—or maybe just Farquhar—were amazed to know about. Jason Glass wondered what the law thought of the Menzies.

Then he got a chance to find out. Weary of the single-lane roads and the roundabout loops of the Lochs named Ewe, Maree, and Torridon, Glass entered the town of Shieldaig driving on the wrong side of the road. He almost hit an oncoming car head on, avoided it only because the other driver had swerved violently to the American side of the road. Unfortunately, the vehicle he almost demolished turned out to be an unmarked police car, which was immediately spun around and launched into pursuit by what turned out to be an unmarked policeman as well. Glass pulled his car off the road to the right, still the wrong side, and waited while the driver got out and sprinted up to him. He was dressed in a dark blue business suit, a tall, handsome brown-haired man who dangled a leather-cased badge in front of him from the moment he sprang from his car.

"What in the bloody hell are you doing?" This seemed all he was prepared to do about it, get the answer to this question and not bother to issue a summons. He was flushed, clearly rattled by the experience, happy enough to be through it unscathed if he could just find out why.

"I'm sorry—I'm not used to driving on the left. I was tired. I forgot."

"Are you a Yank, then?"

"Yes. Glass, Jason Glass. I'm living down in Loch Killilan while I work on—"

"Yes, yes, Glass. I know who you are, actually. *Gratuitous Glory* and all that sort of thing. Now the Menzies." He seemed repelled too. "Mr. Glass, my name is Ross, Detective Inspector Ross. I'm with the Royal Scottish Police in Kinlochewe. I wonder if you might consider helping me with a case I am working on—have been on and off for some years now. It involves the Menzies, and I thought your research might turn something up."

"About what? My research is already turning up more than I had hoped."

"About the death of Mr. Farquhar Menzies' wife, Catherine, back in 1970. She died of exposure to the elements according to the coroner, and I have no reason to doubt that verdict. It's just that I have never figured out why a mature woman would have been cavorting around outside the Castle Menzies on a subfreezing winter night wearing no more than a nightgown and a flimsy nylon robe. I have always suspected there was more to it than there appeared at the time, that someone had gotten off who shouldn't have."

"You had an autopsy done?"

"Of course: exposure, pure and simple." He placed his hands on the doorframe and looked vacantly over his right shoulder. "I have always felt that she was either shoved outside or at least locked out once she stepped beyond her doorway. That would constitute second-degree murder, you see."

"I am surprised that after five years, Mr. Ross, you would continue to harbor suspicions about a case that is otherwise dead."

"Not so, you see. There was another death of someone closely associated with the Menzies in 1972. A death by poisoning that was less convincingly ruled a suicide."

Glass took out his notebook to record the name. "I'll let you know if I come across anything, though research for a book and police investigation are not really working with the same clues most of the time. What was the name of the second person?"

"Macgregor. Mrs. Annette Macgregor, widow of the local doctor, mother-in-law of young Clyde Menzies."

"Mother of Ann Macgregor as well? Yes, I heard something of that suicide from Sybil Menzies."

"Yes, that's the one. Ann is the daughter who gave up her medical career almost the same day she took her diploma. She works in London now. Left immediately after her mother's death, actually. I wanted to question her more than I did at the time, but she made herself rather hard to find about the Lochs."

Glass blew through his cheeks. This Menzies disease was not only congenital, it was contagious. He had heard almost too much for one day. "Inspector Ross, I will give you anything I get, though frankly I do not know how much longer I will be here or on this project. This family, if I can speak openly, is a bit different from what I had been led to believe it was before I accepted the assignment. I might get out of here before anything else happens."

At this Ross laughed loudly from the belly. "I don't blame you in the slightest, Mr. Glass. At least in my job I can divert myself with shipwrecks, drownings, car crashes, and bank raids. You would have to think, eat, and sleep Menzies. I don't know if I could bear all that much Menzies." He was still laughing, despite the content of his next sentence. "I say, though, Mr. Glass, if you go, take care they don't send you out in a box."

Glass's stomach dropped. "Dead?"

"No, alive. You heard how the clan chief before Farquhar—Mr. Bruce Menzies—arrived at the castle for the first time, haven't you?"

"No."

"I suppose they wouldn't tell that one, would they? Well, he came by train in a dog crate. A five-year-old boy shipped from Glasgow and probably points beyond that as well, stuffed in a dog crate like a mongrel."

"Who did it?"

"Oh, I have no idea on that one. In 1904 or 1905 it was, long before my time. His mother perhaps."

Glass reflected on this. "No, his mother died at Ladysmith years before. It couldn't have been she. But it could have been—"

"His father, perhaps?" He was snapping his fingers to massage his memory for the name.

"Roberts? Yes, perhaps Roberts." But then Glass resisted himself again. "No, not Roberts—not that too!"

Ross pushed himself back from the car. "Well, at any rate, don't underestimate them, Mr. Glass. They are a peculiar lot." He waved, then returned again. "And drive on the right side of the road—the correct side, I mean: the left one."

For the remainder of the distance back to Loch Killilan, Jason Glass had trouble recalling, with each oncoming car, which side of the road he was supposed to be driving on.

When Glass arrived back at the cottage that evening, a letter from Ann Macgregor awaited him. Her plans had been changed. She would be away from London on assignments in Brussels and Paris for the next two weeks but would visit the Lochs on Friday the twenty-third to "see how you are getting on." She had enclosed a clipping from the *Telegraph*. Perhaps her purpose was merely informational, perhaps sadistic, perhaps just an attempt to keep him in the Lochs despite his ever-growing inclination to get the hell out: AUTHOR'S DESERTED WIFE FORCED TO SELL HOME.

7 *ROBERTS MENZIES IN ST. LOUIS*

ON FRIDAY MORNING TWO WEEKS LATER, Duncan woke Glass and informed him that Ann awaited him at his writing spot along the Gap lake. The pleasure such information would ordinarily have afforded him was severely undermined and in fact redirected by the utter rage that now brewed within him. For the half-hour from the time Duncan had awakened him until he finished showering and dressing, he fought to alter what he would say to her, but he knew he needed a target and also knew he could not help making it her when the time finally came. He picked the crumpled piece of paper off his writing desk, stuffed it in his shirt pocket, and set out for the lake five minutes away.

Ann was already there as he approached down the sloping green-and-azure-and-silver bank. When Glass first caught sight of her, she was in the final stages of kicking off her nylons and girdling her light blue dress around her thighs to wade into the shallow waters, which, as always, perfectly reflected the day's sky.

"Hello there, Jason," she called cheerily as she started back out. "I hope you don't mind if I use your private waters now and again."

"No, anytime. Any time at all." His voice was as he feared it would be, reflecting his impatience to be on to something else.

She tried to keep her good humor, did so to a point, but knew there was trouble, could guess at least its category if not its precise dimensions. "More news, I suspect, that fits into what you've been referring to as 'troublesome'?"

"Ann, *this* piece of so-called news is so ludicrous that it would scandalize 'troublesome' even to associate with it. But as far as I am concerned, this is what might finally be labeled the 'last straw' as well. I'm packing my bags on this one. Sit down." The last two words were too harsh. She sat down quickly but resignedly on the grass, tugging her skirts tightly beneath her as she hit the ground.

"What have you got this time, Jason? Was Roberts peddling the crown jewels to the Boers on nightly flits out of Ladysmith?" Her tone was only slightly miffed—more of it suggested that she would not be particularly surprised at anything now, seemed in fact to be trying to invent something so totally ridiculous that the most recent "truth," whatever it would turn out to be, would pale before it.

"I wish it were even that sensational." Glass plopped down too now, kicking off his shoes and socks to run his toes in the grass as she was doing. He removed the piece of paper from his shirt pocket but did not give it to her or unfold it. "You know that reference I found in the diary to the city of St. Louis, the one I could not figure out at all?"

"Yes?" She had, perhaps, expected this to be the current cause of Glassean unrest.

"Well, I tried to get on with positive thoughts about our friend Roberts, just as you asked me to. But I cheated on you, I'm sorry to say. Now, the year in question in the diary was 1904. In the St. Louis in Senegal there was a typhoid epidemic that year that some of the Western nations, the British Empire among them, sent medical supplies and personnel to help combat."

"Good, Jason, so you followed that lead. Where did it take you?"

"No, you see, Ann, I didn't follow it. For two reasons. First, I had no contacts there, but I did know this guy in St. Louis, Missouri—so I wrote to him instead."

She was disappointed. "They needed outside medical personnel there in 1904?"

Glass glibly shook his head. "No, in 1904 they had a World's Fair in St. Louis, Missouri."

"And now you are going to tell me that Roberts simply went on holiday, journeyed to the middle of America to ride carousels and experience transported European culture?" She tried to divert him with her irony, but she knew the record was already complete. It was just a matter of waiting to have it revealed.

"No, no, no, my dear Ann. Not a bit of it. Our friend Roberts would not exert effort for such as that. At first the Fair was to my mind just an isolated coincidence, but then, on one of my walks to town, it became less so. I had seen the St. Louis World's Fair mentioned in one of the Boer War books I've been steeping myself in over the last few months. So I did not even finish my journey to town, in fact sacrificed my bottle of Scotch to go look it up."

"And you found?" Totally serious now, her beauty suddenly austere.

"I found, Ann"—his tone was becoming almost giddily cynical—"that the Boer general who handed the British their first major victory of the war—"

"Yes, Cronje—Piet Cronje—at Paardeberg. Go on."

"You've been reading as well, I see. Yes, the infamous Piet Cronje, who could have escaped Lord Bobs and Kitchener of Khartoum by using the great Christiaan De Wet's cover and diversion to lead his men out of their trenches to safety, but was too cowardly or demoralized or whatever to do so: this selfsame Piet Cronje turned up, it seems, at the St. Louis World's Fair. And you know what he was doing there? Do you, Ann?"

"No, what?" There was a snicker embedded in her terse response.

"Putting on a show twice a day in an arena. Reenacting his ignominious surrender at Paardeberg no less, the acknowledged beginning of the Boer downfall! So I thought about it. It couldn't be accidental, could it, that both Roberts and Cronje turned up in places called St. Louis in the same year, both so far from what they were calling home? So I thought about it some more, and asked myself which one would *our* Roberts turn up at: the one where there was a plague in a strange land he probably had never even heard of before, or the place at which there was a fast buck to be made? I chose the latter, on a hunch." With this he responded to her disgusted look by pulling out the wrinkled letter from Professor Mentosi, who lived in Missouri and not in Senegal, and left her to unfold it herself, to handle it as if a wasp might fly out of the final crease.

Courageously she read it aloud:

"Dear Jason Glass: Very nice to have heard from you again. Your Annie Daly book was superb, worthy of every honor accorded it. I envy your being in Scotland on yet another. I am teaching summer school this year to get ahead on my alimony. Sorry to say I hear that you are *way* ahead on yours."

She glanced up and smirked at him, knowing that her own problems would begin with the next paragraph.

"I managed to uncover several daily programs from the Fair which are dated August, 1904. Piet Cronje *did* perform the surrender of Paardeberg twice daily seven days a week, apparently over a long period of time. He was clearly listed in the programs I found. Assisting him in an outdoor arena was a variable cast of some three dozen horsemen who apparently shot it up a bit at the beginning of each performance, then reenacted the surrender. I found no Roberts Menzies in the cast, but don't lose heart, Jason. The person who played the part of *Lord* Roberts, who accepted Cronje's gun, was listed as 'Bob Menzy.' The conclusion is yours to draw. I have actually seen a blurred photo of him, or at least his left side and back. Cronje is a very squarely built man with a black broom beard and a wide flat-brimmed hat. He is holding a white horse with some covered voortrekker wagons just behind him. The man identified as Bob Menzy is of much more slender build, a shortish man, smaller than I am. His hair is white, but that could easily have been powdered to make him look like General Roberts. He is wearing a crisp khaki uniform with high black riding boots, black leather belts, and what we used to call in the military a 'cunt cap' on his head. A snappy figure in contrast to Cronje. Sorry I could not send the picture—it is a rarity apparently and is not allowed out of the collection.

"One other thing, however. You did not mention that this Menzies was an amputee. Now, unless General Roberts himself had no left arm and the actor was pretending not to for realism, I can tell you for certain that the actor's left sleeve has no hand sticking out of it. Does that help?"

Ann knew there was no reason to read the closing compliments, so she passed the sheet back to Glass without refolding it.

Now Glass fell backward on the soft downlike grass and started to laugh, at first quietly, then out loud. He wished he could control himself. Ann was as distressed as he had yet seen her.

"You did not seem a few moments ago as if you found this so funny."

"No, I didn't. But now my unfortunate fiction-writing instincts are grabbing me—I'm beginning to create a context."

"Such as?"

He sat up and began to gesture broadly from his shoulders. "Ladies and gentlemen, in this corner, wearing the baggy clothes, the ratty hat, the bug-infested beard, we have that great Boer general who surrendered Paardeberg with hardly a shot being fired—the great Piet Cronje." He began to laugh again, to the point that his eyes watered. "And in the other corner, playing the part of Field Marshal Lord Roberts, missing one arm instead of an eye but otherwise a perfect replica of Lord Bobs, a hero in his own right, the man who single-handedly saved hundreds of lives within the Ladysmith perimeter with his expert medical attention, and who—also single-handedly—deprived thousands of others of theirs at Colenso and Spion Kop by selling the Boers the codebooks which made the heliographs and searchlight signals as secretive as a babbling mynah bird, here he is, ladies and gentlemen, the great Roberts Menzies!" Here Glass stopped to applaud and cheer. "Now watch, ladies and gentlemen, as the great Boer patriot, for the sum of ten dollars a performance, will fire blanks at these fake British troops played by Missouri farmers who get a dollar fifty apiece and then hand over his horse, and gun, and wagon to that great Scottish patriot, Roberts Menzies—alias Bob Menzy for today—who gets five dollars a performance to pretend to be a loyal British subject to make up for the fact that when they needed him to be, he wasn't. Watch as they fire guns at each other and pretend to do what they should have been doing four years ago, then go out for dinner together and do again what in fact they were and have been doing all along! Yes, ladies and gentlemen, Bob Menzy is from the same Menzies family who a century and a half ago deserted the field at Culloden Moor because they couldn't stand where they wanted to, the same family who a few years after that sold the land out from under their own clansmen and turned it over to London capitalists who in turn handed it over to sheep to get fat and woolly on, the same family who rerouted an entire rail—"

"Stop it!" She yelled this at him, did not shriek it. She threw herself forward on the grass, face down, cradling her head on her arms, her shoulders bouncing rhythmically from her sobs. "All right, you win. The project is a fiasco. I finally agree. I have agreed for a long time." She tried to look up now, but the bright sun hurt her burning, teary eyes. "So what do we do? We go to your cottage, gather up all the diary pages and all letters and clippings and photos and other detritus, and crush it to our breasts and dump it into a cardboard carton and drive it to Castle Menzies and storm the guardhouse (which like everything else Menzies is fake), manned by a near-paraplegic, and trot it up to Farquhar and tell him to stuff it, tell him that his ancestors—from Culloden to Ladysmith to today—are all frauds, that his family should never have scourged the face of Scotland, or perhaps the earth either, that his single son is a derelict married to a young slut who could not keep her pants pulled up since she was fourteen, that his grandson is a near-idiot who will be capable of engendering, if anything, a string of more idiots? Is that what we do now? Is that what the truth requires?"

She put her face back to the earth and commenced to cry again, but Glass snatched her by the left shoulder and spun her over on her back. She wrestled to pull away from him, to get face down again so she would not have to look at him or the glaring light of the sun, or perhaps at the truth. She flailed wildly with her arms and legs, anything to wrestle free of him. Finally he lay on top of her, pinning her arms to her sides with his arms, her legs together with his legs.

"Suppose I say no to that, Ann." He could feel her breathing hard beneath him, but she had relaxed her muscles. "What, then, *does* the truth require: That we pile up everything we have into two stacks? We weave a story from the good things—some of which are undoubtedly true, some undoubtedly not? We spend thirty pages on how Roberts moved the wounded from Dundee to Ladysmith; a hundred on what he did by day within Ladysmith for almost four months, how the patients he brought with him and those under his care died at an exceptionally low rate in comparison with the overall statistics; that somehow he got his dying and motherless son out of Ladysmith and—though it took five more years—back to Loch Killilan; that he served bravely in World War I—though we now know that that is *not* where or how he lost that left arm; that he returned to Loch Killilan a hero, even though he had been missing for a score of years, bringing with him a German wife whom he saved from her own people's military madness, and lived in pastoral bliss with her for the remaining half-dozen years they each had left? Yes, Ann, a very nice story can be made of that—and there's probably more we could find in the way of ornaments to hang on it as well. But what *do* we do about all those soldiers' lives that were lost because the Boers were reading the British searchlights and heliographs like headlines on a newspaper? What *do* we do with the fact that he did not bother to come home for twenty years or notify his family where he was? What *do* we do about his reducing the whole miserable episode to a money-making farce in St. Louis? What *do* we do about his own son's apparent rejection of him when he finally decided to come home? Do we pretend that never happened?"

He now became more physically aware of her long and supple body beneath him, that her pubic mound was pressed tightly against him. She was calm, so he slid off her. She looked at him carefully, as if she had become aware of their contact at the same moment as he had.

"Jason, I think you have three choices. You can pack your bags and leave, as you have threatened to do several times. Or you can write the lies that Farquhar wishes you to. Or you can try to make sense of all this." Now she sat up and pulled her dress down slightly from where, in the struggle, it had ridden up over the left hip of her white panties. "If you choose the first course, you go back to your wife and her demands for money and the poverty you must have to live in so long as you insist on keeping it from her. Back to your children who have apparently more loyalty to her than they have to you. If you choose the second, you will disgrace yourself in your own eyes and eventually in the world's. If you choose the third, you not only can live in comfort here but you can also do for the Roberts Menzies story what you did for the Daly one."

"Farquhar won't let me take the third option."

"He will if he doesn't know about it, won't he? Write him a first chapter along the lines he wants. I will give it to him, and he will be satisfied that you are in line. He knows nothing of literary style. Dash it off for him. He will accept it as a rough copy that you will turn into a proper one later."

"And with the rest of my time I keep digging, hoping that the *full* truth will clean this whole matter up?"

"It will at least *explain* it. That is all you did for Annie and Peter Daly. You explained why it happened the way it did. People are sympathetic creatures, I have found, if only they can understand and identify the reasons *for* behavior that seems wrong or indecent. Isn't prejudice a form of purposeful ignorance? We could assume that Roberts Menzies is totally as we now know him—a traitor, a deserter, a moneygrubber, an errant father. But before the Boer War, he had no history of that, did he? What happened to him in Ladysmith? Did he lose his mind as he lost his wife? Why did he not come home—a home he once loved—for twenty years? Do we accept that a youthful skirmish with his father would explain all that? Why did he later come into conflict again with his father, whose heir he was, and his own son, whose life he saved, when he finally showed up? There are reasons we don't know, Jason. We can pretend that all we've found out is all there is or we can act as if we know that we have only found the worst that we—or at least you—have been seeking since you noticed those missing and altered pages in the diary."

This woman, Jason reflected, had a rhetorical gift which could not have been learned in medical school, had to be, in fact, a personal attribute which would not allow itself to be wasted on the staccato conversations of an operating room. She knew he could not tell the lies, but she also knew even more that he could not return to dogfight with Margot, her attorney, and his manipulated children. She knew too, from the way he had spoken of it at other times, the essential thrill he got not so much from uncovering the dirt of the past as from establishing its context. She was right. The story of Roberts Menzies would be neither so clean as Farquhar wanted to have it nor so foul as he, in his eagerness to retaliate, was insisting it was. Margot was, to his mind, the only totally corrupt and selfish person he had ever met, and perhaps what had attracted him to such a personality in the first place was the same instinct that dug for more and more dirt on Roberts Menzies. He decided to give Roberts yet another chance and reluctantly said so. In giving Roberts a chance, he was giving Ann a chance and, most of all, himself a chance—with many things. What she had suggested was in his own best interest.

They seemed about to kiss to seal the bargain when they heard Duncan hailing them from the road above.

He was running as fast as he could down the grassy slope, flailing a shovel over his head against the backdrop of the magnificent rock-and-heather walls of The Gap. He was winded by the time he reached where they sat ten feet from the lake. He did not even try to speak until he had sufficient breath, but it was clear from the expression on his face that he had something significant to say.

"Aunt Annie, I just . . . heard my father say to my mother that . . . there are things in Great-grandfather's grave that are secret." Without further ado, he shoved the spade toward Glass.

"What?" Ann and Glass queried at the same moment, half-smiling as they did so.

"He said secrets were buried . . . with Great-grandfather! Let's dig them up." His eyes were wide.

Ann rose to her knees now, laughing tenderly as she grasped the tousle-headed boy by his shoulders and focused on his slightly vacuous eyes. "No, no, Duncan, that is just an expression people use. It means that sometimes people die knowing things they have not told anyone. Which means that things die with them. They will never be known. They are 'taken to the grave.' " She swatted him affectionately on the backside.

Duncan backed up indignant, holding his rear end with his free hand, banging the shovel on the ground with the other. "That is not right. I heard him say things were buried . . . in Great-grandfather's grave. Things that would not be nice to find out. Dig, Mr. Glass." Again he thrust the shovel forward. This time Glass took it, trying himself not to laugh, smiling instead.

"Well, perhaps, Duncan, but I don't think I will do it in daylight. Your grandfather would get angry with me if he knew I was doing it, don't you think?"

Duncan frowned in disgust. He stammered senselessly for a moment, at which Ann tried to embrace him from her kneeling position, to calm him. He pushed her on her shoulders, causing her to fall backward into a sitting position. He stepped up to Glass and ripped the shovel from his hand. "You are afraid." He looked at both of them carefully, then sped away, back up the hill, almost as quickly as he had come. Ann and Glass watched him helplessly until he disappeared around the bend in the road. Duncan had the most literal of minds and would be destined to make its consequent mistakes. Because of this Glass pitied the boy, probably loved him.

Part Two

AMBIGUITIES

8 THE EXHUMATIONS

THEY PARKED THE CAR ABOUT A HUNDRED YARDS down the road and tiptoed along the gravel berm the rest of the way. The moon reflected brightly off Loch Killilan, but the mist was rolling in thickly now, frequently obliterating the Loch entirely and then revealing it again several seconds, sometimes minutes, later. Glass, who carried a six-battery flashlight, still wore the same clothes he had worn to the pub earlier in the evening, but Ann had changed into a pair of jeans which were far too stylish for wear in underbrush that, at midnight, could often scarcely be seen. By the time they reached the turnoff for the small church, built nearly upon the banks of the Loch, the mist had lifted a bit, allowing them to follow the driveway without the help of the flashlight. They moved as quickly and softly as they could, watching carefully before them for potholes which could sprain an ankle or crack a shin. When they reached the church itself, they tightened themselves to the wall and eased around to the rear. There, in moonlight and mist, they saw what Glass had expected to and Ann had not.

When he returned from The Angus Bull at eleven, having consumed more beer than was probably wise, Glass had heard the phone ringing even as he was unlocking the door. It had rung eight or nine times before he could get to it in the dark living room. It was Sybil. She sounded almost but not quite drunk.

"Jason, I've come home to find that Duncan is not in his bed. Is he there with you, by chance?" She did not seem worried, though she was not unconcerned either.

"No, Sybil, he's not. Clyde doesn't know where he is either?"

"This is Tuesday, Jason. Clyde is out whoring tonight."

"Have you called Henrietta or Ann? Perhaps he got . . . lonely . . . and went up there for company. I understand they have a big new telly to watch." He hoped this was all it would take to find him.

"Yes, I've called there. I don't know where else to try. And I don't feel well." Her voice did sound woozily shaky.

"Go make yourself some coffee, Sybil. Let me check a few things out. I'll ring you back." He hung up without saying good-bye. Even before he could remove his finger from the button, the phone rang sharply again. It was Ann this time.

"Jason, Sybil's just called. She says Duncan's not there. If I pick you up, will you help me look? Henrietta's gone on horse-back along the high road toward the pony farm on the other side of the crest. I think we should look the other way." She went on to list several alternatives, including the ruined house along the Gap road which Duncan sometimes called his "own" home when he'd had enough of Clyde's being Clyde and Sybil's being Sybil.

So they had stopped there first, using the headlights of Henrietta's truck to illuminate the yawning gap at the junk-strewn end of the house, then Ann's flashlight to scan the more enclosed sections at the other end. No movement, no sound. So Glass insisted that they try his theory next, which, to Ann's reluctance, they did.

Now, in the foggy moonlight behind the church, against the backdrop of the chrome-colored lake, they could see the boy's shoulders and head sticking out of a hole which by this time must have been three to four feet deep. When they saw him, they tossed care and secrecy aside and sped up to where he worked, guided by the moonlight, the flashlight, and a kerosene lantern which Duncan had brought to illuminate his work.

"Duncan," Ann said softly but firmly when they attained the edge of the hole, "what are you doing?" She knew, of course.

They could barely see his face in the darkness. "I am not afraid." He never missed a stroke. "I will take the secrets out for you." Incredibly, the tip of the shovel had already struck something that sounded hollow and wooden. Glass knelt at the side of the hole and snatched the shovel from the boy's grasp before he could take another stroke against the wood, which must by now have been well rotted. This remote burial place and a wooden coffin attested too succinctly now to the bitter hatred Bruce Menzies must have felt for his father at the time of his death.

"Duncan, I tell you, you have made a mistake, damn it. Now

get out of there. There is nothing except a dead man in this hole." He yanked the boy out by the arm and swung him wide of the grave to set him down beyond the pile of earth his efforts had produced. The fog was getting very thick, and Glass was anxious to refill the hole as quickly as possible. He pointed the flashlight toward the thin stone grave marker, which was now on its back, and saw immediately that there must be two bodies in the grave instead of one:

ROBERTS MENZIES
(1872–1925)

AND

MARIA MENZIES
(1881–1925)
Her dust will be scattered
but her soul will live.

"A woman's body first, I suspect, Jason," Ann said through a noticeable shudder. "Maria died several months after Roberts and would be buried second."

"On top of each other!"

"It might be done that way at times, perhaps, especially among poorer folk who cannot afford more than one plot."

"The Menzies are *not* 'poorer folk,' " Jason said with pragmatic indignation.

"When it came to Roberts and his unwanted German wife, they were, I fear. My father told me once that their burials had been oddly conducted."

Jason merely shook his head and tossed the first shovelful of earth back on top of the exposed casket. At which Duncan bellowed, "Get the secrets first!" He tried to snatch the shovel from Jason, slipped his grasp, and stumbled feet first back into the hole, his arms extended for balance as he plunged in. He hit the wooden lid with a thump first, then with a splintering crack as he dropped another two feet through the lid of the coffin. Ann shrieked now, but the air was so heavy with moisture that she could not have been heard by more than Jason, Duncan, and perhaps Maria Menzies. Jason was paralyzed with horror for a moment, then found himself pulling Duncan, who had become hysterical, back out of the hole, which was now deeper than he was tall. The boy's mind had accepted reaching into a grave to remove "secrets," but not standing in an open coffin. He cried uncontrollably and threw himself into Ann's arms. In the dark, Glass could hear her sobbing as well, felt as if he would like to himself. Then he was hit from behind.

More horrified at the thought of falling into the grave himself —he would have gone face first—than by the unknown identity of his attacker, Glass fought himself back from the edge first, only to lose his flashlight over the side instead. He clutched at Duncan's lantern to illuminate the darkness behind him, to find his adversary.

"Charlie," Ann's voice, still shaken, called as firmly as it could. "Charlie, come here. Here, Charlie." It was Duncan's sheepdog, who must have been wandering around other parts of the graveyard and responded to his young master's cries. The dog seemed quickly consoled by Ann's familiar voice, for he backed off from Glass and took up a stationary position somewhere in the dark mist, panting heavily and liquidly.

"Jesus to goddamn hell, Duncan!" Glass was more frightened than he could ever recall having been. "This was the most idiotic stun . . ." he hated himself for his phrasing. "Goddamn it, Ann, hang on to him and his mutt until I can get this damn hole filled up." He tossed in another shovelful, but it was underfilled, since he could now not see the pile of dirt from which he was digging. He repositioned Duncan's lantern to give himself a better view.

"Jason, get Henrietta's torch out of there before you bury it, will you?" This involved reaching into an open coffin, and he noted that Ann had stepped back after making the request.

"Ann," he snarled with some impatience and much anger, "that I do not plan to do. If you want Henrietta's flashlight—torch—*you* get it. Call me a pantywaist if you wish, but I have gone about as far as I plan to for one night. My advice is to leave it. We'll get a replacement at Sciennes' in the morning and tack it onto Farquhar's account." He paused to see what she would do. "You're the doctor—or at least, were. You've fooled with dead people before. I let my words do that so my hands won't have to."

Unsure of what she would do, she edged forward and peered into the hole and beyond it through the foot-square gash in the middle of the coffin lid. Its interior was fully illuminated now by the still-lit flashlight, like the inside of a mummy case Glass had once seen in a Boston museum. What it lit up was unmistakable: bones.

"Shit. Shit." Glass was first nauseated, then sick. He released Duncan and spun into the thick mist to throw up his beer and supper. When he turned back to the hole, mopping his foul mouth on his sleeve, he saw Ann, incredibly, *in* the grave, kneeling carefully on the remainder of the coffin lid. She had her hand inside, even though she had already removed the flashlight. With her free hand she pulled out a bone. Again Glass tried to vomit, but he had nothing left to spew up.

"Jason." Her voice was much calmer than he had expected. "Jason, these are the bones of a dog." She reached in for a handful. "There is not a human bone in this box." She re-inserted the flashlight and scanned around. Many ribs and leg bones were visible, also a skull that even Jason would have suspected to be a dog's.

"Ann, now, look. I grant you that this is a very interesting piece of information, well worth thinking about. But not now and not here. Look, it's starting to rain. Let's get this thing filled back up before the dirt turns to mud and I can't move it."

"Give me the shovel, first." She continued to stand on the coffin lid. She inserted the point of the blade inside the coffin, scattered the bones to either side of the center, and began to tap on the bottom of the box. A hollow thumping sound, as if there were space below it. "I think, Jason, that since we have come this far, we should go all the way. Come in here and let's try to break through the bottom into the next one. The wood is very rotted."

"Ann, I will not pursue this. If we lucked out to find dog bones in Maria's coffin, I am quite sure that we will find Roberts' bones in the other. That I do not wish to do."

Now the rain, which had just been a drizzle for two or three minutes, began to fall in a downpour. Duncan's and Jason's hair was quickly matted to their foreheads, and Charlie was losing much of his husky round shape. By the lamplight Jason could see that Ann's was becoming straight and stringy just as quickly, and a puddle was forming at the bottom of the coffin.

"I doubt from the sound that we will find much at all in the next coffin, but we shall see." Now without his help, she raised the shovel and slammed it hard against the bottom of the box. It penetrated immediately, disappearing the full length of its blade before she controlled its downward thrust. Then there was splintering, and she tried to pull herself up on the side of the hole, but the rotten now-wet wood gave way, and like Duncan before her, she shot down another two feet so that her head was now below the top of the hole. With this she lost her courage, so Jason leaned over the side, prone on his stomach, and used his arms to give her leverage to climb the side of the pit. In passing up through the double level of wooden coffins, she tore the side of her soaked and muddy jeans. Since this last penetration had been her idea, she fought to control the whimpering that had once again taken hold of her. Jason wrenched the flashlight from her hand and, without asking himself why, pointed it back toward the boxes.

There were a number of bones in the bottom box, but not enough for a body, even a one-armed body. On further inspection, Jason decided they were dog bones from the upper coffin which had fallen through when Ann plummeted downward. Water was now cascading over the sides and seeping, indeed splashing into the bottom box, filling it quickly. But he could see that there was something inside the box, something that looked like a woman's purse. It was submerging rapidly. He had come too far now; convinced there were no human bodies in this grave, Glass jumped in carefully and distributed his weight in the first coffin so that he could reach into the second to retrieve the purse. But the wood gave way again, and Jason went through to the bottom and hit on his knees, scraping his hands and forearms as he dropped. His right hand was slashed on the palm when he reached sideward to steady himself and accidentally placed it on a sharp protuberance which, when he pointed the flashlight at it, turned out to be the skull of the dog. He gritted his teeth, stuffed the leather pouch inside the front of his pants, and then reached his hands up so that Ann and Duncan could assist him up. He almost hit Charlie lip to jowl when he thrust himself out.

He found himself not speaking or thinking now but panting, heaving hard and futilely at the shovel as he tried to return the dirt to the hole. But it was thick, heavy, impossible to move except in small amounts. He was drenched, and beyond the glow of the lantern, so were Ann and Duncan and Charlie.

"Jason, no one will open this church until Thursday evening. You can't see this place from the road, so let's come back tomorrow and fill it in. It's too much to do just now."

He didn't answer but yielded to the tug of her hand on his as she took up the flashlight. Duncan grabbed the lantern and they began retracing the path around the church to the main highway, and then the hundred or so yards along it until they reached the truck. There was no moonlight left, no sign of the Loch, no sound other than the hissing splash of the torrent as it struck the ground around them. Glass was still heaving and panting. He felt Ann take the shovel from his grasp and toss it in the back and then saw her insert Duncan and Charlie inside behind the seat and then felt her push him into the left front and shut him in while she circled the front of the truck to get to the driver's side. And he sat low in the seat, his knees against the dashboard, while she threaded the narrow Gap road and spun her tires in the gray dirt to climb the steep grades and round the tighter bends. And then he felt her stop in front of Clyde's and take Duncan and Charlie from the rear and heard them move toward the front door, which opened and, in thirty seconds, closed, and then she returned and they drove to his cottage. Not until he heard her shut off the engine in front of it did he open his eyes for the first time since he had gotten in. He had said "Shit" out loud at least a dozen times.

Whether from fear or tension or sheer physical discomfort, Ann unashamedly stripped off her muddy sweatshirt and jeans at the door and stood trembling in her panties and bra until Glass could retrieve a quilt from the upstairs bedroom and wrap it around her. He heated some coffee, then removed his own wet clothing and donned his robe. By the time they had settled together in front of the fire and warmed themselves inside and out, Ann was already trying to analyze what this all meant, as if the physical horrors of the last hour had been dreamed rather than having actually taken place.

"I have been trying to formulate an opening question for you, Jason, but I have been unable to come up with one. Nor am I sure that you would have any answers if I could."

"Let's start with the obvious. How long have those graves been empty? Would there be any way, medically or even archeologically, to tell when in the last fifty years those two bodies were snatched?"

"I can't speak archeologically, Jason, but I think I can say with some degree of medical certainty that the bottom coffin never contained *any* body whatsoever at any time. The upper one never had more than the dog in it. If you feel your stomach is up to it, I'll tell you what you would have found in there if there had been."

"Skip it, I'll take your word for it. So let us work on the assumption that they were empty graves all along—fake ones. Which required two fake funerals in the same year of 1920—"

"Nineteen twenty-five. According to the records, Bruce Menzies buried his father, whom he had rejected despite his presence for the last half-dozen years, in January of that year, then his stepmother, whom he never deigned to call that, in June. Thus the grave was opened twice for the deposit of two empty coffins."

"And now opened three times for the desecration of both of them. Could Bruce have murdered—or have *had* murdered—one or both of them?"

"His father I doubt. You see, Jason, clan feuds are historically notorious throughout Scotland—rejections, disinheritances, reunions, then the whole cycle again. But patricide? There is not much record of that. Blood ties are too strong. I suspect Bruce genuinely hated his father for any number of reasons but also probably saw to his well-being, however clandestinely he did so."

"Look. Roberts was the true clan chief and reappeared just when Bruce had reached his twenty-first year and was celebrating his own impending assumption of those duties with his grandfather's blessing. If what I know of Roberts is any clue, Roberts showed up and said 'Mine' right in the midst of Bruce's bar mitzvah, or whatever the Scottish call it."

"We don't *know* any of that, of course, but I can accept it for the sake of argument, certainly." She shuffled her chair closer to the fire and tightened the quilt more closely to her neck and breasts, shivering slightly as she did so.

"Bruce must have been glad to see Roberts in one way. If I had been delivered to Kyle station, even at the age of five, in a dog crate which was probably bounced and slung on and off freight trains all the way from Glasgow, gagged so that I could not tell the world that I was a human and not a cocker spaniel, urinating all over myself and waiting for it to run out the holes that somebody had humanely drilled in the bottom so it would —if all this had happened to me, I might have a wooden box ready for that person myself. And I am supposedly nonviolent!"

"No, Jason—by the time Roberts arrived, he was nearly fifty

and looking nearly twenty years older than that, according to my father. He was without his left arm and his right eye. He was a sick man. Like Farquhar, my father felt that it was the reason he married Maria after the war—he needed a keeper. He knew he was dying. He simply came here to do that. Any threats he made to assume the role of clan chief would have been idle talk only. He probably could not have performed even ceremonial functions, much less practical ones. Bruce could simply have waited it out." She was about to begin another line of reasoning when she noticed some barely contained eagerness on Glass's face, heightened by the flicker of the firelight which intermittently exposed and disguised his features. "Okay, Jason"—she laughed slightly—"let your fictional imagination have a go at this one."

"Yes, yes, It's ready to. I'll go along with you for a moment. It may be that Roberts is *not* the villain of *this end* of the piece. Nor Bruce either. But somebody had an empty coffin buried. Who are the suspects?" He raised his hand in the air, ready to tick them off as she named them.

"Angus, Roberts' father, is one—but I deny that on the same grounds. He could not kill his son to convenience his grandson. He was also sick and dying himself—he died sometime in the spring of 1926. He's out so far as I am concerned. Not to say he had any love left for Roberts, however."

"I'll go for that. Not his father, not his only son. Who's left?"

"In the family, two. One would be Aunt Elizabeth, whom you met so auspiciously that first night at the castle. Not likely either, do you think?"

"How old would she have been in 1925?"

"Mid-twenties, no more than that. She's in her mid-seventies now, though she's been unbalanced for as long as anyone can recall. At least since the early 1950s, which is my first recollection of her."

"Who's the other?"

"His German wife, Maria."

"Good," said Jason, fairly clapping his hands as if he knew a plot that could be assembled now—just for the sake of argument. "We need to know more of her, I think. Would there be some reason for her to be involved in Roberts' death and then have an empty coffin stuffed in the grave?"

Ann waved this off. "The first half of that I don't know. But five months later she died also. Too much coincidence, don't you think, that whoever buried her decided not to place her body in the ground either?"

Glass whistled, surprised to see steam come from his mouth as the room was beginning to chill again. He threw another log onto the fire. "This is bizarre, Ann. What's our best source of information on Maria, at this point in history?"

"The only one left living now who would have known her would be Aunt Elizabeth."

"Great. There's a mind that does not make much sense at all. We could be off on a wild-goose chase in an instant with her information. What's our next choice?"

"The only person who has shown any interest in Aunt Elizabeth for the last twenty years: Henrietta. Perhaps she has sifted something out of her soliloquies that might be of use. The only other person left who ever sees her is Farquhar."

"Whose information would be more misleading than Aunt Elizabeth's. Yes, Henrietta it will have to be, and she has already indicated to me that she knows more about all this than she will *tell*—though I got the distinct impression that she would verify anything of worth that I found for myself. Perhaps Henrietta would like to go to dinner tomorrow—it's bargain night at The Bull, isn't it?"

"Bargain if you mean they'll charge you less. No bargain in what you'll eat."

"Ann, my dear, I am not going there to *eat*." Now he paused and spun his neck to the right so fast and hard that he could hear it snap. "That pouch we took from the grave. Did we drop it on the way to the car?"

Ann smiled wryly and produced it from beneath the quilt that she continued to clutch tightly around herself. "No, Jason, you dropped it when you dropped your trousers. Here 'tis."

He handled it carefully, both because it was delicate and because it was foul to touch and, most of all, smell. Despite the fact that he undid it very carefully, the rusty buckle crumbled in his hands. The odor drew him back to the dank corner in his father's basement where he used to sit as a boy to look at the naked breasts in *National Geographic*. Inside the pouch were papers, roughly five by eight inches in size and not clipped or bound together in any way, numbering perhaps two hundred in all. As he riffled through them their smell intensified, almost as if they disdained being tampered with. At first afraid they would crack and fall apart, Glass realized that they were simply too damp to do that, though they would become very delicate when they dried out. They were covered very tightly, one side each, with minuscule handwriting in black ink which had blurred badly into the paper.

They knew, of course, that they held in their hands perhaps the best piece of source material they had yet come upon, given the fact that Farquhar had so badly decimated Roberts' diary. But age and dampness and murky calligraphy made the thing virtually illegible. Their initial dismay, however, gave way to renewed hope when they discovered that the top and bottom pages were much worse than the ones in the middle. Glass leaned closer to the fire to try to read it.

"It's not in English. It looks like German to me. Maria was German, correct? I don't read the language; do you?"

"No. I have only much Latin and some Greek and a bit of French to bring to occasions such as this."

They studied it further. It was clearly some sort of daily record, perhaps a diary or maybe just an almanac; it was impossible to be sure without translating it. All the breaks in the writing opened with a date, however. One at the middle of the stack read 23/11/11—twenty-third November, 1911. They turned back to the earliest pages but could not read the dates there. On the fourth page they finally could make out 2/11/99—November second, 1899. There could not have been entries much earlier than that, for upon sampling the middle pages they could tell that rarely had more than three or four days in a row been neglected by the writer, almost certainly Maria. They went to the bottom of the pile next to determine what the latest date was. Again the same problem: they were too blurred to read.

"Here is one several up that says"—Glass squinted to read it—"2/1/25—February first, 1925."

"No. January second, 1925. You Americans are the only ones I know of who list the month first. Judging from how low you are in the pile, it was not attended to much after that date."

They agreed, perhaps just because it suited their purposes to believe so, that this must be a diary kept by Maria Menzies from some arbitrary date in her younger life up until just before the time of her death in 1925. But they could not determine why she would have buried it in Roberts' empty coffin, almost as if she knew that she would die herself before long. It was almost as if she had buried *her* life instead of his.

"And that's not all," Glass continued to muse with a mixture of annoyance and exasperation, "but then somebody buried a goddamn *dog* in *her* coffin! Hell, Ann, the only human being that I know of in this whole spooky district who ever got into a coffin was poor Bruce Menzies, and he was a *live child*! Say, do you folks in the Lochs play with a full deck or even by the same rules the rest of us do?"

She let this go unanswered. "Obviously the only thing to do is get these translated—though there will be a good deal of time and expense involved in that."

"Surely there's somebody around who can read German who would like to make a few bucks—quid, that is?"

She shook her head. "The more I look at this the less I think it's German. Look at all these double vowels. It must be Dutch or a sister language from the Low Countries." Now she stood up and began reinserting the pages into the foul-smelling, soaked, mold-covered leather pouch. "I'm off to bed, Jason. The train to Edinburgh leaves at eight, so I can perhaps get three hours' sleep before that. I still have enough connections at the University there to find someone who knows Dutch and will be happy to make a few pounds doing this. In fact, I had a Dutch professor there for abdominal surgery who I'm sure can steer me to someone reliable." She looked around for her clothing, then recalled its location and condition. The rain still fell steadily outside. "May I purloin your robe to get back to Henrietta's in?"

"Certainly"—Glass laughed, rising also—"but won't that look suspicious?"

"Not nearly as suspicious as me strolling in my bra and panties, now would it? And I certainly have no intention of getting back into my miserable things." She smiled at him brilliantly, her hair still straight and matted, her face, though, still awfully pretty.

"You could stay here."

She continued to look at him, still smiling, though now more ironically. "I have a long day tomorrow, Jason. I need sleep."

"So do I."

"Then we'd best get to places where we're assured of getting some." She kissed him, the first time she ever had, lightly on the chin, very lightly, so that he wondered whether in fact she had made contact.

"I promise you can trust me." He didn't believe his own words.

"Well, unfortunately, I can't."
"Trust me?" He was hurt.
"No, promise."

9 PER STIRPES

THE ANGUS BULL'S WEDNESDAY-EVENING "bar snacks"cost three pounds fifty apiece and consisted of re-stewed potatoes, orange vegetables that Glass could not identify, and a sauce-soaked gristly lump of meat which the establishment billed as "steak." Henrietta showed no visible displeasure when served, hammering at her food gamely, though Glass, who had had no breakfast or lunch, was severely disappointed. They drank more pints of beer than either had intended, perhaps to wash down the "food," perhaps to fill themselves in its place. The beer, however, served to loosen Henrietta's tongue more than Glass had dared hope.

He had awakened at two that afternoon, ashamed of himself because he knew that Ann must already have arrived in Edinburgh and be well on with her mission by this time. To counter his sloth and guilt, he phoned Henrietta immediately and offered her the social occasion he had once before promised her during a chance encounter along the Gap road. She had accepted willingly, even eagerly, and said she did not mind preparing the Menzies genealogy that Glass said he required to be on with his work. He frankly felt that by this time he could piece most of this together by himself, but he wanted to see what her version would be. When she picked him up at seven, she was dressed in a neat white blouse and black skirt, the only time he had ever seen her not in blue jeans; had, in fact, combed her hair, so that if she did not look younger than her forty-five years, she looked a handsome representation of them. She even wore perfume, which Glass had noted immediately when he climbed into her pickup truck for the three-mile ride to Loch Killilan.

Henrietta had finished most of her meal, though Glass had managed only half of his before giving up. She mopped the table clean with her napkin, spread their beer glasses aside, and unfolded a foolscap sheet of paper on which she had constructed the genealogy. The chart was so clean and neat that it could not have been a rough copy. Oddly, given her general attitude toward Glass's project, she had expended a good deal of effort on this.

"Okay now, Jason. From the top. Stop me if you need clarification. I could have traced Menzies back ten centuries with some research, but I felt you would rather have it from Angus forward. Correct?"

"Correct, at least for now." He was conscious of her staring at him intensely anytime he spoke. There was a pause before she returned to the sheet.

Henrietta, it quickly turned out, had prepared this chart as much to criticize and editorialize as to assist Jason Glass. Glass, though, took notes quickly as she spoke, using her frequent discursions into personal opinion to catch up with her facts.

Angus, as the chart showed, had been born in 1848, had died in 1926. In 1870 he married Margaret Gunn, 1852–1925, the last of three Menzies to die in the same year. A proper wife for a clan chief, she was a passive figure who took it very hard when Roberts failed to return after the Boer War, even harder when he emerged the way he did from World War I. Roberts himself, 1872–1925, had married the Edinburgh nurse Catherine Clyde in 1897. An apparently sterling woman, she bore him one son, Bruce, while they were under siege at Ladysmith and died a few days after his birth. Sometime later, probably at the conclusion of the Great War, Roberts married the "German woman" named Maria; and she was destined to be hated by virtually every Menzies in the clan, both because she was the "enemy" and because she was not the perfect mate for a clan chief that Catherine Clyde had been.

The son, Bruce, 1899–1943, was one of the few newborn infants to survive the Siege. Five years later he had to survive as well his shipment to the Lochs, by whom and from where it was never determined, nailed in a dog crate. Infuriated at Roberts for not returning after the Boer War, Angus raised Bruce as if Roberts' generation had never existed and planned to hand over the chieftainship to Bruce on his twenty-first birthday, which would occur during Christmas week of 1920. When Roberts

THE CLAN MENZIES

(as represented by Henrietta Menzies to Jason Glass on Wednesday, May 28, 1975)

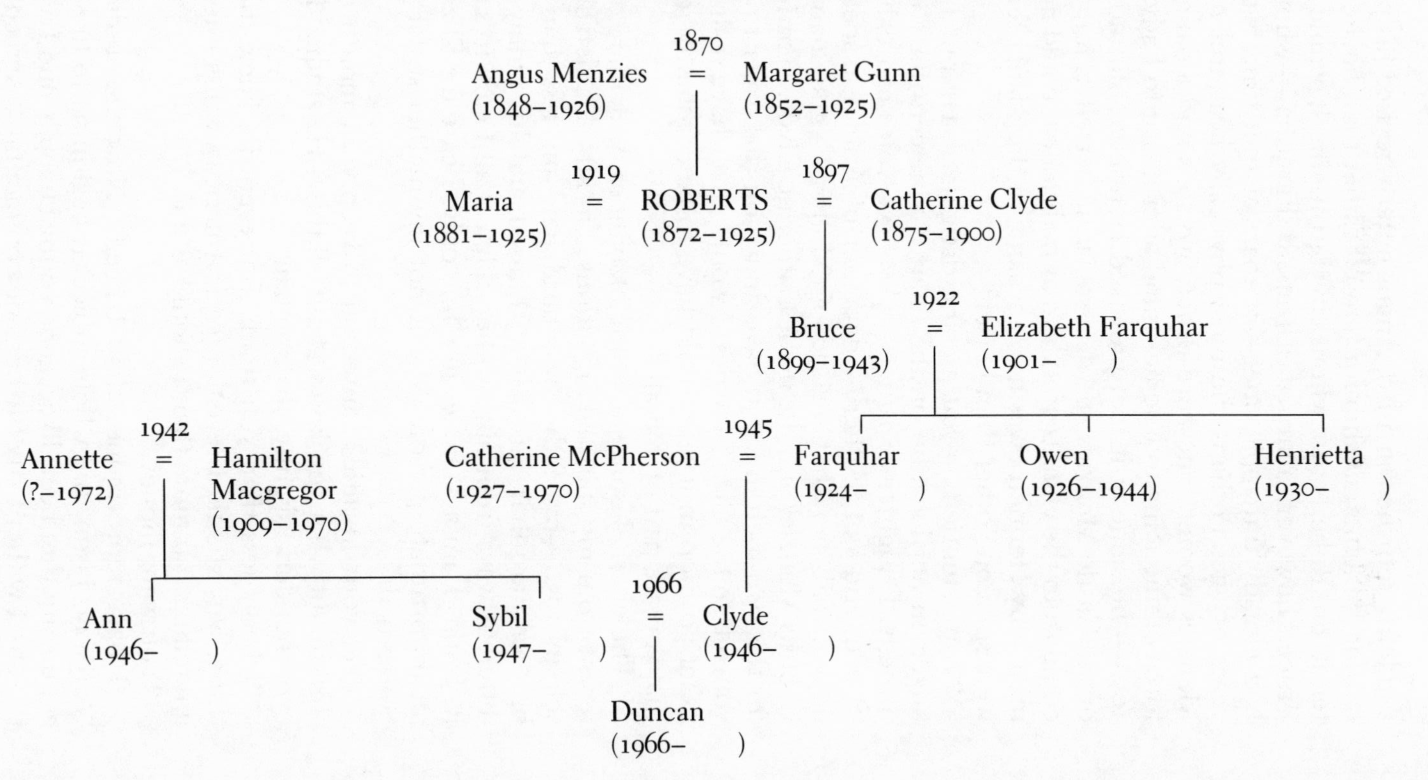

suddenly returned in 1919, Angus bitterly revised his plans, retaining the chieftainship for himself rather than having to confer it on Roberts, to whom, by birthright, it would belong. Bruce, however, married Elizabeth Farquhar—whom Glass had already unhappily met—in 1922, at that time twenty-one years of age. Perhaps the most physically beautiful of all the Menzies women, she bore Bruce two sons and a daughter before commencing to lose her mind after a visit to Ladysmith in 1950—the same visit that provoked Henrietta into moving out of the Castle Menzies and disassociating herself as much as she could from the clan itself. Glass, as he listened, could not determine why Henrietta was now speaking of the "daughter" as if it were someone other than herself.

"You, Henrietta—*you* are the daughter." He put his index finger on her location on the chart. "Nineteen thirty until the present. Daughter of Bruce—why have you been calling him 'Bruce' and not 'Father'?—daughter of Aunt Elizabeth—why do you call her that instead of 'Mother'?—granddaughter of Roberts Menzies and the noble Catherine Clyde. Henrietta, but for this two-inch line you have drawn on this paper to connect yourself to the Clan Menzies, I would never have realized your exact position in it and would have to be constantly reminded that you are part of it at all."

"The chart, Jason, shows my bloodlines, which are quite different from my spiritual affiliations, I'm afraid. I detached myself in 1950—my father was dead, and my less-than-beloved brother Farquhar was driving himself and his family mad in different ways from our mother. That is all I care to say about it, Jason. I am a Menzies in name only. I care for Elizabeth as an unfortunate person—she is not my mother so far as I am concerned."

"Yet your loyalties cause you to keep your mouth clamped shut about what you know about all this." He studied her gray eyes, her dark, slightly silvering hair.

"I know less than you think. But even if I knew the whole thing, why should I reveal it to an American writer—for free? I am telling you more than I should as it is."

"You want money?"

"I have more money than I need." Now she studied him. "Anyway, Jason, the whole subject is beginning to tire me. Do get me another beer, like a good young chappie, and I will finish the chart without any further side commentary. Agreed?"

He rose and stepped to the bar and ordered two more pints from the sullen male bartender who shared nothing in common with the rather pleasant young girl he had met there on his first night in town. He appeared the type who would have chefed and sold for three pounds fifty the sort of slumgullion they had been fed for supper. While he waited for the man to draw the beer, Glass watched the fog collecting once again around the rain that had been falling all day.

"Now, Bruce's dates, as you see," she said crisply after he had placed the dark beer before her and waited until she had sipped, "are 1899, born on the twenty-ninth of December in Ladysmith, until 1943, killed in May in the North African campaign. He was in his forties, he needn't have gone at all, but it was as if he had war in his system—spawned by the Boer War, killed by the Second World War. With this, Farquhar, who was eighteen and about to go to war himself in 1943, was allowed to remain at home and tend to his father's lands. His father had connections in the British War Office which facilitated this, you see. But the second son, Owen, born in 1926, left on his eighteenth birthday the following year—beautiful Owen, the loyal, the patriotic, the last vestige of the Catherine Clyde strain of Menzies. He was severely undertrained at Aldershot through the summer, and then got himself permanently killed in the invasion of Germany in September. So much for Owen the Good. Had Farquhar the Lesser gone in his place, as he should have, the Menzies would have traveled a different sort of course these last thirty years. Owen would have been chief of a clan, as Scottish leaders once were, instead of what they are now—chiefs of sheep and cleared land and capital investments."

"Ann has told me of Owen, at least briefly. She implied that her father was very devoted to him even above the other Menzies."

"Everyone was devoted to Owen, Jason. Since he was the second son, he was not in line for the chieftainship unless Farquhar was done in, as all of us except poor Owen occasionally hoped he would be, so, had he returned, Dr. Macgregor was going to set him up in medical school in Edinburgh after the war. I am sure that Ann has told you that the tragedy of Owen's death was that his stomach wound was highly fixable, not necessarily fatal at all. But because of the heavy shelling, they could not get him to the field hospital, and he bled to death over the course of several hours."

Glass noted that this was the first Menzies, with the exception of Roberts' first wife, of whom Henrietta spoke with any admiration or sympathy whatsoever. She resumed her narrative with no further comment.

"Now to the bottom. Farquhar married Catherine McPherson in 1945, within a month after the end of the war he never troubled himself to go to. He was, of course, clan chief by default now, and has been ever since, though he's been trying to patch up the clan's faults to lessen his de-fault."

"Catherine McPherson, 1927–1970. Dead at forty-three. I don't believe I've ever heard Farquhar mention her."

"Probably not. She had served her purpose by then. He married her after knowing her only two months. I can recall her vividly as a young woman—the most beautiful woman in the Lochs, it was said, though generally the most chuckleheaded as well. She knew Farquhar did not love her, but she was content with his castle, his money, the clothes he bought her—which is everything Farquhar wanted any wife of his to be anyway. She was a walking portrait—have you ever read Browning's poem on Ferrara's last duchess?—used to establish beauty, image, decorum, and glamour for the Menzies name, and of course to produce a male heir as quickly as possible—which she did a year after their marriage." Henrietta pointed now at the name of that heir: "Clyde, 1946–present. Quite a success, wouldn't you say? You've met Clyde?"

"Not really. Only saw him in the dark one night."

Henrietta now grinned at him. "Yes, so Sybil said." She continued to grin. Glass wondered exactly what Sybil had said and how far around she had been saying it. He pushed her attention back to the lower lines of the genealogy.

"Catherine is the one who was found dead of exposure in the interior courtyard of the castle, wasn't she? I was told she had gone out on a cold winter night for some unknown reason, dressed only in a nightgown and a robe. No foul play was suspected?" He knew Inspector Ross at least supposed some.

"Dr. Macgregor, of course, had died himself just a few days earlier, so a doctor had to be imported from Fort William to examine the body. But there was no reason to doubt him. It was exposure pure and simple. Apparently she had fainted or fallen and hit her head on the stairs or something, lost consciousness, and died before she could regain it."

"And no one knows why she was outside dressed like that?"

"Somehow I suspect Farquhar knows, but he's never said. I'm not sure if anyone ever asked him. I haven't. Why don't you?"

"Sometime, I am sure I will. And so to finish. In 1966, Clyde married Sybil Macgregor and young Duncan was born to them that very same year?"

"Since the wedding took place in February of 1966 and Duncan was born in June, I am sure you can guess the circumstances surrounding that marriage. Farquhar was furious; of the two Macgregor girls, it was Ann he wanted for Clyde. Sybil was a slut, slightly dumpy, definitely not interested in anything like decorum or a family name. Farquhar even tried to claim that Sybil had been so loose from the age of fifteen on that no one could pin her pregnancy on Clyde. He almost had him off the hook."

"Who put him back on it?"

"Clyde himself did. He was sure that Sybil could have been fooling around with no one else since she started up with him, was sure that the child had to be his. I think you'll notice enough Menzies features in the boy's face to accept that now, but Farquhar would not give up till the day of the wedding—which was conducted in a civil service in Kyle. He had not only gained the unwanted Sybil, he had lost the beautiful Ann—whom I suppose he hoped Clyde would use just as he had used his own wife: for image and to inject some physical beauty into Menzies countenances."

"What, though, about Duncan's mental deficiency? Is it hereditary?"

"I think not, though no better explanation has been offered. Having known Dr. Macgregor and his wife, and Ann and even Sybil, I see no signs of it there."

"Wait, Henrietta: why not trace it on the Menzies side? Surely Roberts acted in some pretty strange ways. Then you inject Elizabeth Farquhar, the woman you've disowned as your mother, into the family—a woman, I am sorry, who spooked me severely the night I saw her. Then you look at her oldest son, Farquhar, whom you've called mad yourself. Why can't we have a Duncan turn up? And Clyde himself does not seem particularly sharp of eye, wit, or tongue."

"You'll have to ask Ann about that. She's the medical expert. It seems to me, though, that one can be born deficient, as Duncan was, or one can be driven mad by circumstances. I cannot speak for Roberts—I never knew him; he was dead five years before I bothered to be alive. But I can speak for my Aunt Elizabeth. She raised me almost single-handedly into adulthood. She was a loving and caring mother despite, first, Bruce's neglect of her and, second, his decision to get himself killed at forty-three in the last war. It was not until we came back from Ladysmith in 1950 that she came apart mentally. At roughly the same time that I moved out."

"So tell me, Henrietta—what happened in Ladysmith in 1950 to cause both of those things?"

"If it is any of your business, you will have to find that out for yourself."

"And would you agree, Henrietta, that perhaps Farquhar's—shall we call it derangement?—began in 1950 also?"

Henrietta smiled patiently, again squeezed his knee. "No more, Jason; this beer has made me tell more than I wanted. You are the researcher."

"Researchers need cooperative sources."

"Cooperation must be induced. You've had all you'll get from me for now, maybe ever."

"You're still a Menzies, Henrietta."

"No more than half a one, I assure you."

At this point the pleasant young bargirl, who had by now taken over for the sullen male, leaned over the counter and signaled toward Jason.

"Mr. Glass, a trunk call for you."

It was Ann, who knew of his plans to bring Henrietta here this evening. She seemed very businesslike, perhaps troubled. Maybe only exhausted.

"Jason, I need your advice rather quickly." The pub room was noisy, the connection somewhat poor. He pressed the phone tightly to his ear, stuck his index finger in his other one. "I located my Dutch professor late this afternoon; in fact, had dinner with him at the Doric Tavern this evening."

"I'll ask you when you get back what you ate. It had to be better than what I did." The bargirl gave him a sheepish smile.

"I've got the diary back in my hotel room, but I took two photocopied pages to supper so I could show them to him. He looked at them and told me that they were *not* Dutch, Jason."

"Not Dutch? Then what are they? They don't look Swedish, definitely are not Norwegian or Finnish. How can we find out what they are?"

"My professor *knew* what they are. They are written in Afrikaans."

"And Afrikaans is an African language spoken by the—"

"By the Boers, Jason." She paused to let this sink as far into him as it already had into her. "Maria, if this is her handwriting —and I think it will turn out to be—Maria was a Boer, not a German."

"Shit!" The bargirl glanced at him with some annoyance now. "That means he did not pick up a poor war-torn creature during the Great War. He could have married her in South Africa anytime from . . ."

"Actually, Jason, anytime from January second, 1900, onward."

"Well, let's give Roberts a few days of mourning for his dead wife. Also let's give him till the last day of February, 1900, when he managed to get out of Ladysmith legally and by daylight rather than sneakily and by night."

"Jason, there will be much time for speculation when we don't have a phone line between us. What I need to know now is how you want me to proceed. Dr. Krause has located the roommate of one of his medical students—the chap is a South African studying political theory at the University. He speaks both Afrikaans and English quite well. Perhaps, if the price were right, he would translate this for us. Shall I explore that in the morning?"

"Yes, yes. By all means. Check him out. Meet him. If you are satisfied, offer a pound a page to translate it for us. Let him take you a bit higher if he tries to. But look, don't give him the original. Bring that back here. Get the whole thing Xeroxed beforehand, okay?"

"Fine. I have one other piece of information that might interest you. Professor Krause was able to get through enough of the material to give me the author's last name. It was De Jager." She spelled it out for him, and he wrote it on a beer mat. Repeated it to verify it.

"Now, Ann, when will you get back here? I have been talking Menzies bloodlines with Henrietta all night. I've gotten a few random facts to go along with it, though I hope I can remember them all when I get back to the cottage. I'm taking few notes—you know how sensitive Henrietta is about such things."

"Yes. And I suspect that you'll recall more if you slow down on the pints for tonight. You sound a bit thick-tongued now." This was somewhat lightly said, though not entirely so. Ann was not teetotal, but he recalled her restraint on the occasion of Farquhar's potential bacchanal, the night they sang "Marching to Pretoria" and "The Road to Mandalay" together. "At any rate, I'll hope to be on the late train tomorrow. I'll call you from Henrietta's when I get there."

They rang off. When he returned to the table, he noticed with chagrin that Henrietta had already ordered and received two more pints. Jason was looking to get home to his notebook. He decided to make use of the extra half-hour, if he could, by working in some of Inspector Ross's conjectures about the Menzies.

"Just do one more thing for me, will you, Henrietta?" She looked at him boozily, gave his knee still another squeeze underneath the table. "Fill in the bloodlines about Sybil. She is currently . . . ?"

"Twenty-eight. That would make her born in 1947." She wrote this under Sybil's name, not as neatly as she had done the rest of the chart in earlier hours.

"And her only sister is Ann? Yes, a year older." She drew in "Ann, 1946–present."

"And Ann never married?"

"No, never. She finished her medical degree in 1972, but never did her residency. She has been in London, with the same employer, for the last three years.

Jason saw he was going to have to urge each step now. Henrietta's eyes were puddling. "And their father was Dr. Macgregor, correct?" He, of course, knew this much without asking.

"Yes, Hamilton Macgregor. Died in 1970 just before Ann finished school. Was sixty-one." She scribbled "Hamilton Macgregor, 1909–1970" on a slant above Ann and Sybil's names, drew crooked lines connecting them all.

"And his wife's name?" Now Jason took the pencil from her hand and did the writing himself.

Henrietta took a long sip on the beer. "Annette. Don't know her family name. Died in 1972, though. Don't know exactly how old she was. Fifties, anyway."

"That too is young. How did she die?" Glass, of course, had already heard.

Henrietta now stared into his eyes as directly as her clouded vision would allow her to. Her head pivoted a bit on her neck, her mouth grinned unwillingly. "Suicide." She started to slide clumsily from behind the table. "Enough for tonight, Jason. I fear I am going to be sick. Perhaps we should leave."

Glass vaulted up to settle his account at the bar, did not wait for the few coins he had coming in change. He rolled up the chart to protect it from the rain, then snatched Henrietta around the right biceps and led her outside. The cold air and rain seemed to clear her head a bit, and she got cleanly into the passenger seat on the left side of the pickup truck. When Glass sat down behind the wheel, she handed him the keys. He could not get the engine to catch until she reached under the dashboard and choked it for him. As they began the mile-long journey down the highway to the turnoff for the Gap road, she definitely began to feel ill, demanded finally that he pull off to the side, and got out in the rain and retched into the darkness. While she was doing this, Glass looked ahead and could see the flashing blue bubble lights of two police cars five hundred yards ahead, roughly in front of the churchyard he and Ann and Duncan had visited the night before. Only now did he realize that, because of his late rising and the steady downpour during the day, he had not returned to fill the grave. He hoped Duncan had, but even that would not be enough to hide the fact that it had been recently opened.

Once Henrietta had climbed back in, he planned to get by the scene as quickly as possible, but soon realized as he approached the church that one policeman was on the roadway signaling him to halt with a red plastic wand. When Glass had done so, the policeman, a man with a much thicker Scottish accent than Ann or the Menzies had, leaned toward the driver's window.

"Good evening, sir," he said in such a way as to induce calm despite the blackness and storminess of the night and the unlikelihood of being stopped by a policeman amidst it. "Are you locals?"

"Yes, we live in The Gap, just ahead."

"Mr. Menzies?" The policeman seemed startled.

"I am Henrietta Menzies," Henrietta spoke up, apparently feeling better after jettisoning her miserable supper and excessive amount of beer. "This is Jason Glass, the famous writer."

The policeman did not act as if he were acquainted with Jason Glass's fame. "Have either of you noticed any peculiar activity in the vicinity of the church down below of late?"

Henrietta, of course, did not. Jason, of course, claimed he did not. He bravely inquired why the question was asked.

"Well, there's been a grave-robbing, actually. A double one, apparently. I am sorry to say, Miss Menzies, that the stone indicates it was the grave of one of your ancestors—Roberts, in fact, and his wife! The grave is nearly filled with water and mud. It's been open for a day or so, I would say. You've heard nothing of this?" He acted as if she should have.

Now Henrietta stared at Jason, as if she not only suspected but *knew* he had done it. She said nothing for a moment; then she looked back at the policeman, whom, in the dark, she could hardly see. "Well, Constable, that, I assure you, is no problem of mine. I have no truck with corpses. Call Farquhar Menzies at the castle, will you. He'll be disappointed, I am sure."

The policeman did not give them leave to depart, but Glass took advantage of his speechlessness to do so. He navigated the truck into The Gap, up the difficult slimy roads, through the narrow bends between the boulders, scraping two of them with his bumper tip as he, somewhat beered-up also, misnegotiated the nature of several turns. Finally he was on the more open road around the lake; passed Clyde and Sybil's house, which was dark, then the two ruined houses; next passed his own cottage, as dark as they were, then up the gliding turns toward Henrietta's, near the top of The Gap. She seemed to be sleepy when they finally got to the lay-by before her door. He climbed out, then more or less pulled her out the other door. The amorousness which she had kidded about, hinted toward, now became real.

"Why not come inside for an hour or so, Jason?" She kissed him sloppily on the cheek as he steered her toward the door to her cottage. There were no lights, and he was managing to guide her and himself through every puddle available. "Have you ever tried an older woman? I'm not that much older, am I, Jason?" She was trying to pretend she was joking, but in essence Glass knew she was not. She unlocked the door and flooded her tidy, rustic parlor with light. "How old are you, Jason?" She giggled and shut the door behind him, though she could surely feel the stiffening and resistance in his limbs as she tried to pull him farther inside.

"I'm thirty-five, Henrietta."

"Only ten years! You'll be forty-five before you know. And

you won't change much, nor have I." She spun around with her arms extended girlishly, flaring her skirt.

"Not tonight, Henrietta. Maybe some other time. We've been drinking too much."

"I am *not* drunk, Jason. Nor are you. It is because I am old, isn't it?" She seemed hurt.

"No, of course not. Now just get some sleep, Henrietta." He turned and opened the door, but she shrieked at him so violently that he froze where he was.

"You didn't mind getting Sybil's pants off her, did you? She says you still have them, too. You didn't mind getting Ann's clothes off her, did you—and that's a hell of a lot tougher than Sybil's, I'll tell you. At least she managed to wear her pants home, you bastard."

He could not understand what had come over her, was in fact somewhat frightened by it. But then he got angry, reached into his raincoat—which was the same outergarment he had worn the night he was with Sybil—and found her pink bikini panties still wadded up in the pocket. He pulled them out and threw them gently but directly in Henrietta's face.

"Not tonight, I said. Now sober up before you hate yourself, Henrietta, and give those to Sybil when you see her. Tell her to strap them on next time."

With this Henrietta's fury increased. "You son-of-a-bitch. You think I'm too old."

"I think you're too drunk."

"You think I've dried up, don't you? Why, I haven't even gone through the change yet. You think you're some sort of stud horse who can do better than a forty-five-year-old bag like me. You bastard, I still wear the same size dress I wore when I was twenty. My tits don't sag."

"Come on, Henrietta. Calm yourself. You're not going to like yourself in the morning. I'll see you then. Let's forget this ever happened." He stepped outside into the rain but could not close the door because she blocked it open with her foot.

"It was probably too dark to get a good look at Sybil, wasn't it? She had a cesarean—her stomach's an ugly mess." She braced the door with her hip. "Look at mine, damn you!" She pulled up the front of her black skirt with her left hand and her nylon briefs down from her waist with her right, exposing several inches below the navel. It was indeed the body of a younger woman.

"Lovely, Henrietta. I mean it. But not tonight. I am too tired. Maybe I'm the drunk one." He simply walked away now, not bothering to try to wrestle the door shut. He reached into the truck and pulled out the chart, then disappeared down the road into the darkness for the mile walk to his cottage. He could hear her shouting obscenities at him for at least a hundred yards. The last thing he heard her yell clearly was ". . . and half of Scotland has been inside Sybil, you shit. You'll be the first inside of me if I bother to wait for you." She called him something else but he could not hear it. Perhaps it had been "grave robber."

Yes, they are all crazy, he thought as he trudged downward through the rain, with the possible exception of Duncan.

10 *THE RUINED HOUSE*

THIS WAS PROBABLY A SHEEP BONE, but Glass had seen enough of all varieties in the last several days to be getting easily spooked by any bone. The morning was suddenly hot and sunny, and Duncan perspired freely from his efforts as they stood examining what he had found. He was beginning to carry his shovel around the district as regularly as Robin Hood must have lugged his bow.

"What made you start digging here, Duncan? I frankly would not have thought to look here myself." "Here" was in the gaping section of the ruined stone house toward the bottom of The Gap.

"I saw some people . . . who lived in a . . . tent down by the . . . lake once . . . climbing around in here. They found a . . . bone too. They said it was a . . . people bone. Belonged to somebody . . . who was inside when the house . . . fell down." He pointed upward now to the nonexistent second story and the roof, of which only the trusses remained.

"I don't think this house fell down with anyone in it, Duncan. I think it was probably abandoned by whoever used it. Probably some shepherds over a hundred years ago. It just started to fall down when no one took care of it any longer." Glass believed what he was telling the boy, yet still, this end *was* much more ravaged than the two other sections. The heap of gravel at the center of this section was strange, and stranger still was the yawning hole in the front which obscured the outlines of the door and windows that uniformly characterized the lower floors of the other two sections. Since the rocks from the facade that had fallen were nowhere in evidence, one could almost imagine the sort of implosion that had pulverized those mighty stones and reduced them to the pebble-dust pile atop which he and Duncan currently stood, turning over in their hands a bone which could have been a human rib but was more likely that of a sheep. Several sheep in fact poked their black-and-white bodies around the corner of the opening to watch them intently as they sifted thorugh the top of the pile.

So for more than an hour, he and Duncan took turns digging in the pile of detritus and debris in the north end of the ruined house. At first Glass had planned to do this just long enough to convince Duncan that no more bones were there. But within a half-hour he had discovered another, and Duncan had two more. Now Glass dug furiously, happy at least that it was daylight and dry now.

All the bones they initially uncovered seemed identical—rib-like, though they had fairly well mangled one with the shovel and split it into three parts. It was near noon when they came up with a leg bone.

On this discovery Glass's sheep theory would have to stand or fall. He explained to Duncan what he had in mind. They would temporarily "capture" one of the larger sheep that idled nearby defoliating the land, measure the bone against its foreleg, then release it.

Duncan was all for this. But instead of approaching a very docile ewe who probably would not have minded a bit of human attention, he made for a rather suspicious-looking ram, apparently because the creature came equipped with two circular handles with which Duncan could grasp him. This animal was not tremendoulsy big—he stood no more than three feet high at the top of his head—but he commenced to bleat and scream and wrench his neck violently back and forth the second Duncan took hold of his curving horns. Glass could see that the horns were not chipped or cracked or scarred, so Duncan had at least the advantage of having taken on a young, inexperienced fighter, but the animal proved to have more native strength than either of his captors had presumed. With a sudden wrenching spasm he flipped Duncan atop his back; but the boy held on gamely, calling now for Glass to complete his end of the bargain as quickly as possible.

This was not an easy chore, for the ram kept dancing and bucking, tossing Duncan's weight off his back first on one side, then on the other. To his credit, Duncan never lost control of the horns and kept remounting the beast until Glass could hold the legbone they had exhumed from the silt pile up to his front shin. This was a waste of time, for the animal had a foreleg that was barely half the length of the bone he held: the hind legs were longer below the knee joint, but even these fell short of the length Glass held up to them. The animal's right hind foot dealt Glass a stunning blow to his own right leg in the commotion, and in the same motion he finally freed both his back and his horns from Duncan's weight.

"Are you all right, Duncan?" Glass panted as he rubbed his sore shin tenderly, the beginnings of tears creeping up into his eyelids from the pain. Other than being winded, the boy seemed unhurt. "Well, you are correct that these are not sheep bones, and they are surely not big enough to be the leg of a horse, or its ribs either."

"I told you they . . . are people bones. Been here a long . . . time, I think." He drooled slightly down his chin as he spoke, encrusting the dirt and dust on his face into rivulets of mud. Glass took his handkerchief from his pocket and dried the boy's lower jaw.

"Well, then, what do you say we go up to my cottage and have some lunch? Then we'll come back and dig some more."

"More toast?" He inquired eagerly. "Popshine?"

Glass laughed and ruffled the boy's hair. "Yes, more toast in the popshine." So they hid the shovel from the view of a passerby and stashed what bones they had in some thick brush and departed to Glass's cottage a mile farther into The Gap, higher up the road.

They returned an hour and a half later with a canvas bag that Glass had found in a shed adjoining his cottage and stuffed the six ribs, one shinbone, and one broken bone of some sort into it and recommenced digging in the silt pile, which they had already reduced from four feet to three. But as they worked down farther the material became more resistant, harder, heavier to move—also less productive of the bones they sought. In the first hour of renewed digging they found only another half a rib. But they did not plan to quit until they were convinced nothing more remained. It was almost four o'clock when they found most of a human skull. It stared straight up at them, seemed to guffaw because its lower jaw was missing.

"Jesus Christ!" Glass was surprised that his tolerance for ribs and leg bones stopped short when it came to a skull. He fought off fright, could feel himself panting as heavily now as when he had fallen into the double grave just two nights before. Duncan simply stared, eyes wide, saying nothing, as if he too had hoped to come up short of a skull. "Bring the bag over here, Duncan, so I can put this head in it."

The boy did as he was told, seemed to act as if one of them had a duty to fetch the bag, the other to lift and insert the head. He deposited it at Glass's feet. His end of the transaction was complete. Glass eased the skull into the bag. When it struck the bones inside, it sounded like the end of a sawn plank dropping into a pile of other ends of sawn planks. Glass winced at the noise.

Again Glass looked up into the upper reaches of the house, out through its roof beams at the still-clear sky. Then back at the pile of pebble and sand and rock at his feet. Then at the gaping hole in the front wall of the house. Then, for the first time, at the other building, opposite it across the road—one that because it was less imposing, gained less immediate attention.

Though just as vacant and just as useless, this one was probably a product of the present century. The building was smaller, but it had been divided in thirds as well. There were three doors with three identical windows to the right. Instead of rocks and boulders, this one was constructed of cement covered with a substance that reminded Glass of stucco. Its roof was intact—wood covered with orange tar paper or shingle—but its door and window fittings were missing. Glass could look right through it, even from where he stood, and see the lake glistening behind and slightly below it. On the end nearer him someone had written in red spray paint: 2/8/74 JOHN FARRELL FUCKED KAREN FRANCE. Which was all well and good—certainly a more pleasant thing than what someone had done to somebody else in the house across the road.

Glass returned his attention to the pile, and before long he had come up with fingers, probably a forearm, and—at five o'clock—a nearly complete pelvis. Each of these was placed more carefully in the bag than the head had been. Finally, though his courage had returned, Glass decided that they had found enough for the time being. With Duncan using his feet as rakes, they covered as well as they could the fact that they had been digging there, then started back up the road toward Glass's cottage.

Behind them they suddenly heard a car engine and, in the distance, could see the blue bubble lights—not flashing but clearly evident in the sunlight—of a police car working its way through the last boulders at the bottom of The Gap, its occupants almost surely still investigating the grave robbery they had discovered the night before. Glass did not have to think twice about the consequences of being found dragging a gunnysack of human bones down the road the day after a grave robbery—Duncan seemed to understand the general dangers of a bag of bones anytime—so they sprinted off down the bank to the lake, out of sight of the patrol car almost the whole way. At the bottom, without being told to, Duncan shed his jeans and T-shirt and—naked—plunged into the lake, dragging the bag with him. About thirty feet offshore a single tree grew from beneath the water. Duncan dived underneath at this point and fastened the bag by its drawstring to the base ot the narrow trunk. Even while he was still working at this, the police car slowed visibly as it passed the two ruined houses, but did not stop.

"We won't move those until tomorrow, when the police have gone, okay?" he asked the boy as Duncan tried to force his wet, undried body back into his jeans and T-shirt. "And don't go get them yourself, hear me? Come for me first, and for heaven's sake don't mention this to anyone—not your mother or your father or Aunt Henrietta. No one, hear?"

The boy nodded assent, though it was less comprehending, more offhand than Glass would have liked. He decided to remove them himself at the earliest opportunity.

So they parted—Duncan back to his parents' house lower down The Gap, Glass to his cottage upward in the other direction. Above him, in the distant reaches of The Gap, he could see the setting sun flashing off the chrome and glass of the police car, parked now in front of Henrietta's cottage.

11 *THE SECOND LADYSMITH DIARY*

FRIDAY NIGHT BROUGHT INTO TOWN all those people who were otherwise never seen in or even near Loch Killilan. Glass was hard-pressed to find a place to sit in The Angus Bull when he got there at nine thirty. He had to settle for a rickety stool and the barest corner of a small table which two drunkenly generous field hands offered him when they noticed him balancing his pint in his hands at mid-room. He thanked them, but clearly this would not be the best place to discuss his newest discovery once Ann arrived.

Glass had had Thursday night to himself. Duncan arrived within an hour after they had parted at the lake to tell him that Ann had called from Edinburgh to say that she was remaining there yet another night but would be on the late train to Kyle the next day. Duncan had no reason for her delay, but Glass managed to employ the evening in writing several pages of the placebo they would shortly hand Farquhar to assure him the project was going smoothly. He also wished to reorganize his thoughts and notes, and so listed questions in order to get ready to pursue the truth in the directions Farquhar would not be told about.

Ann entered the doorway from the hall and began to slide between the standing drinkers who jammed the middle of the pub, spotting Glass only after she had done much tiptoeing and searching about the room.

"My dear Jason, how are you since our little night of horror?"

Glass gave her a quieting motion, though he had hardly heard her over the noise of the crowd. "The police are investigating a certain open grave these days. Understand?" She did, paled just slightly, but quickly regained her color. "We'll talk about other things later, including a big find your nephew led me to. Now tell me about Edinburgh."

"Lovely, as always, Jason. I told you I had dinner at the Doric on Wednesday, then at The Royal Scotsman last night. Dr. Krause and I saw the Tattoo after that and . . ."

"I think you know, Ann, that Edinburgh means something else as well." He was not sure why he could not sit through a few minutes of travel chatter—perhaps it was because she seemed for some reason to be steering away from the point at hand. He softened his tone. "I'm sorry. But you must know I've been a bit tight waiting for you to get back. You extended it a day, in fact, which made me still more anxious. Just give me a quick summary, and then you can get back to your meals and sights and spectacles."

She laughed as if unhurt by his urgency. "The summary, Jason, is that I looked up the South African chap yesterday morning. He was definitely interested in the money—looked as if he badly needed it—and the pound a page seemed more than he ever dared hoped for. I did, though, offer a pound twenty-five for the pages that are blotted or in bad condition—most of which are at the top and the bottom of the stack. And the Xeroxed copies do not help things, either. I asked him to post me the translation in groups of thirty or forty pages as he finished them."

"Now, you're sure he can do it?"

She reached into her purse. "He speaks Afrikaans and English fluently, Jason, and I had him do two sheets from the middle—the cleanest I could find—to test him." She unfolded them and placed them on Glass's knee, since they had no more table space than what their glasses occupied. "He had no trouble at all with syntax or grammar or vocabulary—only with handwriting. You'll see several places where a word is either missing or noted with an interrogation point to indicate that he is not sure of himself there." She pointed to two such instances. "A real scholar, Jason. I don't think we shall have to fear carelessness."

"You say he's studying political theory? I suspect they could use some of that in South Africa these days, especially some that's been taught somewhere other than there. Or is he one of them in his thinking?"

"I did not examine his politics—just his English. His name is

Paul Krige, if you want to set your CIA to him. Or you could probably get to the bottom of his barrel pretty quickly yourself if you cared to, couldn't you, Jason?"

Glass let this go, though he could tell it was intended in fun. "So anyway, Ann, you have given me the first two pages of what will probably turn out to be a summary of a quarter-century of Maria De Jager's life. What does this bit tell you? You've read it, I'm sure?"

"About a hundred times by now, I expect. Long train ride, you see. But let me not summarize. Read it for yourself. See what you deduce. Can you concentrate in all this noise?"

"Well, I am too anxious to wait to finish my beer, so let me at least try. Can you give me a context, datewise?"

"Yes, it came from the middle of 1918. July."

While she turned to speak some works of acknowledgment to a field hand who seemed to know her, Glass squinted at the two tightly written sheets of translation before him. Krige's handwriting was itself difficult.

but Queen Street was the wrong place they told us, so we had to walk another half-mile carrying all the things, and cry some more with people looking at us except that Piet was not crying but she was and I was—and I cannot understand why it was hurting her so badly since he said he had only just met her. But we walked down Renfield Street and it was crowded and people were bumping into us because we had so much to carry and I would not walk behind or in front of him and she would not either but finally we got to the other one and they said yes this was the right place to go to war. And he had to go upstairs behind the windows where they announced the train departures and get his free coupon to go to war with rather than have to pay to do it the way the people going to Stranraer had to. And I watched where he went and when he came back and went to her to quiet her I went to the same office and told them that they should not permit him to go, that he would not be eighteen for another two months yet and maybe the war would be over by then. But they said they needed him and that was acceptable, that he would be in training for more than the two months it would take to get to be eighteen. So then I told them that he was not going to join a British unit but a South African one and they said that he should not have been given a train pass if he was not a British citizen. But then another man said he had examined Piet's papers and that he was a British citizen so why was he going to fight with the South Africans and he mentioned "traitor" and I got angry and reminded him that the South Africans were on the same side the British were even though they should not be—and then the man got angry too and called me a "traitor"—and I told him that nevertheless the South Africans would take boys under eighteen when the British wouldn't and that was why he was going where he was. So I walked out though I should have argued more so that they would take his free rail pass from him and none of us would have had enough money to buy one instead. And we heard the train being called just when I got back to where they were, and she started to cry harder and so did I and so did Piet a little bit but then he ran through the gate and never looked back and when I turned around she was gone and I walked all the way back to the flat and I never stopped crying until I got well back along Gallowgate.

Friday, 5th July 1918. Received a postcard from Piet in London saying that the South African Embassy had booked his passage as a civilian to Germany.

Monday, 8th July 1918. She called to say that I had to help her, that she had no money. When I asked her why she ran off at the station she said she was too sad to watch him walk toward the train without looking back at her. I said I would not help as I did not even know her name and he did not know her more than a few weeks. So she told me her name, which I almost did not even remember five minutes later, but I think it was Wallis, and then she said she would insist

Here, to Glass's annoyance, the sample translation stopped. He flipped the sheet over to see if there was anything on the back, knowing full well there would not be. Ann had finished her conversation with the two young men to her left when she saw he was approaching the bottom of the second sheet.

"I wish I had read the whole thing while I was still in Paul Krige's presence so he could have completed that whole episode for you. But I simply scanned the sheets to make sure of his English and then stuffed them in my purse. Sorry."

"You pretend as if your interest were academic."

"I try to pretend that, don't I?" She laughed lightly, though he could not hear it over the roar of the taproom. "Actually I can't wait until the next installment—which won't pick up there, I suspect, but rather back at the start. We'll have to allow ourselves to be teased by all this for the present." She sipped her sherry. "Now, you will at least be happy to know that I put enough postage on the envelopes I gave him to have them specially delivered when they arrive."

"Fine." He took a long thoughtful swig at his pint. "Now, how much have you deduced from all this?"

"Well, a few things. I thought we were onto something when I saw the name 'Piet,' but that cannot be old Cronje, as I had at first hoped. Obviously it is a boy who is still seventeen and is off to lie his way into the war in Europe."

"You forget, South Africans have no age or sex restrictions for soldiers—or at least, they did not in Boer times."

"Boer times were nearly two decades earlier, Jason. They were British subjects by this time, governed by some version of British law."

"Yes"—Glass chuckled—"however reluctantly. I gather from my research that British law was never at the forefront of their minds. What else?"

"Well, then, the second thing is that Piet must be a relative or exceptionally close friend—he is not Maria's lover, for she would have been in her high thirties by this time. The 'she' referred to is more likely the girlfriend, however recent a one."

"And apparently an annoyance to Maria."

"Yes, I suspect we shall find that she is when we get more pages." Now she leaned more closely toward him, to point at various places on the page. "I am fairly sure I know *where* this all took place, as well." She tapped the paper. "These street names—I showed them to the guard on the train to Inverness—are all to be found in central Glasgow. 'Queen Street' in fact is the name of the smaller station there, and the other station—Central, which serves the South—is about a half mile away."

"So we can possibly deduce that Maria De Jager was a resident of Glasgow, that Roberts met—and wed—her there after the war rather than during his years in South Africa as we speculated?"

"That's the conclusion I have drawn, though needless to say it will be revised a hundred times as we get through the earlier pages."

At this point a particularly loud and ruddy young man who had been laughing obnoxiously at the center of the room raised his glass toward the ceiling and—in response to the bargirl's call for last orders—shouted out: "Last orders on old Fuckqueer Menzies, blokes." A loud cheer broke out. "I understand that Mr. Glass here has an open charge at this place that he can sign us all drinks on."

Ann seemed to know the man and stood to confront him. "Here"—she pulled several bills from her purse and stuffed them into his shirt pocket—"buy a last round for yourself and your mates. I know all about your difficulties. Now is not the time or the place to bring them up."

The man reached into his pocket and unfolded the bills and made a slight turn toward the bar. "Tell Menzies for me, Miss Macgregor, that me dad and mum's gettin' old. They'd like to 'ave a trip to Montana to see Brian and Thomas afore they die. Or maybe"—he was snarling now, though he seemed to acknowledge that Ann was a symbol and not the proper addressee of what he was saying—"maybe 'e'd like to give Brian and Thomas and their wives and bairns a trip back here—where they belong. A one-way trip." About five other men his own age turned to the bar with him, and slowly, the hum of chatter began to return almost to its original crescendo.

"There, Jason," Ann said as she slowed the truck for the turn off the highway into The Gap, "you have an example of the familial past Farquhar is trying so desperately to live down."

"I'm not sure I follow you." He was still a bit shaken and very angry—angry at the troublemaker, angry at himself for having allowed Ann to settle it.

"The Clearances—one of your favorite subjects several weeks back, remember? That was Charles Peebles. The Peebles family was one of those cleared generations ago by the Menzies. They went to America and eventually worked hard enough to buy a small ranch in Montana—where they have raised sheep for the last hundred years. Ever since then, each son goes to Montana to work with the branch of the family there, staying here only long enough for the son behind him to become old enough to manage the small feed business they run here. Charles is the current victim, with no more brothers behind him. Brian and Thomas have been in America for at least a dozen years now and have never been back. The parents are somewhat indisposed and becoming more helpless by the year."

"But none of this is Farquhar's fault, right?"

"No, of course not. But it is felt to be the fault of the current Menzies, whoever that one happens to be at the time."

"Perhaps, then, this is one reason why Farquhar—and frankly, several generations before him—is so obsessed with reinterpreting, even reorganizing and rewriting the past?"

"Now, Jason," she said with no small degree of triumph as she threaded her way through the boulders at the head of The Gap, "you seem to be getting the point. Your Annie Daly was a figure from your family's past. Roberts, Angus, Bruce, and even those before them—and the things they have done—are factors of Farquhar's present! Simply because he is a Menzies. Most of us like to think that if we cannot control the past, we can control the present. It's a matter of definition. Of semantics, I suppose."

They were approaching the lake now, and Jason told her to slow down and turn off the road in front of it, with her headlights pointed out across the water. When she had done all this, he reached over, shut off the ignition and the lights, then quickly summarized for her what he and Duncan had found in the ruined house earlier in the day.

"Do you think these bones were removed from the graves sometime, however far back, before we got there, then buried in the ruined house?" Her tone suggested that in case Glass was going to claim that, she did not consider it likely.

He wasn't. "No, the bones were too scattered around the pile for a one-time stash, Ann. And they were in there for a long time, judging from the difficulty we had even getting down very far into it. The stuff was more like cement and mortar and gravel than dirt and vegetation. Whoever the poor guy was, I think he died right on the spot we found him. Perhaps one of the last tenants of the house?"

"To the best of my knowledge, no one has lived in that house in this century. But bones last a long time before decomposing. You say you were able to extract them whole, without their crumbling?"

"A couple split easily when we struck them with a shovel. But the ones in the sack down there"—he pointed toward the water they could barely see in the quarter-moonlight—"are all in good shape. Including the skull, save that it came without a jaw."

"Well, I guess we had better get them out and have a look at them, hadn't we?" She opened her door and slid out from behind the wheel into the darkness. "You're sure they're human bones, Jason?"

Glass reached back in and flipped on the headlights, using the low beams to aim downward at the water's edge, and got Henrietta's flashlight out of the glove box. "All I can tell you is that they are *not* sheep bones. You're the doctor. You tell me what they are."

When they got to the water's edge, Ann reached under her dress and undid her nylons, kicking the first off as she pulled down the second. Glass had intended to be the one to swim out for the bag, but now he watched Ann step into the water. "Guide me to the tree with the torch, Jason." She pulled her skirt up around her hips.

"You're not going to swim out fully clothed, are you? Here, let me go." He began to kick off his shoes without untying them. He could hear Ann laughing.

"Swim? Jason, between here and that tree you claim guards your treasure, the water is not more than two feet deep." Then something dawned on her. "Ah, yes, when Duncan goes skinny-dipping he *does* try to act as if it were the Marianas Trench, doesn't he?" He watched her walk out slowly. If the water was deeper than two feet, it was not by more than a few inches; she kept her skirt just at the bottom of her underpants. Glass edged out into the water to try to keep the light beam as directly and brightly on the tree as possible. When she got there, she worked awkwardly to hold her dress above the water with one hand and untie the canvas bag with the other. Glass was ashamed to feel a definite twinge of lust as he watched her. Within three more minutes she had returned, towing the bag through the water behind her.

When they got back to Glass's cottage, they lit a fire to take the chill off the room, then spread out the contents of the bag on the floor before it. Both ignored the limb bones, which dropped puddles on the stone floor; but whereas Jason became immediately interested in the skull, Ann noticed the pelvic girdle. Feeling the same grisly feeling overtaking him that had upset his stomach in the graveyard three nights before, Glass indulged in a bit of lame levity. "It is easy to see which of us is the more cranial, which is more carnal." He cradled the skull in his left palm and prepared to recite what he remembered of Hamlet's Alas Poor Yorick lament when he realized that Ann was deeper into the issue than he was and was not in the mood to joke.

"Jason, I can tell you one thing about this person that you

have not as yet determined." She turned the pelvic structure around in her hands, much as she must have done in medical school a few years earlier. "This person was female—the pelvic bone structure is always an easy form of identification." She detailed several differences, though she fell quickly into professional terminology that Glass did not follow. He took her word for it.

"So it's not Roberts after all."

She cocked her head. "You expected it to be?"

He laughed slightly ironically. "Not really. I guess I just hoped he would turn up to fill the void in this project I see developing now."

"The void?" She set the bone down on the floor and hoisted herself up to the sofa. Glass sat down beside her, noticing beforehand that she had placed herself in such a way as to be closer to him than she need have been. Perhaps too quickly after he had positioned himself he put his right arm around her shoulders. She did not resist.

"Yes. You see, I am stuck until I get some of that translation. I've got an empty double grave on my hands that I dare not inquire about lest it draw suspicion to me—it would not take too much to place me there that night, I suppose. Then I've got a pile of bones from an unknown female that I plan to keep to myself for a while as well."

"You are not fooling me with your excuses for delay, Jason," she replied somewhat sternly, even though she let her head rest on his shoulder as she approached what was to be some sort of reprimand. "You have not turned a word over to Farquhar as yet and you've been here more than a month."

"I'm researching."

"Ho, ho, you certainly are, aren't you. Nosing about in all the places Farquhar is expecting you to stay out of. I would get him something he wants to see rather quickly, if I were you. I spoke with him just before I went to Edinburgh. He's getting anxious."

"I'll have you know, Ann"—now he squeezed her a bit—"that I wrote five pages just last night, just the sort of thing Farquhar will want, all lies."

"Then write about twenty-five more and get it to him during the next three weeks, will you? About then the translation should start arriving and you can spend your spare time on that."

"What is so important the next three weeks?"

"Well, I want you kept busy, for one thing, so you don't get into trouble while I'm gone."

"Gone?"

"Jason"—she turned toward him now, yet kept her forehead in contact with his right cheek—"I have a job, you know. I have several assignments back in London which require my presence. Two novelists and one biographer are coming in to go over revisions and whatnot."

"When do you leave?"

"On the morning train from Kyle."

"But you've just come that route today. Tomorrow's Saturday. Give yourself a holiday before going back, for Christ's sake."

"Can't, love. I've left all the manuscripts in my flat there. I did not expect this side trip to Edinburgh, you see. I should have been back long ago. Not only does Farquhar not know I am doing this piece of related research with you, neither do my employers. You see, they want the same book Farquhar wants, not the one you wish to write. They are expecting Roberts to be another Annie Daly."

"So I guess I'll have plenty of time to write away on that version for them. I can just transcribe Roberts' edited diary and beef it up a bit to account for the missing pages and then improve the style—he wasn't much of a rhetorician, you know—and everyone will be happy. Except me."

"You know, Jason, the week's activities you just outlined are the very ones Farquhar is *paying* you for. You are theoretically *not* self-employed, though you tend to act as if you are."

"You don't have to remind me of that. It's just that I haven't faced up to telling thirty pages of straight lies as yet. When do you get back?"

"I'll try for three weeks from Sunday." Now she bounced up and confronted him squarely. "I'll bring two satchels full of manuscripts and work here for as long as they last me. Being in London is not as important in the summer."

Glass smiled, as if he could cope with the three weeks of lies with this to anticipate. "Then we'll do all the things—non-Menzien, of course—that I thought we might do this coming week."

"Such as?"

"Such as, wait and see." He leaned forward to kiss her quickly, and she met him halfway, then jumped up, as girlish as he had ever seen her.

"Must get home to Henrietta's, Jason. Long day today, another tomorrow. Ah, how I have come to hate trains since I've met you." She picked up her purse and advanced directly to the front door. "Oh, and sorry that I haven't got you your robe back. I'll ask Henrietta to drop it off tomorrow."

Glass balked at this. "No, no hurry. Don't have her make a special trip."

Now she looked, if anything, coy. "Oh, Jason, never. No special trip. She'll be going by this way anyway—it seems she has something of Sybil's to drop off as well." The look on her face, however ironic and uncritical, suggested she knew exactly what it was that had to be "dropped off" and how it had been delivered to Henrietta's in the first place.

Glass tried to make reply, but found he had none. He smiled sheepishly instead.

Ann started toward the truck, but paused and called back: "Oh, Jason, I've been meaning to tell you and keep forgetting. Be sure to leave Saturday the twenty-first open—the whole day."

"For whom? For what?"

"For Farquhar. He's getting lonely for you. Wants to make sure you're still around, perhaps. It's the day of the annual Dunedin Games on the Isle of Skye. The Menzies always go, have never missed. Some rather spectacular carryings-on that might interest you, but I'll leave Farquhar to tell you about that. He'll be by for you at six that morning." She raised herself into the cab and deliberately started the engine before she could hear Glass's reply, which she must have feared would be peppered with epithets. It was.

Glass retired inside, felt suddenly weary, and gave himself only enough time for two quick jolts on the Scotch bottle while he cleaned up his boneyard and stashed his bagful behind the logs in the woodbin. He would find a better place tomorrow.

12 *ROBERTS' HUNDRED*

THIS WILL BE A LONG DAY, GLASS thought groggily as he slammed off the old wind-up alarm clock which was enthusiastically obeying its instructions for 5 A.M. Long in hours, long in company—Farquhar Menzies had seemed a person who could inflate the psychological experience of sixty minutes into at least twice that. The only thing that had made him bearable on their one previous meeting was Ann Macgregor, and now she was five hundred miles away in London and not due to arrive until late tomorrow, if then—he had not heard from her in three weeks. Nor had he heard from Paul Krige, so the project had stalled.

Yet not shut down. On the previous Sunday and Monday he had dashed off a full forty pages of the placebo version of history he was writing for Menzies, the version based mainly on Roberts' edited diaries of the movement of the patients under his care from Dundee to Ladysmith in the week before the Boer investment. Even this was not a total waste of effort for Glass, for only one page was missing here and this was the period in which Roberts and his pregnant wife seemed to be unquestionably heroic, creating calm at a time of general panic, treating both aged citizens and young soldiers wounded at the early battles of Talana Hill, Elandslaagte, and Rietfontein. It had been a very bad time, and the two Menzies had done well in it. Glass had found to his joy that he would probably be able to use these placebo pages even in the real version. Roberts had apparently met no Boers with whom he cared to associate as yet, but Glass's history had still not reached the point of the actual siege.

Glass wished he had written this part sooner—it might have stemmed some of the initial cynicism he had been unleashing against Ann and Farquhar. Roberts and Catherine were so far heroic victims of history, geography, politics, and even nature. The growing abrasions between Briton and Boer, which were by 1899 nearly a century old, were being intensified by Cecil Rhodes and Alfred Beit's greedy quest for mineral wealth in South Africa, by the political shenanigans of the British governor of the Cape Province, Alfred Milner, and by ill-fated and ill-advised paramilitary actions such as the Jameson Raid. Now the British were actively provoking the Boers to war, and on October 11, 1899, the Boers declared it and invaded the British province of Natal from the Transvaal to its north. One of the ironies of history is that this invasion was provoked so that the stronger British forces would immediately have an excuse not only to repulse the invasion but also to return the favor by marching into the Transvaal and the Orange Free State—rich with gold and diamonds—and so reannex them to the British Empire as they had been twenty years earlier before the British disgrace at Majuba Hill. They would eventually do all this, of course, but surely they had not expected to lose the lives of so many innocent civilians—and innocent soldiers—before it could be brought about. Or, as it is tempting to think, maybe the number of civilians and soldiers lost did not matter to the likes of Milner and Rhodes.

Roberts and Catherine were two of the innocent. They had met in 1897, during Roberts' last year at the University of Edinburgh Medical School, and married that same year. He twenty-five, she twenty-two, they answered the call of the British Government for doctors and nurses in the Cape Province and Natal. They hired on to work in the civilian hospital at Dundee, in extreme northern Natal, for three years, at which point they would return to Loch Killilan to assume the practice of the local physician, Dr. Scott, who had announced plans to retire in 1900. Glass reflected that Angus Menzies must have had mixed emotions about this. On the one hand he would retrieve his son, his only child, who had been long gone from the district, first in school, then in service to the Crown. And his son would render a vital service to this sparsely inhabited reach of Scotland, which surely considered itself fortunate to replace an aging doctor with a young one so easily. Though Angus would have been only in his early fifties then, he must also have foreseen eventual difficulties in getting his son to set aside his professional duties to assume his place as chief of the clan, to see to its economic and territorial well-being. In fact, he must have assumed that this might be impossible, which is another reason perhaps for his early grooming of Bruce when he showed up at the Kyle station in 1905 nailed in a dog's shipping crate, crying as any five-year-old would be.

But Roberts. Roberts did nobly before Ladysmith was invested, and this was detectable not only in so biased a document as his own diary but also in the military records of the British Army.

It was estimated that thirty thousand Boers marched into Natal on October 11 and 12, a province as yet defended by only nine thousand British troops. And the bungling began immediately. The British subjects in Dundee and the four thousand troops garrisoned at Glencoe Junction were ordered to fall back from the Transvaal border, not the hundred miles that would have made them safe and free to operate below the winding Tugela River and the terrible heights that hugged its northern banks, but a mere forty miles to the vulnerable, though larger, garrison at Ladysmith. Ladysmith was a terrible choice; even General Buller on his way from England had been sending messages to his subordinates to get out of there and position south of the Tugela as quickly as possible. The town itself was surrounded by high hills in all directions and indefensible.

Perhaps one reason those who were eventually invested in Ladysmith did not move more quickly to get out in time was the sheer difficulty they had had in getting to it in the first place. According to Roberts Menzies' diary, communication between military leaders at Dundee and civilian officials in the town itself had almost totally ceased from the moment when the Boers invaded Natal near Acton Homes on the twelfth of October. In the ensuing week, there was much talk about leaving Dundee for the south; whether this would in fact occur and, if it did, how *far* south they would venture was all rumor among the civilian population. Then, on Wednesday the eighteenth, notice was given from General Penn Symons' office that trains were being sent from Ladysmith to evacuate those civilians and military wives who wished to go, though the troops would stay on to defend the town, the huge military stockpile stored within it, and—more generally—the morale of the whole of northern Natal. The people there had begun to fear not only invading Boers, but also rampaging blacks who (rumor had it) would be inspired to carnage by the absence of the military force. Here Roberts records a fragment of a conversation he had with his wife on the matter:

Normally I would not even have suggested that Catherine leave Dundee. Not only was her commitment to the patients too great to be at their sides one day and fleeing for her own safety when the non-ambulatory ones could not be moved the next. But also there was the sheer folly of abandoning one indefensible position at Dundee for another, perhaps worse one, at Ladysmith. General White had already chosen, we were told, to make his stand there instead of backing across the Tugela to Pietermaritzburg. Catherine decided, on her own, that the military blundering we were familiar with (Penn-Symons') was better than that of the doddering newcomer from Britain (White). So for every reason, she was determined to stay. Furthermore we had personally come to feel that the Boers were a decent folk, whatever our political differences, who would respect the white flag (which we were already fashioning several of from torn bedsheets); the red cross, which was clearly in evidence all about the building; and the professional neutrality of civilian medical personnel who could be of as much assistance to them as to their enemy in the event Dundee were taken.

But I did suggest she leave. She was in her seventh month to term and, though she was strong and hardy, never sick, she might not remain that way were supplies to run short. We already had evidence that some Boer medical personnel were more given to faith healing and witch-doctoring than we were. Were she able to reach Ladysmith before the rail lines were cut, she could persuade General White to allow her to pass on—as certainly he would allow any civilian to pass on—to Pietermaritzburg or Durban or I hoped even London. Our term was up here in July in any event.

But she would not go.

Here, according to the diary, the whole matter dropped.

But as quickly as the order to evacuate was posted, it was pulled down on Thursday the nineteenth. Which was highly curious, both for Glass in retrospect and for Menzies on the scene. The Boers were getting closer, the general panic greater, Boer spies more plentiful, not only at Dundee but also at Glencoe and, almost surely, at Ladysmith. Throughout the day on the nineteenth, word came back from the outlying areas that the Transvaal Commandant General, Piet Joubert, and his army were closing in from three directions. The most pressing problem was the force of five thousand under General Erasmus, whose sole responsibility it was to capture Dundee and the military supplies there. Why had the order to evacuate the civilians been withdrawn? Menzies' diary proved to be historically accurate on this point:

In their disarray, the generals feared that no train would get through before the Boers cut the line. Apparently, a force under Kock had already been sent to do this. The decision was made to fight it out—probably tomorrow—to trust the will and spirit of Tommy Atkins to get us out of trouble.

Friday, 20 October 1899. Tommy Atkins did it, apparently. Early this morning word came that the Boers under Lucas Meyer had taken Talana Hill less than a mile to our northeast and Impati Hill about two miles to the northwest. They had got guns, big Creusots apparently, to the top of each and had virtually the whole British force pinned down on the veld between them. They gave quite a pounding for a bit, according to one of the chaps they brought in who'd been taking it.

This is the first time I have ever seen war casualties. May I never see them again, though surely, in view of what must be about to happen, I will not be so fortunate. The first I treated were two NCO's, terribly trampled by stampeding horses when the Boers opened fire just after dawn. Then a bugle boy who died in my arms—69th battery, I believe—whose head was crushed by a Maxim 1-pounder which was so wet it could not even explode, merely kill on impact like a caveman's rock. But this was nothing compared to what followed. The Boers are deadly shots with a rifle, and many of the officers complained that Penn-Symons' decision to attack in close order rather than loose made the men impossible to miss from the hills above, rain or no rain. A townswoman was killed by a random Creusot shell while she stood in the streets urging on the green troops who were hurrying out to battle—the whole lower half of her body was severed from the upper, right in the middle of a crowd of civilians.

Around noon, however, Major Donegan, the field hospital commander whom I have mentioned on other, happier occasions, summoned me to assist him on the scene. I was terribly frightened to go, of course, but I rode out amidst the Mauser bullets, holding my red cross flag as high as ever I could, and when I got there I saw the source of his call. General Penn-Symons himself had been wounded in the stomach whilst rally-

ing his forces to scale Talana Hill in the face of the devastatingly accurate rifle fire. He was in terrible pain, but kept asking over and over if his Dublin Fusileers had taken the hill. Ultimately they did, though I fear we cannot pull General Penn-Symons through. His upper intestines are almost non-existent.

But this was not the only loss. In the rain the British artillery must have lost sight of their own infantry going up the side of Talana Hill —these khaki suits and brown-painted belt buckles have some strategic advantage, I suppose, but they caused many deaths today. Captain Nugent was hit through the knee by his own guns on the hill, and then again through the hip and thigh as he tried to crawl back to us for treatment. We could not even get out to help them until someone fortunately got word of their error to the gunners a full half hour later. I do not wish to know the body count of our men, either that inflicted by the Boers or by their own mates.

So the Boers are driven off at least for today. But they will be back, for our cavalry failed to pursue them—which anyone knows is the third and last Aldershot procedure for any victorious battle. Perhaps they could not find <u>them</u> *in the rain, either.*

Glass had noted the change in tone that distinguished this entry from the one Roberts had made the day before. While it might be the very explainable reaction of a young man who had never witnessed war before, it seemed something else. He read on.

I was particularly appalled tonight to hear the savage anger among the troops at the fact that wounded Boer prisoners were being treated by British civilian doctors such as myself, almost as if they expected us to let them rot and die on the field. Perhaps it is too much to ask them to shoot at Boers by daylight and pity them by moonlight, of which there is none tonight, but I can only think that in the long run, it is by daylight that we make our sole mistake.

The entry for Saturday the twenty-first was less bitter, though only momentarily.

We found one chap on the field today who had been overlooked yesterday. He was drenched and shivering, covered with dried blood from head to knees. Yet, when we brought him in and cleaned him up, all we found was a broken leg, no wounds at all. When we asked him about this, he said, in as few words as he could utter, that the blood with which he was saturated was that of his sergeant, whose head had been exploded by a Mauser shell and sprayed all over him. He was so blinded by blood that he stepped in a shell hole by accident and snapped his leg in two.

The next entry was dated the same day, though written apparently at a later hour:

Our communications with Ladysmith were severed sometime yesterday, in the vicinity of Elandslaagte, we learned this afternoon. General White had sent some troops north from Ladysmith this morning to investigate the situation, and word has come of a bloody battle fought there early this morning. A British victory apparently, though I hear more gleeful talk of "pig-sticking" by our troops and even of one of our officers, who made a captured Boer run across the veld so that he could overtake him on horseback and sever his head from his neck with a slash of his sword. Perhaps this did not happen—it could be simple battle myth.

It rained terribly hard all day today. General Penn-Symons lingers, but I examined him this evening and know that he cannot live more than forty-eight hours.

The entry for Sunday, October 22, was the first of the missing pages. Glass's research in the *Times* history of the war indicated that this was the day that General Yule, now commander in Dundee in place of the dying Penn-Symons, had fallen back from Dundee to Glencoe, where he heliographed White in Ladysmith to send him help against the Boers. Boers were thick indeed, apparently, in the Glencoe-Dundee vicinity, having been driven back twice now from Talana and Elandslaagte. But White could already feel the imminent squeeze on Ladysmith. He flashed back that he could not afford to release any troops to the north, that Yule should pull out of both Dundee and Glencoe and fall back on Ladysmith, where, when he got within range, White could send out a force to escort him in. Glass simply could not determine why this page might be missing from

Roberts' diary, especially in view of what he found in the entry for the next day, Monday the twenty-third.

The handwriting was very ragged here:

We have camped for the night along the Helpmaaker, about twenty miles south of Dundee I would estimate. We are still less than half way to Ladysmith, though my patients are holding up well, as is Catherine, who works as if she were not carrying the weight of a seven-months baby in her womb. We are very cold and wet—the rain did not let up for an instant all day. Our clothing is caked with mud, which was nearly knee deep along the road at places. The wagons bogged down continually, and the fact that we should not be with the column is frequently made clear by the members of General Yule's staff and by the soldiers who are forced to dismount to help us extricate our ambulances.

But at least we are out of Dundee. Kaffirs have brought word that the town is now entirely in Boer hands, that people who attempted to defend their homes were shot in cold blood. They brought no word of those still left at the hospital, save that Penn-Symons died this morning. The Boers have found the supplies we had to leave behind, enough to feed ten thousand men for two months, I am sure. Perhaps this and the goods train they captured last week near Elandslaagte—full, I am told, of whisky, chessboards, and polo sticks—will be enough to bog them down and accustom them to the British comforts so they will not pursue us to Ladysmith and then, we hope, across the Tugela. I will not be content till we have reached Pietermaritzburg, the next location where there is a sufficient hospital for my needs.

While the Boers enjoy our rich food in Dundee, we have only hard biscuits and bully beef to subsist on, though at least we have enough of that.

As I said, however, I am a pariah because of the deal I forced them to strike in the dark of the morning. We were not supposed to be along, and every soldier knows that. They resent us, but they know that there was no choice.

Glass's imagination, of course, feasted on this latter paragraph. Farquhar must not have known the meaning of the word "pariah"—had perhaps mistaken it for something else because of the rough scrawl, undoubtedly the result of Roberts' using a barrelhead or a wagon floor as a writing table. There was something covert and clandestine suggested in that last paragraph on the twenty-third—and like so much of what Farquhar had chosen to remove from the diary, it was not all that hard to project what it might be.

Glass's scenario was built again upon facts from the *Times* history. Having been heliographed by White that he was out on a limb in northern Natal, surrounded on three sides by Boer forces, Yule decided to leave Glencoe for Ladysmith. But his supplies were two miles back in Dundee; they had to be retrieved. All this was fact. Also fact was that the army could not afford civilian panic, nor civilian accompaniment to Ladysmith. It would slow them down, not to mention calling the Boers' attention to the imminent retreat. So Yule had sent a party back to Dundee under cover of night (actually early morning on the twenty-second) to snatch enough stores for a moving army to last a week. Then, without the knowledge of either the Boers or the loyal British subjects sleeping soundly in Dundee, they fled to the south, to join with the garrison at Ladysmith. All this was done. All this was fact.

So where did Roberts fit in? It could only be some sort of blackmail, for a later page in the diary indicated that he had brought more than a hundred patients in twenty ambulances out of Dundee hospital, and this would never have been allowed unless Roberts had them where it hurts. He was a doctor perhaps making his night rounds when he spotted the movement in the British encampment nearby, had gone out to check on what was happening, had discovered that he and his wife and unborn child and his hundred or so patients were to be left in the lurch, ditched outright. Perhaps he had threatened to blow the whistle on the whole operation unless they took him. So they did—this too was fact—while the other patients were left behind and the citizenry was left to die in significant numbers the next day trying to act in the place of military forces who had deserted them. This Roberts was certainly a mixed bag. Uncompromising at one moment, totally compromising at the next. Perhaps he had been the author of the plan, also fact, to leave lighted candles in all the tents to fool the Boers—and, of course, the citizens of Dundee as well—into thinking the army was still there. Roberts could think of such as that.

24 October 1899—Tuesday. We reached the Washbank River today and camped there. The men are beaten and demoralized, though they are at least dry for a change, for the sun shone today. My patients are still intact—I have lost none. Catherine coughing now but otherwise in good spirits. So much of their welfare is a result of her good judgment. It is times like this when one thanks God—if not for one's present predicament, at least for one's past choices. What if I had not chosen Catherine?

25 October—Wednesday. It is raining again. I lost one patient today to pneumonia. We were lucky not to lose more—five others have it as well—but one is one too many. I have begun to treat the soldiers and perhaps am more acceptable now, though not many speak. Their feet are in bad shape—they have blisters, gangrene, and who knows what else, and some have worn the soles off their boots and are marching on their bare feet when they cannot bribe one of the cavalrymen to make room on the back of his precious mount for a few hours.

But we are within range of Ladysmith, less than eight miles to go tomorrow.

Then, on Thursday, the twenty-sixth, they got there:

26 October 1899—Thursday. We reached safety in Ladysmith today. The front of the column began entering at eleven this morning, though it was mid-afternoon by the time our ambulances passed inside the British perimeter. If General Yule was not happy to have us with him, General White was surely less so to see us arrive. I demanded hospital facilities and got them in the Town Hall, no less, when White removed his own headquarters to the top of Convent Hill behind the town, a place whose height gave him a better view of the surrounding hills.

Roberts spent several pages now outlining the arrangements he made for his patients in the Town Hall hospital—Farquhar had not removed any of these—and then concluded the entry for this important day with the following lines:

White has established a fourteen-mile perimeter, though even with our troops this is too thinly defended. He is angry that reinforcements he had expected to get have been held back at Pietermaritzburg. While this is a wise military move, I am sure, it has spoken only one thing to the civilians and military at Ladysmith—we are to be left to fight our own battles for the time being, and our force is not large enough. There is fear of a siege. Every train moving south is full of women and children, though some insist they will not leave. Communications—both rail and wire—will not remain intact much longer. Every necessary message is being sent out as quickly as possible. White is reputed to have asked today for several naval guns from the HMS Powerful to match against the Creusot Long Toms which the Boers invariably bring with them. There is no panic as yet in Ladysmith, but there is much uneasiness.

It is very late as I write this, in the midst of a meeting-room ward of our Town Hall hospital. The patients are quiet for the night, and the only sounds I hear are the sisters whom White has allowed us to help look after them. The reek of iodoform permeates the place, and we have begun to receive wounded soldiers in our midst. I will do my best for them as well, though much of what I see I never expected to and must reach back into the farthest depths of my professional memory to know how to treat.

Catherine is sleeping, dry and safe for the first time in days, but how much longer will our security last? Perhaps she should leave on tomorrow's train—but I cannot do my work without her.

So this was how Glass had spent the early part of his week, creating from these facts the placebo version he would hand this very morning to Farquhar Menzies, a version devoid of suggestions of blackmail, favoritism, and—even—of the monomaniacal, perhaps egomaniacal devotion to "his" hundred patients which Glass was beginning to smell in the diary's pages. Still, these pages were easier to work into acceptable shape. What came next, Glass already knew, would not be.

As he awaited Farquhar and various other Menzies for the outing to the Dunedin Games this morning, with sunlight just now beginning to suggest itself over the Gap walls, he reflected on the one other success he had had this week as he awaited both the first translation pages from Paul Krige and the return of Ann Macgregor.

On Thursday, two days before, he had ridden in Duncan's pony cart into Loch Killilan for the purpose, ostensibly, of buying a week's worth of food, but really to get some beer and Scotch. He had been reluctant to return to The Angus Bull since the night he had had his run-in there with Charles Peebles. Yet before his morning in Loch Killilan ended, it was Charles Peebles whom he had most wished to see and, in fact, wound up seeking.

As he pushed his trolley repetitively around the short, narrow aisles of Sciennes' Store, to this day still unable to detect any order in the placement of goods upon its shelves, he was sought out by the same woman, apparently the manager, who had greeted him his first day in town. She wanted the same favor this day she had wanted then: more autographed copies of *Gratuitous Glory*, which she could sell for a pound extra apiece to those who did not understand that Glass would have signed anyone's free of charge. She bore an armload of about fifteen and set them down on the floor in front of a row of cornflakes boxes and began handing them one by one to Glass to sign. Glass decided to get something for himself out of this round.

"I was wondering," he began his inquiry, ashamed that he still did not know this woman's name, "if you could tell me anything about those two ruined houses near the lake in The Gap. That is, how long they have been vacant? How long the stone house has been in ruins? Anything at all, really."

She was a fond, motherly type, not at all reticent about divulging information. "Well, surely you knew, Mr. Glass, that the newer one, the one which is still in one piece and backs onto the lake, is the one in which Roberts Menzies and his second wife lived before they died in . . . well, whatever year it was. Forty-some ago, I expect."

Glass stopped signing for a moment, slightly stunned by this. "No! No, I hadn't known that. I had presumed they lived in the castle."

"They did initially, from what I've heard, but there was too much friction in the family in those days. They were a bit corked, I imagine, that Roberts had stayed away so long and then returned with a German woman just after at least a dozen young men from the district had given their lives fighting them in the Great War. Other strife as well, but I don't know much about it. At any rate, Angus had that house built in the early twenties for them—the site had the advantage of being a good ten miles off from the castle, you see."

"And it's never been reinhabited since Roberts died?"

"Just by his wife, but she died not long after." Now her face darkened. "Wasn't that quite something, Mr. Glass, about their bodies being stolen from the churchyard? How much of them could have been left, do you suppose?" Like several others he had encountered round about, she looked at him as if she presumed that he, being Roberts' official biographer, knew something more about it than she did. He deflected the question.

"What about the ruined house across the road? That's much older?"

"That dates from quite early in the last century, I'm told. It was a shepherds' house—it could hold three families. I haven't seen it in many years. I've heard there's not much left but the stone walls today."

"Not much. But while most of the decay is natural, there is one unit which has a gaping hole in the front and a heap of pulverized stone in the middle of the ground floor. The two others are still fully standing with nothing more than weeds growing inside. Do you have any idea what happened to it?"

Happily, she was nodding affirmatively to this. "Lightning, Mr. Glass, though some of the older folk around here insist that it was not a bolt that struck it but that it was just rattled to pieces by thunder. I accept the lightning version myself."

"Whether lightning *or* thunder, it must have been *some* bolt —or clap!"

"Oh yes, the Great Storm of '25—June twentieth, 1925. I was only ten years old, Mr. Glass, but I can honestly say that I have never been more frightened of anything in my life. The rain clouds rolled in down the Loch in the late afternoon and kept pelting water for at least twenty-four hours. But that night there was the most severe thunder we have ever heard hereabouts—at least ever since then! Several fishing boats that were moored on the Loch were sunk, a house right here in town had its roof burnt off when it was struck by lightning, one car was even blown over on its side by the wind. The house you're speaking of was the tallest structure on that end of the Gap floor and it must have taken the lightning bolt full on its face to smash that hole in it. But much as I don't believe it, the thunder was so bad that night that it could have shaken down a mountain, much less the front of a house. Because we are ringed in by hills here, the reverberations are much worse than you would normally expect. One claps rings back about five or six times before it exhausts itself. My late husband was a war veteran—he said it sounded like the German artillery in the Argonne Forest it was so bad."

Glass had finished signing the books, and returned the woman's pen to her. "And no one lived in it at the time?"

She shook her head. "Not since the '80s, I don't think, when the last shepherds left."

"Where did they go?"

"Two of them went to Montana with their families. They had relations there. The third opened a feed store here in Loch Killilan. Their name is . . ." She groped a bit for it.

"Yes. Peebles."

So that was why Jason Glass went looking for Charles Peebles before returning to The Gap in Duncan's pony cart that morning. Glass had not been a superstitious person to this point in his life, but as he walked quickly two blocks along the Lochfront in search of the Peebles feed store, he began to feel that Fate was somehow hemming him in. The more questions he asked, the more he discovered, and not just the factual information he sought, but how much this factual information was now connecting with his own extraliterary life. If the story of Roberts Menzies and the story of Jason Glass had heretofore been separate things, they seemed to be becoming intertwined into different facets of the *same* thing. For every step he took into Roberts Menzies' strange life, Roberts seemed to take one, and perhaps two, into his. In the back of his mind, Glass was even bothered that the day was June 19, 1975—one day short of the golden anniversary of the Great Storm of Loch Killilan. He found the burly redheaded young man taking inventory in the back room—actually shed—of his parents' store. Charles recognized him instantly, even smiled sheepishly, put his clipboard on a stack of burlap feed sacks, and thrust his hand toward Glass.

"Sorry abou' the other night at The Bull, Mr. Glass. I was a bit pissed up, you see." Glass shook hands willingly. Fate apparently was already backing down a bit.

"Don't worry about it, Charles. Call me Jason, will you? I have done enough research into this case to understand your anger."

"Then why are you goin' ta paint it up all white?" He was still friendly, but clearly wanted to know. "Those Menzies bastards have screwed our lives—and I just don't mean Peebles' lives—for a hundred or more years. We . . ."

At this point a much older man, stooped and ancient, came around from behind a pallet load of corrugated boxes. He wore pince-nez spectacles on the tip of his nose, a long, pointed, Dickensian one. "You're Glass?" he scratched. Glass nodded.

"My father, Mr. . . . Jason." Whatever tirade Charles had been about to launch into on the subject of Menzies was now discarded, as if his father had the right to speak not only by age but because he would say it all better.

"Glass, when you're done writin' that pile of horse paddies, I plan to go down to Sciennes' and nick a copy. And I don't mean to say buy one, either. I will turn to the index at the back. I had better not see the name Peebles in any form in that book, do you hear?" The old fellow was truly angry. "If Farquhar Menzies hired you to make that one-armed, one-eyed treasonous witch doctor and his krauthead wife into sterling examples of Scottish bloodlines, I say Annie Daly was a whore who probably spread clap all over New York while all her grateful kin was gettin' fat on her earnings. No less a liar than that, sir, could even get started on Roberts and stick with it for more than five minutes after he started asking questions." Now he stared at Glass and defied him to suggest otherwise about either Roberts or Annie.

Glass decided not to be angry about the reference to Annie Daly. The man did not believe it, had in fact probably gone and read the book just for the sake of constructing such a line when and if he ever ran into its hatefully anticipated author.

"Mr. Peebles, please. I understand about the Clearances. I would—"

"The Clearances!" The old man looked at Glass as if he were a total fool. "The Clearances took place many generations before I came along. Those were other people in other times. No man can change the past, Glass. No matter what folderol your ancestors get into, there's nothing you could've done about it, is there? Only you and Farquhar Menzies go around trying to make it look better than it was! I don't give a bloody hell about the Clearances."

Young Peebles stepped in. "That's right, Jason. I myself don't know much about that. My father doesn't either, I don't think. We are angry about what the fuckin' Menzies have done to us in our lifetimes."

Yet another new angle. Glass hoped it did not lead far. "Such as?"

"Such as this, Glass." Though it seemed as if he might have a long list, the old man knew exactly what the top of it was. "I am seventy-six years old. That's exactly as old as Bruce Menzies would be today if he hadn't got bumped off in the last war. I knew him almost from the time he showed up here sittin' in his own shit in a dog crate. We grew up together. Since he came late to the Castle Menzies, he never seemed to understand that he was better than me, even when old Angus said he could make him clan chief on his twenty-first birthday. We played football together, drank pints together, had our first pieces of arse in the same field on the same night."

Glass looked sheepishly at Charles, though the young man was engrossed in his father's story, which he must have heard many times before.

"Right after the Great War ended in 1918, and everyone from the Lochs who made it was comin' home and needed a place to live for the family he was late gettin' a start on, Bruce told me that I could fix up the house in The Gap that the Peebles family had been run out of two or three generations before."

"The stone one on the left side of the road."

"That one, yes. It was just a shell, but what a stout shell it was. He said that if I fixed it up and lived in it, I would be in charge of all the sheep in The Gap—about seven thousand, then. So I worked at every odd job I could find in the district, diggin' cesspools, fixing up barns and houses, to get the money to rebuild it. So in the summer of '19, I bought the lumber and spent the summer working on it. I was going to move my wife and myself and our firstborn into one section and fix the others up for my two older brothers who had gone to Montana. They even started making their plans to return to Scotland. And then . . ."

The old man paused to control his temper, and Glass's researcher's mind intruded upon him before he could start again. "And then Roberts Menzies came home with his German wife."

"Correct you are, sir. Just after I got all the flooring back into the place and had thrown up all the roof beams, Angus came riding up the road one day in his Rolls-Royce touring car, with this poor one-armed weasel and his fat wife in the back seat. They stopped across the road from the house and looked at the land and the view for a while. And even while I was still sitting between the roof vaults, nailing the last one in place, Angus crossed over to me and told me not to drive any more nails; that Bruce had no right to give me the property—*or* the job; that his long-lost son was to build a house across the road and his wife would not want neighbors that close. Would not, in fact, want neighbors in the whole bloody Gap!"

"Couldn't you appeal to Bruce?"

"I tried, Glass, but Bruce had changed, overnight. Now he was not interested in giving things away, he was trying to recover his losses to the father he had never expected to see and didn't want to. A few months short of becoming clan chief, he had been shoved to the rear to wait until his father died. I was told never to return to my building site, and in the very next week a crew from Inverness happened along and started surveying and digging for Roberts' house. He moved in at Christmastime, while the wife and I moved into the loft of this store." He pointed upward to a high storage area where burlap sacks were thickly stacked. "In order even to make this place livable, Glass, I've had to ship each of my sons to Montana as soon as they were old enough to tend sheep. Charles here is the last. He had to stay."

Now Charles spoke. "We have had it worse than that, Jason. When Roberts died around '25, Bruce again told my father to fix the place up. Said he didn't care what Roberts' wife thought about having Peebles across the road from her. Not that it would have mattered much, since she did not live much longer herself. But then God Hisself did us in. That same summer a storm wrecked the house for good."

Glass was interrupted in his thoughts now by a horn honking outside his window. In the early-morning light he saw quite a crowd inside Farquhar Menzies' Rolls-Royce, but they were busily shifting to make room for him. He stepped outside, waved slightly as he locked his front door. In the front seat were Farquhar, driving, Sybil, and Clyde; the latter seemed to glare at Glass as he approached the rear door. In the back were Henrietta and Duncan, the former eying him ironically, the latter blankly, as he always did. Only Farquhar seemed genuinely delighted to see him, though Sybil looked as if she might have been had not Clyde been present.

The Rolls had a small open-bedded trailer attached to its rear bumper. In the bed, strapped tight to the sides by three different chains and a half-dozen ropes, was a cannon with at least a fifteen-foot barrel.

This would be a long day.

13 HOMO LUDENS

JASON GLASS WOUND UP HAVING A GOOD TIME this Saturday—too good a time. Somewhere around midafternoon, Glass, like everyone else in the Menzies party except Duncan, had gotten drunk. He had not intended to—though clearly they had—but had not bothered stopping before he did either.

The trip to Dunedin, in the western extremities of the Isle of Skye, took a full three hours that morning. They waited nearly a half-hour for the ferry at Kyle of Lochalsh, were slowed by the narrow, winding, fog-enshrouded roads on the east side of Skye, were further slowed by the several-ton cannon they were towing to their rear, which reduced the Rolls's efficiency to four miles a gallon, and were finally thwarted when Sybil misread the map and routed Farquhar through Portree, the long way to Dunedin, rather than through Bracadale, the shortest one. It had been depressingly foggy the entire route, though they found the field of the Dunedin Games totally sunlit when they arrived.

Dunedin Castle was the ancient stronghold fortress of the Oliphant family and boasted visitors over the centuries ranging from the monarchs of the day to Sir Walter Scott and Boswell and Dr. Johnson. The castle itself was erected on a rock overlooking a miniature seaweed-strewn harbor too shallow for any sort of boating whatsoever. In size it was slightly larger, perhaps, than the Castle Menzies, though not nearly so picturesque or attractive. Heavily assaulted throughout centuries of Scottish feuds, the castle had been repaired with red brick and modernistic window fittings, giving at least one side of the edifice, despite its name of Elf Tower, the general overall appearance of a Bronx tenement.

The Dunedin Games served the same purpose as summer games throughout Scotland from Braemar to Blair to Glamis: to bring together members of the clan and all the residents of the district for reunion and friendly competition. Indeed, the games were so popular an activity that a good number of families toured them from week to week in caravans, and apparently the schedule never varied. The third Saturday in June was always Dunedin's turn, just as the first Saturday in September was always Braemar's.

From what Glass learned in the painfully slow car trip that morning, the Oliphants and the Menzies had always been on friendly terms; though Farquhar had not said as much, Glass recalled that the Oliphants had followed the Menzies off the field at Culloden because of some sort of mutual-defense alliance. And for the last century, again according to Farquhar, the Menzies had dragged their clan cannon, itself towed from Culloden before firing a shot, to the Dunedin Games for a ritual firing at four o'clock. In the old days it had come by oxcart, later pulled by horses and tractors, now—in the 1970s—towed in style at the rear of a black Rolls-Royce with the remaining Menzies riding in air-conditioned comfort before it.

From the moment he arrived Glass was a pariah, for he was virtually the only person present who did not wear a tartan. Both Henrietta and Sybil had skirts fashioned in the Menzies yellow-orange-blue-and-green, while Farquhar, Clyde, and even Duncan wore kilts and belted plaids. Glass wore blue jeans and a sweatshirt. At least a thousand other participants wore at least two dozen other patterns, and quite a few men carried bagpipes, which they blew into all the more regularly as the day got older.

During the late morning and the early afternoon, Scottish tradition was completely in evidence, and the Menzies were prepared to be completely traditional. Farquhar was to make his yearly attempt to win the bagpiping contest, and Clyde was to enter the various athletic events which typified Scottish games. Neither had done particularly well in the past, and before long it was apparent to Glass that they were not destined to this year either.

The *piobaireachd* competition, or piping contest, was judged on three points: the tuning of the instrument, musicianship, and fingering. A contestant actually had to enter two different rounds, for a "rehearsal" was held in the morning during which the judges could select the best pipers to participate in the actual public event that afternoon. All entrants were expected to play the same *piobaireachd* in the morning, but each could select one he preferred during the afternoon. Glass, as he listened to those pipers who came immediately before Farquhar and immediately after, could distinguish no difference among them. All seemed to produce the same exact notes with the same degree of redness of face and absence of tune. The judges, however, took copious notes on each contestant, and he could tell from the expressions on their faces and on Farquhar's that Farquhar was not doing well. When the finalists were announced, Farquhar was not named among them. Nor, according to Sybil, had he ever been in the last twenty years.

To Glass's inexperienced American eye, it was easier to tell that Clyde was not succeeding either. He finished seventeenth among the twenty-five of his own age group who took part in the hammer throwing. He did worse still in putting the stone. Glass was sure that he was trying his best in each event—there was a look of severe intensity etched on his face each time he assumed his position—but he was totally unemotional each time he failed, as if he had fully expected to. His best event was the race up the hill, in which he finished eleventh; his worst was the tossing of the caber, a 20-foot-high, 120-pound pine log, in which he came in last. But he had some very bad luck in the caber toss: as he ran forward with the log cupped vertically in his locked hands and steadied by his head and shoulder, a momentary gust of Skye wind broadsided him at the peak of his run and caused the giant log to sway violently to the left as he prepared to launch it. After release, it seemed more as if he had dropped than "tossed" it. Still he took things stoically, said nothing to anyone, and strode dejectedly from the field. His year's work was done. Glass felt sorry for him.

Sybil, however, won one of the dancing events. Though she had not done spectacularly in the strathspey or the simple reel, she spun her way to a first place in the Highland fling. In this competition, two dancers competed against each other through the furious deerlike dancing steps on a high platform. One of the two was selected as the better and passed on to the next round. Glass, each time Sybil succeeded, was not entirely convinced that Sybil had been the winner. He also noted that whereas the other competitiors had protected themselves beneath their swirling kilts with cut-off jeans, swimsuit bottoms, or modest white cotton underpants, Sybil wore a pair of garish orange bikini panties that had the words PRIVATE STOCK printed in luminous green lettering on the backside. In the final, the other woman's wild spins revealed blue gym shorts. Though Glass thought she was better than Sybil, more gracefully built, more soft of foot, Sybil won—as she had for several years running. Applause for her triumph was muted.

By midafternoon, however, the amount of Scotch and beer consumed had turned the crowd from totally traditional to fairly elemental. Hordes of young men and adolescents loitered together clutching one, sometimes two beer bottles by the neck, clustering with their mates who wore the same or at least aligned tartans, calling otherwise aligned, differently tartaned groups rather fundamental epithets. Less bellicose youths found themselves rather pretty young lassies, some of whom incestuously wore the same tartan they did, others of whom forecast future unions between families, and had selected the shade of various trees to conduct their eventually quite physical courtship. While some proceeded with a modicum of dignity, others rolled together in the grass with reckless abandon.

Glass knew his compatriots were drinking too much as they sat in the sun observing the games, knew as well that he was too. After three o'clock it became customary to pour Scotch into each new cup of beer, not just for Farquhar but for everyone else, whether he be Menzies, Macleod, Oliphant, Farquharson, or Jason Glass.

Shortly before four, Farquhar signaled Clyde, Glass, and Duncan off the lawn where they sat observing the activities and led them toward his car and, of course, the Culloden cannon, which still stood erect and ready in the trailer at its rear.

"Here, Glass," he said slurrily, handing him a ring of small keys, "unlock the binding chains on the wheels. Clyde, help me knock the blocks out. Duncan, climb on the trolley and be ready to push when I give the command." Within five minutes, all this was accomplished. A crowd was gathering around them now, though no one said much or offered help. This was a Menzies enterprise, and clearly a popular one. When Farquhar gave the order, the cannon, mounted on a carriage with wooden wagon wheels, rolled with surprising ease down the two metal ramps at the rear of the trailer and halted itself at the bottom. With this Clyde stood at one wheel, Farquhar at the other, Glass and Duncan at the rear of the cannon, and all four began pushing it forward. No directions or guidance were needed, for the crowd of onlookers opened a path just ahead of it now, knowing from years past exactly where it was to go. Untartaned, Glass felt like a hired hand. All that united him to the Menzies and the other Scotsmen who had gathered this afternoon for the games was that, as they were and the Culloden cannon would be, he was loaded.

Under the strength of the three men and the young boy, the gun was wheeled into position overlooking the shallow, vegetated harbor which nothing more threatening than a salmon could ever have navigated for invasion. Everyone in the crowd now, including those who had not attended the wheeling up of the gun, assumed a position along the wall or down the grassy slopes which descended from it. An elderly man wearing an Oliphant tartan moved toward Farquhar and told him that it was five before four. Already, at the far end of the harbor where it bent toward Loch Dunedin and Little Minch, a wooden boat with a white sail, the shape of a Viking ship but a good deal smaller, was eased out into the water and stringy grass by two teenagers in swim trunks. They did not have to moor it or anchor it—it moored itself into the slime and seaweed. Back at the gun, Farquhar was loading the powder magazine and inserting a fuse, while Clyde rolled a round metal ball down the mouth of the long barrel, after which he forced it to the cannon's base with a ramrod. Duncan by now merely stood aside with his fingers in the ears while Farquhar, at the signal of Oliphant, lit the fuse with an ordinary kitchen match which he struck on the heel of his shoe.

Everyone who was near him, Glass noted too late, had inserted his fingers in his ears as well—including Farquhar once he had extinguished the match. Everyone but Glass. The BOOM that erupted when the fuse hit the powder was literally deafening. It clapped once from the muzzle of the gun, then three or four times off the stone-and-brick walls of Dunedin Castle. Glass, who had been dropped to the ground by the gun's report, did not see the ball hit the water, but he could see the resulting geyser which shot up over the heads of those behind whom he was sprawled. His ears rang as he got back to his feet. Sybil, who had taken up a position behind him, helped him up, laughing as she did so.

"Jolly unfair of them not to warn you of that, actually, Jason." Glass did not so much hear this as he read it on her lips.

He could also tell, again with his eyes rather than his ears, that the tartaned army amidst which he stood was disappointed. The ball had fallen short of the targeted Viking ship and just sprayed it. It continued to lurk in the seaweed, its white sails now speckled with green slop.

"More powder, Father," muttered Clyde with seeming embarrassment. Clyde had said very little, generally looked surly. Farquhar did indeed remove more powder from the wooden keg, though he spilled a good deal of it down the side of the gun carriage in trying to pour it into the magazine. Again the fuse, the ball, the ramrod, the ignition, and the group's ears, this time Glass's included, were covered again.

Fingers in ears actually did little. The blast was nearly as loud as the last time, the reverberations just as many. The ball, however, traveled no farther than it had before. For the third shot the trajectory was lowered, the powder increased without as much spillage this time. Instead of lobbing the shot at the Vikings, Farquhar was planning to fire it as if he were using a high-powered rifle with a telescopic sight. The clap was much louder this time, but the ball struck far short of its mark and at least entertained the crowd by skipping three times across the swampy water before sinking some twenty-five yards short of the ship.

Farquhar was clearly frustrated, Clyde annoyed, though so far liquor seemed to be softening the blow of their failure. They had, however, only three balls left. Duncan continued to stand with his fingers jammed in his ears, never removing them, as if he did not even want to chance hearing his father's profanity, which was now erupting quite freely.

"Haven't missed with three shots in a row since 1951, Farquhar." This was Oliphant speaking. If he was trying to quell the fires in Menzies, he was actually fanning them. The crowd was getting restless, as if it needed to get to the beer stands or the toilets.

"Pack the shitting sod fucker to the gills, damn it!" Clyde snatched the horn from his father and poured a whopping load of powder into the magazine, then another, then tamped it all down as if he were filling a pipe. Sweat ran down his meaty purple face; his kilt spun like a square dancer's skirt as he bent up and down from the powder keg. He jammed in the fuse, then flung himself to the front of the gun and rammed the fourth ball inside. "Now light the bloody thing, but up the angle first."

With Glass's help, Fárquhar did so, his red pageboy in sweaty ringlets now. Then he lit the fuse.

The blast was incredible. Sybil reeled back into Glass, Duncan into Henrietta. Several people sitting on the wall to the right and left of the cannon muzzle simply dropped off the front of it and hit the turfy slope four feet beneath them, unable to break their falls because their index fingers were still stuck in their ears with all the applied pressure of champagne corks. Some almost reached the water's edge before their kilted forms stopped rolling. Those who did not go over looked simply, and finally, shell-shocked.

The cannonball itself took off like a black golf ball, even sliced hard to the right at the top of its flight. It landed at least a hundred and fifty yards beyond the Viking menace, not even in the water, cracking through tree limbs and underbrush and striking the muddy embankment with a sucking thud that was the first thing the throng heard after the last reverberation of the gun.

"Haven't missed four straight in this century, Menzies." Oliphant again. He was not needling Menzies. He wanted results. Glass had not been prepared for this sort of monomania in what he had at first taken to be an annual equivalent of a fireworks display.

Farquhar's hand was trembling. He looked pathetically at Glass, his eyes bloodshot. Glass, his eyes no better, stepped up to him. The heat of the sun was beginning to make him sick to his stomach.

"Look, pour the powder in till I tell you to stop. I think I know how much you need." Farquhar, seemingly happy to have help, if even from the only attendee of the games not in a tartan, scooped up the powder and began letting it drizzle into the opening. When Glass called "Stop," he stopped instantaneously. He stood back. Glass stepped forward and cranked the gun trajectory down about four degrees. Duncan helped him turn the handle. Crossing his fingers, he gestured to Farquhar and Clyde to go about their work. Clyde inserted the fifth ball —without enthusiasm now, though Farquhar was handling the fuse eagerly.

When he lit it, the cannon simply seemed to *sound* right this time. After the previous blast, few even had their fingers in their ears—perhaps they could not even hear this one. The shell was on line the whole way, the crowd commencing the cheer in expectation even before it hit. When it did hit, the throng roared in jubilation as the ship shattered to pieces, spraying torn sail and lumber in all directions. Farquhar looked at Glass but said nothing. His gratitude was unmistakable, as was Clyde's anger.

Only Clyde spoke. "We still had one more left, Glass." Glass did not know what to make of this. He could count. Clyde returned to the gun to prepare it for its return to the trailer, but Farquhar just walked off alone into the milling crowd. Sybil stepped up to Glass grinning broadly at him. She offered him a swig from her flask, which he willingly, though awkwardly, took. Then she put her arm through his and guided him off in the direction of Henrietta and Duncan. Glass could feel Clyde's eyes hot on his back.

It was after dark when the games broke up. Farquhar's contingent had done much more drinking, enough to have an unending singalong most of the way back. Farquhar, slinging his car and trailer recklessly along the narrow and winding Skye roads, led the patriotic songs, and even Clyde joined in. Only Duncan did not—perhaps he did not know the words to "Razors in the Air," "Soldiers of the Queen," and, of course, "Marching to Pretoria."

They stopped at a hotel near Broadford so the ladies could use the toilets, then along the road some ten miles later so the gentlemen could use the weeds. It was here that Glass realized that the day's ritual was by no means over yet.

"Blasted bad firing, damn it," Farquhar muttered in the darkness. "Gives us only one shot left." He was pulling up whatever he had on under his kilt. Glass, zipping, wondered more than vaguely what they needed *any* left for. "One should be enough if we're careful with it, however." Glass did not inquire about this, presumed he would know sooner than he wanted to what it meant.

They got back into the Rolls and spun on toward the ferry, the cannon bouncing and rocking behind them with sufficient force to jerk the back end of the car violently up and down. Glass was beginning to get very sick when, luckily, Farquhar turned off the road again, this time into the drive of a rather formal manor house which had all its windows lit in apparent expectation. Farquhar alone got out and approached the front door, was briefly admitted, then returned with another man, also kilted, who must himself have just arrived home from the games.

"We had some bad luck today, Gavin; only one ball left. So give me the best position you can." The other man nodded affirmation as he passed beyond the lights of the house out into the moonlight, leading the car down a dirt drive to the rear of the house. After about two hundred yards he stopped, turned around, and pointed to a wide spot at the right side of the road. Farquhar swung the car into this and back out of it, stopping so the gun carriage could occupy the wider spot. Glass could contain himself no longer.

"What are we doing?" he whispered to Henrietta, who, though distant, had been generally pleasant all day.

"Farquhar has to shoot the last of his wad, Jason," she said too loudly, probably to badger Clyde, for Farquhar was already out of the car discussing matters with the man called Gavin. "We always visit someone on our way home from the games each year who needs some buildings cleared. Why don't you get out and have a look?"

Actually now everyone got out. Gavin was pointing down a sloping hill in the full moonlight, gesturing toward a clump of trees. "It's right behind those trees, Farquhar. If you can hit the trees you'll get the hut without any difficulty."

Glass could barely see what looked to be a small building with a rock base and wooden sides peeking out from the right side of the copse. Farquhar did not plan to detach the gun this time, but rather moved the car slightly so that it would point the right way from its carriage. Clyde told him when to stop. Then they loaded the cannon and rammed the ball home exactly as they had done at the games.

"Your trajectory's too high, Father, and you'll go over the top. Better lower it." Glass agreed not only with this but also with the amount of lowering they did. Now Farquhar struck his match and was about to light the fuse. Glass did not agree with something else.

"You're too much to the left. See, the house is at the right side of the trees, not in the center. You'll just wing it the way you are now."

Farquhar was about to respond, but Clyde took over, his burly form immobile in the moonlight as he spoke. "I think it's quite satisfactory as it is, Glass." This was all he said, but it was forceful.

"No, Clyde, I think he's right." Farquhar moved back toward the driver's seat. "Mount the gun, Glass, and tell me when you think it's on line." Glass climbed the spine of the cannon and laid his right cheek along the cold steel barrel. Menzies started the car violently and moved it forward with a lurch that threw off the aim entirely. Under Glass's direction, he eased backward until Glass felt the gun was on line, slightly to the left of the part of the house he could actually see. It was about a hundred yards downrange.

"Why don't they just get a wrecking crew to remove this thing?" he muttered to Sybil after he had dismounted.

Sybil tittered boozily. "This gets their rocks off, Jason. About the only thing that will for Clyde, too." She pinched the fleshy outer part of his hand now.

"It's not on line, Father. You're going to miss *again*." The last word was heavily underscored.

"Quiet, son." Farquhar mounted the cannon, decided that Glass's estimate was correct, dismounted, and prepared to fire. He lit the match on the heel of his shoe, put it to the fuse, and —like everyone else—stepped back, with his fingers jammed in his ears.

Since the distance of the shot was comparatively short, the powder supply was not great nor the blast severe. It did, though, rock the Rolls-Royce forward about three feet despite its parking brakes and transmission lock, and the whole assemblage of gun, carriage, and car continued to bounce up and down for fifteen seconds.

The shot itself was perfect. It cracked through the trees, then clearly struck the building beyond. Planks and stones sprayed out to either side of the copse of trees, and sounds of other collapses continued for nearly thirty seconds after the ball had struck.

"Damn good shot, Menzies," said Gavin with a happy laugh. "Now, then, all of you come by the house and have a nightcap with Margaret and me." Glass prepared to drink some more.

Gavin escorted all of them—Duncan included—into a warmly heated, spectacularly appointed sitting room. Though the outside temperature was still around sixty, Gavin had a blazing fire in the fireplace, and over it hung a kettle of what turned out to be the "drinks": mulled wine. Each took a seat in a soft chair or couch, though Glass made the mistake of selecting one too close to the fire. His flagon was filled twice before he had even realized he had emptied it once, in fact was not sure whether he had drunk or spilled the previous round. He could hear the conversation buzzing around him, was even vaguely aware that some statements might have been directed toward him, was uncertain whether or not he had answered, had heard Sybil mention without concern that she had not seen Clyde since they

he could feel the car lurching up and down again though now he was on his back on the back seat with his feet in Duncan's lap, his head in Henrietta's, her hand stroking his forehead, only two heads in the front seat now rather than the three they had come with

could hear the door opening in the front and then the one at Duncan's end by his feet and then Sybil and Farquhar with an arm apiece pulling him forward up and off Henrietta's lap

and then felt himself walking across the gravel toward the door the stones thick and pointed through his shoes

and then she had his pants off and she was naked above him in the dim light of his desk lamp alone

and could feel her breathing in his ear

and then he woke up alone and naked in his bed and the phone was ringing like last time.

14 THE RIDDLE OF THE ROCK

THE PHONE CALL THIS TIME BROUGHT TWO VOICES from the past—or at least, announcements of them. The postmaster in Loch Killilan reported, with early-Sunday weariness, that he had not one but two special-delivery letters for Glass and inquired whether now might be an appropriate time to bring them by. Glass foggily agreed.

One was, as he expected, from Paul Krige in Edinburgh, an envelope addressed in Ann Macgregor's handwriting. The other, as for some reason he had feared, was from Margot on Cape Cod and addressed in her own.

Jason Glass had lived near Boston almost his whole life and had never been to Cape Cod, nor had Margot. Now she was renting a summer house there near Truro. Summer houses near Truro went for something like $1,100 a week—which was why Jason had never been there. But Jason had also just won the International Book Award, and this was why Margot *was* there. Her letter was to the point and reflected little time away from her sewing machine:

> I called Larry in New York and he told me where to find you. Don't be angry with him, Jason. At first he wouldn't, but I told him Patricia was deathly ill (Don't worry about this either, because she isn't and never was), so he told me. He also told me what you're doing there, without my even asking. My regards to the Clan Menzies.
>
> What I want to speak with you about is money. You can forget the divorce if you want. Frank and I have just moved in together—without your legal permission—to try ourselves out for the summer. Patricia and Elizabeth are spending the summer with his sister-in-law in the West. They would send their best, I am sure, if they knew I was writing.
>
> You *must*, however, come to your senses about money. The courts are giving me only $700 a month for Patricia and Elizabeth, on the basis of the fact that that was all you usually cleared a month on your miserable free-lancing jobs. You can do better than this, Jason, for your own kids. So far I've been able to make ends meet by selling off some of our things. Your desk went for $250, though I thought it should have brought more given the fact that you wrote GG at it. The copy you "autographed" for me brought $500 in itself, especially since it contains that gloriously gratuitous inscription which made all the news. Harvard paid a couple of grand for the manuscripts and notebooks for the book, though they cannot release them for public view without your or my permission each time someone wants to see them.
>
> Which is the point.
>
> A professor and a graduate student want to see them. They have a federal grant of some sort to do research on, apparently, anything they want to. They feel there are some loopholes in GG that they might like to close for you—such as

the fact that never in the history of Phalon & Son Perfumeries was there anyone employed there named Annie Daly. They seem to think that Annie Daly just got hold of a piece of their stationery from someone to write herself a puff letter —or have somebody else do it, since they suspect that it might be a man's handwriting, not a woman's. They have found records of seven other Annie Dalys in New York in the 1870s, and they want to see if the handwriting samples in your papers resemble any of those. They said not to worry, that this might be just a small stain on your otherwise "marvelously splendid" book. On the other hand, Jason, it might unravel the whole thing, mightn't it? They have offered me $3,000 to allow them one day's access to the papers. I don't know whether I will take it or not.

They might go higher, but no matter how high, it would be a one-time payment and it might destroy your book. Why don't we settle this child-support thing right now, and I promise you can have sole access to the papers. I am not raising my initial demand for $2,000 a month, nor am I lowering it. It seems fully equitable, given the sort of life the girls and I had come to expect after our success with GG.

If we can't come to an agreement on this now, Jason, I will have to take their $3,000 or whatever they will give. I am freeloading on Frank too much and owe him for the girls' plane tickets to the West. Prices are very high here.

Please respond before July 1st.

As always,
M.

Jason Glass cursed out loud for nearly a half-hour, without being entirely sure exactly what he was inveighing against. Surely somewhere in there was Margot, probably right at the front of it. Also there were those damned academic snoopers who would take apart anything to see what made it work and, once they knew, would publish an article or a book about it so that the entire world would know and not have to think about the whole entity anymore. They would get promotions and reduced teaching time as a consequence—maybe even a job for the as-yet-unemployed graduate student—and then rest easy indulging in intellectual masturbation until the next occasion arose for scholarly rape. Glass had hated these people—Boston was full of them—and now they and his also-hated wife had fallen into natural allegiance, they to destroy his reputation, she his earnings. While she sunned herself on Cape Cod and his daughters rode horseback in "the West," he labored through the mists, physical and intellectual, of the Scottish Lochs, trying to write two books instead of one—one a lie, one not—in order to accrue money that Margot, his daughters, her lawyers, and "Frank" would not know about. Having reflected upon all this, he cursed aloud for another half hour. He kicked the unyielding stone walls of his cottage, but was careful not to damage anything that could be damaged. He still had that much self-control left.

Yet he was equally angry with himself. While all of this could have been contrived on Margot's part, there still was the wide possibility that it was true. Since he had technically "deserted" her, she could legally sell off what he had left behind to support herself and the children. Only the fact that he was still alive (or at least had not been declared dead) was enough to require Harvard to give him some say over who got to see his papers. But as long as he was not available to referee them, Margot would again have the final word. Jason Glass cursed himself for not having thought of this before leaving, on the sly, for Scotland. He could write his lawyers, of course, and tell them to get hot on it, but he had already paid them more than $12,000 this year and the only advice he had received from any of them was to do what Margot asked, the judge ordered, and Internal Revenue insisted. It was like paying to go along with Fate, like tipping the hangman before he kicked open the trap.

Yet he was furious with himself for still another reason. The two things whose authenticity he had never checked in his *Gratuitous Glory* research were Peter Daly's Army discharge certificate and Annie Daly's recommendation letter from Phalon & Sons. The latter looked absolutely authentic, and the company had been bought up by a larger concern nearly seventy-five years back. There was virtually no one to contact, and no apparent reason to try. Now, without his papers and notes, he could not be sure how much other research might be called into question on the basis of this possible loophole, and the presence of seven *known* Annie Dalys in New York at this time continued to haunt him as well. What if he had, however unintentionally, misrepresented the Daly legend? Not only would his name be disgraced, which was bad enough, but his whole moral stance on not telling Menzies lies would be a comic sham. He cursed some more.

He felt the need to take immediate action, yet what could he do? The written word seemed the only means available, yet whom to write to and what to write? He sat down to his typewriter, still woozy and hung over from the day before, and began with a letter to Harvard. He did not even know whom to address, so he put it in general care of the Harvard libraries with the statement "This is from Jason Glass, whose papers you just purchased" typed boldly across the bottom border of the envelope:

> To Whom It May Concern:
>
> My wife has informed me that she has just sold you the manuscript and research notes to my recent biography, *Gratuitous Glory*. Please be advised that I am alive and of sound mind and may be contacted via general mail in Loch Killilan, Scotland. Though my wife, with whom I am currently involved in several legal disputes, has seen fit to fill her pockets by selling you this material (which to a degree I am flattered you thought worthy of owning), I wish to inform you that I intend to exercise final right of decision as to who shall have access to those papers so long as I am alive. For the present, the only other person authorized to do so is my literary agent, Mr. Lawrence Asbury of New York. Any violation of this privilege will result in legal action's being taken by my attorneys.

Here Glass paused. Harvard would probably laugh if he put his attorneys' real names in here, for surely they must be the same joke all over Boston that he had found them to be in the courtroom when they handled his case. Rather he made up a firm name in New York City and used that instead. Then he finished with a final paragraph which belied the legal professionalism he tried to instill in the rest of his letter:

> Lastly, I would suggest that you keep your eye out for other persons and institutions turning up with duplicate sets of these papers. Margot Glass is a crafty bitch who is second to no one in her devotion to all things Phoenician. I don't know whose face is on a thousand-dollar bill, but this is her god and she is a polytheist many times over. She has probably Xeroxed all this stuff and will sell it again and again. She is not a nice person.

Ashamed of this ending, he signed the letter *Jason Glass* anyway, sealed it in the envelope, and affixed airmail postage before he could think of changing anything.

Skipping breakfast, he dressed quickly, got his sunglasses, and stepped out into the vivid morning sunshine, bent on getting into Loch Killilan on foot as quickly as he could to make the mail truck's eleven-o'clock departure for Inverness. It was now ten—though he had forgotten to wear his watch, he could hear the Sunday churchbells in town announcing the hour.

Glass knew, of course, that his letter was a feeble gesture. Even if Harvard kept this professor and his graduate student out of the Daly material, the professor could raise such a public stink that Glass would be examined with a scrutiny rivaled only by the Watergate prosecutors. Failure to comply and examine his own sources would be equivalent to an admission of guilt, or at least of scholarly misrepresentation or neglect. And he honestly felt his story would stand—he would have to check one or two things more carefully than he had done as yet, of course, but he had no real doubt that his Daly story was accurate.

Yet as he cut off the Gap road onto the back path to town that Duncan used for his pony cart, he had to admit that while peripheral details could be easily cast to the dogs, Annie Daly could not. She once could have—but now that the record was down, she could no longer. The past simply *had* to shape up the way he needed it to, the way he claimed it had in his IBA prizewinner.

Before he reached Loch Killilan, Glass had made three other decisions. First, he had to leave for America and attempt to save the one achievement he might ever have as a credit to his name and the reputation of Annie Daly from what might become a gratuitous and pointless exposure of her a century after her death. There would be no point to that. The only ones who could possibly benefit would be the professor and his graduate student, and surely, Margot, who would have the last laugh. He wondered if Margot was sharp enough to realize that the demise of his book would be the demise of her hopes for long-range child support, which, Glass had already figured, would amount to $258,000 over the next eleven years.

So Jason Glass's second decision, as he moved down the path behind Sciennes' Store, was that he would settle with Margot once and for all. He would give her a lump-sum payment of roughly half that—or, put another way, all the money he had made on *Gratuitous Glory* to date. She would take that. Margot operated on the bird-in-the-hand principle—get everything you can now and fly away later if you need to. He might sign her Mexican divorce as well.

The third decision he made as he tapped on the closed post-office window and slipped the letter to Harvard through the mail slot in the door. He would take the Roberts Menzies diary back to America with him and simply whip out, at the most furious pace he could achieve, the very story Farquhar Menzies wanted told. It would be exactly the way he liked it. Glass would not even open Paul Krige's envelope; he would simply leave it behind for Ann Macgregor to do with what she would. In the last hour he had come to see Roberts Menzies in the light in which he should have seen him all along—the very one in which he now viewed Peter and Annie Daly. What was the good of pointless exposure? The man had stepped earnestly into adulthood, done some good, made some mistakes, and died having achieved less than he had planned to. This was exactly what Jason Glass himself had done and, somewhere down the line, would do. Most humans follow that pattern, so why chastise Roberts Menzies for having followed it as well?

Glass continued down the deserted Sunday-morning street, the houses and closed shops on his right, the sky-blue waters of Loch Killilan and the Kelly-green grass banks beyond it on his left. Without knowing why, he turned suddenly and entered the front door of the Scottish Rite church, the only one in town.

Inside he saw Henrietta Menzies sitting alone in a pew near the back and slid into it beside her. He wished it were Ann Macgregor instead. In front of him were a young couple, cleanly scrubbed if not exceptionally attractive, he in a well-pressed though ill-fitting dark suit, she in a lacy white dress and straw bonnet. They linked pinkies together as they listened to what Glass could tell was the tail end of the sermon. Glass, the most shabbily dressed of the group—and undoubtedly the only agnostic present—felt ashamed to walk out in the company of the others. They were, for the day at least, spiritually uplifted where his own spirit had been broken. If they lived far distances from each other during the week, these people formed a community on Sunday mornings. Glass was alone, against Margot, against a professor and a graduate student, against all those who had read and been inspired by his book, against History, perhaps against the Truth.

"Was yesterday sufficient to bring you back to the Lord's fold, Jason?" Henrietta chirped cheerily once the service was concluded and they were out in the sunlight again. Only now did Glass realize that he had not taken off his sunglasses during the ceremony. Henrietta had noticed it too. "Why the dark glasses, Jason? Are you afraid that God will ask you to autograph a copy of *Gratuitous Glory* rather than pay the extra pound for one at Sciennes'?"

Glass laughed at this as well as he was able, then accepted Henrietta's invitation of a ride back to The Gap in her truck. Perhaps because they were alone, she was less distant than she had been at the Dunedin Games the day before. When she inquired about his being in town on a Sunday morning, especially after "so exhausting a Saturday night" (he was curious about her phraseology), he summarized his decision of an hour before.

"I've got a lot of trouble on the home front, Henrietta," he said wearily as she slowed for the turn off the highway. "My wife has sold all the manuscripts for my book to the Harvard library, and now there are those goddamn—or, at least, damn, for Sunday—academics trying to get into them to scour for errors. I just sent a letter warning Harvard not to let anyone see them without my permission."

"And what would they find if they did, Jason?" Her curiosity seemed mild enough; perhaps it was sympathetic, he could not tell.

"I'm not sure. Nothing perhaps. But I may not have done enough to verify the authenticity of one document in the Daly papers." He paused, rethinking himself before he spoke more. "I've decided to go home, Henrietta." She glanced quickly to the side, her face serious, though she had to look back to the winding boulder-encased road almost as fast. "I have more at stake in keeping the Daly story intact than I do in running poor Roberts through the shredder of historical research. I'll give Farquhar the tale he wants—since it relies so seldom on historical fact, I could write it in Bechuanaland as easily as I could write it here. So I'll write it in Boston and mail it back to him. It won't take three months as long as I don't get bogged down trying to put Annie Daly back together again."

"Jason, neither Annie Daly nor Roberts Menzies nor Humpty-Dumpty can be put back together again once they've shattered. Roberts I know has been broken; so has Humpty-Dumpty. If Annie Daly was too, there's nothing you can do. Accept that."

"I can at least stop those academics from breaking her image, can't I?" Glass was talking too loudly, he feared a bit hysterically now. "And in turn, I will stop trying to knock Roberts off the wall to see if he breaks."

As they approached the lake, Henrietta pulled her truck off to the side of the road and turned off the engine. They were on the far side, looking across at the two ruined houses, the stone one yawning from the gaping hole in its facade.

"Jason, Roberts fell off the wall somewhere between fifty and seventy-five years ago. Annie Daly, if she did, did so almost a hundred back." She turned toward him. "You flatter yourself in thinking that from this late date you have the power to reach back and prevent them from doing what they've already done."

"That's not what I mean, and you know it, Henrietta. I mean I can let the pieces lie unexposed. What does uncovering them do for anyone?"

"Why, then, did you uncover Peter and Annie Daly when you thought the story—as it still may be—was true and laudatory?"

"To hold them up as examples of human conduct. To reveal good people doing good things that would otherwise not have been known about." He was parroting.

"So that later generations could emulate them?"

"Certainly. I'll just quote my reviews: 'To re-create an awareness of the concept of family, etcetera etcetera etcetera.' "

"So is there not equivalent reason for exposing the evil of the past?"

"So that the reviews can say: 'Jason Glass has shown what these people did, shame on them, don't you do that, reader.' "

"Exactly."

"Well, you're the first one around here that I've heard say *that*."

"You seemed to be saying it for yourself for a while."

"Yes, yes, I did, didn't I, Henrietta? It seems to me, too, that I tried to get you to help me out by giving me what you know about the Menzies. If you are so big on the antiseptic powers of the truth, why don't you start applying what you know—if not to me for my book, then to the open wounds that plague this family? Henrietta, if you can remain silent, can sin by omission, I can write my quickie placebo and sin by commission so that I can get back to guard Peter and Annie Daly against these academic hacks who are already circling around the Harvard Library like buzzards around carrion."

Henrietta snapped open the door to her right and got out. She did not walk away or speak in reply. She leaned against the front fender of her truck, staring out across the lake toward the ruined houses, as if rethinking her position. From the back she looked terribly strong physically, as tall as Ann though not as statuesque. For the first time, however, she looked vulnerable despite her dark blue Sunday dress and white broad-brimmed hat—the only time, save the night at The Angus Bull, that Glass had ever seen her in other than blue jeans and a sweatshirt.

"As I was going to say, Jason," she said squinting into the sunlight now, "and as I have said: I don't *know* everything."

"Tell me what you do, then."

"Just as you plan to go back to America and let new information come to light on *your* relatives?"

Glass was silent. Henrietta began to walk slowly down toward the edge of the lake. Glass followed carefully; the weeds were thicker on this side, the ground rougher. By the time they reached the water's edge, Henrietta's dress and stockings were littered with dried vegetation which she did not bother to brush away. She proceeded carefully on till she had gone about half the length of the small lake, then sat down on a conveniently placed and sized boulder. She made room for Jason beside her. There had been other places to sit down; Glass wondered why she had led him so far.

The day was so lusciously beautiful, the sun so warm, the sky so cloudless, it simply did not lend itself to the sort of philosophical argumentation in which they had somehow become engaged. Henrietta, perhaps simply because she was the less depressed, was the first to notice this and to act.

She stood and removed her hat, placing it carefully on the rock next to Glass after she had dusted it clean with the palm of her hand. "Jason, when someone is murdered, why is it that the police and the public insist that the killer be caught and brought to trial?"

"So that he can't do it again, obviously."

She rested against the rock and gazed toward the water reflectively. "Yes, but suppose it is obviously a crime of passion. Perhaps just manslaughter, not even semi-intentional. The public and the police both know they are not dealing with a hardened criminal, someone likely to do it again."

"I think you know the answer as well as I do, Henrietta. To let such a person go unpunished would be an invitation to others either to act under the guise of excessive emotion or to not bother controlling their bestial instincts. He still must serve as an example."

"You are still being noble in the abstract, Jason. There is more, isn't there? Suppose you were the victim. Suppose you could choose whether the killer was caught or not. Tell me, how would you choose?"

"To have him caught, of course."

"Why? Say it honestly."

"Revenge. To make him pay as I had paid." He looked at her curiously now. "You are leading me over the hurdles, Henrietta, but I'm not sure why."

"Yes, but you should ask yourself one further question, Jason. Suppose the criminal turned out to be one of your own family—say a fictitious person named 'Joseph Glass.' Would you actively reveal *him*?"

"No," he said after some hesitation, "I suppose I would not. I would feel sorry for him in ways I could not care about a stranger."

"Piffle, Jason, it would be yourself you were feeling sorry for."

"Myself?"

"Certainly yourself. Your innocent name would be dirtied forever if he was caught."

"Somehow, Henrietta, I have become the case in point when the case in point is really you. You are the one on the horns here. You, or at least half of you, is a Menzies who is embarrassed by what the Menzies' name has been associated with almost since the time Scottish history was first recorded. The other half wants revenge—revenge against a lot of people all of whom are also named Menzies, unfortunately—for what they have done to a lot of other people, the ones who died at Colenso and Spion Kop for example, because Roberts had turned over the codebooks, which left them—"

She waved these hundreds or thousands off too easily. "Yes, if you wish, Jason. But I was thinking closer to home actually." She put on her sunglasses now, even though the bright daylight had not altered in any way.

"Who?"

"A lot of people, both alive and dead."

"Such as?"

"Farquhar's wife, for a start. Ann's mother for another. Aunt Elizabeth, *my* mother. Roberts' wives—plural, not singular. In the long run, even Ann and Sybil and poor Duncan. Perhaps even—"

"Perhaps even you, Henrietta?"

"Perhaps."

"Come on, Henrietta, all those victims are women except one, and he's a retarded child. I hate to say this, but you are beginning to sound oddly like my wife."

"Which, Jason, is the very reason I keep my mouth shut. Your wife, what little I know of her from you and from the periodicals I've read, is exactly the sort of person I do not wish to sound like or be like. Yet hatred festers within me. It would be easy to become like her with a little less discipline than I've been exerting. Which is one of the reasons I have never married."

She expected Jason to be surprised at this, but he chortled instead. "Which means what? That your poor husband would become the scapegoat for all the disgrace that Roberts has brought upon the Clan Menzies over the last three-quarters of a century? Spare me such a marriage, will you?"

She spun off the rock and confronted him. Despite her sunglasses, he could see that the look in her eye was the same one he had been suddenly confronted with the night after they had left The Angus Bull. "You are a bloody fool, Jason, if you think it's just Roberts. I did not even *know* Roberts. But I did know Bruce, and I do know Farquhar . . . not to mention my glorious nephew, Clyde!" She became louder and tougher, totally out of control. "These disgraceful, self-righteous bastards—and I won't omit Angus, even though I didn't know him either—who marry women for their decorative qualities or their functional ones, who drag them to bug-infested, louse-ridden places like Dundee and Ladysmith, who force children upon them they don't want or aren't ready for or shouldn't have had in the first place, who use them to populate the Menzies stud farm to prolong their name and retrieve their glory (which is, by the way, entirely irretrievable), who, with the exception of Owen the Good, squirt their semen wherever they need to squirt it whenever they wish to."

Glass stepped forward and grasped her by the shoulders to settle her. "Easy, Henrietta. You're getting overwrought. You are falling into the reverse of blind antifeminism—antimasculinism: there must be such a word."

"Antimasculinism! Jason, the last thing I am," she was yelling at him now from less than a foot away, "is a man-hater. Have you forgotten Owen? When I was a child, I had little or nothing to do with Farquhar, not because he was the Farquhar we now know—he wasn't then—but because he was not Owen. From the time I was five and Owen was nine, I wanted to be with no one but Owen. Because he was my brother? No, for I rued the joke God had played on us that made us siblings. I loved him—because he was male and good and no other male I had ever encountered had linked those two qualities together. I lived for the warm days of summer when he would bring me to this lake, this very spot upon which we now stand, Jason, you and I." She backed away from his grasp and turned to the lake as if to command it. "We would take our clothes off—all of them—and we would swim together, and I would look at his body, at his penis, even though he knew I was. I liked to pretend that he looked at me that way too, even though he probably just thought of me as his little sister and nothing more. Every year his body would be larger, stronger, and mine would be larger and more ready for his. Then one year he had hair around his penis and I had no hair so by the next year I had grown some too just because I wished to have it so Owen would see me as a woman and not a girl because now he was a man. And he laughed the first warm day that spring when he saw what I had managed to have. And I made him touch me, and he did, even though he said he shouldn't have." She was weeping bitterly now. "And we came here the rest of that summer, and again the next and the next, and finally in 1944, when he was eighteen and I was fourteen, he went to war and within two months . . ." She could no longer speak, was sobbing without restraint and pressing the palms of her hands to her eyes. "Oh, Owen, Owen."

Now Glass embraced her and she clung to him tightly, uttering her brother's name, shifting its intonation, Glass soon became aware, from lament to supplication to, almost, direct address. He was unsure of what his next move should be, but he knew it would have to be a cautious one.

"And because you lost Owen, you never sought another man?"

"And because there were too many Farquhars and Bruces and Clydes. And Robertses and Anguses." She had lost entirely the dominating quality which her size and bearing usually lent her. She backed her face away from his; her cheeks were tear-soaked, her eyes burning from the sun, her gray-black hair streaming recklessly in the breeze from the top of The Gap. "And never since has a man seen or touched my body. And I am forty-five years old. Never since that boy who had your dark coloring and your brown hair and eyes and your high cheekbones and your wide smile. Oh, Jason, the moment I saw you in Sciennes' I thought I was being tricked again, that I was given my brother back, that I was being mocked with a man who was not my brother, did not have the blood obstacle between us, yet who was an outsider who would leave me, who was younger by ten years and so would not love me. I resented all that." She stared into his eyes imploringly now. Glass was not sure what her mental state was, was uncertain whether to break her trance or let it see itself through to the end. And in a second he had almost no decision left to make.

"Love me once more, Owen?" It was not a request; it was a plea.

"Henrietta, I have never made love . . ." And then he realized that she had not used his name and therefore had not mistaken what they might not as yet have done.

"How old were you then, Henrietta?" He tried to use the pitiful tools of verb tense and past adverb to lure her back to the present.

"Fourteen, Jason. I was a much more beautiful girl than I am a woman. I wish you could have seen my body and my face at fourteen, for you are good like Owen was and you would have wanted them too, as he did."

"And he made love to you?"

She nodded, never removing her eyes from him.

"Just once?"

"Just once. He promised me that we would again someday, but he died first. Until now." She kissed him softly on the lips, then guided his hands under her skirt, where she, not he, removed her panties in the same motion with which she guided herself and him carefully to the ground amidst the uncut grass which was as soft as the maidenhair to which she had brought his hand.

And he hated himself because he did not love her; because he wished she were Ann if this had to be; because he was playing a role in her life that she had created for him rather than one that he had chosen for himself; because he was not man enough to resist—or perhaps was too much a man to be able to; because he was being once again forced forward by the past. He resented Henrietta, despite his pity for her, and he hated himself, whom he refused to pity.

Glass had lost track of time, but they must have lain together embraced for at least a half-hour. Then, across the lake, they saw Sybil's Mercedes back out of the drive. Knowing that she would spot Henrietta's truck along the roadside on her way out of The Gap, they got up and fixed their clothing. Henrietta was quickly the Sunday churchgoer again, Glass the random hiker who had wandered in. He said he wanted to walk the rest of the way home around the back side of the lake—he had never been on this side before. He wanted to be away from her as quickly as he could. But as they parted, just as they heard Sybil's car shut off back at the road, Henrietta, in command again as she normally was, decided not to let the morning terminate yet.

"Before you leave here, Jason, be sure to examine the stone against which we were leaning a bit ago. Then, after you do that, take care not to stub your toe going home." She stepped forward and kissed him quickly on the cheek. "Cheers now, Jason. I'll have Ann call you as soon as she gets in this evening." She acted as if nothing had happened.

Glass watched her pick her way among the high grass to intercept Sybil before she saw them together. And again it struck him that in less than twelve hours, he had—perhaps—made love to both of them, and neither had he intended to nor particularly wanted to and the one whom he wanted to very badly he never had and perhaps never would.

He reluctantly examined the rock as she had instructed him. It was so covered with lichen that at first it seemed no different from any of the other gray-green rocks that littered the Gap floor and walls—but then he noticed that it certainly was. Apparent even through its mossy covering was the fact that something had been chiseled in this rock, long enough ago that it took him several minutes to clean the surface enough to read it. The lettering, as on an old tombstone, was no longer sharp. But it could be read:

M.D.J. IS DONE
20-6-1925
A.M. & B.M.
DONE AGAIN
11-5-1944
O.M. & H.M.

NEVER DONE AGAIN
11-5-1945
H.M.

These nine lines occupied almost the whole horizontal surface of the stone. Three different hands had set to this on three different occasions. The last six lines made sense rather quickly. Total sense where an hour before they would not have made any. The first three made none, but within several more hours, because he *did* stub his toe as he had been cautioned not to, they too made sense. Horrible sense if his guess was correct.

Ann would not believe what he would soon tell her. But finally she would have to.

Part Three
PERCEPTIONS

15 MARIA DE JAGER

PAUL KRIGE'S ENVELOPE CONTAINED A TRANSLATION of roughly one-third of the material he had been given. So Jason Glass spent the rest of Sunday afternoon and evening reading what Krige had decoded, waiting for Ann to arrive, suspecting now that he knew the end of Maria Menzies' story and so should begin learning the start of it and its middle. The arrival of the diary translation, plus the inscriptions on the rock, had conspired, for the time at least, to keep him in Scotland to pursue the truth of Roberts Menzies and Maria De Jager rather than to vacate for the sole purpose of defending Annie Daly against it. He was not at all sure he was making the proper choice, but Margot was not in Scotland.

I wish I were a man, but at least I am not a British woman. They are not allowed to go to war as my mother and sisters and I are. I am glad I am a De Jager, for our wagon has only six of us inside. The Doorn wagon has thirteen and it is terribly crowded and no bigger than ours. I thought the ride would be bumpy, but the roads are still muddy from winter and getting muddier with the early spring rains. We spend much of our time outside pushing. It is the 30th of September today, a Saturday. I will write something down every day till the war starts and after that until I cannot.

Sunday, 1 October '99—Probably not every day. Today was just more pushing and watching other wagons as full as the Doorns' get stuck worse than ours. I will write when something happens—perhaps in two days, when Father says we will reach Pretoria. I hope I will see Christiaan there.

Tuesday, 3 October '99—Pretoria is not what I thought it would be. Perhaps it is because there are wagons everywhere that wouldn't be here if there were not going to be a war. But the streets are very dirty with horse droppings and all sorts of other trash that people have thrown from their wagons. Many of the buildings have tin roofs on them, and there is no place with the big buildings I have seen in pictures of Johannesburg. We went to see President Kruger today—even he has a house with a tin roof. He sits on the porch acting as if he were some common trekboer on a Sunday rather than the President of the Transvaal. He should have looked more important. And he is ugly. His face is like bread dough and his eyelids and the skin under them are so heavy that I don't know how he can open his eyes far enough to see. He has no thumb on one hand. Father said that he fought at Blood River against the Zulus and had it shot off there, but I heard President Kruger say to another girl who visited him in front of us that it happened in a gun accident and not in battle at all. He should not be so honest. But he did fight at Blood River and he was a voortrekker. He is what the Boers are. But he is very ugly. Ours is not a pretty people. Next to the President, Father and Christiaan, despite their fat stomachs and dirty beards, are handsome. Beside Mrs. Kruger, I am pretty. I am pretty next to most Boer girls, I think. But I would not be pretty next to an English girl.

Wednesday, 4 October '99—I am excited by the prospect of war, but I don't understand why we must fight it. President Kruger said that diamonds and gold are not riches for the Boer people but blood and tears for them instead. Why do we not give them to the British? Why must we make them fight for them, be killed and kill us? I expect to die, and I expect Father and Christiaan to die. But why should we die for the diamonds and gold which we don't need or want? We should die if they try to take our farms, which they do not seem to want. Perhaps we must fight because farms are not exciting. War is. Maybe gold and diamonds are. Why must the British fight? They have so much. But so much is not exciting either. War is.

Thursday, 5 October '99—There is word that the men will depart tomorrow or the next day—without us, we have heard. I do not want to stay in Pretoria. We came because we thought we would go to the battles. We will go. We will wait a few days, Mother says, but we will go. Helena does not want to go—she is cowardly, afraid of death, wishing to just marry, since she is fifteen. She would rather be on the farm, but she was also too cowardly to stay alone. Piet wants to go desperately—he has heard that Boer boys will be allowed to fight in the bigger battles or when the number of wounded gets too great or when those who are cowardly simply desert and go back to their farms. Piet is prepared. Mother and Katerina want to go too. Mother says we will.

Friday, 6 October '99—The men will depart tomorrow—Father is to go with his commando under General Joubert to the Natal border above Dundee, perhaps to invade. They should not invade. God would not want us to. But they say that the British are not ready to fight, that they must be attacked before they are strong rather than after. Their soldiers are still on the high seas from England and India and Australia. Their commanding general is still in England himself and cannot possibly get here before the end of the month. But if we invade we will lose God's favor, and we have always thought that worth more than military advantage. I wish our soldiers had uniforms, red ones like those the British will have. But they have no more uniforms than their farm clothes and the only thing that will mark them as Boer fighting men is their great slouch hats which is the same thing that marks them as Boer farmers. There is no difference between a Boer farmer and a Boer soldier, which is why it is foolish to fight for anything but their farms. Give them the gold and the diamonds, save us the blood and the tears. But it is the excitement. Boerhood is boredom!

Jason Glass wondered how carefully this aphorism had been translated from the original and how much was Paul Krige's attempt at stylistic gymnastics. Glass hoped there would not be too much of this.

Father exchanged his rifle today for a German gun called a Mauser which fires shells automatically and these shells must be three inches long, perhaps four. He has been told that he must bring two horses with him into battle, so he will take Piet's as well as his own. He must bring eight days' rations as well, and Mother is trying to get this together, trading things we have extra of with families of other wagons for things they have extra of.

Saturday, 7 October '99—There was a great prayer meeting at sunrise this morning, so large that many different predicants led prayer at the same time so that all the families could hear. Then President Kruger made a speech to the men and their families that none of us could hear but it seemed as if he might be crying and he was very stooped over when he walked away. Then the trains were loaded, first with thousands of cattle for meat for the soldiers, then with the soldiers and their horses and their equipment. Many of the men, including Father, had a very difficult time getting their horses to enter the boxcars. His own went on happily enough, but Piet's was afraid, more because of the sound of his hooves on the hollow ramp than of the tight conditions inside. But eventually Father got him in and then the door was shut to prevent any of the animals from bolting and we did not get to kiss him goodbye because we did not know the door would close with so many cars still to be filled. And we may not see him again and he will be jammed with other men and horses inside for the next three days, which is how long others have said it will take the trains to reach the border at Sandspruit. The only stops will be at stations along the way where ramps have been built to remove the horses and there will be only one of these each day. As small and rough as our wagon is, I am glad I will go to war in that instead of one of these boxcars. (There is word among the women that they will leave tomorrow.) When the train finally started to move toward Natal, the band struck up the Transvaal anthem and played it over and over again until the trains were out of sight to the south. It was hard to imagine the men inside, the farmers, the traders, the boys of the high veld, all packed together, Christiaan among them though I have not seen him, instead of loose and free, spread so far across the veld that they hardly ever see their neighbors without trying to, much less be jammed together with them where even the most private things will have to be done in public.

Sunday, 8 October '99—A Mrs. Botha, who is the wife of one of the generals, took charge of the families today and said that those who wanted to go to Natal should line their wagons up behind her and follow her. She seemed angered that Mrs. Joubert was permitted to accompany her husband but that she had not been. Mother could not decide for a moment, but then she decided that we should go and soon so had almost everyone else.

It took the party of women and children ten days to traverse the roughly 180-mile route to the Transvaal border at Volkrust. Maria De Jager's entries here were sporadic, and those she made were replete with boredom and meaningless accounts of set-tos with her two sisters and her mother. As the oldest child, at eighteen long a woman by Boer standards, she was often charged with guiding the oxen, which, if anything, she found more tedious than merely riding because she could not sleep. When they reached Volkrust on Wednesday the eighteenth, they learned that the Boer commandos had invaded northern Natal fully a week before and had proceeded as far south as Dundee, where, it was expected, they would encounter their first resistance from the outnumbered but well-equipped British garrison there. Some rumors had it that the British forces had already fallen back on Ladysmith, 60 kilometers to the south of Dundee, but better-informed sources discounted this. On Thursday the nineteenth the caravan of women itself crossed into Natal, unafraid of the British troops (There were none this far north), unafraid of the British subjects who resided there (There was known to be heavy Boer sympathy in this part of Natal), but constantly wary of the overmythologized but very real danger of armed kaffirs who, it had long been feared, would take the occasion of white upheaval to pursue their own long-frustrated ends.

A passage from Maria's diary entry of the nineteenth caught Glass's special notice:

Majuba Hill. We passed it today, actually saw it. Fought on the day of my birth in 1881, the last my ancestors thought they would ever see of the British. And it was the last—for a time. For fourteen years. Then they came back with the Jameson Raid, my teachers had told me at least forty times that winter, and they were dispatched back to Bechuanaland that time too. But now four years later they are back again, in the thousands they will come this time, and we must live with the truth that there is not a single British soldier in the Transvaal at this moment, but because we invaded them, even though we were provoked, they will come in thousands whenever they finally get enough soldiers here to enable them to do it. We will have successes for a time—we must already have—but they will come and eventually we will suffer for disobeying God's call of peace, for not just giving them diamonds and gold they want that we seem to have no use for, for accepting the blood and tears that President Kruger said we would have to accept. For seeking excitement.

That evening the wagon train stopped at Ingogo and the next at Newcastle. It was, according to Maria's diary, Sunday the twenty-second when the women finally overtook their men in the hills behind Dundee, and so she and Roberts were for the first time within a mile of each other, though of course they had no reason to know that as yet. This was the day of the mysterious omission in Roberts' own diary—the crucial missing page of October twenty-second, the day on which Roberts engineered the forbidden removal of himself, his wife, and more than a hundred of his personal patients from the Dundee hospital to their ill-fated internment for four months at Ladysmith.

In Maria's entry for the twenty-third Glass found a hint as to exactly what might have occurred the night of the escape. He found the clue amidst wondrous descriptions Maria had taken to writing about life in the laager with the Boer commandos:

Tuesday, 24 October '99—I was allowed to go with Father and Piet this afternoon to deal with the flesh corporal. He is in charge of taking the meat that has been butchered from the herd and distributing it to the burghers. He actually turns his back to those coming forward for their portions so that he will favor no one, by accident or design, so that those he likes and those he dislikes approach him from behind and accept the portion doled to them. I was allowed to step forward for Father and Piet because their shoulders are so bruised from the recoil of their Mausers that they can barely move their arms, much less carry the weight of four days' meat on four days' bone. So I carried it for them. I am strong, but I must strengthen the muscles of my arms and shoulders because the women before much longer will have to be the ones to move the ammunition and even perhaps the earth that will create the trenches.

They say we will go south tomorrow in pursuit of the British army that has sneaked out of Dundee in the night and is already a day or two on its way toward Ladysmith, where they will try to regroup their forces. There is some hope of overtaking this column before it arrives there, for Father and Piet were told by a doctor at the hospital that over ninety patients in ambulances are with them. Father said to this man how foolhardy attempting to move a fighting force with ambulances full of sick people was, but the doctor said that another medical man threatened to reveal the army's night maneuvers if he was not taken, and his patients too. He had a bugle that he had taken from a dying bugle boy and had threatened to signal us with it if he was left behind. Father says he is the sort of coward England breeds who can be counted on to undermine them for us with his own blundering and stupidity and fear.

To Glass's mind, Roberts was the "medical man" in question. He sardonically formed a mental picture of this man whom he was being paid to mythologize leaning out of a hospital window, the horn an inch from his lips, with Yule or his emissary negotiating so that he would not sound the notes of retreat or even of attack. But Glass was already becoming more careful about the conclusions he would draw and how he would draw them; he would label this speculation in his final draft of the "real" biography.

Maria's discussion of British lack of character at the end of her entry for the twenty-fourth formed the transition to the opening of her entry for the next day. She and her father's commando unit were several miles to the south of Dundee now in pursuit of General Yule's ambulance-laden column and its flight toward Ladysmith:

Wednesday, 25 October '99—We have traitors of our own. I had thought that traitors were just those who told the enemy your plans, but they are more frequently, I think, people who simply have plans of their own who resent or just tire of doing what everyone else does or what they are supposed to be doing. There are families among us who say even this soon that they must leave for huis-toe, but we know that they will never come back to the war. They will not bother. It is not even so much that they are afraid—they are just not used to living so close to one another, so close they can hear babies not their own crying, children not their own bickering and laughing, dogs and cocks not their own barking and crowing. They have lived so far out on the veld that they have never heard that before and it makes them worried and defensive to hear it so nearby. But they are traitors, for they will sacrifice their nation to their own wishes to be alone, have become so accustomed to being alone that their own individual wishes blind them to anything else.

Others, though, are traitors because they are afraid of being killed or wounded, and wounded to them seems worse than killed. It is easy to know who these men are, for they mark themselves with blood in order to pretend they are not afraid of it. They will steal a chicken from another family if they have none of their own, and they will take it beyond the laager and slay it and bury the entrails so they may smear its blood upon their faces and show that they are wounded and how brave they are, as if bravery once were enough to satisfy the need for bravery twice. And they leave too, also pursuing their individual purposes or their individual cowardices at the expense of the rest of us who will fight on to defend our common homelands.

An entry on the twenty-seventh, the day on which she witnessed her first battle, reveals that she found herself to have little stomach herself for the essentialmost reality of war.

Friday, 27 October '99—I have today despaired that this journal shall ever be read all of one piece. When I am struck by an English shell my pages will be scattered farther than my blood and bones will be, for that is the thing one most notices about a battlefield when the fighting is done. Paper. White paper is strewn everywhere, floats on the breeze if there is one, lies still on the veld if there is not. They are mostly handwritten pages scribbled by the now-killed hearts and minds and souls of dead Briton and Boer alike. There are logs and journals and diaries such as mine, written in two different languages to keep account of individual selves in such a dreadful endeavor in which any self matters little. There are letters to home and letters from home all in English, letters which profess and receive love, which inquire about the well-being of grandparents and children and wives and even pet dogs, all in the hands of people who will neither give nor receive love ever again. Their wives and children live on and pray for the physical well-being of their men, not knowing even as they pray that it is already too late for that and can only be directed toward the salvation of their souls. Dying old people in England will never be told so that their own deaths may be more peaceful. Children will be told slowly and by degrees. Some of the papers are photographs, pictures of the same people who wrote and were to receive the letters that were never mailed and perhaps only hastily read. Some of the papers are pages of Bibles, all King James versions, half written in English, half in our tongue. Some of the papers are pages from newspapers which remind us that our terrible battlefield is but a dot of fly excrement on the face of the earth, that it matters little except to those of us on both sides who are here and those far away who stand to gain by our deaths. Some of the papers are pages torn from books, books which the soldiers read to pass away the long hours between fighting, the hours in which they would otherwise sit and wonder what it was like to die and whether the next fight would be the one after which they would no longer have to wonder.

The dead horses are there and they stink but they are hard to see at first glance because they blend with the veld. The broken lances must be stepped upon to be noticed because of the depth of the grass. The bodies of the men blacken in the sun and look from the distance like anthills rather than the remains of human beings. Some of these too are hidden in the grass, but we know they are there because of the vultures cawing and circling above, waiting for the field to be free of the living so they may be about their business with the dead.

And so that is what is left after a battle. History books and storybooks never speak of this. It is impossible to describe what it looks like for a hundred men of the British light cavalry to thunder on toward a trench filled with Boer riflemen, hitting no Boer because in their firing they can see no Boer to aim at, few if any staying on their horses when the charge is over. Nor were any of us prepared for the terrible noise of the battle which is not the individual pops of single rifles but the continuous and unbroken snapping of Mausers and the thunderclaps of the Creusots and the pom-poms and the howitzers which are all about us. And finally the new gas they call lyddite which is black and yellow and green and horrible of stench but which floats upward and so is harmless if you keep your head down in your trench.

And so this is what I saw of war today and fear I will see every day. I must strengthen myself to stand it and I must educate myself to know why it must be, why there are at this moment graves being dug on both sides, doctors from both sides meeting together without animosity at the center of the veld on which the battle was fought, why the horses who were so highly trained are reduced to carrion at the pull of one trigger apiece. And the paper is adrift on the veld, scattered like the dust from which our Creator made us and to which He, in His wisdom, this day chose to return so many. May my pages, I pray, not be scattered apart when my flesh and bones will be.

And so the entry for Friday the twenty-seventh, and Glass was amazed at the difference in tone Maria De Jager's diary reflected in less than a month of writing. The airy Boer girl who sought excitement and glimpses of British soldiers seemed already to know that enough of both would soon be at hand, maybe already was. The next entry was for Monday, the thirtieth of October, "Mournful Monday" so-called, the day on which the British forces tried to block the Boer encirclement of Ladysmith by taking key positions at Nicholsons Nek and Pepworth Hill and Lombards Kop and in fact took none of them. It was also the day on which the Boers prepared their seige and on which the De Jager commando was assigned to the top of Umbulwana Mountain to the east side of the town, the position that would become the anchoring point of the whole Boer circumference that was to seal off the town in just three more days. As Jason Glass scanned the rest of the pages that Krige had sent him, he could see that Maria, after this entry, had returned to the trivial affairs of life as the Siege settled into place. What was to be so terrifying a one hundred and twenty days within the town was to be, with few exceptions, an almost unbearably boring four months in the hills beyond it. But nonetheless, the entry for the thirtieth still had the reflective and maturing Maria speculating on what this war really meant.

Monday, 30 October '99—The younger officers have come into conflict with the older ones and for now the older ones are in control. They say we shall halt our invasion of Natal now rather than pursue the British troops still south of the Tugela and pin them against the sea. The younger men like Botha say we must strike now before the British reinforce themselves, take all they have so they have not an inch of ground upon which to land their soldiers when they finally get here from England and India and Australia. But the older generals like Joubert and Prinsloo say that we must not be greedy, that God does not mean us to have everything at once, that He will continue to bless us if we are patient and take what He offers as He offers it, not try to reach behind Him and take it before He is ready for us to have it.

Perhaps the British have too much and this is what will weaken their wills and their characters and their bodies. When we capture their supplies we are hip deep in liquor and polo sticks and only ankle deep in medical supplies and things to repair the spirit as well. But the British have a purpose for being on this earth, however wrong it may be, if it is, whereas the Boers treat this earth as if it had no end of its own, as if it were only an unhappy halfway house to heaven.

That's what the English in Ladysmith will know if we lock the door upon their town—what it is like to have no other purpose than to rise each day and look at the world as a Boer does and wait to fall asleep at night and wake again tomorrow.

The Boer claims he is God-ordained, that the hand of God reaches out to him with daily gifts because He approves of him. Yet who has more aspired to do the work of God on earth than the British, however wrongly they seem to go about it? Has the Boer ever sought to eliminate hunger or disease or misery beyond his own family? Has the Boer tried to civilize the world by bringing foreign lands full of cannibals and backward peoples under the reign of a culture which at least understands what civilization is, even if it does not always live up to its understanding? No, the Boer stays where he is and does not move unless his land goes bad or the black men rise against him and then he simply slaughters the black men or moves away and abandons the places he has already civilized. Only the Boer could take war with all its pain and suffering and horror and make even that dull. As long as the English cannot move also, the thinking now will be, the Boer will be happy in his trenches, swatting all day at the bluebottle fly, at mosquitoes, at the tsetse if he sees one. He is content to squat atop his own droppings rather than soil his hands by touching diamonds or gold or by conquering Natal.

There must be some way to seek something different and better in life without, as the British do, taking what is someone else's to have it for themselves. Life must be something else than just staying the same as we were born so that God will recognize us when we step before Him.

With the experience of Roberts Menzies' diary behind him, Jason Glass could not help looking askance at the document he held in his hands. The pages Krige had translated ran through roughly the middle of November, six or seven weeks, in other words, of a young woman's life, weeks that recounted her first emergence from a life to which so flat a word as *static* even lent dignity and power. In the first pages she sounded like a girl, and in the mid-November pages she did as well—"*I hit Helena in the mouth because I had seen it first and she would have it for herself instead*" (Monday, 13 November 1899); but by the middle pages, even given the fact that she seemed to have more than the normal amount of schooling for a Boer at the time, she was indulging in some rather subtle speculative reasoning on history and metaphysics and even theology—subtle, that is, given who she was and what she was apparently destined to become. It all seemed highly unlikely and inconsistent, and Glass had no way of knowing whether Krige might be tampering here. The diary pages were, unlike Roberts', all the same hand, though Glass could not be certain that Krige had not embellished or otherwise misrepresented what she was saying to herself in this crucial week before Ladysmith was shut off.

As he continued to read on, he began to doze over the pages. But in his waking moments he was becoming more convinced that the girl named Maria De Jager—whose end he now suspected he could account for—was not a bickering Boer girl who had too much of riding in a covered voortrekker wagon, but was rather a girl who became, in stages, fed up and so took action and then took more and more and still more and had finally been absolutely resented for it by yet another group of people who, though they would not like to admit it, depended on the repetitive status quo just as much as any bushveld Boer did.

And finally Jason Glass fell asleep at his desk, sure that Krige was right and had not mistranslated a word. Krige was unwittingly exposing the roots of Maria De Jager's ruin, which came twenty-five or twenty-six years after those roots were planted and took hold.

Part Four

FACTS

16 THE MEANING OF THE ROCK

He knew it was Sunday, the twenty-second of June—the calendar pad on his desk told him that. He knew too that it was either before dawn or after dark, remembered after a few moments that it had to be the latter as he recalled where he was. The translated sheets of Maria De Jager's diary were sleep-scattered about the desktop now, and he would probably have disarranged them some more had not the hand running through his hair persistently kept at the task of waking him. He blinked his eyes clear and looked up to see the beautiful face of Ann Macgregor beaming down at him from where she sat atop his desk.

"What was it this time, Jason," she chided, "the local alcoholic product or simple overwork? I'll accept the latter if you claim it."

"It *was* the latter, Ann," he chuckled back as he rubbed his right cheek along her thigh—something he could not as yet have brought himself to do if he had been fully conscious. He let his head continue to rest in her lap as he brought her up to date on his recent problems at home, where he was not, and abroad, where he was. She listened patiently, though there was little coherent order to what he was telling her. He heard himself even admitting without intending to that he was prepared to tell all the lies that Farquhar wanted, that he had to get back to America as quickly as he could to shore up his story of Annie Daly, unraveling as no more than unintentional lies itself. He began to babble metaphysics which had been "proved" by both the Roberts Menzies and Annie Daly stories, that most human beings were finally filthy at the core, no matter how polished their surface veneer. Only three people he could think of might not be, and one of these, he forthrightly announced, was Ann herself. She laughed at this, embarrassed for him and for her.

"You don't know a thing about me, Jason, that I haven't wanted you to know!"

"I'm not sure you're right there, Ann. You see, I don't know anything about Maria De Jager that she doesn't want me to know either, seeing as how she is the source of all the information I have about her life. But I can already tell—and I've read a good deal of her diary now—that she's got what we call during our American maturation process 'hot pants.' She tries to cover herself with noble statements about the Boer cause, about the folly of war, about the pointlessness of arguing over diamonds and gold. But I'll tell you for a bloody fact, just by what I got between the lines, that she is bored stiff being a Boer farmer's oldest daughter, that she finds the Boer race an ugly lot physically, that she considers herself a superior Boer specimen, and that she wants little more out of her trip to war than excitement and a British husband. Krige has translated to the point where she and her family are camped above Ladysmith on Umbulwana; her father and brother gun away at the town all day while she catches her beauty nap in the wagon. Then, at sundown, she pretties herself up and accompanies them out onto the battlefield to exchange wounded and bury the dead with the British. She is becoming remarkably hardened to the sight of blood and death in her nightly writings, perhaps because she does not see much of it in her casting about for live British soldiers. If Krige were trying to write a serialized novel, he could not have broken off in a better place this time—Maria has realized that even British soldiers get dirty and stink on battlefields, so she has spotted 'someone else' who is trying to do some business with the Boer officers which her father has so far been too noble to get involved in."

"You think this someone is Roberts?"

"That, Ann, I have little doubt of. For three reasons. First, doctors would be the only people whom the two sides would tolerate on a battlefield at the close of day—or stretcher-bearers sent out to aid them in carrying the wounded back. Second, we know—or pretty well suspect—that Roberts did some negotiating with the Boers during the Siege. And third, and most obvious of all, we at least know the end of this story to the extent that Roberts and Maria got together somewhere along the line. This would seem an apt moment."

"And have you managed to determine as yet exactly what Roberts was negotiating with and for?"

" 'With' I have little doubt will turn out to be the codebooks that the man in Aberdeen suggested when I first arrived here. He would have had access to them, since he was General White's personal physician."

Ann shook her head negatively. She seemed to be ahead of him again. "No, no, Jason. While I'll buy the codebooks as his barter, they cannot be White's own. He would have missed them, wouldn't he? And it would not have taken too long for Roberts to be on the list of suspects. Those were not penny dreadfuls or pornographic magazines, Jason. They were not mass-produced or left to lie around. Nor were they infrequently used. They had to belong to someone high up who would have both *had* them and, second, not known they were gone."

"Or somebody in the Signal Corps he bought them from—but that would have been too dangerous, ripe for blackmail." He smacked his knee with the palm of his right hand. "Damn it, Ann, you're right! You've got to be. I know whose they were! They would be a dead man's. They had to have been General Penn-Symons', the general who was mortally wounded at Talana Hill and whom Roberts treated on the battlefield." He blew through his cheeks. "Which makes him a very calculating fellow, doesn't it? Instead of swiping something off a table for whatever immediate purpose he might have had, he took them and stashed them away for whatever future purpose he might have wound up having."

Ann leaned forward now. "Yes! I had not thought of Penn-Symons, but that is a good guess. But if we are to make him *that* calculating, we cannot, I fear, presume he did not know what his purposes would be down the line for their use. He has a dying general in his arms and he nicks his codebooks. I say he *knew* what he would want in exchange. But what?"

"Initially I thought money, at times I still do, but I gather that coins and currency were not something the Boers put much stock in, much less carried into battle with them to buy codebooks or souvenirs. Now I think it was probably *not* money, though my corrupt nature, being as I am a member of the other, dirtier half of the human race, had decided that that would be the most likely." He winked at her. "Now tell me your guess."

She shrugged, as if her guess, at least her first one, were purely a hunch. "How about his wife's passage to safety—whether from Ladysmith or wherever things finally went wrong? You recall the ambivalence he had about giving up her services on the one hand—which he did not want to do—and having her trapped amidst danger or disease or both when she was in the final stages of her pregnancy—which he did not want either."

Glass shook this one off. "Wonderful motive, Ann, and typical of your part of the race to hatch that one instead of money. But we know that she died in Ladysmith and we know, or think we know, that he handed the codes over. Thus, those don't add up, unless the Boers tricked him and did not make good on their end of the bargain."

"Give me another, then."

"I don't have a good one. Usually if it's not money, it's a woman, and we know there's a woman involved here. A not unwilling woman, too."

Now Ann rejected his theory, even more quickly than he had hers. "If you are saying he traded the codes to Maria for the use of her body, that collapses in all directions."

"Remember that Roberts' wife was entering a three-month sexless period, my dear, and he was too much the doctor to toy around with that for his own pleasure."

"It still collapses. If she were willing, as you infer, he would have needed no codebooks and would have saved them for another occasion. Hardly likely he would have had such long-range plans with Penn-Symons dying in his arms either. And if her father would not deal with Roberts, as you also have inferred, it is not likely that Maria would have done so for the reasons you are speculating upon, Jason. And what would an eighteen-year-old Boer girl want with codebooks which broke one code and turned it into good English, which to her was a code as well since she could not then speak it? No, that is not good, and you know it."

"I see you have an alternative, but remember that Roberts is a Menzies before you dip into your admirable soul for yet another."

"Yes, Roberts was a Menzies. What do Menzies spend much of their lives doing?"

Glass laughed. "Cleaning up after other Menzies, it seems to me."

"Exactly! Roberts was a doctor. Even the Aberdeen professor admitted that he had tried to convert sheep-grazing land into a hospital site. He dedicated himself to a South African hospital rather than live in Scotland under terms he could not accept.

He saved almost every patient he brought into Ladysmith when other doctors were losing at least a third of theirs—when theirs were healthy to start with and his were not. What would he have traded for, given all that?"

"Medicine?"

"Yes. Bandages, iodoform, antiseptics, painkillers."

Jason smiled at her. "Oh, I've projected even more wildly than that, Ann. Serial writing insists that readers do, you know, so that they buy the next issue, pay the next admission, watch the next program. Krige has promised that shortly. So we shall see who is right. I won't even tell you the rest of my suspicions., but I'll write them down and seal them in an envelope so you can check my powers of foresight when the time comes."

"And what will it prove if you are right?"

"Exactly the point I am after—that I can think such things up about people because I am one of the majority that knows what people will do to get what they need."

"And I am so good that I am not?" She seemed tired, even weary now.

"Exactly."

He kissed her as long and as lovingly as he allowed himself to, then swept her into his arms and carried her across the threshold of the spare bedroom and placed her gently on top of the spread. After covering her with a quilt, he left the room and shut the door softly behind him. She was sleeping soundly even before he did so.

He got quickly into his own bed and fell asleep before long, cursing Margot and Roberts and Maria De Jager and the human race out loud for as long as his conscious mind could remember to do it. Would that they lived their lives in anything like the way Ann Macgregor assumed they did.

The next day, as they walked the west shore of the small Gap lake to circle to the site on the eastern side that Glass had "visited" the day before, he decided the time had come to probe Ann Macgregor's background. Her statements the night before suggested that she was ready to have it probed—or at least as much as she "wanted him to know." He talked quietly, never sure what fragments Duncan would pick up and accidentally misuse.

"What I have never been able to understand, Ann, is why you took a medical degree and then did not do the residency, racing off to London as if you had studied for the publishing trade instead."

"The answer to that, Jason, is quite easy. I entered medical school in the first place in 1968 because my father and mother wanted me to. I was the so-called 'obedient' daughter, you see."

"Trying to make up for Sybil?"

"In a sense, I suppose. She had been forced into marriage two years earlier, and I fear my staunch Calvinist parents had felt the finger of God pointed against them. I never believed much in that sort of thing really—my father and mother did so much good in this district that I cannot believe that they thought God would suddenly give them the sign they were damned—but subconsciously I decided that I had to make their spiritual lives look otherwise to them. When my father died in 1970 and my mother . . . also . . . died in 1972, a month after I had taken my medical degree, I saw no reason to go on with something I had been doing for two now-dead people anyway. I offered myself to several London publishers as an editor of medical texts and chose the job in which I had the best opportunity to move laterally into more creative areas—which I did within a year."

"I don't know whether you've ever noticed it, Ann, but I see a certain similarity between your father and mother and Roberts and his wife—his first one, not his second."

She laughed quietly as she jumped a small rivulet that fed into the lake. "Now, on that one, Jason, you are *not* ahead of anyone else. The devoted doctor and his faithful, hardworking nurse. Yes, they filled the role for three decades that Roberts and Catherine were supposed to have filled when they returned from South Africa, except that Catherine died there and Roberts didn't bother to return for nearly twenty years. In fact, medical services in so remote a place as this were very bad until my father returned from medical school in the mid-1930s. And he had no trained nurse until my mother arrived from Glasgow just before the Second World War began."

"And a doctor–nurse romance ensued?"

"More or less, I suppose. But they had other things in common as well. They were both very religious people—both Calvinists, as I said, both always with an eye on heaven and doing the good on earth that assured them that they had been preselected to go there. Hard work is part of all that, you know. And they were both lonely people. My father was an only child whose parents had both died when he was young. My mother was the product of a Glasgow orphanage. It was a natural liaison, I suppose."

Glass grasped her hand as they threaded a narrow place between the water and some rocks. Duncan drifted ahead of them, plunking stones into the unrippled waters to stir them up.

"How was it that your mother left Glasgow after her nurse's training? Must have been a lot of jobs there, at better pay."

"Yes, my father always did consider himself quite fortunate on that score. He had advertised in both Edinburgh and Glasgow for four years for a nurse, without success. But what he needed was someone who *wanted* to be in the Lochs, and Annette Wallace was such a person."

"Why did she *want* to be here? Had she ever seen the place?"

"No, never. But why do any of us think we would like to be someplace we have never been? The second I knew I was not going to practice medicine, I wanted to live in London—I had never been there either. Some romantic picture which seldom materializes the way we had hoped. Though I don't mind London."

"And she did not mind the Lochs?"

"No. She wanted the family she had never had and she found it. First with my father, later with two daughters, but in between with a surrogate son."

"Owen Menzies?"

"Yes. You've been talking with Henrietta, I see." She did not notice Glass's wince at the verb. "Owen the Good, as he is called. The one Menzies in generations whom the clan could have been firmly directed by—save that he was not the oldest son and so was not destined to be that leader."

"I gather that Bruce Menzies was not much of a father to any of his children, Farquhar or Henrietta either."

"Right, apparently. He had some ax he spent most of his life grinding—against his own father, Roberts, I suppose. He stayed close to Farquhar because he was the oldest son. Henrietta was never apart from her mother for many years. This left Owen almost parentless himself. My mother was very fond of him, but my father absolutely adored the boy, from what I've heard. He allowed him to help out in his surgery to the point that Owen got quite good at the simpler medical procedures even in his teens. When he went to war, he went with a letter from my father attesting to this fact so he could join the Hospital Corps. My father was going to recommend him to the University for medical study when he returned. But Owen was not used in the Hospital Corps. He was sent to the front lines instead."

"And killed there."

"I am sure you have heard that it was not exactly *there*. His wound in the stomach could have been repaired, but his mates had such difficulty getting him to an aid station for treatment that he died several hours later before he reached it. A common occurrence in war, I am told."

They walked in silence for several minutes as they rounded the end of the lake and proceeded toward the rock on which he and Henrietta had sat the previous day.

"Henrietta does not seem to have ever gotten over that," Glass remarked, annoyed at himself for allowing yesterday to slip into at least his side of the conversation. Ann seemed to know nothing about the episode.

"No, she never did. There was some relationship between them that went beyond a brother/sister sort of thing. I am not sure it was destined to be healthy. But the other person who never got over it was my father. He was crushed. He never said it, but I am sure he would have liked either Sybil or me to have been a son whom he could have named Owen and raised to aid him in his surgery and go to medical school. He got a daughter who did all that instead. 'Ann' and 'Owen' are not pronounced too differently around here, are they?" She smiled shyly at the inference. "I began to worry about him the older I got, for he devoted his spare hours to some experimentation he could never perfect—something to do with slowing down the vital functions of the human body in crisis situations (such as war) in order to have the period between wound and death lengthen itself. He planned to perfect the drug and make it available to every soldier, first in the Korean War, later in the Indochina War, even later still in the Vietnam War. Every combat soldier would carry a small syringe of the stuff to inject into himself or a comrade in the event of serious wound. The heart rate would slow; hence bleeding, gastrointestinal functions, and even awareness of pain would decrease. He had planned to name it after Owen, but he could never work the bugs out of it. The worst bug was that it slowed mental processes down as well. In the lab animals he worked with, he could revive some of the vital functions to their normal rate later, but he could never get a few—including the mental processes—to move forward properly again. At times he became almost obsessed with the whole thing—you would have thought he could have brought Owen back to life with it—and I think he killed himself with anxiety in the long run."

They reached the engraved rock now and Glass gestured her to sit with him upon it. He had two more things he wanted to find out and so did not show her yet what he had come to.

"Ann, I know your father's death is a tough thing to talk about, even at five years' distance. But I must ask you one more thing. Farquhar's wife died just two days after your father, walking around outside on a cold night with no more than a nightgown and a light robe on. I am told she collapsed in the castle courtyard and died of exposure. Is there any connection between the two deaths?"

He could tell from the look on her face that she had long ago considered that. "I don't know, Jason, but I have always suspected there must be. Despite the fact she was married to Farquhar, she was a very intelligent and apparently happy woman. She would not be traipsing around underclad. With the exception of my mother, Sybil, and me, Catherine was the last person my father spoke with on his deathbed in the hours following his heart attack. He requested that she appear, made us leave the room while he spoke with her for no more than five minutes. When she emerged, she tried to cover the fact but she was terribly shaken by something that had occurred in the room. We went back in, and within the hour he passed away. Within two more days, so had she. She was only forty-three."

"So you never discovered what went on between them."

"No. But I know my mother tried. You see, I hate to mention this, but in the last several years before his death, my father was spending ever more time around the castle. I think my mother suspected something between him and Catherine. She was so beautiful and married to a rather uninterested husband in Farquhar. But I am convinced she was wrong. She devoted her own remaining two years to trying to find out, however."

"If he was dead, what good would it have done her to know?"

"Annie Daly and Roberts Menzies are dead too."

"Touché. But perhaps it is your goodness, your naiveté coming to the surface again, that prevents you from imagining your father as male along with father and professional."

She darkened a bit at this. "I suppose we could say that she took her own life when she verified that it had all gone on, couldn't we?" Rather than let Jason respond, however, she continued. "But no—my father was a Puritan, of the strictest sort. He would not tamper with his soul to that degree. I never missed a Sunday of church, nor did he, until he died. No—my mother's death followed a telephone call, from whom I don't know, from Glasgow. She retired to her room for the rest of the day. When she did not rise in the morning, I went to see about her and discovered that she must long ago have unloaded half the leftover capsules in my father's vacant surgery and stashed them in her room to be there on the day the call finally came."

"And you don't know anything about that call?"

"I have never investigated it."

"Why?"

"For the same reason Farquhar wants *his* version of Roberts written, the same reason you now are prepared to do it, and the same reason you will leave me and go back to America to make sure that the college professor and his student don't get into the back rooms of the Harvard Library. Few of us want to know the truth—it is too terrible to live with. It takes more courage than most of us have."

"You know I am vulnerable to such suggestions, Ann. But we must face the fact that the one asset the truth has going for it is that it *is* the truth—it can never be made nontruth. The truth can be Good or it can be Horrible—but it is always fact." Her eyes were filled with tears now, tears she would not let fall. He kissed her and could feel her trying to swallow the tears. He felt that she loved him, and he knew he loved her. She was stronger now than the night before. "The truth has a way of demanding that it be recognized, Ann. If you don't go looking for it, it seems to come looking for you. Stand up for a moment."

He pointed at the inscriptions in the stone, still clearly visible because he had scraped the lichen off the day before. She read them aloud with no trace of recognition in her voice. " 'M.D.J. IS DONE. 20-6-1925. A.M. & B.M. DONE AGAIN. 11-5-1944. O.M. & H.M. NEVER DONE AGAIN. 11-5-1945. H.M.' What does all that mean, Jason?" She looked at him quizzically.

"I really am only interested in the first three lines—the last refer to Henrietta and Owen's last day together before he went to war and Henrietta's commemoration of that day a year later. Now, does the date June 20, 1925, ring any bells for you?

"None. I wasn't along, you see, till twenty-one years after that."

"No legends you've heard about it?"

"Come, come, Jason, give me a better hint if I must guess at all this!" She was excited to know what he had to tell her, was becoming impatient with him.

"The Great Storm of '25?"

"Yes, I have heard of that. The thunder-and-lightning storm which destroyed so much property and killed so many sheep. Yes, though I did not know it was June twentieth."

"Yes, it was—I have it from someone at Sciennes' who lived to tell the story."

"Surely you do not think two people were out here carving their names in a rock at the height of that storm? They would have to be mad!"

"Or drunk, perhaps."

"Very drunk."

"June twentieth, 1925, was a Saturday."

"So what, Jason?"

"The third Saturday of June."

She paused on this. Then her face lit up. "The Dunedin Games!"

"Good, you're catching on. Now, walk over here with me. Careful not to stub your toe. Duncan," he called to where the boy was picking sprigs of heather higher up the hill above them, "you come too."

Together they walked approximately twenty-five yards, Glass guiding both Ann and Duncan alongside him so that both would stub their toes as he had. They did, and both uttered squeaks of pain at the same moment. Duncan dashed his hands into the deep grass to see what he had struck and pulled up a round, solid metal ball. "Four," he uttered with a good deal of glee, even though it was rusty and far from being shiny.

"Yes, Duncan, four. And pretty shortly I expect we will find a fifth, though not on this side."

"Jason," Ann said, as if to summarize what she knew quickly so that he could fill in the rest just as quickly, "I have been to the Dunedin Games enough times to know what that is. It's a cannonball, and I presume you will tell me that it fits the Menzies' Culloden Cannon."

"My dear, it certainly does." Why was he imitating Stan Laurel at the present moment?

"Are you going to explain this, Jason, or must I wait until you twist it through your almighty typewriter to read it?"

"No, let us go back to our rock and sit on it till I tell you to stand again." They did so. "Now, picture the Clan Menzies at four o'clock in the afternoon on Saturday, June twentieth, 1925. First, who would have been there that year as the cannon was being rolled into place to fire into the Oliphants' dismal swamp?"

"Old Angus was still alive then. Bruce would have been there. Roberts?"

"No, Roberts died earlier that year, in January."

"All right, but Maria could have been there."

"Yes, possibly. And Aunt Elizabeth, and maybe even Angus' wife, Margaret, and Farquhar, though he would still have been in diapers. That would about do it. Now, who would have fired the cannon that year?"

"Angus."

"Who would have assisted him?"

"Bruce."

"Stand now." She did so, and he pointed to the third line of the inscription, which read "A.M. & B.M." "Angus and Bruce, perhaps?"

"Perhaps."

"Now, what mental frame would they be in at four o'clock?"

"Sloshed."

"Yes, quite so, I am sure, Ann. Two days ago it took the current Menzies—Clyde and Farquhar—five shots to hit the Viking sailboat in the bay. Do you know how many it took in 1925?"

"That's ridiculous. Of course not."

"Well, I do."

"How?"

"Because I placed a trunk call to old Oliphant yesterday to ask him. He remembers every detail of every games in this century apparently."

"How many, then?"

"One. Now, tell me what Menzies do on the way home from games?"

"They fire their remaining rounds at preappointed targets to clear unwanted buildings."

"Here, sit back down, but be ready to stand again when I tell you. So they came home in 1925 with five useful shots. The storm commenced, I am told, just at nightfall and was vicious from the start. Now, would Angus and Bruce pause at the height of such a storm to clear buildings?"

"No, certainly not."

"Hah. Your naiveté again, Ann. I told you you were too good to be one of the rest of us. Of course they would. They were totally jacked out of shape—as we all were Saturday. They would have loved it, to pound back at the gods' thunder with their mighty Culloden cannon, which never got fired at Culloden, of course."

"But no one else would have gone out to guide them to the targets."

"Precisely. So they would have had to come home with five good shots still in hand."

Ann was beginning to enjoy this but now jumped in to wreck his chain of reasoning. "No, Jason, you are wrong. They could not have gotten back that night, for they would have had to use the ferry to cross from Skye to the mainland. No one would have operated it for them at the height of that storm."

"Incidental, my dear Watson! Would a reluctant ferryman stop two drunk Menzies on Culloden Cannon day from crossing the high seas—or at least several hundred yards of them—their tartan kilts flailing in the wind and with their mighty gun to defend them?" He grinned widely.

"I can't accept that, Jason." She shook her head negatively.

"Well, then do so for the sake of argument. Suppose they made it to the Castle Menzies, the rain slashing in their faces, the gun bouncing up and down to the rear of their 1925 Mercedes-Benz touring car—or whatever they had that year—the lightning cracking like a broken electrical circuit, the thunder pounding as the Lochs had never heard it pound before. What would they do when they reached the castle?"

"They would leave Aunt Elizabeth and Maria and Margaret and young Farquhar, if he was even with them, and then they would . . . no, they would all stay until the storm ceased."

"Not a bit of it, my dear—for three reasons. They would not have let the hated Maria in for a night at Roberts' ancestral castle, they had five good shots still left in the gun, and they were drunk. No, they would have driven Maria home and gone out to unload their gun. Now, do you know where Maria was living in those days?"

"No."

He slid next to her and put his arm around her shoulder and pointed out across the lake to the low green stuccoed house, the one that said JOHN FUCKED KAREN on the side, though they could not read that from where they sat. "There."

"No, I hadn't known that. A pathetic little place at the bottom of so vast a Gap, isn't it, Jason?"

"Yes, very much so. Not much of a place to survive the storm in, especially with the lake waters so close to the rear doorway."

"What, then, are you driving at?"

"Just this. Why not go to higher ground, to a mighty rock house not fifty feet away, partially refurbished and comfortable enough, till the storm subsided?"

"You are suggesting she crossed the road, took up residence in the ruined house, and then was ironically struck by lightning there? That's how that giant hole occurred, you know."

"No, it did not, Ann. Picture now Angus and Bruce, hate-filled, resentful, drunk, armed with a cannon with five shots left. Picture them dragging it back around to this side of the lake, ramming it backward into this clearing with their touring car. Picture them then getting out and wrenching the mighty gun into position, pointing out across this lake the same way it had pointed earlier in the day into Dunedin Harbor but now with only flashes of lightning to help them aim. Imagine them loading the first shot, firing with a boom as loud as the thunder and so indistinguishable from it, but, never having fired from here and barely able to see, missing badly—say short. Then badly again, say left. Then badly again, say right. Badly enough that forty-five or fifty years later a young retarded Menzies would stumble upon these three loose balls and carry them home to play with or contemplate or, eventually, to line his mother's garden with. You've seen those three, Ann?"

"Yes." She was very much chastened now, and Glass was losing the sleuthful glee with which he was telling the story.

"So the ball we just stumbled over and with which Duncan is now playing is the fifth one, not the fourth."

"And the fourth—"

"The fourth, dear Ann," he interrupted so she could not beat him to the point which was his and not hers, grasping her around the shoulders and again pointing across the lake, their ears joined together so they could both sight down the barrel of his arm, "the fourth was right on target. It ripped right through the end of the house and left a giant gaping hole in it, and brought down timbers and debris and shattered stone on top of the lone occupant, who was an unwanted foreign woman in her mid-forties whom the Menzies would never, in their own minds, even allow to share their name."

"Maria De Jager! You are suggesting that the skeleton Duncan found buried there was actually her—"

"Stand." Glass bent over and put his finger on the first line of the inscription, which read "M.D.J. IS DONE."

At noon this same day, Duncan interrupted Ann and Jason as they ate lunch in silence at his cottage. He merely wanted to say that he had found the last ball at the rear corner of the ruined house, exactly where Glass's arm trajectory had estimated it would be. Then, without even asking permission, he went behind the woodbin and removed the gunnysack of bones that Glass was hiding there. And without saying goodbye, he left the cottage. They could see him dragging the bag down the chalk-white road, its string tried to his belt so he could tote his shovel over his left shoulder and a rudimentary cross made of two nailed planks over his right one. His head was earnestly lowered as he trudged toward the ruined house a half-mile on.

17 MULIER LABORANS

IT WAS A CLEAR NIGHT THIS TIME, still light even at ten o'clock, no sign of fog as Glass and Ann Macgregor approached the gatehouse. He walked so quickly, perhaps so furiously, that she had to run several steps at a time to keep up with him as they crossed the three-arched causeway. They could already hear the sharp spatting sound from the power plant in the lower reaches. Glass snatched the bottom of the gate knocker and slammed it heavily against its metal plate. A face finally appeared through the peephole.

Glass spoke first. "Jason Glass, here to see Mr. Menzies."

"I'm sorry, sir," came the old-man voice of the fake gatekeeper who never seemed to be off duty at Menzies' fake castle—or rebuilt one, anyway. "I have orders not to accept visitors this evening." This was to be final, for he was even now closing the peephole without further ceremony.

Glass snatched his pen from his breast pocket and jammed it through the hole before it could be fully shut. "I'm not a visitor—I'm an employee. Jason Glass. You ought to know me by this time, damn it. It would be in Mr. Menzies' best interests to let me in. Miss Macgregor is with me as well."

The latter name seemed to give the man pause for a moment, but he denied them again. Then, with strength Glass had not expected the man possessed, he forced the pen back through the opening with the flat of his hand and shut the hole completely.

Glass uttered a curse he hoped Ann had not heard. "Stay here; I'll be right back." He turned to recross the causeway.

"No, Jason, I don't want to. I'll go with you." She kicked off her high-heeled shoes and trotted after him, her hair and dress blowing in the firm breeze of Loch Duich. Since she was essentially barefoot, Glass skipped the idea of sprinting to the inn several hundred yards back along the shore and used Sybil's Mercedes to drive that short distance. When he got back to the small village that rested on a promontory facing the castle, he passed quickly into The Sheepshead, Ann, still shoeless, right behind him, and found a pay phone next to the public bar. He had no coin. Ann did and gave it to him. The butler answered.

"This is Jason Glass. I would like to speak with Mr. Menzies, please."

"He wishes no callers tonight, Mr. Glass. Perhaps tomorrow you—"

"Look, chum"—Glass had been angry all day and was getting angrier still—"today is Thursday, June twenty-sixth. I have a plane ticket back to the States for Saturday the twenty-eighth. Which means I'm on the train in the morning. Tell Mr. Menzies that there is no tomorrow."

The butler went to relay this information and returned to say that Menzies would see Glass. They returned to the castle gate, where Ann retrieved her shoes. The gatekeeper, foiled, grudgingly admitted them. He hunch-shouldered ahead of them across the interior courtyard and led them up the narrow exterior staircase, the irregular snapping noise still issuing from somewhere below them.

Menzies met them in the Banqueting Room. He wore only a

dressing gown and slippers. Glass was surprised at this, especially given the fact that Ann was there.

"What is this I am told about your leaving, Glass?" Farquhar looked as if he had been asleep—he was more groggily annoyed than intellectually concerned. "You have only produced a fourth to a third of what we contracted." He was still oddly ignoring Ann's presence, as if she were a fixture or a decoration instead of a guest. "I found that work to be very acceptable but I want it finished."

Glass was so angry he could not contain himself. "Look, Mr. Menzies, I have a life of my own to keep together. Earlier this week I had planned to take all the Roberts crap back to America with me and mock up the lies there. But now I don't even plan to do that. This is a bad story from start to finish, Farquhar, and the more I find out about it the worse it gets. Yours is an evil bunch, sir, and I plan to get the hell out of here before I get further caught up with the lot of you, dead and alive."

Farquhar's florid face became redder still as he listened to Glass inveighing against him and his. "Now, here, here, Glass. Watch what you say."

"I will *not* watch what I say. We are going to have this out right now and I am going to be on the early train out of Kyle in the morning." He noticed Ann sitting quietly in the corner, her eyes to the floor, her hands folded in her lap. He had hoped she would join in with him, but it seemed now as if she were going to remain neutral. "Let's start from the top, Farquhar. To tell your story the way you want it, I have to condone, among other things, murder. I will not—"

"*Murder?*"

"Don't give me that sheep-dip, Farquhar; you know what's going on as well—"

"Speak clearly, man. What murder?"

"Maria De Jager, for one. I suspect Roberts, for another." He noticed Menzies' face react with disbelief to the first name, scorn to the second.

"Poppycock." The scorn had taken over. "Who are the murderers?"

"Do you really want to know, Farquhar? Then I will tell you, though believe me, it hurts to say this even to a Menzies. Maria was done in by your father and your great-grandfather, by means of the great Culloden cannon—which surely never killed anybody else, did it?—on the night of June twentieth, 1925." He recounted the circumstances, the evidence, to the point that Farquhar seemed unable to respond. It was clear to Glass, however, that all of this was new information.

"All right, Glass, I will have all that looked into. But now, Roberts. What proof do you have that Roberts was murdered?" The scorn was again overcoming the simple shock.

"I have none, Farquhar, and I am getting out of here before I bother to go looking for any—which I can't seem to help myself from doing so long as I stay here. You know the big 'grave' robbery several weeks ago? You know who did it? I did." He purposely omitted reference to Ann's and Duncan's roles in the matter. "Now, I have already proved to you that Maria De Jager's body—no, why don't we call her by her proper name, Maria Menzies—never got lucky enough to get into any grave; at least, any subsurface one. But there never was *any* human body in that grave at *any* time. There was a dog's body—a bit of research tells me that Maria had a sheepdog named Botha whom she acquired when she arrived in 1919 and who probably was her only other companion in The Gap than her one-armed, one-eyed, prematurely senile husband. Louis Botha was a foremost Boer general, Farquhar, who died in 1919—I would love to know whether, in naming the dog, she was out to memorialize him or screw the condescending Menzies who had relegated her to a small cottage ten miles from the center of clan action. Anyway, when Angus and Bruce staged the funeral for Maria De Jager, they had to bury something, so they probably killed the poor mutt and let its hundred-pound weight do the job in the nice wooden box they bought for her. And, as I said, there never was anything in Roberts' box because, unlike Maria's death, which was a secret between the two of them, everybody in the family knew the story about what had become of Roberts and no phony weights would have been needed."

"And just what *was* that story, Glass—about Roberts, I mean?" Glass knew that Menzies *did* have information on this one, was testing him to see what his score would be.

"I do not know the story, Farquhar. I presume we might drag the lakes and dredge up a few bones or maybe dig around your castle here—but fifty years is a long time to hope to still find anything." At this Menzies laughed, though it was more forced than hearty.

"Now let me tell you some other things, some of which you

may know, some I'll bet will be surprises. We did find one other thing in Maria's grave besides dog bones, and that was a diary—Maria's diary which she kept from the day her family set out for the Boer War in September, 1899, almost until the time of her death. I cannot figure out why Angus and Bruce would have buried it instead of destroying it; perhaps it was senility on Angus' part—he was seventy-seven then—or perhaps Bruce at twenty-five was still unjaded enough to bury at least some morsel of the human life he had cannoned apart. Maybe Angus' wife—who apparently was their sole champion in those years, a champion for nothing other than their human dignity, not even Roberts' claim to the clan chieftainship—perhaps she knew what her dear husband and grandson had done and slipped the diary in on them when they were drinking at the wake. She was dying herself then, and I suspect that that in itself provoked special sympathy with another of her ilk."

"And what tidbits have you gotten from the diary, Glass?" Menzies clearly had known of no diary and, though he pretended otherwise, was concerned about it. Glass decided to strike to the heart immediately.

"Well, Farquhar, to a great extent it fills in the gaps you yourself made in Roberts' diary—you see, I am convinced it *was* you, Farquhar, who did it. Let me summarize the good points for you."

Glass had received the second installment from Paul Krige just that morning, and he and Ann had read it the entire day, sitting tightly together against the lakeside rock, exclaiming to each other with each unsuspected piece of information. Glass had to admit that some of it even he, less good and naive than Ann, had not projected.

One of the most glaring omissions, or deletions, made in Roberts' diary had been nearly a week's worth of pages in mid-November which, on the basis of the information contained in Krige's translation of Maria's journal, turned out to be—probably—the record of an escape attempt Roberts had made in mid-November, 1899, about three weeks after the Siege of Ladysmith had begun. This, in fact, turned out to be the first occasion on which Roberts had encountered the De Jager family. Throughout these pages, Roberts Menzies is referred to, always, as Bob Menzy—presumably because, since there was only one of him, the Boers with their rudimentary English could not understand the pluralization of both names. Bob, of course, was a shorter, friendlier, more easily written name for Maria to handle in her diary. In Roberts' own diary, Farquhar, or whoever had censored it, must have felt that the act of escape looked like cowardice—here was a necessary doctor slipping out of the perimeter with a kaffir he had paid to guide him, leaving behind more than a hundred of his own patients and an ever-increasing number of wounded soldiers, not to mention a pregnant wife.

A patrolling commando, of which Maria's father and brother were a part, had left the immediate perimeter of Ladysmith after receiving a heliograph signal from Botha's forces to the south. He needed assistance in extending secure Boer territory beyond the Tugela River, to this point the natural barrier between British and Boer forces. Since the main British forces were still not entirely massed in Durban, and General Buller was still on his way by sea from Cape Town, Botha had decided that the British would have to fight their way to the Tugela rather than have that much geography given to them without resistance.

Roberts, of course, could not have known this, was himself probably assuming that he would reach safety once he had crossed the Tugela—which, within two days on foot from Ladysmith, he and his kaffir did. According to what Menzies told the Boers who later captured him, he immediately became aware that he still was far from safe, so he discharged his kaffir and proceeded south along the railway through Colenso and Chieveley, destined ultimately, he claimed, for the hospital at Pietermaritzburg. He did not walk the tracks—he kept to the hills around them, but never out of sight of them, for they were his sole guide.

And he probably would have made it, but he was undone by his own people. Steaming north that day came a British train with a locomotive and six cars attached containing a forward observation team of several British officers and noncoms and a couple of newspaper correspondents. The train was so far north, in fact, that Menzies presumed that he was now in space the British Army had tightly secured. He was not. Rather, when he ran to the tracks to flag the train down and travel back with it to Pietermaritzburg, he was told by a correspondent that at his own urging, they had probed farther north than they probably should have. Within the next couple of hours, virtually everyone on the train, Roberts included, had been taken prisoner. Though he was not named in Maria's diary, Glass knew exactly who the correspondent involved was because of the similarity of the details of this encounter to another description of it he had already read in his general research on the Boer War. It was Winston Churchill.

Not clear from Maria's diary was why Roberts was sent—indeed, escorted—back to Ladysmith while Churchill was shipped off to prison in Pretoria, a prison he escaped a short time thereafter. Perhaps it was a humanitarian gesture on the Boers' part, though they refused Menzies' request on the spot for medical supplies. (Ann had been gratified to see the beginnings of her interpretation of Roberts' ultimate "trade" taking shape.) Perhaps it was the reverse—they wanted everyone inside the perimeter the way a zookeeper wants all his animals in a cage. Perhaps it was Maria's doing. This was the British man she wanted. It is also not clear whether Roberts' escape attempt was an act of cowardice or an attempt to get supplies back from Pietermaritzburg before the actual fighting for the relief of Ladysmith began. Maria did record much discussion and questioning done by her father in which Roberts catalogued supplies he needed—bandages, iodoform, medicines of various sorts. It was interesting, however, to Glass that according to Maria, Roberts spoke continually of the "sick," never of the wounded. Glass was not sure, however, whether or not Krige in translating had been concerned with what might seem to him a fine distinction but was, actually, a large one. The "sick" were the hundred-and-one patients Roberts had blackmailed the British army into removing from Dundee the week after the war started; the "wounded" were the soldiers who were trying to fight their way out, the ones Army doctors took care of. That same curious dichotomy which Glass had discovered in the early pages of Roberts' edited diary continued to persist even in Maria's.

After Roberts had been returned to Ladysmith in late November, he became a familiar face to the De Jagers. At first it was just on the battlefield during the white-flagged mop-up operations in the evening as each side buried its dead and carried back its wounded. The Boers were quite gentlemanly about this. But then other meetings began to appear in Maria's diary. Oddly, Roberts turned up at a Sunday religious service—which itself was not unheard of, for a certain extramilitary camaraderie had developed between some members of the besieging forces, there with their women and children, and some of the besieged, there alone, familyless, otherwise forlorn. The Boers were not a fighting people, and they just could not keep up the sham twenty-four hours a day—ten or twelve for sure, but not all the time. On two such occasions, when Roberts had slipped out by means Maria could not or just did not describe, he attempted again to negotiate for the ever-needed medical supplies, always without success. At one point he offered to spend one day a week treating Boer casualties and sickness and, incredibly, was rebuked by Maria's father for treasonous conduct to his own side. Boers on the whole were reputed to be a terribly moral race, but the extent of this stunned Glass. So they would not then have suggested or even agreed to the codebook exchange which later eventuated.

Maria's diary was never specific on the matter, but Ann and Glass had stopped to discuss it as they sat against the rock on the lakeshore reading the translation that afternoon. As the main British forces began moving north in late November and early December, winning all the minor skirmishes in thinly held Boer positions south of the Tegula, it became clear that the British would have to be stopped at the major natural barrier they had to cross for the relief of Ladysmith—the twisting Tugela River and the sheer upgrade they would encounter once, and if, they had crossed it. The question in the Boer camps as mid-December approached, the end of the rainy spring and the start of the bitterly hot South African summer, was *where* they would try it. Yet suddenly General Louis Botha *knew* where they would try it and, on December 15, was fully in position behind the tin-roofed river town of Colenso. Within two hours that auspicious Friday morning, he had routed the British troops back toward Frere, had inflicted a thousand casualties, had captured Colonel Long's guns, had mortally wounded Field Marshal Lord Roberts' oldest son, and had set the relief of Ladysmith back by months.

Somehow Botha had known too much too soon, had a strategy for victory mapped out that could have been stolen from the map rooms of Aldershot and, in the long run, probably had been. It must have been Botha who had accepted the codebooks, an officer not so much less honorable than the De Jagers but one who, to quote the Boer phrase of the early war, recognized "when the hand of God was being extended to him" and, unlike General Joubert two months earlier, was not to be satisfied with taking a finger alone. And Maria would have had a personal reason to go to Botha with what she called "English strategy books," though apparently she never understood that all these books contained the means to see through the heliographic and searchlight messages, not the whole grand design itself. Her own brother was to fight at Colenso, as was her heretofore "lover" Christiaan, and she thought she could save them. History had to this point accepted that someone in General Buller's relieving forces had accidentally or purposely tipped the British hand at Colenso. It seemed now, however, to have been done from within Ladysmith by a British doctor who was either a great, if misguided, humanitarian or an obsessed monomaniac. And it was done through a Boer girl who was either a devoted sister and girlfriend or an opportunist eager to find any way at all to establish an ongoing liaison with the British doctor who was to replace the Boer lover she had and the mythical red-coated soldier she had concocted.

Nor did she mention her *romantic* liaison with Roberts at all, but near Christmastime she suspected she was pregnant. At first Glass and Ann thought this was the too-quick misestimation of a high-veld Boer girl who had little knowledge of the laws of nature or even of her own body. But, as later pages proved, she was accurate. No other men but Roberts were mentioned, and Christiaan had been removed to the Tugela in late November and had, ironically, been killed at Colenso after all. This death, amidst reflections of "Bob Menzy," was barely noted in Maria's diary. Christiaan was, after all, "a homely man of the Boer race." Roberts, still whole, was not.

She could not, of course, tell any of this to her Calvinist family or to Boer doctors who would tell them for her. In a vaguely worded passage dated Christmas Day, mixed in with an odd account of the Boers' loading their cannon with tins of plum puddings and shelling them into the heart of Ladysmith with affectionately ironic greeting cards for the besieged town, she mentions telling Roberts about her problem and, apparently but unclearly, Roberts suggesting that he could "have me not have the baby, since he was a doctor." Yet this abortion was never again referred to in this section of the diary, and Roberts, though his name is mentioned frequently, did not reappear in the Boer camp for several weeks. As Ann had pointed out that afternoon as they read, the reason for this was obvious, though perhaps Maria did not know it: on December 28—just three days after the abortion plan was hatched—Catherine Clyde Menzies, "the best of us," Henrietta had called her, gave birth to her own son—Bruce—and a week later, on January 2, 1900, died of now-rampant enteric fever. Not only did Maria not know any of this: it seemed that she was totally unaware that Roberts had a wife, pregnant no less, with him *in* Ladysmith or, even, that he was married. With his wife close to term, locked up in Ladysmith with women who were mostly dying or at least very sick, Roberts' libido seemed to have yielded to this buxom, clearly ready Boer girl.

Then, in the entry for January 17, 1900, Roberts' first return to the De Jager camp atop the mighty Umbulwana, from which the Boers commanded the little town below them, is graphically portrayed. Maria describes herself as being torn between aborting the baby and insisting that Roberts marry her, of fleeing the Ladysmith perimeter together and going then to England to forget about the war in particular, South Africa in general. But Roberts had two main problems with this. First, the idealistic streak which he could never, no matter what he did, seem to quash said that he should stay with his patients. The searchlights advertised another offensive from across the Tugela—to both the British and the Boers, of course—and his record for keeping his patients alive was exceptional (thanks in great part to his private supply of medicine). Perhaps the "idealistic" is also properly termed the monomaniacal side. Then there was the practical Roberts Menzies, the one who was the schemer, the rule bender, the traitor: this Roberts Menzies had a three-week-old motherless son whom he needed away from the typhoid, the enteric fever, the malnutrition.

So they struck a deal—Glass's glossing, not Maria's phrasing. Yes, her diary said, "Bob" would marry her, would give her son his name, in return for a favor that would benefit them both. Maria does not recount the particulars of the scene in which Roberts revealed to her both his dead wife and his still-living baby son—the entry for Thursday, January 18, suddenly just admits to it. More exciting to this Boer girl is his ultimate proposition:

Bob said we would marry as soon as both of us reached England but that I would have to go there first, that he had a professional duty to his patients in Ladysmith until its relief. But the British forces advance and fight so clumsily I fear it will never be relieved, leaving him down there for years and us up here on Umbulwana. What foolishness this all is. I will do as he asks. I will take his living son, Bruce, away with me and our unborn son, whom I will name Piet after my brother and General Joubert, and we will flee to England and wait for him there. He is not a soldier doctor so he can leave Africa as soon as Ladysmith is relieved and his patients can be taken to Pietermaritzburg. He will come tomorrow with money for me and a place for me to go when I get to England.

On Friday, January 19, Roberts did indeed show up: not just with an address, which at this point in the diary Maria does not bother to mention, and not just with money—though somehow he had come up with a hundred pounds in gold sovereigns—but also with a three-week-old male child who never ceased crying in hunger, Maria said, until she had found him another breast than her own to nurse at. She was not clear on the details of this, but she apparently tried her own and later struck a deal, another one, with a Boer woman whose own child had recently died at birth.

She apparently kept the child a secret from her own family for yet another week, leaving him probably in the care of the woman who was nursing him. Then in the entry for Friday, January 26, 1900, she speaks of appropriating a wagon from the stock of those whose owners had perished in battle, of sneaking out of camp before daybreak (and she had apparently not seen Roberts since the day he had entrusted his son to her), and setting out on the road by which she, her family, and other families had come from Pretoria. This would not have been hard to do once she had crept away from her own family, for Boer soldiers and their families frequently left the siege lines to go home on *huis-toe* to plant crops or for any other reason that suited them. It was not illegal—all Boers were volunteer soldiers for the length of their desire to stay and fight. Many had already left, in fear or boredom, and never returned, even close neighbors of the De Jagars at home in Tuinplaas. She, the month-old Bruce Menzies, and her two-month fetus had made their escape.

And now the diary entries became ever so summarial and brief. The idle girl no longer had time to be scribbling; she had stepped into the life she had so far just planned and fantasized about, knew she would have to endure several months of hardship to earn the life of happiness that seemed, now, within her reach if she extended her arm far enough. The hand of God had reached out to her individually now, and she planned to reach hard to grasp it. She got to Johannesburg on Sunday and rested in a hotel there overnight. In the morning she bought a rail ticket eastward and reached Lourenço Marques, on the Indian Ocean, on the morning of February 6.

Here she was stalled for nearly a week seeking passage on any ship headed west around the Cape that would take her. She was recognized as a Boer by virtually every British captain or sympathizer she encountered, and passage was denied her despite the fact that she was claiming to be a British officer's wife returning to England with their newly born son. She recounts long periods of sickness each morning, something she could look upon as another extension of God's hand in that it made her not want to eat and she was able to spend more money on feeding Bruce Menzies. Finally, on Tuesday, February 12, she bribed a cabin boy on a British freighter to slip her on board for the ship's passage to Durban. At the height of summer, she slept in a horizontal storage compartment just below the main deck, sweating profusely, mopping Bruce's brow as she again tried to feed him from her as-yet-unfilled breast. When they reached Durban on the fourteenth, the boy allowed her to stay between decks, for another ten pounds sterling, for the three-day passage to Cape Town. On the seventeenth she disembarked unfed, unwashed, clutching Bruce Menzies weakly to her belly, tight against the other child, who might or might not now ever get to be born. She heard at the docks of a British troop ship which had discharged five thousand soldiers and was taking dependents away from the war zone back to England. She had no papers and at first was denied passage; but she found a Red Cross worker to whom she told the entire truth, and the Red Cross worker had heard one word—just one word—that could get Maria De Jager passage with or without papers. That word was *Ladysmith*. Anyone who had escaped Ladysmith, especially a woman carrying a six-week-old baby, was a national hero by definition. Not only was Maria accepted now as a passenger, she was celebrated. She constantly feared, her diary shows, that her minimal English would be what would finally expose her for what she was—a member of the siege force, not of the besieged as she was pretending to be. However, enough British officers had married Boer women in South Africa over the last several decades that she was not, by definition at least, an anomaly.

She reached England on the H.M.S. *Tantallon Castle* in the

early morning of Thursday, March 1, 1900, underclad because it was winter there. It was five weeks since she had stolen the wagon on Umbulwana, six since Roberts had entrusted her with his son. She was given a warm coat, threadbare though it was, by the Salvation Army post at the Southampton Docks and placed on a special train for Waterloo Station before seven o'clock that morning along with all the other women and children evacuated from South Africa. And so, in the drizzle of a winter dawn, she saw the fabled England for the first time, green in some places, raw in others, terribly wet. The train rolled quickly over the Sussex Downs and she fell asleep as it sped on for Waterloo Station, suddenly finding herself in the drone-echoing canopy of this most enormous of all London railheads. And when she detrained, she saw more people in one tight place than she had ever seen in her entire life—not just the incoming passengers and those trying to be outgoing ones, but crowds who just stood packed together, milling about, crushing into one another so badly that she describes having to carry Bruce Menzies above her head and being unable to defend or protect the unborn baby in her womb. And the crowd was yelling, cheering, and singing—"God Save the Queen" and a new song called "Marching to Pretoria." Those people who could move were shoving in the direction of newsboys who stood atop baggage carts and could have sold more papers than they had, could have charged triple the price for the ones they did have—and, in fact, were doing so—and Maria De Jager, in what minimal English she could read, knew what the three-inch-high headlines in the *Daily Mail* said:

LADYSMITH RELIEVED!!
Buller Joins White at Town Hall
Tales of Disease and Malnutrition
At Boer Hands Proliferate.

But the crowd in Waterloo Station did not wish to hear those tales—Ladysmith was relieved, soon Mafeking would follow suit, and the time to crush the Boers was at hand.

As Jason Glass recounted this tale for the mute Farquhar Menzies, with Ann Macgregor sitting quietly in a corner of the Banqueting Room, fifteen feet from either man, Glass found himself entering the summarial part of this portion of the story, the very part that had sent him driving too fast for the narrow Loch roads that night between Loch Killilan and the Castle Menzies, that had had him pounding on the front gate demanding entrance and finally threatening on the phone to leave entirely if he did not get it. Now he would ram home the *coup de grâce* so that with luck, perhaps a Menzies, even a Menzies, could understand what it truly meant to be one.

"So now, Farquhar, she reached into her purse or pocket or wherever she carried it and discovered that the address Roberts had given her was not in England at all; it was in Scotland, in Glasgow, on Gallowgate Road. So she asked whoever would answer amidst the jubilant throng, and found out that you got to Glasgow by crossing the heart of London and boarding still another train at still another station, called Euston and not Waterloo this time. So she loaded whatever she had her earthly possessions in into a hackney coach and probably had to pay the driver extra to carry her and Bruce to Euston Station because the celebrating crowds in the streets were jamming the crossroads. But she got there and probably found the cost of a ticket to Glasgow higher than she had ever thought a ticket on a train to anywhere cost. And she nursed Bruce again with her still-unsupplied breasts, probably trying to hide in a corner of a third-class car so that she would not offend this civilized nation she was in with what she had to do to keep the travel-weary child alive. So she got finally to the flat on Gallowgate Road, and I still do not know how Roberts came to send her to that one, and she set up housekeeping there, in a land whose language she only partially understood, with young Bruce Menzies first, then later with a Menzies we did not know about until now called Piet. Then, she waited for Roberts to get back.

"But Roberts did not get back for another eighteen or nineteen years! That's your Roberts, Farquhar, deserting the woman upon whom he had fathered an illegitimate son and who had saved his legitimate one, undoubtedly one of the few babies born during the Siege of Ladysmith to get out alive! And then, Farquhar, and then, twenty-five years, three months, and nineteen days later, Bruce Menzies—resentful, hate-filled, drunk, in command of an ancient cannon with five shots left for the day, wheeled that cannon across the lake at the height of the most frightening storm the district can recall. He knew that this woman who had saved him would have to take refuge on higher ground from rising waters, waited till she got there, with no more than her dog to keep her company (which is not to say even *protect* her). And then he fired four cannon shots at the house in which she was holed up, missing once, missing twice, missing thrice, but—probably because a lightning bolt had lit his target for him or because his grandfather who was helping him had fired this cannon for over a half-century and would not miss four in a row—he hit with the fourth, toppling a wall and a roof upon her. And so ends the story of Maria De Jager—no, Maria Menzies."

Farquhar was terribly shaken, but not out of control. "An amazing tale, Glass, edited at least as heavily as the diaries I gave you to start with. By your own admission you have only part of this woman's diary. You omit convenient details. Yes. So she brought my father out of Ladysmith all the way to Glasgow. I obviously owe her my own existence, don't I? But five years later, in 1905 if I am correct, she nailed that same child up in a common dog's shipping crate and mailed him to Angus, leaving him without food or water for the two days he was in transit." Farquhar was shouting now, on the verge of standing up from his chair to pace the floor in his slippers and robe. "Never until today did *I* know how this had all come about—but now I do. I am not sure my father *ever* knew. Maria was a stranger to him when she came here in 1919 with Roberts."

"I doubt that. The memory forgets nothing, Farquhar. It may have taken months or years for young Bruce's associative memories to join with his present perceptions, but I am sure they must have. He hated Roberts for deserting him, her for doing the same thing when his father proved unreliable.

"She was a vain young girl, Farquhar, who, under pressure, discovered a heroic streak in herself which she exploited for the benefit of at least four different people. Some of us start weak and find strength—like Maria; others of us start strong and discover weakness—like Roberts. It is unfortunate that the weak side, first or last, usually winds up in control in the long run. Yes, she reverted to type and shipped Bruce in a dog crate—not to hurt Bruce, but to gesture obscenely at Roberts, whom she had not heard from in five years. I can't tell you much about his five years from 1900 until 1905, Farquhar—for one thing, he couldn't have worked into Maria's diary much; for another, you subtracted the pages from his that would have told me."

"All right, then, do you wish to have a summary? I'll give it to you; then I'll give you all the missing pages so you can check it for yourself." He was still shouting as he vaulted from his chair and crossed to a bookcase in a far corner of the Banqueting Room and removed a loosely gathered, rattily dog-eared stack of papers from a top row of books. He stalked back across the room, his robe flapping broadly despite the presence of Ann, and tossed these flatly on Glass's lap. "Take them home; read them all."

"I'm leaving for America tomorrow."

"I doubt that." They stared at each other menacingly for a moment; then Menzies continued. "After Ladysmith was relieved, Roberts transported his patients by train to Pietermaritzburg."

"I know that—you left those pages in. Don't toot his horn. Get up to December, 1900, where the whole thing just about stops in my copy."

"Yes, that *is* the most significant omission, isn't it. Yes, when Lord Kitchener took to burning farms to force the submission of the Boer guerrillas who were holding out despite the capture of Pretoria the previous June, Roberts disavowed allegiance to the British Government there. He became a doctor with a roving guerrilla band and was soon not only repairing the scoundrels but firing upon his own countrymen who were trying to bring peace and order."

Glass felt as if he wanted to laugh at the ironies now, but he did not. "So Maria had junked the Boers for the life of British ease she had anticipated; Roberts rejected the comfort in favor of the principle the Boers were now fighting for. The deeper you look, the darker it gets."

"I don't know what his principles were, Glass, but I do know that he temporarily lost his mind. He attests in those pages on your lap to having participated in the demolition of the three different blockhouses manned by six British soldiers apiece along Kitchener's barbed-wire lines. When he regained his senses, he left the service of those illegal forces and took up residence in the concentration camp at Bloemfontein, in the Orange Free State. His experience at Ladysmith was apparently invaluable to both the British and the Boers in treating the same dysentery and typhoid and malnutrition among Boer women and children that had existed during the siege. He was still there when the whole blasted war finally ended in May of '02. He did some good, apparently." Menzies quieted now. He seemed weary.

"All things to all men," Glass mused. "So why now did he not come home?"

"I can't answer that. His diary ceased with the war, except for several random and meaningless entries made over the next one or two years. You have those pages, not I. What does Maria's version say?" For the first time Farquhar appeared to really want to know.

"The translator has not completed those pages yet. I'll know in a week, I expect. I do know, however, that somewhere along the line he met up with the Boer general who surrendered Paardeberg to Kitchener and Lord Roberts back in March of 1900—Piet Cronje. They went to America together in 1904 and staged a shoot-'em-up act at the St. Louis World's Fair for a while." Now Glass recalled something else. "Say, you know the left arm that Roberts supposedly lost in World War One? He didn't lose it there. A friend of mine saw a picture of him at the St. Louis Fair; he didn't have it then either."

Farquhar was truly surprised by this. "Read all the pages you have there, Glass. Nowhere does Roberts account for the loss of his arm during the Boer War. Surely he would have mentioned it, would he not? It has to have happened between May 1902 and whatever day in 1904 the picture you mention was taken."

A long silence ensued now. Finally Ann rose from her chair and walked to Jason's. "Let us be on our way, Jason. This has been a long night."

Glass stood wearily, though Menzies continued to sit. Glass tossed the diary pages unceremoniously back into Farquhar's lap. "As I said, I won't be needing those. I'll be on my way in the morning."

"And as *I* said, I doubt that." Still very quiet, almost defeated. "We can yet come up with some version of this whole thing which will satisfy both of us."

"I doubt *that*. But I'm not interested in any event." He offered his hand to shake once before they parted. Menzies ignored it.

"Your wife is a very crafty woman, Glass." Menzies looked at the floor.

Glass's heart literally jumped at this. "My wife? Margot?"

"Yes. She wrote me, you see. To discredit you in my eyes. But actually, her letter had the reverse effect. She showed me exactly how good you are—in making poor excuses for mortals become immortal in the end."

Glass was very nervous now. "Just what in the hell do you mean?"

"She told me of the work of an American professor named Feldman and a student of his. It seems that they have gone back into the records of the company which bought out Phalon and Son and have determined that no one named Annie Daly ever worked there. So they pursued a number of other Annie Dalys who lived in New York at the time—found something like a dozen, I'm told—then were able to find one such person who not only had the required number of siblings—seven, wasn't it? —but who lived at an address adjoining another in which the young Mr. Phalon's secretary lived. The further they pursued this, Jason, the worse it got, you see. Pity, too."

"What is it that's a pity?" Ann had spoken for him when she saw Glass all but frozen at the center of the room. She was firm, highly annoyed, speaking more directly to Menzies than Glass would have presumed was diplomatic.

"Annie Daly's the pity. They also have proved that this same girl died in the same year as your Annie Daly did—1894, correct? You see, she must have been given Phalon and Son stationery to launch herself on a career which might have been more respectable than the one with which she had until then been advancing her family's fortunes. That string of temporary employment your book wades through, Glass, is apparently going to turn out to be entirely fabricated. She had virtually only one money-making occupation throughout her adult years, and as a result she caught the clap, shall we call it, and died. So you see once again the dangers, do you not, of relying too heavily on people's personal diaries and on fond recollections of those who stand to benefit by recollecting fondly? There is only one way Annie Daly can now be saved, and hence only one way Jason Glass can be saved from the attendant embarrassment."

"And that is?" Again it was Ann who spoke. She glowered at Menzies as if she already knew.

"I am prepared to offer Professor Feldman five thousand pounds to suppress what he has found. In fact, I have already initiated contact, and he has sent me an outline of his proofs. You will find photocopies of that material at the bottom of this stack of papers." He extended the missing pages of Roberts Menzies' diary and the missing information about Annie Daly at arm's length toward Glass. Glass let them hang there, suspended in space. "You will not have to repay me the five thousand pounds or even say thank you. All you will have to do is—"

Now Ann crossed the room and snapped all the pages from his grasp. "Yes, I'm sure he knows what you will expect." She turned her back to him with almost symbolic forthrightness, took Glass by the arm, and led him from the room without further remark.

18 ROBERTS ALONE

FRIDAY MORNING GLASS TRIED SEVERAL TIMES to bring himself to cancel his airline reservation, but each time he approached the phone he caught sight of his haggard face in the mirror above the sideboard and could not do it. When Ann called at noon, she asked him if he had, then told him she would take care of it, said also that she would be at The Angus Bull after nine that evening if he cared to meet her there. She admitted she was not sure he would be up to it, and he admitted he was unsure himself.

Yet, at nine thirty, he did. He had sat at his typewriter the entire day, writing what about what he could not plan from moment to moment. He started a letter to Margot, but he realized it was on its way to being highly "publishable" and so destroyed it. Then he began again on the placebo version of the Roberts Menzies story, found the prose ridden with syntactical clumsiness, bland word choices, and unmitigated lies—but he did not destroy it, for every page completed, no matter how wretched, was one step closer to the end. He tried a letter to his agent to suggest the latest information on Annie Daly, but here it was the truth, not lies, that backed him down. Glass felt almost nauseated when he realized that now he could live with neither the truth about anything nor the lies. Making some tentative decision, to be in effect for at least the day, Glass decided that lies, since concocted, could be more easily dispensed with than truth, and so decided to pursue truth for at least a while. Which he consciously thought at first to mean he would return to writing the real version of Roberts Menzies with the latest information from Maria De Jager's diary, but which produced no more than a list of various things that truth suggested. When he slid onto the bench next to Ann, who had successfully saved him at least half a seat against the Friday-night throng, he tossed the list on the table before her. He was too tired, too dejected to rise to buy himself a beer. Young Peebles noted this from another table and bought and delivered one to him.

The list read:

MENZIES VICTIMS

1. Maria De Jager—murdered
2. Elizabeth Menzies—driven mad
3. Catherine McPherson Menzies—prematurely dead, of exposure
4. Owen Menzies—killed in war
5. Henrietta Menzies—turned hermit
6. Duncan Menzies—born retarded
7. Annette Macgregor—suicide
8. Piet (De Jager) Menzies—abandoned by his father
9. Roberts Menzies—unclassifiable!
10. Jason Glass—generally defeated

Glass had intended to place himself last on the list—the climax, the innocent sacrificial victim who had just happened upon this whole mess; but suddenly the list extended itself:

11. Angus Menzies—failed by his oldest son
12. Margaret Menzies—witness to internecine warfare among three generations
13. Catherine Clyde Menzies—taken to South Africa, impregnated, killed by circumstance
14. Bruce Menzies—fatherless, shipped home by his stepmother in a dog crate, whole life consumed by bitterness and hatred, killed in war (perhaps wanted to be)
15. Clyde Menzies—just isn't "up to it"
16. Sybil Macgregor Menzies—isn't either
17. Hamilton Macgregor—lost his "son" to the war, failed in his lifelong research
18. Ann Macgregor—adrift

He had also compiled a list of victimizers, but he began to find many of the names from his first list reappearing on his second —at which point that endeavor became so tangled and confused that he destroyed it. He concluded finally that "things" were at fault, that no one on the whole chart of Menzies that Henrietta had given him, nor the one extra name—Piet's—that she did not know about, nor Jason Glass (who did not belong in the Menzies genealogy), nor other names which could be added as well—no one was a nonvictim. To the extent that one victim was also a victimizer, it was, had to be, simple reflex against those who seemed to have victimized him. It was all so mechanistic that no one could be blamed for being himself a mere spring or wheel.

He could not tell what Ann's reaction was to this cheery piece of work as she read it, but he knew from the start that she was trying to pick him up, would react in as upbeat a fashion as she possibly could. She even laughed slightly when she read the word *adrift* next to her own name.

"Would you mind, Jason, explaining how it is that I am 'adrift'? You make me sound as if I were a loose woman." She was fairly yelling this above the roar of the pubroom, though it came across almost as a whisper to Glass's ear not two feet away.

"I should have erased it before I showed you all that. Maybe I shouldn't have shown it to you at all. What I meant is that you spent the first two dozen years of your life being the dutiful daughter, to the extent that dutiful daughtering took you all the way through medical school before you no longer had to dutiful-daughter because all of a sudden you were no longer a daughter. So, at twenty-six, you seek the role you wish for yourself, think it to be an editor in a London publishing house, yet you seem to flee London at every chance you get. You are beautiful but unmarried, and are now getting yourself smeared with Menzies crap for reasons which are basically contradictory and which you barely understand."

She was silent on this for several minutes—a silence that was hardly meaningful, for silence in this room was absorbed like a dewdrop.

"Jason, if your list reveals anything for me, it is that I am a better person than I had heretofore credited myself with being."

"Ha, ha. Ann, I have at long last won a single victory in Scotland. I have been trying to convince you of that for weeks, now, haven't I?" He leaned over and kissed her ring, not entirely in mockery.

"Now, Jason, at least see my point despite your jesting. Though I am glad to see you jest for a change. All I meant was that seeing life as a tangle of unrelated threads—perhaps a spiderweb, as Schopenhauer's metaphor would have it be—I decided, without knowing I was even deciding, that it was the response one made *to* life which counted, *not* the foolish plan we all think we have *for* life. Circumstances are what they are, Jason; they cannot be changed. With a medical degree in hand that I no longer had any use for, I simply responded by trying some other positive course, whether or not it was the right one. Which it probably was not. But analyze your victims list. Classify the sorts of responses you have there. Am I not at least as adept at responding as anyone else, perhaps better than most?"

Glass put his hand on her knee. She wore a black skirt of a shiny material which played erotically on her stocking below it. "Well, I suppose I'll rate you higher than Bruce and Angus—at least you did not wheel out a cannon and gun down an enemy which could be no more than symbolic, a scapegoat for every frustration life coughs up. Yes, you did better than that."

Ann caught the forced irony in his voice, but she was still insisting that her point be recognized for what it was. "Yes, and I could have committed suicide; I could have toyed with madness; I could have made myself available for what your list terms 'premature death'; I could have taken down my pants and made myself available to anyone who wanted me, for recreation alone or for money"—she saw Glass wince almost imperceptibly at the latter implication—"or, like you, I could write myself off as 'generally defeated.' Instead, I tried to make a constructive response. Who else on your list of wrecked lives has—except my father?"

"Ann, once again, I would love to put you atop that list of wonderful company you have previously tried to convince me does not exist. And I will. And I will put your father there as well; but it seems to me that perhaps Angus' wife and the noble Catherine Clyde—one even hates to admit that she had become a Menzies, doesn't one?—also belong there. Owen and Duncan can be removed entirely, just because they did not have much chance to try."

"Yes, *try* is the word, Jason, isn't it?" She was becoming a bit shrill, both in her insistence and in her attempts to have Glass hear her over the din. "Certain of us are fortunate to have the opportunity to *try*, and so, unlike certain others of us"—she slanted her eyes directly into Glass's—"we therefore do. We *respond* rather than, like certain others of us, *react*."

"I am a reactor, I take it?"

"Not in essence, just in performance. Respond. If Annie Daly turns out to have been a whore, stand forth and admit it. Go from there, wherever that has to be! If there is something to be said to the world in getting Roberts' story right, say it! You list him here"—she tapped the victims list sharply—"as unclassifiable. Classify him, damn it. God, Jason, can't you see by this point that Roberts is, after all, the most interesting and, in the long run, valuable person on your list? Not in the way Farquhar means it; in the way I mean it." She clasped both his hands on the table. "Whom do we know more conflicting facts about, and who has a better record of both responding and reacting? Whom have we encountered who did more clear-cut good, and who likewise did more banal self-serving things, than anyone else? Roberts. That is why he is important—he is the worst of us all and the best. Which is why we can't figure him out, and why we can't figure ourselves out."

"I am not ready to deify even half of him yet, Ann. The dirt and the snow were soaked together in every action he apparently ever performed."

"Oh, yes, Jason," she replied with a good deal of cynicism, "there undoubtedly will even turn up something virtuous about his trekking off to St. Louis after the war to sign autographs instead of home to his family. You see, he was probably just as big an attraction as Piet Cronje there. Who else—not even Cronje himself—could say that he had endured the great Siege of Ladysmith? No one else in St. Louis, Missouri, that's for certain! But Jason, be patient; something 'good' will turn up about that. Just as something 'bad' will turn up about the way he lost his eye and his arm—which I now know about."

"You *know*?"

"Yes, I do. As of one o'clock today."

"Even before you tell me how it happened, tell me how you found out!"

"You see, I read a book called *Gratuitous Glory*. What I learned there is that battlefield heroism and battlefield cowardice are immortalized in the words of the common soldier who has never demonstrated particularly great amounts of either. So

I went through the local Army records until I found the names of ten other men from the Lochs who served in South Africa. None was still alive, of course, but *two* families had an oral tradition of a British doctor who was known to be serving with Boer guerrilla groups and who lost an arm. The details I received from both a family in Ullapool and another in Kinlochewe were the same. Neither had a name for the doctor, of course, but both match awfully well with facts we already know about Roberts." She looked tremendously satisfied with herself.

Glass, with the fading picture of Annie Daly in his mind, decided to rule cautiously on what she had discovered. "Tell me, then." He was openly suspicious.

Ann reached into the large handbag she frequently carried with her, a bag that was a cross between a large purse and a briefcase and was large enough to carry a number of manuscripts; rooted for a moment; then produced a handwritten letter from the correspondent in Ullapool. She handed it to Glass, and he read it, concentrating on it intently despite the riproar of the packed pub.

25 June 1975

Dear Miss Macgregor,

Thank you for yours of the 23rd. Yes, my grandfather, Thomas Douglas, did indeed participate in the Boer War from 1901 until it ended in 1902. He never used the word "fight" because he was one of those poor unfortunate soldiers who were assigned by Lord Kitchener to man the blockhouses which were erected to trap roving bands of Boer guerrillas. According to Grandfather Thomas, very few were ever caught near his station and the lines of barbed wire strung between them were a greater problem for him and his mates than for the Boers.

There was one terrifying story he had to tell, in fact told many times, that may well relate to the person you are interested in. It happened near Klerksdorp in the western Transvaal near the Orange Free State border. Since there were usually six or seven soldiers and three native sentries assigned to a blockhouse, which you may know was no more than two circular corrugated water tanks set inside one another with the space between them filled with gravel and a canopy over the top, the men spent as much time outside them as the sun would allow. It was not unusual for them to stray in twos or threes down the fence line, often as far as the next blockhouse to inquire whether the boredom there was different in kind or degree. According to Grandfather, it never was.

One day while walking back from a neighboring blockhouse, my grandfather and another chap encountered a man whose name they did not remember, if indeed they ever asked it, but he was Scottish and he was a medical man. He claimed to be lost with a contingent of patients whom he was attempting to move to the British military hospital at Bloemfontein, so Grandfather advised him of the proper route and even parted the wire so that he could bring his ambulances through. A half-hour later, when the wagons appeared on the veld, they turned out to belong instead to the Boer guerrilla fighter Christiaan De Wet, with whom this Scots traitor had apparently aligned himself. The so-called "patients" were actually some Boer families whose farms had recently been burned as a result of Kitchener's scorched-earth campaign to bring the Boer bandits to their knees. De Wet and several of his men came through the wire lines firing, killing Grandfather's companion and badly wounding him. The gunfire attracted the soldiers of the two nearest blockhouses to the scene, and a skirmish ensued. Several men, women, and children were killed on the scene, but De Wet managed to get the larger part of his group through by hiding them at the bottoms of wagons and beating the horses—which turned out to be stolen British mounts and not the starving Boer animals—as hard as he could. Outnumbered, on foot, and fearful of being led into one of the Boers' notorious box-canyon traps, the soldiers elected not to pursue.

And here, Miss Macgregor, is the truly gruesome part. The Scotsman was struck in the cheek by a bullet—actually in the lower part of an eye socket, or so Grandfather said. When he staggered backward from the impact, he fell into the tangle of barbed wire which had been loosened for his passage. His left arm became hopelessly ensnarled in it, so much so that flesh and muscle were being torn from it each time he tried to pull himself free—except that there was no pulling free, for each coil he escaped simply led to another coil beyond it. Grandfather spoke as often of the man's bravery as of his treachery, however, for he never uttered a cry of pain, despite the situation his arm was in and despite the fact that his right eye was a pool of blood!

So anxious were the soldiers to get their own wounded to care that they overlooked the Scotsman and his predicament. As Grandfather was being removed from the veld in a captured wagon, he said he could watch the doctor for quite some time. As soon as the British soldiers left the scene of the fracas, the vultures arrived. Grandfather often spoke of the horror of vultures stripping the meat from a dead horse, so the sight of them at work upon humans must have been devastating. Grandfather could never forget what he saw that day—not only the awful creatures croaking maliciously at each other as they fought over the "best" morsel, the attack upon the necks and the eyes of their victims, the flapping wings which beat continually to ensure their sole command of their food, the chalky white excreta which they voided even as they continued to eat—but also (perhaps if anything more terrible still) the sight of a living man, not twenty feet from these vicious creatures, his arm being stripped of its flesh and tissue as cleanly as if the vultures themselves were doing it. Still worse was the sight of this poor creature, traitor though he was, forced to employ his medical skill to amputate his own arm just below the shoulder, with no other painkiller than fear!

Miss Macgregor, this story has haunted both my youth and now my middle age. At first I did not wish to retell it, but now I note I have retold it even at length. For all the instinctive reaction against a traitor I have always had, I could not but pity, even admire, the man—his ability to endure pain in the most frightening situation imaginable; the way he was in fact attempting to aid families made homeless by the brutal Kitchener; the way he sacrificed himself for their ultimate freedom. I cannot, however, imagine that the man lived through this. The last Grandfather saw of him he was running, now with only one arm, across the veld for several hundred yards, only to collapse after several minutes and not rise again. A well-fed vulture was even attempting to fly over to survey his body, but the beast was so full it could not even take off! The last Grandfather saw, it was, though, still trying.

I hope I have been of help in your research. Perhaps Mr. Glass would post me a copy—signed, of course—of his next book when it is ready. I remain, your obedient servant,

Mary Douglas (Miss)

Glass knew that Ann dared drive no faster on the winding roads into The Gap, but he wished she could. He had drunk his beer quickly, both to avoid wasting it and to numb himself at least a bit to what he had just read. He had made her finish her sherry at a speed much faster than anyone, especially Ann Macgregor, was supposed to, all this so they could get back to his cottage to locate the pages in Roberts' now-complete diary in which this might be alluded to. Now more than ever, Glass wanted to know the *exact* story of this man, for if there were examples of treason in it more despicable than he had imagined possible, the bravery, the generosity, and the horror were greater than he had conceived of as well. Glass *would* tell this story, could perhaps tell it well enough that even the now-emerging variations on the Annie Daly story might be understood and accepted by his readers as well. Mankind, especially members of it possessed of the dynamism of Roberts Menzies and Annie Daly, was a mixture of the most dreadful and the most glorious; and these two individuals perhaps possessed dimensions of each extreme which verged on the mythopoeic.

The night was becoming chilly and loch-damp as they arrived in front of his cottage, so he built a fire quickly and lit it with the help of a paraffin block as Ann began to sift through the sheets of Roberts' diary that Farquhar had finally brought forth. The details of Miss Douglas' letter suggested that the season of the incident she described was probably summer—say December of 1901 or the first two months of 1902. In January, the last week, Ann detected that Roberts had already reached Bloemfontein and was not in the British military hospital there, but in the concentration camp for Boer women and children. She paged back to early January and found much reference to Christiaan De Wet and his plan for saving the victims of Kitchener's farm burnings from the fate of the concentration camps, in which the death rate was even higher than it had been at the height of the Siege of Ladysmith. She paged forward, and under the date of Thursday, January 16, she began to recognize the parallels between the Douglas legend and the Roberts diary. When Glass finished with the fire, he sat down beside her and she began reading aloud the page she had selected. It was, they now realized, the last one written in the "Real Roberts" handwriting before the horrible "Non-Roberts" scratch scrawl took over.

We did some farm burning of our own today. I confess that I was fully part of it at the time—the house was full of British officers, and we took some perverse pleasure in routing them out of it with a taste of their own methods—but all in all, in retrospect it amounts to the same thing as if they had burned it themselves, as eventually they would have: one less Boer farm when this whole miserable experience is over, if it <u>*ever*</u> *is. As we rode away, there were four pillars of smoke on the horizon, only three set by the British.*

We must move south now, for we are short on medicine and the tsetse fly is very thick here. We have 40 women and 73 children, many more girls than boys, in thirteen wagons. We have enough food for only one meal a day—we eat it at noon, as we now are—unless we are fortunate enough to be able to steal some British horses and eat the weaker ones. I am sought as an expert in this by the very Boers who forced me to eat it two years ago when that was the only meat we had in Ladysmith. The ironies of life! Occasionally De Wet suggests that perhaps we should allow these 113 suffering people to be placed in the camps and stop dragging them all over the veld as we seek our prey, but I am against it and so far I have prevailed. Though the figures I have heard on the death rate in the Transvaal and Orange Free State camps must surely be exaggerated, I am sure I can predict the conditions in those camps which would make their individual deaths more certain there than even here on the veld amidst frequent gunfire.

At this point there was a break in the writing, and the passages that followed were torturously written in the almost-unreadable handwriting that swayed up and down its horizontal lines like the flight of a seabird. Ann read much more slowly, more haltingly now, in part because of the difficulty of the handwriting, and in part because of the emotion which suddenly began to force its way into her voice. For the first time both she and Glass realized that Roberts Menzies must have been left-handed and was now trying gamely to write with his right hand. The entries, as a consequence, became more cryptic, more direct, more stark.

I will be half a surgeon. This was all the entry for Sunday, the nineteenth of January, said. Immediately after it on the page was the beginning of the entry for Monday, the twentieth of January, 1902, which went on for fifteen sheets of Neanderthal scrawl:

Bloemfontein. In town Boer girls dance with British soldiers, waiting to marry them as soon as their fathers stop resisting and let them go home. In the military hospital, sick and wounded are treated with proper care. In this camp, there is nothing that could be called proper in the slightest. My people, all 113 of them, are here as well, though De Wet and the others, they say, got away. Now these women and children who have lost their furniture and Bibles and homes and dogs, now they will lose their lives to these squalid conditions. It is a city of bell tents, the hospital tents at one end, the tents for living, 16 to each, at the other. Each day another living tent is converted into a hospital tent. More than half the children who have been brought here have already died. Some children have hanged themselves from the bluegum trees rather than wait for death any longer. Women menstruate without protection and steal each other's laundered rags when possible. Families re-form to units of four or five women and twice that many children. Masturbation is open and rampant. They sing "Sarie Marais" hopefully after they eat each day, but then depression sets in again. Women fight physicially with other women, children with other children. The civilized Boer women try to teach sanitary habits to the bushveld Boers, but they insist upon force-feeding horse dung to counter their children's sore throats, sewing up their sick children in the skins of freshly killed goats, on urinating and defecating in all the wrong places. I have only been here two days, but the place is ablaze with measles and whooping cough and pneumonia and scarlet fever and, always, enteric. The camps are ovens in the day, ice lockers in the night. There is almost no medicine, little sanitation, no warm clothes or blankets, poor food. And I have been appointed their doctor, I who can half-see them and half-treat them, I who need treatment myself. I have lost two stone in the last week alone. From Bloemfontein drifts the music, sung by soldiers and the Boer girls who are fortunate enough to be pretty, to be docile, to not have fathers who fight with De Wet or De la Ray or Smuts. "Rule, Britannia," they sing together, "Soldiers of the Queen," "The Absent-Minded Beggar," the songs we sang at Edinburgh and London and Cape Town and Dundee and Ladysmith but which I shall never sing again.

Ann turned the pages, sorted back and forth through them, found there to be no more entries until Wednesday, the twelfth of February. Ann read it aloud again, holding Glass's hand firmly now as she encountered the ongoing story of human suffering and degradation that unfolded through these final pages of Roberts' diary, the pages Farquhar had withheld, the pages that worked their way down toward the photocopied research sheets which claimed to document that Annie Daly was a whore in the most professional sense of the word.

More arrive every day, some from as far away as farms at Wesselsbron and Hoopstad which now no longer exist. But there is no increase in the overcrowding any longer. Thirty of my own people have died in the last three weeks, as have hundreds of others. All my medicine is gone, and I have not the ability for the surgery I need to perform. The news the new inmates bring with them is horrid. Smuts is rumored to have made it all the way to the west coast at O'Okiep, but their horses are dying under them and they are becoming foot soldiers rather than mounted guerrillas. They are savage killers of British, almost as savage rapists of anything female. The only clothing they can replace their rags with is uniforms off British soldiers they have managed to kill, and these very uniforms have gotten many shot by other bands of guerrillas. Kitchener has rounded up Judas Boers and is paying them to spy, to kill their brothers, or, if they are too honorable to do that, to at least keep the British supply trains on the move. He is also using their sharp eyes to help him scan the veld at night with searchlights mounted on trains. This will go on through the summer, but then the fall will come, and then the fear of the winter and it will have to be over. If I am alive then, I do not know where I will go and no one will care.

If Farquhar had withheld nothing, there was only one more entry in this severely underkept diary which covered the last gruesome stage of the Boer War. This was the detritus which history has forgotten in favor of the memorable Boer sieges at Ladysmith and Mafeking and Kimberley, of their great victories at Colenso and Spion Kop, of the British relief of those three towns and the three-pronged march under Roberts and Buller and French to Johannesburg and Pretoria, of the flight of Kruger and Steyn and Schalkburger, of the annexation of the Transvaal and the Orange Free State as British colonies to join Natal and the Cape Colony as the Union of South Africa. All of that, history has forgotten, happened in the *first* year of the war; there was still another year and a half to go, the year and a half of scorched earth and barbed wire, of guerrillas and blockhouses, of concentration camps and starvation, of general devastation and a million personal tragedies.

The British commander, Lord Horatio Kitchener, in fact, became the focal point of Roberts' last war entry, dated Friday, May 30, 1902.

Tomorrow the gates of the camp will be opened by the last remaining British soldier, if there is one left beyond them, for the singing has long since stopped and the handsome officers and the pretty Judas Boer girls have left for England and their society weddings. Perhaps there is one left out there to open the gate for us, and perhaps it will be Kitchener, whom none of us has sufficient strength left in our bodies to attack but whom each of us still has enough saliva in his mouth to spit upon. But it will not be Kitchener of Khartoum, for he is too important, too British, too godly to deal with such as us. He has spent the week of Vereeniging persuading Smuts and Botha to lay down their arms, that the winter will be too cold to go on, that the women are starving and naked, the land ruined, the children dead, the kaffirs rebellious. Kitchener will convince them that he has done his job, that it cannot be undone. He will ask those who can write to sign a surrender, those who can't to make crosses. He will demand that they turn over their ammunition, perhaps will allow them to fire it all off at the sky, just as they set fire to it all as they fled from Ladysmith rather than ever have a Boer bullet find a Boer heart. I will walk out that gate tomorrow, along with the 49 of mine who have not died, and they will go to their homes, if they can find them, but I will not, for it no longer exists. I will stay.

And so concluded the final pages of Roberts Menzies' account of the Boer War, a journal of treason, of heroism, of success, of heartbreak; a story of the loss of a beloved wife and the near-acquisition of a new one he now planned on abandoning as if she had never crossed his path, or more accurately, he hers, atop mighty Umbulwana, from which the Long Tom commanded Ladysmith; of the fathering of two sons—one born in Ladysmith, the other, apparently, born in Glasgow late in 1900; and of the abandonment of both of them as well.

As Glass and Ann sat before the warm fire in his cozy cottage in the Scottish Lochs, nearly six thousand miles and three-quarters of a century from where all this had happened, there seemed to be no distance at all. The fire snapped cooperatively, the brandy they now drank was warm in their stomachs, the love in their hearts for each other was more real by the moment. Yet both were crying, for themselves because they were human, for Roberts because he had been as well, for the Boers who died and even those who had lived, for individuals like Catherine and Maria, and for groups like those who had lost their homes and those who had been forced to fight for the greed of individual men and of an empire which was made up of and governed by men. Perhaps they even cried for the greedy—Rhodes and Milner; the warriors—Buller and Lord Roberts; the final adversaries —De Wet and Kitchener. They had all been men too.

And perhaps they shed tears—it was more that they did than cry—because they knew something of the future of these men since, for Jason and Ann, it was already past. Many of these same men would be in another, more terrible war in less than a dozen years. Kitchener would die at sea, his ship struck by a German torpedo. Bruce Menzies and his son Owen would die in still another war. Roberts would be forced home with nowhere to go and only one arm and one eye to get there with, and he would meet a mysterious end, perhaps at the hands of his own son. And Maria would be killed by the same son, whom she had saved, and by the boy's grandfather, for whom she had saved him, even if she did ship him home in a dog crate. They wept, perhaps a better word still, because Roberts Menzies had saved a hundred, more than a hundred, sick and injured in Ladysmith, but caused the deaths of the same number at Colenso; that he had loved one wife intensely but left another to rot in a foreign country; that he had had the courage to amputate his own arm on a mission to save others but would, within just two years, make a mockery of his cause by performing one of its bleakest moments twice a day, for five dollars a performance, in Forest Park, St. Louis, Missouri.

Jason Glass wept for his wife, for his children, for Annie and Peter Daly, for himself. Ann Macgregor wept for her mother, a suicide; for her father, a failure in his most cherished endeavor; for her sister, a slut; for herself and the secret she hid and could not tell to Jason Glass, whom she loved.

They wept because they were human, all of them.

19 ROBERTS MENZIES IN LADYSMITH: THE ARMORED TRAIN

THEIR HEADS HEAVIER WITH BRANDY than they wanted them to be, their eyes sandy with tears, they had fallen asleep. Ann had been the first to wake, and Glass felt her kiss him as she gathered her things to leave. He vaguely saw her place another log on the fire, felt her tuck a quilt firmly around him on the couch, heard her shut the door softly behind her ten seconds before the engine of Sybil's car turned over. Glass waited another ten minutes for his mind and eyes to clear—he was sure that he would not go back to sleep—and then got up and made himself a cup of coffee. It was three thirty in the morning. He ascended to his study, brought down all the pages of the placebo version of Roberts Menzies' story, and threw all but the first chapter into the fire. Everything in the first chapter he felt to be accurate, for Farquhar had recognized little but heroism and good intentions during the Dundee period. The exception, of course, was the omitted pages concerning the night of October 22, 1899, when Roberts had "persuaded" the evacuating British troops to remove him and twenty-one ambulances full of patients from Dundee to Ladysmith. Now Glass planned to outline three more sections and so compose the biography, not of a hero nor of a coward, a patriot nor a traitor, but of a real man who would be more meaningful to whoever read the story than the overcelebrated Annie Daly. Vaguely, he planned one day not long off to say to the world that there never could have been such an Annie Daly, save in his own idealistic imagination, just as there never could have been such a Roberts Menzies, save in Farquhar's.

The Legacy of Ladysmith would be divided into four parts:

I. Roberts Menzies before Ladysmith—his general background, his medical training, his assignment to South Africa with his wife, his removal from Dundee.

II. Roberts Menzies in Ladysmith—his actions under siege for four months, his care of the wounded and, especially, the sick, his negotiations with the Boers, his affair with Maria De Jager.

III. Roberts Menzies after Ladysmith—his alliance with the Boer guerrilla forces, his disfigurement, his actions in the concentration camp.

IV. The later Roberts Menzies—his movements after May, 1902, in South Africa, his American escapade with Piet Conje, the dark period from 1904 until he went to World War I in 1914 with a South African regiment, his return to Maria, his reappearance in the Lochs in 1919, his still-mysterious demise in 1925.

Part One was more or less already written, and Part Two was greatly available to Glass via a collation of Roberts' now-whole diary and Maria's. Part Three would lend itself to such a collation as well, though it would be briefer, more sketchy, and research of the sort Ann had just attempted would be required. Part Four might be very difficult indeed.

Within the next four days, a time during which he was almost never away from his desk and typewriter and during which Ann and Duncan delivered food to his kitchen but never came upstairs for fear of disturbing him, Glass had written the first draft of Part Two. On the fifth, he slept almost the whole day, but he left the typescript on the kitchen table so that Ann could read it. In return, she left the final installments of Maria's diary, which she had just received the day before from Paul Krige. She had already marked the most important passages.

And so, on a bright early-July afternoon, she sat by his rock at the lake and read what Jason Glass had written:

Part Two
Roberts Menzies in Ladysmith

Mournful Monday, October 30, 1899 * * * By Sunday, the 29th of October, fear of a Boer siege had severely intensified among the civilian population of Ladysmith, and more and more sought passage on the next train, perhaps with each new one the *last* train, out of Ladysmith to the safer areas south of the Tugela. Others vacillated. Roberts Menzies had been in town for three days now, and his diary during this period suggests nothing but professional concern for his patients and tender devotion to his ever-working, seven-months-pregnant wife.

By 11:30 this Monday morning, White had decided that the

offensive north and east of the town was doomed and ordered his cavalry to withdraw from where it was operating around Lombards Kop. Menzies, now at the center of town, writes of observing the first cavalrymen racing back into town "as if they sought the finish line at Ascot," of the dust from their horses' hooves nearly filling the air to the point that one could hardly see across the street from the Town Hall to the Royal Hotel. As more and more horsemen packed the streets, however, the rate of entry slowed, though there was no hesitancy to ride horses up onto the sidewalks in order to allow more room for those men still exposed beyond the town to push their way in.

The only hope the civilians and military in Ladysmith could draw upon on this dark afternoon was the arrival by rail of the awaited four naval guns from the H.M.S. *Powerful*. These were moved immediately to Limit Hill, where they squared off against Umbulwana Long Tom, but within minutes Long Tom had destroyed one of the four and killed the sailors who were firing it. This bad news was somewhat mitigated by later word that the Long Tom on Pepworth Hill had itself been put out of commission by British artillery.

But this did not in the long run help the Nicholsons Nek column, which had hopelessly failed. Under White's constant heliographing, various sections gave up and made their way back into Ladysmith all afternoon; but 1,100 soldiers and 200 mules bearing supplies and gun parts and ammunition did not return; the latter stampeded, and the 1,100 were captured. Some said that Boer buglers had blown the surrender at the height of battle to trick the British into throwing down their arms, then taken them all prisoner. Such behavior was not typical of Boer fighting men, however. Though the siege would not be complete for another three days, the events of Mournful Monday had ensured that it was unavoidable. The British Army had taken none of the hills it needed to. More civilians crushed onto the trains to flee.

That same evening, a Boer messenger with a white flag rode into Ladysmith and asked to speak with White before the Town Hall. Roberts was present on the steps nearby and overheard the conversation:

The man, who spoke rather respectable English, said that the prisoners they had taken were being shipped to Pretoria, but that there were a good number of wounded soldiers, as well as dead ones, on the battlefield whom we could collect without opposition. A contingent was quickly made up of volunteer soldiers and every available doctor, volunteer or no.

We rode out about four miles to the east, where the worst of the battle had been fought around Lombards Kop. The dead were all around—dead men, dead horses, dead mules. The smell of their sunburnt bodies was foul, and I must admit that I was glad that my duties, as a messenger of life, were with the wounded instead, though often the two categories were hard to distinguish from each other. I was gratified that those less wounded were willing to wait for treatment so their mates more badly hurt could be handled first. All they wanted for the interim was a match and help lighting a cigarette, which most removed from cigarette cases they had carefully placed in left breast pockets before the battle to protect their hearts. Several cigarette cases I saw were smartly dented.

By nightfall we had managed to load all we could find into ambulances, which cycled in and out of town. As darkness approached and we feared we would not complete our work in time and would have to leave a great number until morning when we could again locate them, five Boer doctors rode down from Pepworth Hill to assist us in finding and treating the ones who still remained. Why must we be civilized with each other, one asked me, at the close of day and act like animals with each other the rest of the time? The irony confuses me as much as him, and I had not a shred of an answer. I was, however, so gratified by the help that I vowed not to miss the first opportunity to return the favor in the direction of his wounded.

As we picked up the last man, a lance corporal from Dalkeith, this same doctor said a very curious thing to me, which I took to be humanely and not chauvinistically motivated: "Your town and your people are in a very bad position, Doctor. The war is young. Virtually every Boer farmer who has wanted for a short time in his life to do something other than plant and reap is in those hills. They are heady with victory, so heady they may on their own overrule General Joubert and attack to crush all of you. Joubert wants a surrender instead. If you are wise, you will grant him one, for you cannot get out now." I could not reply, so he waved and rode off into the gathering darkness.

On the next day, Buller arrived in Cape Town and telegraphed White to go on the defensive, to entrench, to tighten his perimeter to a protectable distance. Either his own appearance via Colenso with the relief force or an imminent offensive against Bloemfontein which would draw the Orange Free Staters off in defense of their homeland could serve eventually to give White the opportunity to break out. Buller also said that the key to keeping the relief route open was the protection of the railroad bridge at Colenso, 15 miles to the south. White tried to send a column to guard it, but the roads south—and in every other direction—were being sealed off by Boers one by one. At midday on Thursday, November 2, Buller telegraphed to White to send General French out before the rail lines were cut so that he could lead the relief force toward Kimberley. So with French hiding beneath the seats of an otherwise empty coach, the last train from Ladysmith thundered southward into an ambush at Pieter's Station. But the engineer ran through it and French got away, leaving the frustrated Boers with no recourse but to pull up the tracks behind it.

With this action, however, the Siege of Ladysmith was now under way.

November, 1899 * * * On the night of the first of November, the day before the Siege had fully begun, Roberts apparently made one last suggestion, far short of an appeal, that his wife leave Ladysmith, for even now they could tell that they were in their last twenty-four hours of access to the outside world. But again she declined and, in that very act, doomed herself at twenty-five to only two more months of life. Instead, she went to the railroad station and assisted with the dispatch of the last women and children, all nearly hysterical, who would be able to leave for months. Very few men this time would be allowed to go.

On the second, as the tracks were being torn up to the south, the Boers on Umbulwana began shelling the town steadily. Roberts was attempting to confine himself to his own patients at the Town Hall, though by now he considered his "own" to mean anyone in the building rather than just the hundred he had safely brought with him from Dundee. But he was frequently sought by military messengers for external duties as well. On this date he writes of performing a double amputation on a young soldier who had been struck in the legs by an unexploded shell. With Catherine assisting, he amputated one leg at the thigh, the other at the shin. Before going under the anesthesia, the boy remarked calmly, "I guess my cricketing days are over."

As early as the third, both Roberts and the military doctors realized that hospital space and medical supplies would become a severe problem before very long, so a military emissary was sent to General Joubert to request that the noncombatants—that is, the remaining civilians—be allowed to leave Ladysmith immediately. But Joubert respectfully declined the request, simply because such was not the strategy of a siege. Roberts suggested that the sick and wounded currently on hand be allowed out instead. General Joubert's staff officers found this to be unacceptable also. What Roberts and the military chief medical officer, Colonel Exham, therefore decided to request of Joubert was that he allow the establishment of a separate hospital camp beyond the British perimeter that would not be shelled. Though the rationale here was ostensibly an attempt to ease the pressure on the already-strained hospital facilities inside the town, Roberts knew that it was only a matter of time before they would also be besieged by typhoid and enteric fever, that once these cases passed a certain stage the victims would simply die lingering deaths. These, then, were the real cases for which the outlying hospital camp was being sought, and Joubert agreed to a "safe" area almost at the foot of his own Umbulwana. Hence, the Intombi Camp was established, and one train a day was allowed to leave Ladysmith station under a white flag to travel the four and one-half miles from the town to the camp to deliver medical supplies and new patients, all of whom, the town soon came to realize, were "doomed." Another sort of patient the British military authorities envisioned for Intombi was wounded Boer prisoners, who they presumed would soon be infected by the available diseases and so also die off quickly. Roberts Menzies was particularly bitter about this decision:

Exham is well aware, both by statement and by action, that Boer doctors make no distinction in treating both battlefield wounded and sick prisoners—Boers and English receive equal attention. That we, who as an empire have taken it upon ourselves to civilize the world, should act in this manner is unconscionable. Better to have sent Jameson and Rhodes and Willoughby to Intombi, for they would be better eliminated than incapacitated Boers.

The "Jameson and Rhodes and Willoughby" of whom Roberts writes were, with the exception of the military high command of White and Ian Hamilton, perhaps the most noteworthy figures besieged in Ladysmith. Leander Starr Jameson had been the leader in the last days of 1895 of the foolish Jameson Raid upon Johannesburg, designed to draw off Boer forces so that Uitlanders in the area could overthrow the Boer government and have the gold and diamond fields for themselves—the incident, in other words, that was to have accomplished four years earlier what the current conflict was now about. The "Rhodes" Roberts mentions, therefore, is rather Frank Rhodes, Cecil's brother, himself a Jameson raider, as was the other named, Sir John Willoughby. These three men had used their subversive and entrepreneurial talents to accrue many comforts for themselves and were, it seemed, destined to have the easiest time of it through the Siege. They had the plushest rooms at the Royal Hotel, a cache of champagne, an inexplicable access to better foods while everyone else in the town had been put on rations immediately. The tone of Roberts' diary suggests near-glee when, one day early in the Siege, Jameson approached him for the diagnosis of a "minor illness": where Roberts initially supposed it would turn out to be gastrointestinal, it was diagnosed as typhoid. Roberts' retributive satisfaction, however, was tempered by his professional understanding that one case of typhoid quickly produces more.

Which leads to a very curious episode. Roberts' diary for Sunday, November 12, 1899, speaks of a meeting he had on the main street in front of Harvey Greenacre's store with a man named Oscar Meyer. Meyer asked Roberts where to find Jameson, Rhodes, and Willoughby. After several murky lines describing the exchange with Meyer, Roberts acknowledges that he told the man they were in rooms on the top floor of the Royal Hotel, at the southeast corner of the building. The descriptive terms are all geographical—this as opposed to "third floor, last room on the right." Since Sunday was a holy day for the pious Boers, they never shelled the town on that day—but the very first shell launched from Umbulwana on Monday the twelfth struck the southeast corner of the Royal Hotel. Fortunately, or unfortunately, the three were downstairs at breakfast at the time and escaped unscathed. On another occasion they were nearly struck in a shelter along the Klip River, on another while standing near the post office. On Friday the twenty-fourth, Oscar Meyer was declared a Boer spy, the order for his arrest went out, and Meyer was forced to steal a horse and ride out of town under the cover of Boer long-range rifle fire.

If anything, this contact between Roberts and Meyer on November 12 seems to be the first occasion on which Roberts had clandestine dealings with a Boer sympathizer—all the more interesting since it occurred only three days before Roberts was captured by the Boers in the train incident near Frere, a full twenty-five miles to the south. Roberts' entry for the twelfth, totally unsuspicious, mentions his delivery, with his wife's assistance, of the first Siege baby born in Ladysmith, and it also describes the appearance of some Boers under the white flag in Ladysmith to buy or borrow some chlorodyne. Colonel Exham, Roberts writes, denied it to them. Yet after the entry for the twelfth ends at this point, the one for the thirteenth already has Roberts and his kaffir guide well along on their way to the Tugela. He does not detail how the escape was made.

The entry for the thirteenth indicates several times that the goal of his escape was Pietermaritzburg, the location of the nearest well-equipped military hospital. From everything available in these pages, it seems that Roberts was not deserting but was fully prepared to return with medicines and surgical supplies. He had already seen the beginnings of typhoid in Ladysmith; an entry for the tenth suggested suspicion that he might have enteric fever on his hands as well. Supply estimates made by the military at this point had already stated that while there was food available for eighty days, the medical supplies could not be stretched nearly that far.

Three versions of the armored-train incident exist—one from the famous Boer War journal of Winston Churchill, another from the sketchy rendition of it given in Maria De Jager's diary, and finally a fuller one given us, now, by Roberts Menzies. There is no entry for Tuesday the fourteenth, the day it occurred, but there is one for the fifteenth written in the Boer laager on Umbulwana.

I began moving again with the first light, keeping always within fifty yards of the railroad line, now my only guide. I was unsure how far south the Boer presence existed, so I resolved to stay under cover until the first indication I had that the English were in control of the area and then ask their assistance for the rest of my trek to Maritzburg. I had skirted what must have been the town of Chieveley, clearly in Boer hands, just after seven o'clock and was progressing on foot toward Frere when I saw an armored train moving northward. This was a British train, but I knew it was destined for trouble at Chieveley, apparently (if the train had got this far) the first sign of Boer strength. I came out of hiding and sped for the line, hoping to be seen by someone on board. A man in the engine caught sight of me and, after several moments of confusion, signaled the driver to stop.

I cautioned them to turn around, that there were strong Boer forces just ahead. This was discussed among a Captain Haldane, the driver, and a young reporter I learned shortly thereafter to be Lord Randolph Churchill's son. So the train reversed its direction and, now with me aboard, started back toward Frere, where, they assured me, I could find transportation to Maritzburg.

We were within two miles of Frere when the Boers sprung their ambush. They had taken command of a small hill just above the line and had also pushed an enormous boulder across it just round a sharp bend. The riflemen atop the hill opened fire the moment they could see us, and though we tried to duck to the floor of the engine and run the gauntlet of fire, we found ourselves halted by the shattering impact against the boulder. The first truck uncoupled, overturned, and rolled down an embankment. The first armored car derailed onto its side, and the one behind it lost hold of the track with its wheels and came to rest still half on, thus blocking the line. The engine, the tender, and the two other cars were still on the rails.

While the soldiers in the one undamaged armored car fired back at the Boers on the hill, and while the ones who could evacuated the two derailed cars, Churchill and Haldane leapt from the engine to estimate the situation on the "safe" side of the train while I tended to the driver, who had hit his head at the impact and was still dazed. Haldane decided that by constant ramming, the engine might blast the derailed car from the line, so this was undertaken. While we all knelt on the floor of the cab, Haldane himself kept thrusting and reversing the engine, each time ramming the derailed car with a tooth-clattering jolt. Progress was obvious but also slow, and it took roughly an hour, under a hail of metallic, rattling gunfire, to clear the lame carriage off the tracks. Toward the end of this process, the steam tank on the engine was punctured by a Mauser bullet and the woodwork of the engine caught fire. Then, just as we were about to resume our run toward Frere, where we knew there would be help, the rear two cars—which is to say our full defensive firepower—became uncoupled. The engine dared not risk going back around the derailed car it had finally scraped by, so many of the soldiers, Churchill, I, Haldane—anyone available who was not firing back—ran to the two disabled cars and tried to push them up to meet the engine. Though we stayed to the guarded side of the train, some of the Boers had now got into position to gun at our legs, and our casualties were mounting by the minute. Our last recourse, then, was to return to the engine, its cab burning still harder now, and all run along its guarded side as it pushed toward some metal buildings about a mile ahead. There, the strategy was, we would take up a defensive position while the engine went the last mile to Frere for help.

But this was too much for one young soldier, so he raised his pocket handkerchief in surrender. Now the Boers, being if anything extremely honorable fighting men, lowered their rifles and stepped forward to accept the surrender. Since this had not been officially done, however, confusion resulted. Some of the soldiers put their hands up, but others continued to return fire, others ran toward the buildings. The last I saw here of Churchill he was scrambling up an embankment several hundred yards ahead under heavy rifle fire, his hand red with blood despite the soaking rain in which we now found ourselves.

At the height of this, feeling that there was nothing honorable left to do but surrender, I raised my own handkerchief and stepped forward into captivity.

I was led on foot with a dozen or so British soldiers north toward Colenso, where we were interned for the night in a metal shed. Here I again encountered Churchill, who spent most of his time badgering his captors about the futility of their fight, telling them that Pretoria would be taken in less than six months. I could not but be intrigued by such bravado as his, for he and I were certainly in no position to be uttering offensive remarks. Not only were we captive, but so were Ladysmith and Mafeking and Kimberley. Take Pretoria indeed! This war, for Britain, was more an exercise in getting back what it once had had than in going off to pursue what it still had not.

What is clear from this point on is that Roberts had quietly made a decision to separate himself from Churchill in the eyes of the Boers so that he might return to his wife and patients in Ladysmith rather than be shipped from Elandslaagte Station to a prison in Pretoria—which was where Churchill was headed. They were marched across the bridge over the Tugela at Colenso and into the high hills beyond it, the very river and hills Buller's relief force was destined to have to cross and climb before they could even think of advancing on Ladysmith. As they slogged on, Roberts began his scheme to have himself returned, with Boer medical supplies, to Ladysmith. At first he suggested the matter to the young son of the man he could see to be the commando leader—this of course would be young Piet De Jager—and he persuaded the boy to intermediate with his father. The father spoke with Roberts for some time, he from horseback, the Scottish doctor on foot below him, but ultimately denied him on both counts. Roberts resolved to keep trying.

After noon that day they approached the Boer investment lines to the south of Ladysmith and could finally see evidence of what they had heard for hours: the mighty Long Tom pounding away from the top of Umbulwana, though Roberts for the first time was encountering it from behind rather than looking down its muzzle. De Jager took his prisoners with him to the top of Umbulwana, where he organized a fresh detail of men to take them the fourteen miles north to the station at Elandslaagte. It was here, as he rested and ate in preparation for the resumption of the march, that Roberts, gazing down at the besieged Ladysmith with its white-flagged hospital train puffing out on its daily run toward the Intombi Camp, first noticed Maria De Jager:

Boer girls are not often pretty, and those who are have distinctly Dutch features which will, ten years hence, run to pudginess and, ten years after that, to distinct heaviness. De Jager's daughter was one of these—blond, blue-eyed, a smiling mouth, perhaps overly dressed this late afternoon, for the stench of a tightly packed commando laager at least, in a white cotton dress that would be more appropriate, perhaps, in a punt upon the Cam than on the top of Umbulwana. Surely the prettiest young lady I had seen for some time, yet the broad cheekbones, the substantial breasts and hips, the surely strong thighs beneath her skirt, these were the areas which would increase in size and make her look eventually like her mother.

I tried to make conversation with her. At first she held back—I was a prisoner, after all—but eventually she began to ask me questions about England, where she said she had never been but would like someday to go. Here, I felt, was the opening for sympathy and understanding I might play upon, for she seemed to take a personal interest in me as well. I told her I was a doctor, had tried to escape south for supplies to Pietermaritzburg but had doubly failed since now my sick patients would not even get their doctor back, much less the supplies.

Roberts goes on to recount how he did not have to *ask* her to intercede for him, that she offered to, even had him make a list of the things he required so she could speak with her father and, perhaps, Boer doctors. His first glimmer of hope came when Churchill and other prisoners were moved out on schedule early in the evening, while he was allowed to stay. One of his guards, however, suggested that he should not take too much comfort from this, for often those to be executed for war crimes were the only ones not sent on to Pretoria. In the morning, however, De Jager and his daughter approached the tent in which Roberts slept, ordered him out, and told him that he could return to Ladysmith. The medical supplies were out of the question for the same reason that evacuation of civilians after the vise had shut was out of the question—sieges did not accomplish much with constant gifts. What Roberts did detect, however, was the suggestion that "exchanges" often occurred; that is, if the Boers found themselves short of something they desperately needed, they might work a trade for something the British wanted.

So, with the assured protection of Boer guns, Roberts descended the west face of Umbulwana, a white flag over his head for combatants of both sides to see, and progressed across the flatlands to the railroad line and followed it past the Intombi Camp and four miles back into Ladysmith. This was Thursday, the sixteenth of November, 1899.

The ensuing pages show no signs that Roberts suffered any ill effects in Ladysmith as a consequence of his midnight flit to the south, so it must have been officially sanctioned. There is some hint as well that he might try it again, especially since searchlight signals at night had indicated that the British were firmly entrenched now as far north as Estcourt and still moving. Medical supplies, therefore, would be available in less than half the distance to Pietermaritzburg that Roberts had originally thought he would have to travel. But other reasons were beginning to materialize as well why Roberts might attempt to cross out of the Ladysmith perimeter, and on the afternoon of Sunday, November 26, he did so.

Several things had happened in the intervening ten days to change the picture entirely for the besieged town. On the fifteenth, the very night Roberts was in their camp, the Boers had started shelling all night long, and this made sleep as precious a commodity now as many other things were becoming. Then, on Saturday the eighteenth, another Long Tom shell struck the Royal Hotel, rolled down the main staircase, and wounded Dr. Stark, a longtime pacifist who had preached on three continents against British involvement in Africa. He had been working hard within Ladysmith to make both sides "come to their heads" and cease these futile endeavors. Many civilians had looked to him, in fact, as the man who might be able to talk the Boers into lifting the Siege. Now that hope, however futile it had been in the first place, was gone. He died that same day. Then, on Sunday the nineteenth, a day on which Boer guns ceased and Boer hymns echoed from the surrounding hills, a day on which Ladysmith expected a recuperative relief, the first case of enteric fever turned up, and during the next week Roberts himself diagnosed five more in his Town Hall hospital: three among wounded soldiers, two among the hundred patients he had brought with him from Dundee. Colonel Exham insisted, over Roberts' objections, that all five be removed from the Town Hall, which sat directly at the Ladysmith center, and transported on the afternoon train to Intombi. Exham, in effect, had condemned them to death. But what must have been the most demoralizing blow of all came that same day in a different form.

The Boers must for some time have been watching the behavior of the kaffir cattle guards through their spyglasses. Each day they took the great herd out beyond the town limits (but still within the defensive perimeter) to the best available grazing land. While the bovine chewing went on all morning, the kaffirs talked among themselves, often with their backs to the animals. On this particular day, the spacing between men and beasts got as wide as the Boers needed it to be, so their guns atop Pepworth Hill began lobbing shells between the kaffirs and the cattle, causing the cattle to stampede away from Ladysmith and the kaffirs to run toward the town. When a military detachment attempted to ride out to save the day, the Boer marksmen drove them back with rifle fire, and the heavy guns continued to drop shells at the heels of the cattle until nearly every available British source of meat had been stolen, and word now went about Ladysmith that the killing of rats would henceforth be illegal for, within thirty days, humans would have to eat them for food.

So, against this backdrop, Roberts made his second journey to the De Jager camp on Sunday the twenty-sixth amidst very mysterious circumstances and with even more mysterious consequences.

He rode out of town on the day's Intombi train, looked in on a few patients there, and then proceeded on to the base of Umbulwana under the flag of truce. There is no suggestion as to whether or not this visit had the official sanction of

General White. In any event, once beyond Intombi it would have been difficult for any British authorities to spot him moving farther south and east. It was no-man's-land, sparsely defended because of the red crosses on Intombi which prevented combat at that site and because of the sheer face of Umbulwana, which would have exposed a descending army in a second; one man, however, would have been hard to see as he approached it and then climbed it—perhaps only the British aerial observation balloon could have done so, and this was never aloft on Sunday. So around the middle of the afternoon Roberts describes his arrival *"amidst all the white dresses, not just the De Jager girl's today, amidst the hymn singing and the feasting, amidst the pretense that, on the other six days of the week, there was no siege and no war."* In his entry for the twenty-sixth Roberts simply says that he was there to *"negotiate more humane standards for shelling"* and to *"barter for medical supplies, especially for iodoform and other antiseptics to combat the burgeoning epidemic of enteric."* He remarks that he had gone with *"something to trade,"* and that once again the deal was *"sharply rejected by De Jager."* Only certain clumsy references in other parts of the diary, of course, allow us to know that what Roberts took with him to trade was the green codebooks which enabled anyone who had them to decipher the heliograph and searchlight communications between Ladysmith and the relieving column at Estcourt. Even in reading the entry for the twenty-sixth, one has the feeling that Roberts was sinning by omission. More had taken place on Umbulwana than he was admitting to.

His four entries for the twenty-seventh may suggest just what. In the first, written apparently early in the morning (in contrast to the other three, which are done on a different writing surface and much later in the day), Roberts pens a long, intercalated encomium to his wife: her loyalty, her courage under pressure, her dealings with the sick and wounded, her professionalism with the enteric cases, her eight-month pregnancy. He reflects forward to the birth of his *"son,"* his hope that he may be born yet in Pietermaritzburg rather than in Ladysmith. In the second, written later, there is a description of a contest being staged by the *Ladysmith Lyre,* one of two Siege newspapers in print: a prize would be given to the person who suggested the most original and miraculous idea for escape from Ladysmith. Though Roberts did not win, his entry, as he describes it, proves to be extremely interesting: *"Have a handsome young cavalryman seduce a pretty young Boer girl, promise to marry her, then teach her the searchlight codes so that she could inform Buller of the proper route of approach and so end the Siege and unite her with her beloved."* How much of this is what Roberts' initial plan had been is unclear, but on the twenty-seventh, according to later entries, the codebooks were still in his possession, not in Maria's.

And then the third entry for Monday the twenty-seventh: For the first time a Boer shell actually struck the roof of the Town Hall hospital, stripping the building of its red-cross flag. Why had this occurred? One patient had been killed, nine others wounded, and Catherine Menzies had had her arm broken by a falling roof beam. For all the bitter passages throughout Roberts' diary which targeted British amorality and ineptitude, we find here his single vitriolic response to the Boers, one that reverberates in many directions:

The Boers speak of honor as if anyone British were unfamiliar with the word. They place honor above human life, make anyone who suggests that certain pragmatic decisions must be made to protect, save, and prolong human life feel as if he had been schooled in one of the lower rings of Dante's hell. They act as if only they had heard of God, or at least heard of the right God, seem to think that God speaks to them alone and they have been empowered to deliver His dicta with their German cannon. Surely it was I their shell sought today, not my wife or my patients. Would bringing the roof in upon me have erased dishonor from the universe or even from the plain of Ladysmith? I think not. I sympathize with these people who have been driven to war against their wishes and against, in the long run, all odds—but they are a simpleminded, self-righteous, gullible lot who, for the moment at least, have decided I am Satan and that God demands my elimination.

And then the fourth entry:

The night sentries are skitterish, and White has been summoned for his advice and decision. The distant searchlights tell that Buller is north of Pietermaritzburg, that he is coming with 30,000 men to relieve us. The Boer searchlight tries as it always does to confuse the signal in the sky so that we cannot read it, not knowing that what Buller signals is merely repeated over and over until we grasp its meaning. All this is normal. But what White and his advisers cannot understand is the other light, the one pointed from Umbulwana straight into Ladysmith, the one which keeps flashing in the simplest Morse code BOTHA YES BOTHA YES BOTHA YES BOTHA YES. *Botha yes, but I must rethink first.*

20 *ROBERTS MENZIES IN LADYSMITH: ESCAPE FROM INTOMBI*

DECEMBER, 1899 * * * "ENEMY LEARNS EVERY PLAN of operation I form, and I cannot discover source. I have locked up or banished every suspect but still have undoubted evidence of betrayal" (White to Buller via searchlight).

Roberts, of course, gives no direct evidence of when he handed over the codebooks, but it is clear that he did not "rethink" for very long, had in fact decided fairly quickly what his moves should be. Rather, the early-December pages of his diary are more summarial about conditions in Ladysmith. The town spirit was becoming generally lower by the day, and only hopeful heliographic messages from Buller's forces could do anything to lift it. The newsmen in town were still publishing their Siege papers, the *Bombshell* and the *Lyre*, both of which contained the last ounces of wit that remained inside the perimeter. Beer and liquor were running out, and the last bottles were being sold at raffle. Vegetables were hard to come by, as was drinking water, owing to the terribly polluted Klip River. Flies swarmed all over the horse dung, then swarmed all over the spoon of anyone trying to eat whatever meal he had been allotted. The town, especially in the heat of the high afternoon, was enveloped in a rancid stench because of declining supplies of sanitary chemicals.

Catherine Menzies continued to perform as if she were not even pregnant, though she was now in her final month. Indeed, Roberts' diary for the month of December makes only two references to the impending birth of his first child. One reason for this is probably the fact that on the third of December, Catherine took up residence at the Intombi Camp hospital instead of the Town Hall hospital, for the latter had an inflexible capacity whereas the Intombi Camp, with facilities initially for three hundred, had already far surpassed that. The staff of nurses had been increased by three to fifteen, and one of those three—by order of the Principal Medical Officer, Lt. Col. Richard Exham—was Catherine Menzies.

Although this is speculation on my part, I would have to suggest that Colonel Exham is perhaps the largest reason of all behind Roberts' treasonous behavior. British history has since labeled Exham one of the most disgraceful blemishes on the record of the Medical Corps, for his behavior not only during the Siege—which Roberts frequently details—but after the Siege, to the extent that Buller himself had him reassigned to the western front at Bloemfontein. Lord Roberts, after watching his actions in the hospital there, simply had him sent home. Roberts Menzies and a subordinate military medical officer named Major Donegan continually tried to circumvent his orders but usually were unable to. Exham's whole four months' activity during the Siege seemed to be devoted to one purpose: the impression his hospitals (there were four: two in churches, one in the Town Hall, and the Intombi Camp) would make on General Buller when he finally broke through. Hence, neatness at the cost of practicality was always the rule of the day—instruments put away rather than near the bedsides where they could be immediately put to use, for instance, and conservation of medicines (particularly painkillers) so that he would have a good supply for Buller to examine later. Menzies was enraged by this, and Exham repaid Menzies by assigning his pregnant wife, her arm still in a sling, to the enteric-infested Intombi.

Why, then, did Roberts Menzies turn the codebooks over to the Boers for the apparently self-defeating purpose of prolonging the Siege? There are several reasons, but I feel sure the greatest was this: denied painkillers, medicines, even surgical instruments and proper bedding for the patients, and living as he was amidst the moans of the wounded and sick, the last gasps of the dying, and the stench of the dead, he traded for supplies—not with the pietistic De Jager, who must have called him a disgrace for his disloyalty to his face, but with Louis Botha, the thirty-six-year-old general who was taking over where the more moralistic commanders like Joubert, Erasmus, and De Jager were failing. Botha was a general who would take anything God offered him and who as a result would thrash the British at Colenso and at Spion Kop. And for these codebooks, Botha, through Maria De Jager, passed on brandy, iodoform, bandages, chlorodyne when he had it, blankets, sheets, and surgical instruments.

The method was this: Kaffir runners were continually exiting and reentering Ladysmith with mail. At the cost of fifteen pounds a letter, anyone in Ladysmith could send a letter home to Britain. The kaffirs were slippery and well paid and, as such, did their jobs faithfully. They would sneak out at night with whatever letters they had, move to the northernmost extension of the British supply line (now in the vicinity of Chieveley), deposit the letters with the military post office, pick up any that were incoming for Ladysmith, and then return. From the beginning of December on, however, select ones returned by way of the Acton Homes road to a cache of supplies amassed at the base of a small kopje to the south of the British-held Wagon Hill. Here, in some bug-infested weeds along a spruit which fed into the Klip, they would retrieve whatever Botha's men had managed to bring Maria De Jager. (She apparently supervised the entire delivery operation, for her father would never have stood for it.) Then the kaffirs would slip through the undergrowth along the spruit, next follow the Klip to the Intombi Camp, and there make the delivery, for this month at least, to none other than Catherine Menzies. She and several nurses in her confidence (for information of this could *not* reach Exham) loaded what they had onto the empty train returning from Intombi to Ladysmith, after first removing whatever was of use to them. At Ladysmith station, Donegan, again using kaffirs, had the remainder removed and delivered to the Town Hall hospital.

Now, there are obvious ethical problems here, and Roberts and Donegan debated them several times. None of these supplies were ever given to the two church hospitals; Roberts had insisted on that. Donegan argued that since he was breaking orders and risking his career, he ought to be doing so in the name of *all* the sick and wounded, not just some. But Roberts simply threatened to break off the scheme unless Donegan agreed, though he did consent to Donegan's alternative: to allot as much of Exham's minuscule appropriations as possible to the two church hospitals and Intombi at the expense of the Town Hall hospital. Even so, the Town Hall was the best-supplied hospital in Ladysmith, and the mortality rate was strikingly lower than at the other three, though the Intombi Camp's collection of terminal patients should hardly be counted.

Why did Roberts hoard the supplies? Was it egomania, that he wanted (especially at Exham's expense) the best medical record in Ladysmith? Was it humanitarian, that he wished the best care for "his" hundred patients and any others lucky enough to have been shoved into the same building with them? Was it guilt, that it was *his* decision, made two months before, which had removed them from Dundee (where reports had it the hospital was still functioning pretty much as usual and was not under siege) and trapped them in the disease-infested Ladysmith? Was it morality, that he had come to believe the Boers in the right in this war and he did not plan to help the British in general any further? Was it vengeance, that he wished to retaliate against Exham for the mess he was making and for having sent his wife, his most trusted assistant, to Intombi? Or was it simple fear that if Exham caught wind of what was going on he would, first, appropriate all the supplies for his Buller display shelves and, second, turn Roberts in for treason and negotiating with the enemy?

At first the Boers used the codebooks with mixed success. For example, there were several vacated farmhouses scattered about the Ladysmith area which White's staff had determined were being used by Boers as bases of subversive operations—observation of troop movements, organization of cattle thefts and equipment underminings, and the like. Toward the end of the first week of December, White's headquarters on Convent Hill had detected three such houses actually *within* the fourteen-mile Ladysmith circumference and had heliographed troops in the field to attack those three houses at daybreak the next morning. During the night, the Boers slipped away, and the British took not a single prisoner for all their firepower that day. Two days later, the headquarters had designated nine houses between the Ladysmith perimeter and the thirty-mile-round Boer circle beyond it; on the night of December 7, last-minute searchlight signals pinpointed three of these for night raids. The Boers in these three houses abandoned them and slipped into the other six.

The foregoing material is not to be found in Roberts' diary—he seems to have turned over the codes and resolved never to give a single thought to how they might be used—but they can be found in all the major accounts of the Ladysmith Siege and are hard to explain in any other way than the one I have offered. But, as I said above, not everything went right for the Boers. There is the incident on Gun Hill, for example.

On the night of the seventh of December, a British night sortie slipped out of Ladysmith under General Hunter to attack the Boer guns on Gun Hill, four miles due east of the town. Despite a horrendous series of British miscues ascending the hill—a commander ordered his men to fix bayonets when they had no bayonets about them, for example—they took the hill with surprisingly little resistance, stuffed explosives into the Boer gun, and destroyed it. As they watched White's parade of celebration marching down the main street in Ladysmith the next day, the Boers were understandably angry. They had been fully prepared for the attack but had understood from the searchlights earlier in the evening that it was to have been launched against Long Hill, not Gun Hill. That evening, as dead and wounded were removed from the field around Gun Hill, a Boer doctor slipped a note into Roberts' hand. It read: "Check. Has the code been changed?" It was signed "Maria."

Roberts made what subtle inquiries he could and determined that it had not, so he let the matter drop. For me, it is rather easy to explain why this mission backfired in the Boers' faces, though not the one at Surprise Hill three days later. On the night of December 7, just hours before the Gun Hill attack, Buller had been searchlighting his first major strategy to White in Ladysmith, and the Boer decoders would clearly have been much more involved in the information they were reading on the clouds in that direction—south—rather than the internal messages in Ladysmith to their northwest. What they took from Buller was, in itself, critical: WILL ADVANCE BY POTGEITERS DRIFT. WILL START TWELVE DEC AND WILL TAKE FIVE DAYS. With information such as this in the sky, the Boer decoders probably got Gun Hill and Long Hill mixed up in their distraction.

Nothing, however, explains what went wrong at Surprise Hill on the night of the tenth. Still smarting from the loss of one gun and knowing that morale inside Ladysmith had picked up because of it, the Boers lost another. The Boers knew of the attack to be launched on the gun position four miles to the northwest this time, had even removed the gun from the hill. Yet only the smallest diversionary force of British ever went up Surprise Hill; instead, the main force went to the east of the hill and discovered immediately the tarpaulin under which the gun was hidden. They blew it up and killed fourteen Boers in the process. Roberts surely knew something was wrong, for the train from Intombi this afternoon of the eleventh had returned for the first time in more than a week with no supplies whatsoever.

That night the skies were ablaze with more searchlights from Buller: PLAN INTACT, DO NOT ATTEMPT TO BREAK OUT

UNTIL I AM AT LANCERS HILL ON THE SEVENTEENTH. Lancer's Hill was seven miles southwest of Ladysmith, and this was the place where Buller had planned to have the Boers fight two battles at once, one against him at their front, the other at their rear against a great surge of troops pushing out of Ladysmith all in one direction. The Boer siege line and the Boer Tugela line were to be squashed into one and then scissored. Except the Boers knew the plan.

The Intombi train arrived back on both the twelfth and thirteenth without supplies. The kaffirs, when questioned by Donegan, said there had been nothing at the cache for three days now. Although he speculated to Menzies that Boer humanitarianism had probably ceased, he openly accused the kaffirs of selling the supplies to private interests or even of taking them the other way toward the free market south of the Tugela. They denied this. On the nights of the twelfth and thirteenth, BOTHA YES lit the top of Umbulwana again. But then on the thirteenth Buller took command of the skies himself: FORCED TO CHANGE PLANS. AM COMING VIA COLENSO AND ONDERBROOK SPRUIT. CURRENTLY IN CHIEVELEY. And in response to this message the British made a major miscalculation: they continued to assume that Buller would attack on the seventeenth, never pausing to remember that the route through Colenso was much shorter and the crossing could take place as much as two days sooner, only thirty-six hours from then.

Since there is no record of Roberts' having gone back to the Boer camp since the day he traded the codebooks—though he may have—December 14, a Thursday, stands as a critical moment in Roberts' entire history. When no supplies arrived for the fourth straight day, he betook himself, after dark, to Umbulwana, aiming all the while at the place on the dark five-hundred-foot mountain from which BOTHA YES once again continued to flash. *"I found her there, as she had been for four straight nights, and she wept to see me, and we dallied longer than we should have at so crucial a moment."* This dalliance probably resulted in the conception of the illegitimate Menzies who would be born in Glasgow, Scotland, at the end of the following summer and named, by Maria alone, Piet, after her brother and the commanding general on Umbulwana, Joubert. *"She told me that too much had gone wrong, that the Boers to whom she had given the codebooks were seeking a scapegoat, that the man they knew as Bob Menzy was it."*

Roberts needed his supplies; he had not been rationing

what he had as the two church hospitals were doing, for he had felt he had no reason to. He asked to be taken to Botha, and at first Maria would not consent. But finally she did, and he was seized by two Boer guards and ridden, this night of the fourteenth, fifteen miles to the south to where Botha was camped on the heights above the Tugela overlooking the tin-roofed town of Colenso.

Imagine his arrival at Botha's camp in the early hours after midnight. Imagine the burly, darkly handsome, bearded and mustachioed Botha, his eyes under his great slouch hat ablaze from the campfire, his bandolier strapped tightly over his left shoulder, his adrenaline already pumping in anticipation of what he knew would be one of the epic battles of the war, to occur now within hours, not two days from now as White still thought. Imagine his mixture of emotion, of forthrightness and confusion, as he met, for the second time apparently, this treasonous Scottish doctor whom he now suspected of operating as a double agent.

"The codes have been changed."

"No, they have not."

"Not entirely, just slightly, enough to have us make slight mistakes that bear grave consequences. Gun Hill. Surprise Hill. And tomorrow Colenso."

"No. They are the same."

"They cannot be."

"Why?"

"I will show you, Dr. Menzy." Imagine Botha—the great Botha—imagine him ordering this man he now suspected of double-crossing him to horseback and leading him to the brink of the Tugela Heights. Envision them as they gaze southward into the darkness at the five thousand British campfires strewn across the veld on the other side of the river, a line of men five miles wide and a mile deep, numbering nearly twenty-five thousand—a figure almost equaling the entire adult male population of the Transvaal Republic and far exceeding the number in the hills above them who would have to stop them, at daybreak, from crossing a narrow but rough and winding river. Perhaps Botha took command of the Boer searchlight that was intimidating the British forces with its constant flickering across the veld and used it to make his point as a coach would use a chalkboard.

"Their signals to each other this evening, Doctor, indicate that they will try three crossing points in the morning. One is the iron railroad bridge at the center of the line." Did he shine the light on it so Roberts could see it? "An inviting crossing—

no one will get his boots wet—but it will funnel them all into our most accurate Mauser unit. And surely they know that that bridge has been mined for over a month and can be blown to bits at a second's notice. No good general would ever cross there, Doctor, yet their coded messages try to make us believe they will." Did he then turn the light slightly to the right and shine it on the place five hundred feet below them where the Tugela looped around a narrow peninsula of land? "Another spot is to be Bridle Drift there on the loop. Yes, that is the shallowest part, but we surround that peninsula on three sides. No sane man would subject himself and his men to close-range crossfire like that, yet Buller's code says that General Hart is to take his men onto that land immediately at daybreak. Dr. Menzy, the stupidest field cornet on my staff would desert, and rightly so, rather than accept an order to suicide such as that would be." Again the searchlight is moved. "The third crossing point is to the left—a much better place than the river loop, for there the river loops against *us* and they could put us under crossfire if we were foolish enough to have men stationed there. But to cross there they would have to have taken command of a high hill called Hlangwane on their own side of the river, lest we take it and bombard them from high positions on both sides. Doctor, they did not bother to take Hlangwane, so we took it without opposition at nightfall. So you see, Doctor Menzy, the three British crossing points are each futile—yet their codes try to make us believe they will use them. The codes have been changed, and you, or others like you, have told them exactly how they should be changed to be maximumly deceptive." Perhaps in the glow of the searchlight Roberts could see the gleam, surely satanic, in his violet eyes, and hear the boyish laugh which nailed on the final irony.

The diary details none of this, of course, but it does suggest that Roberts staked his life on the fact that the codes had not been tampered with, even without being assured (for who knew what went on at Buller's final council of war that evening?) that they had not been. In any event, Botha, according to the diary, promised to see to even an increased flow of supplies through the spruit cache if no deception was proved at daybreak.

The great battle at Colenso, which lasted from six thirty until eight thirty on the blistering-hot morning of December 15, 1899, proved that the codes had remained intact. Back in Ladysmith, White was unable to muster the breakthrough attack to draw off the Boer forces there because, as far as he still knew, the big battle to cross the Tugela was still two days off. He could only watch helplessly the heliographs that announced it, listening to the booming of the big guns, the Long Toms and the pom-poms, thundering over the hills fifteen miles away, quieting so early that he knew Buller had lost, for the river could not have been crossed and the heights scaled by twenty-five thousand men so quickly. Only withdrawal could happen so fast. Back at Colenso, Roberts watched from Botha's command post above as General Hart, true to script, marched his Irish infantrymen into the river loop and was shot at from three sides, his men filling the Tugela with blood as they became ensnarled in the barbed wire the Boers had laid beneath its surface. He saw Colonel Long's artillery being raced to the front on his left, far outstripping the infantrymen under General Barton who were supposed to have preceded it and formed a defensive ring around the ten big guns he brought with him, a tactical error of the most fundamental sort. Once the guns were within seven hundred yards of the Tugela, the trap was sprung. Just the way the cattle were stampeded at Ladysmith, the Boer guns on the Tugela Heights on the north side of the river and on Hlangwane on the south side began dropping shells behind them so they could not retreat.

Shortly after eight, the Boers read the heliographs from Buller's headquarters ordering a retreat—the railroad bridge had not even been attempted by this point—and the terrible banging and booming of the guns, reputedly the most savage artillery battle in the history of the world to that date, began to subside. But the Boers had no intention of pursuing, of abandoning their invulnerable trenches and the safety of the heights above them, so they allowed the great British army to move ponderously off with its incredible amount of baggage. Then, suddenly, at eleven o'clock a small band of men turned away from the main army and raced back toward Long's guns in an attempt to retrieve them. And the Boers shot all of them as well, and one of the dead turned out to be Fred Roberts, son of the man who, because of this terrible defeat, was two days from now to be named commander-in-chief above Buller—Viscount Lord Roberts, Roberts of Khandahar. These guns would now go by train to Pretoria, sent there with the aid of Roberts of Ladysmith.

So the battle was entirely over by noon, and the doctors and medical corps of both sides went to the field to collect their own. Botha sent Roberts Menzies down with his own doctors, and Roberts stood on the field with the 1,100 casualties strewn around him. The entry for this day is the last in his diary for nearly a week and surely is one of the most pitiful:

Something like 150 British soldiers died today, and five times that number were badly wounded, some mortally. More than 200 were taken prisoner and loaded on the trains to ride with Long's ten guns. Only 40 Boer casualties of any sort. The Boers had all the advantages—of geography, of discipline, of generalship, and of intelligence. As I stood on the battlefield and heard the screaming of the wounded, I did not know whether to work with the Boer doctors who were making temporary repairs on these young British men until their own doctors could attend to them or with the British doctors who were trying to save the lives of their young countrymen. I felt that neither wanted my soul, but surely the British could use my skill, and so I joined them. The stench was unbearable on the field and became dreadfully worse when literally a thousand vultures began to circle above as we worked, shitting that awful white bone chalk of their last victims all over the wounded and dead, into our hair, onto our backs as we hunched over them, into our eyes when we looked up to curse them. The men wailed in their pain, and doubled their cries in their fright that when they were temporarily unattended by a moving being, the vultures might move in to destroy them. Finally we had everyone to a field hospital, all of us, doctors and patients, burned red-brown by the sun, covered with sweat and dust and vulture shit, blistered by the heat. And not a hundred feet from where we operated gravediggers worked to bury the dead before the vultures could tear at their eyes and brains and genitals, digging graves so shallow that arms and legs remained exposed above the ground even after they had been "filled in." So the vultures simply snatched onto these extended limbs and yanked whole corpses out of the ground, carrying them to sites a hundred yards away from others of their kind so they could gluttonize them in privacy. Finally I could no longer bear the work on this terrible battlefield, so I fled. I could have fled south to join Buller's column at Chieveley—Botha would not have stopped me—but I fled back across the iron railroad bridge, north of the Tugela again, convincing myself that I had to return to my wife, to my patients, to Maria, to make sure Botha made good his promise; but I was really fleeing because I was no longer British—they ought not to have me—and I was not Boer—they would not want me. Would that Hart had not gone into the loop or that Long had held his guns back from the river. Then Botha could have "proved" that I had deceived him and so could have shot me dead.

And back in Ladysmith this day the feelings were equally nihilistic. Buller had searchlighted FIRE OFF ALL YOUR AMMUNITION AND MAKE THE BEST TERMS YOU CAN—but White refused to surrender, had decided that this was a Boer message using British code. And the Boers themselves signaled into Ladysmith in no code at all BULLER HAS GIVEN TEN GUNS FOR THE TWO YOU TOOK. And new searchlights far to the west announced that the British had been beaten on that front as well, at Stormberg on the tenth and Magersfontein on the twelfth—and now, of course, at Colenso on the fifteenth. Ladysmith and Mafeking and Kimberley would be towns of skeletons by the end of the South African summer.

* * * * * *

Roberts' next diary entry reveals a shaken man in a mental state approaching, perhaps, paranoia. Writing on the twenty-first of December, still more than two months before Ladysmith would be relieved, he seems to have decided that both God and what he has come to call the Righteous Boers were using him as a symbol of all they found despicable in the British character, perhaps in human nature. On the twentieth of December the tallest structure in the town, the four-faced clock tower atop the Town Hall, had been struck by a shell which failed to explode but which did carry away one-fourth of the tower by sheer impact, causing the whole workings of the clock to collapse and plunge through the ceiling of one of the hospital rooms. And in the tower—which stood as tall as ever but with a gash in its side which seemed to suggest that the structure was even defying gravity to remain aloft—Roberts seems to have seen a symbol of himself. Then, on the twenty-first, General White fell ill, and he knew enough not to seek treatment from Exham or anyone operating under his orders so sought Roberts Menzies instead. Yet the spies must have carried this back to Umbulwana as well, for his house on Convent Hill was struck by a shell even while Roberts was attending him. It burst, in fact, in the very room next to White's. Rightly or wrongly, Roberts felt himself a hunted man.

And then the gods took over. On the morning of the twenty-second, word came from the Intombi Camp that his wife, due to deliver any day now, had collapsed from exhaustion and, it was feared, enteric fever had set in. He did not wait for the afternoon train, of course, rather borrowed a skinny rail of a horse from a cavalry officer and rode out immediately—though this was against the agreement with the Boers—bearing a white flag in the hope that they would not take this easy opportunity to destroy him. When he got there, he knew immediately that the diagnosis was correct; she lay broken by overwork, her weight far down from what it ought to have been, infected with fever, entombed now at Intombi with nearly nine hundred other cases of the same disease, nearly all of which would be terminal.

Yet with the same tenacity and cunning with which he kept most of his own hundred and others alive at the Town Hall, he resolved that she would not fail. Tossing caution aside, he hurried back to town, appropriated a heliograph in a manner he does not detail, rose to the shattered clock tower, and, through the western hole where the clock had been, flashed BOTHA YES BOTHA YES BOTHA YES hard toward Umbulwana, to which he received a variety of answers from confused Boer heliographers: WHITE NO WHITE NO, CERTAINLY YES CERTAINLY YES, and even IS THIS A SURRENDER IS THIS A SURRENDER. But there near the base of the hill, far away from the official signallers on the top, came the one he sought: BOTHA YES BOTHA YES BOTHA YES. So he rode with the hospital train back out that afternoon and slipped across the Klip River and the main Colenso road and found Maria De Jager and there had to tell the girl that he had a wife, that she was here with him in Ladysmith, that she had contracted enteric fever and was in danger of dying, that she was pregnant. This was the twenty-second, and according to Maria's diary, it would not be until Christmas Day that she herself would mention the possibility of her own pregnancy to Roberts, though she must already have suspected it. One can imagine the reaction of an eighteen-year-old Boer girl to the situation in which she now found herself.

Then, as she later would in her own five-week flight from Ladysmith to Glasgow, she reacted on instinct. She bore the message Roberts gave her to Botha: "My wife is dying of enteric. I must have more chlorodyne immediately. We have 900 cases all told. Can you help me get just one to Pietermaritzburg?" On the twenty-fourth the cache near the spruit contained all the chlorodyne Roberts had requested and more, but no direct word from Botha.

And then it was Christmas Day, a Monday, so there were

to be two days in a row of no cannonading by the Boers—except that this was wrong. Nonexploding shells began to land in the main street and on the cricket field just after nine in the morning, filled with plum pudding instead of powder, scribbled with charitably ironic messages of greeting from the Christian Boers to the Christian English. An extra train to Intombi, bearing delicacies for the sick and wounded, was allowed to make an early afternoon run, and on it was Roberts Menzies.

Catherine was terribly ill in her tent, sweating drenchingly into her bedclothes, drawn, hardly even a semblance of her normal self, but still courageous. She asked Roberts to take the baby that day, to have it born on Christmas; said she was dying and felt her body could no longer give it necessary support. But Roberts refused, gave her more of the painkiller with which the Boers had supplied him, and told her before she became unconscious that he was trying to arrange for her escape. It is unclear how much of Roberts' treasonous behavior Catherine had known about as she accepted the supplies of medicine through the month of December, but now she could not help being aware of the enormity of it. And Roberts became even more aware himself when, visiting Maria this same evening, he learned of her pregnancy.

Finally, on the twenty-sixth, came the heliograph BOTHA YES BOTHA YES that he had been waiting for, and after dark he went to the place where he met Maria, and with her was Botha himself.

"A wagon will be ready at Lombards Nek at daybreak. You must get her there yourself. From there we will get her to Buller."

"But Lombards Nek is more than two miles from Intombi. Can you not bring it to the main Colenso road?"

"Doctor Menzy, it is the best I can do. De Jager is responsible for the main road and he does not approve of the things you and I do or the methods we use. He might not cooperate."

"But you are the general; he is only a field cornet."

Again the boyish laugh. "This is not the English army, Bob. The Boer army is democratic—rank means little except in battle. You must get her to Lombards Nek—Weilbach will let the wagon through without trouble."

"It cannot be tomorrow. She will not be fit to travel. She is heavily sedated and about to deliver."

"Then the next day. According to your diagnosis, you have little time left, and I cannot keep the wagon and driver available indefinitely. Do not waste more time. Take the baby yourself, Doctor. Do not wait on God to hand it to you. Joubert waited on God, and that is why we waste our time with this siege now when we could have been dining in Durban a month ago. You and I respond to life, Doctor, and control what we can rather than have to react blindly to what we cannot."

When Roberts reached Intombi after four on the twenty-seventh, the nurses were beside themselves with the number of new patients that had been delivered on the same train, and Roberts was diverted for some hours in helping them rearrange the ever-more-crowded hospital. Old patients who were either on the verge of death or somewhat stronger than the others had to sleep on canvas sacks on the floor now, while patients in the middle stages of the disease were given the beds. Catherine herself had insisted that as a staff member she not have a bed and so had a sack. So it was after midnight, in the early hours of the twenty-eighth, that Roberts, one other nurse, and the chaplain—she to assist, he to hold the lantern above them—performed the cesarean section on Catherine Clyde Menzies and removed from her womb the boy who was named Bruce and christened on the spot—the boy who would, a month from now, be spirited out of Ladysmith and Africa through the arrangements of his father (whom he would not see for nineteen more years and then would reject) and by Maria De Jager (whom twenty-five years from now he would, with the help of his paternal grandfather, kill). But now, December 28, 1899, Bruce was swatted on the buttocks as he dangled upside down in his father's hands and cried a healthy yowl and was handed to the nurse and coaxed to full life while his father sutured his mother's abdomen. Roberts appropriated a litter from a supply tent and carried it to the edge of the Intombi clearance and deposited it in some underbrush. Then he found his way back through the darkened maze of tents, navigating almost by the sound of one distinctly terrified moan which Roberts knew to be in the tent next to Catherine's. Once back inside the right tent, which was occupied by eleven other patients as well, he relit the lantern and moved outside to the side nearest Umbulwana and flashed BOTHA YES BOTHA YES by covering and uncovering the lantern with his hand. Then he extinguished it and sneaked back into the tent so as not to wake the other patients and accidentally have them sound an alarm, picked up Catherine in his arms so as not to strain her sutures, and carried her as quickly as he could to where he had left the stretcher. In the darkness he could not find where he had left it—but Maria already had and signaled him to it with a briefly lit match. Totally unconscious now, Catherine was strapped to the litter, and her husband and his pregnant mistress set out in the direction of Lombards Nek, two and a half miles to the east, she at the front because she knew the terrain better than he, he at the rear. They crossed the railroad tracks less than a hundred yards from the point at which the Boers had severed them after General French had gotten away by train on the first day of the siege, then proceeded across the flat plain for a mile and a half to the Klip River. There was only the barest fragment of a moon available to guide them, but it saw them through the most critical places, brush they would have tripped over, holes in which they could have stepped and so turned an ankle or dropped the litter or both. They knew when they were nearing the Klip because of its rancid stench—it had become almost a sewer to the south of Ladysmith now—and when they reached the bank they set the stretcher down, removed all their clothing and tucked it under the straps that held Catherine in place, and then crossed the river, never more than four feet deep, with the stretcher painfully extended at arms' length above them. When they emerged on the other side, they were less than a hundred yards from the Colenso main road, which Roberts had wanted to be the rendezvous point for the wagon—and here they encountered difficulty.

A Boer guard on the road had detected some indication of their movement through the river and had left the road to investigate. He approached with a lighted lantern, and in its glare they could see a bayonet fixed and ready at the tip of his gun. He was a very big man, but alone. Still naked, Roberts and Maria held to the underbrush alongside the foul-smelling Klip, listening to the man's repeated cries of "Who goes there?" in Afrikaans. Then his light accidentally found them as he passed within ten feet of where they lay. He saw them less than half a second before he was hit full force in the stomach by the driving body of a nude man who knocked the wind out of him and then cuffed his hand over his mouth so he could not cry out. But he could still see as a naked woman —only a teenage girl—now jumped out from where she hid and snatched the rifle from his grip and, rather than club him into unconsciousness with it as Roberts had expected, stabbed him three times in the abdomen with the fixed bayonet. In horror, Roberts released his grip on the man and the man struggled to rise to his feet; did so, in fact, only to clutch his stomach violently and then tumble forward into the Klip and remain there face down.

Roberts' heart was pounding so hard he could not catch his breath. In the glare of the lantern, he could see the naked body of Maria De Jager, still wet from the Klip, smelling like it, as was his, weeds and dead bugs pasted to her breasts and stomach and pubic hair and thighs. He could not move, so she did. She extinguished the lamp, pulled her clothing from the litter and jammed his at him, ordered him to dress when he seemed in the darkness to make no move. She wore only a man's boots and pants and a loose-fitting shirt, so she was dressed quickly, waited impatiently for him to finish, then took her end of the litter as he did his, and walked much faster now across the main road, then along the base of Umbulwana and finally to the Helpmakaar Road, which passed between Umbulwana and Lombards Kop through the gap called Lombards Nek. And now, with Catherine beginning to moan and stir on the stretcher, perhaps roused to semiconsciousness by the nauseating stench of their bodies, they awaited sunrise.

At first light the covered wagon Botha had promised could be seen making its way, slowly enough to be as inconspicuous as possible, from a farmhouse about a mile to the east. When it arrived, the driver looked without interest at Roberts, but spoke several lines in Afrikaans to Maria. Then he dismounted, and with her help, not Roberts', he loaded Catherine into the rear of the wagon. And Maria, again not Roberts, reached under the strap and produced the medical kit Roberts had prepared and translated what written directions she could for him, and the man went on his way, turning the wagon in a wide arc off the road and then back onto it and away to the east for the next southerly road to Colenso.

When it had gone out of sight, Maria returned to herself again, became a Boer girl instead of whoever she had been for the last three hours. But the daylight was increasing, and they had to part. She kissed him innocently, before turning to go back to Umbulwana, but her face and hair smelled of the Klip. And for the rest of the day, Roberts would have to hide until darkness behind a boulder through 108-degree temperatures, watching the skeletal Ladysmith oxen trying to graze just within the British perimeter, the horses gamely attempting to do the same and stumbling with every step because of their weakened muscles. And Roberts had nothing else to do but think of his wife, perhaps of Maria, perhaps of his son.

He would not know until he reached Pietermaritzburg on March 4 with most of his hundred patients still alive that Catherine had died in Buller's hospital tents near Chieveley on January 2. He would never know that Maria would die at Bruce's hands on June 20, 1925, or that Bruce himself would fall mortally wounded in the North African desert on May 11, 1943. On this day, December 28, 1899, Roberts vomited at one thirty in the afternoon because he could not stand the sun or the smell of the Klip.

21 *ROBERTS MENZIES IN LADYSMITH: THE BLOODLETTING*

On January 1, 1900, there were 1,350 people hospitalized in Ladysmith's four field locations, and by January 15 the number would rise to 2,400. The death rate on January 1 was eight a day; by February 1 it would near thirty a day. In the Town Hall hospital itself, the total death figure for the entire month of January would be seven; for February, seventeen. This was *bound* to attract notice, and Roberts Menzies knew it, continually planned for it whenever it occurred.

Perhaps fueled by the re-creative powers of a new year, hope for early relief increased among almost everyone except the highest military authorities, who knew better, and Roberts Menzies, who knew the Boers were reading all of Buller's heliographs like headlines on a newspaper. So when Buller signaled on the first that he was giving up on the center of the Boer line at Colenso and moving some ten miles to the west to attack its right, Roberts saw Boer wagons on the mountain roads heading that way themselves. Roberts, however, had gotten to the point where he tried not to notice, wished the British would change either their code or their tactics or both and, most of all, not leave anything around for him to have to take or turn over. He continued taking in his extra medicine at the spruit cache, and on January 2 found an unaddressed and unsigned note attached to it. "Delivery to

Chieveley accomplished 1 January '00. Still intact." Which he took to mean still alive, not knowing that even as he read the note, the information was out of date.

Perhaps the most important day of all in Ladysmith in January was the sixth, for this was the day the Boers almost broke through to take it. Roberts' diary for this day is almost totally surgical—he had been ordered out to a dressing station below Caesar's Camp—but all the history books detail what occurred.

The Boers had decided that the Siege must end, that the troops were being wasted at Ladysmith when there was the constant danger of Buller's breaking across the Tugela and now of Lord Roberts and Kitchener heading through the Cape Province toward the Orange Free State. In fact, the Free Staters were openly honest with Botha and Joubert, saying that their business in Natal would conclude the moment they got word that their homeland was in jeopardy. So the Free Staters themselves chose to lead the attack on Ladysmith on the sixth, to get it over with. The position their strategists had long ago decided would be most important to wrest from British control, the one that would virtually render Ladysmith helpless, was the row of low hills directly to its south which at its west end was called Wagon Hill and at its east Caesar's Camp. Could they take this two-mile-long elevation, the Boers would be within three thousand yards of the town—even between the town and the Intombi Camp hospital—and could pound it mercilessly with their artillery. The one mitigating circumstance in an open attack on these positions was that it was the C-Sector of the Ladysmith perimeter, and the C-Sector was commanded by the ablest of all White's lieutenants, Colonel Ian Hamilton.

Hamilton suspected the attack was coming when he heard the Boers singing hymns just after midnight on January 6. Likewise he knew that Wagon Hill was the most critical point of the Ladysmith defenses, knew it was most likely to be what came under attack, and so, in the dark, placed a gun on top of it—which, of course, the Boers did not know about. But the day's fighting was nonetheless the bitterest of the entire Siege. Several times the Boer riflemen nearly reached the crest of Wagon Hill, only to have Hamilton's men rally to push them back down. The strategic error the Boers made all day long was not trying to work around behind the hill to cut off continual reinforcements from Ladysmith which kept reappearing each time the Boers battered their way toward the crest. Still, with the besieged soldiers in an undernourished and diseased state, it was not at all clear through the day whether they could hold up. White even heliographed to Buller to start his movement northward then; that much of the opposition was pointed at Ladysmith now instead of being positioned along the Tugela Heights. According to Winston Churchill, however, Buller's war machine was so cumbersome that it would have taken a week to gather itself together, much less be ready on a moment's notice to fly north.

The British received assistance from Nature instead. At five o'clock that afternoon, a thunderstorm broke which Hamilton later called the worst he had ever seen. According to his journals, it was impossible to distinguish between the boom of the guns and the crash of the thunder, impossible to see more than a few feet in front of his eyes. Now the Boer artillery, which was shelling the British resistance from Umbulwana and Gun Hill, had to cease firing because the Boers could easily hit their own forces. The British artillery, which was pounding back at the Boer gun sites, had no such problem and so, even at the height of the thunder and lightning and rain, kept it up. Without the Boer artillery to worry about, the British infantrymen were able to mass a final rush over the crest of Wagon Hill and so drive the Boers back to their own lines on the plains beyond it, groping and splashing through the rain and mud. Several were killed by lightning. But the British had suffered 424 casualties for the day, the Boers 183—which included, however, 64 dead. White heliographed Buller of his victory at the next opportunity, but said MY TROOPS ARE PLAYED OUT. I WILL HAVE TO TRY TO BREAK OUT IF YOU DO NOT ARRIVE SOON. Reading this, of course, the Boers strengthened their forces around Ladysmith.

At mid-January as well there came the series of events which, with the exception of Colenso, were most catalyzed by Roberts' treachery with the codebooks. On the twelfth Buller's heliograph appeared in a new direction, to the west-southwest, announcing that he was preparing to turn the Boer line at Potgieter's Drift. Now the difficulty caused by the Boers' being able to read a message such as this was not so much that they would not be surprised by the materialization of twenty-five thousand soldiers at a single location all of a sudden; it was rather that, knowing what the exact location would be days in advance, they could go there and dig trenches. Sharpshooting riflemen, as the Boers by definition were, hidden in trenches are devastating to attacking infantry and cavalrymen. So, late on the twelfth, the Boers began digging in behind Potgieter's Drift.

And yet, as the Boers quickly discovered, trenches here might not be the best strategy—again advance warning had given them time to think things out—for the river looped against them in such a way as to place them on treacherous peninsulas such as Hart's men had gotten on at Colenso. Also, the steep inclines of the heights behind them could serve to have them, first, pinned down and, second, picked off as they went up them in retreat. So Botha decided to *give* the river and the short flatland beyond it to Buller and dug his trenches on *top* of the mountains instead.

At first it might seem foolish for Buller to have tried this west end of the Boer line, a situation in which he would have to send his army up the sheer face of a mountain barrier rather than through the gorges behind Colenso. The plan did have the advantage, however, of being a single effort, great though it would be; for if the row of mountains from Tabanayama at the left to the Twin Peaks at the right, three miles apart, with Spion Kop dominating the center, could be taken, the land beyond, the entire thirteen miles to Ladysmith, was flat grassy plain. The old Colenso route would have had the British Army in a continuous canyon for miles, fighting Boers off hills on both sides, continually under fire. It seemed worth a try—except that the Boers knew all the strategy. So Warren's men were allowed across the Tugela at Trichardt's Drift and Lyttleton's at Potgieter's. But Warren's movements were pitifully slow—it took him two full days just to get his baggage trains across—and the great battle to be fought at Spion Kop did not come about until the early hours of Wednesday, January 24. Since the twenty-second, the people inside Ladysmith had been observing various sections of the siege force moving off across this same grassy plain to join Botha on Spion Kop.

Commandant Viljoen, one of Botha's subordinates, later called the Boer victory at Spion Kop a fluke. Had the British won, it would have been a fluke as well. Each side made terrible mistakes. For the British, their guns on the plain below often fell short of the mark and struck their own men ascending the mountain. When the commanding officer on the side of Spion Kop, General Woodgate, was killed, both General Coke and General Thorneycroft were put in command, each without the knowledge of the other, and began issuing conflicting orders. Despite the terrible losses the British suffered going up the side toward one false crest after another, Buller held back more than half his forces south of the Tugela and never committed them to the battle.

The Boer mistakes eventuated when they presumed they were losing though in fact they were winning. It had been Botha's strategy to conserve losses for the Boers by backing up from the lower trenches down the mountainside if need be, ever concentrating his forces near the top for what he hoped would be an impossible climb for the British over the summit. Each time the British advanced from one trench line to the next, they had to cross open areas and absorb tremendous losses. Yet for some of the burghers, this apparently steady movement was enough to convince them that the day was about to be lost, and so they began to pack up to go home. The British did, then, achieve their goal—they took the crest of Spion Kop.

And then they gave it up. Not knowing the disarray the Boer command and army were in, General Thorneycroft decided that the crest could not be held through the night, that his soldiers would be slain to a man by night rifle fire, and so he backed down the front side of Spion Kop. As this was happening, an argument erupted as to who was in command —Coke or Thorneycroft—and the subordinate officers seemed to wish to believe Coke was, though he was not present, so they would not have to leave the summit they had bled to get. Winston Churchill, as always offering more advice than he had the age, rank, or position to give, suggested they signal Warren's camp at the base to get a clear order. But the searchlight had run out of oil, and Thorneycroft's order stood.

At daybreak, the only men on the crest of Spion Kop were the dead, piled three deep in Boer trenches, and the near-dead wounded of both sides. Then two men appeared on the crest alone, waving slouch hats toward the plain where Botha's army was massed. These two men had "retaken" Spion Kop.

All day long on the twenty-fourth, Ladysmith had seen the smoke atop Spion Kop, had felt the earth rattling from the Long Toms and pom-poms doing their business there, had heard White's own guns "demonstrating" to keep further Boers from leaving the siege lines to go help against Buller. Patients in the Town Hall asked to be wheeled to southwesterly windows on the second floor so they could look out over the low-slung houses of the town to spot the English relief force when it broke through. But the British did not appear on the twenty-fourth of January; rather, they came on the twenty-fifth—three hundred of them, marching across the grassy plain under Boer guard toward Elandslaagte Station and the long ride in freight cars to Pretoria prison.

On the twenty-seventh Buller heliographed full details of his loss at Spion Kop and his future plans to try east of Colenso next—in two more weeks. White apparently lost heart, signaled that he planned to leave his sick and wounded behind and was going to take his remaining able soldiers to break out to the south. The Boers tightened their lines on the southerly roads within the hour. And so the last gasp of hope as January ended was that Lord Roberts and Kitchener would invade the Orange Free State as they had promised and draw off enough of the siege force to allow Ladysmith to be freed. Medical supplies—at some hospitals—were desperately low, and food, especially meat, was almost nonexistent.

And so the horses. The seventy-five most healthy were retained. Others were driven out on the veld to graze, if they could, so that human beings could eat their food; but these highly trained cavalry animals could not forage and kept trying to fight their way back to their men—their individual men, for the relationship of a cavalry horse and his own rider is one of brotherhood. So White employed mounted Basutos with heavy whips to drive them away from Ladysmith. The ones not driven away were shot—to be eaten. The cavalrymen who lay sick or wounded in the Town Hall hospital actually cried when they heard this.

* * * * * *

The change in the tone and content of Roberts' diary after the first day of the new century is startling. There is nothing personal in it, not even the most critical facts of his existence that can be glimpsed through Maria De Jager's journal. It is as if he did not want to admit to being Roberts Menzies, even to himself—this was apparent from the battle at Colenso forward. And surely there was the fear of being caught by the authorities; perhaps he dared commit nothing suspect to paper. Though it is somewhat surprising that he did not destroy the very incriminating things he had already written in the previous two months, it must be understood that for a diarist to destroy his diary is often tantamount to psychological suicide.

Yet what was happening that Roberts was not telling about? We at least know that it was on Wednesday, the seventeenth of January, that Roberts made his first visit to Maria since their removal of Catherine Menzies from the Intombi Camp in the early morning hours of the twenty-eighth of December. According to Maria's journal, it was on this occasion that she made her own first suggestion of his performing the abortion. (Roberts had brought this matter up on Christmas Day but the whole thing had dropped.) In fact, after the Klip River incident on the twenty-eighth, there is some suggestion that Roberts may have planned no more visits to Maria—at least, she feared as much, but she could not figure out why this might happen. Also in this meeting of the seventeenth, she mentioned that they should possibly get married—she seemed to know intuitively that Catherine could not have lived long enough to reach Pietermaritzburg.

So Roberts returned on the next night—all we find in his own diary for these dates is medical discussion and remarks that heliographs had signaled the crossings of the Tugela at Trichardt's and Potgieter's drifts—and offered his plan that he "*would marry*" Maria after the Siege, if he could, but that he had to remain with his patients (the original hundred and one still numbered ninety-one) until it was lifted. So she agreed to flee Umbulwana at her first opportunity, carrying the three-week-old Bruce and her own six-week-old fetus with her. On Friday the nineteenth, he turned up with a Glasgow address, and a hundred pounds of British gold currency. The infant was very hungry, and she made the extremely mature decision to turn him over for wet-nursing to a Boer mother whose own baby had died in childbirth. This would give him a week of strengthening before, on the following Friday—two days after the fluke Boer victory at Spion Kop—she stole the wagon and, on the twenty-seventh, fled before daybreak, leaving Umbulwana Mountain, the Boer cause and nation, and the family who considered the British an enemy but Roberts Menzies a disgrace to the human race. January 27, the day General White reacted to another disappointment by petulantly threatening to break out and then not trying, was the very day that Maria De Jager responded by doing exactly that. Perhaps the fact that the Boer troops had tightened to the south in case White tried it had made it easier for her to escape to the north.

February, 1900 * * * And now the mood of Ladysmith was at low ebb. Three thousand were hospitalized, and the death rate was climbing quickly toward its ultimate maximum of thirty a day. Both General White, aged sixty-eight, and Roberts Menzies, aged twenty-eight, had taken to walking with canes because their leg and back muscles were too weakened to be relied upon. Looming over all of this, because of a tactless heliograph from Buller on the first, was the new threat of a German engineer who had landed at Delagoa Bay and was on his way inland with a scheme to dam the Klip River south of Ladysmith and so flood the town into submission.

Colonel Exham had for some reason given Roberts the duty of seeing to the sanitary arrangements at the railroad shed next to the station in which the horses were being slaughtered and butchered for food. He was to approve the cleanliness of the work area, as well as the readiness of the two giant engine-repair pits which had been converted into caldrons to cook the horsemeat into what was to be called "chevril," or horse broth. But it did not take Roberts long to understand why he had been appointed sanitary officer: it gave Exham an opportunity each day to rifle the medical supply at the Town Hall hospital. And virtually every last label of any of those bottles was printed in Afrikaans. Roberts expected major troubles now, and they were not long in coming. White summoned Roberts to him on the sixth, the same day on which Maria reached Delagoa Bay with Bruce.

White called Roberts before him on Convent Hill and suggested that the young doctor, for all his fine record, had not been aboveboard with his superiors. According to Roberts, they conducted the entire meeting on their feet—both men must have been leaning on their canes—and White wanted to know where the medicine had come from and what had had to be paid out to get it.

"Nothing, sir."

"That is not so, and you know it."

"It is given me by Boer doctors with whom I have become fr— . . . professionally involved during mop-ups."

"I asked for medical supplies long ago. Why were they not given to me?"

"For two reasons, sir. You dealt with the generals, not the doctors. And you dealt with Joubert and Lucas Meyer. The younger generals are more humane in such matters."

"I do not believe this, Menzies. I believe you have been giving them something they need."

"Yes, I have. I have given them advice about treatments which have been available in Edinburgh for five years but would not have reached here for another five. I return humanity with humanity."

"I believe you have given them military information."

"What military information would I have? The only military officers I have dealt with are Colonel Exham and Major

Donegan and yourself. But what information would any of them have—except you? And you have not—"

"Doctor Menzies, are you aware that just this morning Mr. Foss was court-martialed merely for issuing communiqués with depressing language and demoralizing overtones; that he was given a year in prison?"

"All right, then, sir, I will stop accepting medicine from the doctors. In fact, take me off mop-up duty—my time is well used at the Town Hall and at the horse pits as it is."

White undoubtedly flinched at the thought of giving up any medicine, even if it had Afrikaans labeling and was suspiciously acquired. Also undoubtedly, he released Roberts with a severe caution.

On February 8, Roberts records a confrontation with Exham at the horse caldron, the two men trying to stare each other down through the stinking steam of boiled horsemeat on a hundred-degree day, both men in pith helmets and khaki, sweat-stained under the arms and down the back, Roberts on a cane, Exham still disdaining one.

"This is the hundredth day of the Siege, Menzies. We have been counting heads. When you entered from Dundee in October, you were one hundred three strong. You still have ninety patients alive—defying all odds, I might add—you have buried eleven, and you stand here before me. One hundred two. You came with a nurse who was your wife. Where is she?"

Roberts must have scowled without wanting to at the statement. "You, sir, assigned her to Intombi."

"I have checked. She is no longer there."

"She contracted enteric. She died." Roberts of course did not know the accuracy of what he was saying.

"There is absolutely no record of that, Menzies."

"Then what is your theory, Colonel?"

"I am quite sure that she has escaped and is dealing in Boer medicine which somehow gets only to you. Deny it if you can."

"On the contrary, Colonel, prove it if *you* can."

"Watch your mouth, Menzies. Men have already been court-martialed and jailed here for less."

"Not doctors, sir."

Nevertheless, Roberts knew he was being carefully watched. With Buller having announced another reversal at Vaal Krantz, a doomsday mentality had set in, almost as if nothing would matter now, no matter how stupid the action—even imprisoning doctors. But then events conspired, however unhappily, to keep Roberts Menzies entirely safe, at least for the time.

On Friday, February 9, there was no delivery of supplies at the spruit cache, and again there was none on the tenth. With Maria as far away now as Lourenço Marques, he had no means by which to make inquiries, could flash BOTHA YES into the hills till he was blue in the face. The likely sources of the problem were, of course, plentiful: the Boers could themselves be running short; Botha might simply have decided that he had given enough for one set of codebooks received now almost three months ago; perhaps Exham's parasites had found the supplies; perhaps the kaffirs were selling them. And his own supply on hand was low given the fact that he had had several cases stolen by Exham while he was tending the sanitary arrangements at the horse caldrons. Then a way to make contact developed.

On Sunday the eleventh, while examining patients at Intombi, Roberts discovered a major named Doveton to be in his last hours from enteric fever. Doveton, as far as Roberts was concerned, was one of the most despicable people in Ladysmith. An imperialist of enormous dimensions, he had been the man four years before whose role in the Jameson Raid was to stir the Uitlanders in Johannesburg into action at the very moment Jameson and Frank Rhodes, both also still alive and well inside Ladysmith at this very hour, were engaging the Boer defensive forces outside it. Though the whole mission had failed, Doveton continually bragged about the fact that it was simply the opening chapter in the drama, that the current war, Ladysmith's present helplessness notwithstanding, was the final one—Britain would now dominate all the gold and diamonds in South Africa.

The Boers knew Doveton was in Ladysmith as well—Roberts himself had mentioned it to De Jager on the occasion when he tried to negotiate for medical supplies—and there was no individual they hated more, not even Jameson or Rhodes or Willoughby. Yet now, on the day that was to be Doveton's last, his wife (who had evacuated Ladysmith on one of the last trains before the Siege) reappeared at the Intombi Camp to spend his last hours with him. Roberts, who vaguely knew her from a period when the couple had lived in Dundee, was stunned to see her. In her grief in the hours after Doveton passed away, he could not help inquiring how she had gotten there.

Her answer, as best it can be made out from Roberts' diary entry for the eleventh, was that Botha had slipped her in through the same route the medical supplies took—or used to. Roberts' tone here suggests he was stunned by the fact that Botha would aid someone he and every other Boer so detested. He could not help placing his own name in a pair with Doveton's. But Roberts, or at least the highly pragmatic Bob Menzy, decided that Mrs. Doveton would be the means by which he would make contact with Botha, so he wrote a brief note suggesting his difficulties, even attached a list of those supplies for which his need was most desperate. Since Mrs. Doveton was inside the Ladysmith perimeter illegally, she would have no means to turn him in if she objected to delivering it and actually was so grief-stricken that she probably did not think twice about what she was doing. It would be a mere mechanical act. So she took it with her.

The reader might be inclined at this point to ask about British security. Roberts had taken in more than twoscore shipments of medicine; had left the perimeter and returned several times, once even carrying a dying woman, another time a newborn infant. Now Mrs. Doveton was in and out within a matter of hours. The fact is that British security was as tight as it could possibly have been, was even becoming overtight into the middle of February—but *never* around the Intombi Camp. Those people assigned there—such as the three nurses who were receiving the supplies from the kaffir runners—operated by different standards than those four miles off in Ladysmith did. These standards were not entirely altruistic, for the arrival of the supplies in the long run helped keep the diseases distant from the medical personnel who had to deal with them. No one knew what Roberts had done to establish this lifeline to the outside; the nurses did not care; Major Donegan did not allow himself to ask questions. But now, apparently, Roberts had made perhaps his most ill-advised move, as Botha was to confirm.

No supplies arrived on the twelth, but some did arrive on the thirteenth, the very date on which Roberts had expected them, *if* Mrs. Doveton had delivered the letter. She had, and Botha had attached one to the packing cases in response. "This is the last I can send. Exactly as to your list. You will not need them much longer. You have made a mistake that could cost your life. You will be safe to Maritzburg but do not tarry there an extra minute. Heavy birds make loud cries, especially the female. I will see you again. Till then." Unaddressed and unsigned, of course.

On this same day, February 13, 1900, Lords Roberts and Kitchener invaded the Orange Free State from the west, and the Free Staters around Ladysmith and the Tugela Heights packed their wagons and sped away to their homeland, weakening Boer forces in the Natal theater by 30 percent. And on this same day Maria and Bruce lay between decks on a freighter bound for Durban.

All Buller's forces and White's besieged would now need was dogged persistence and wise patience. In Ladysmith, the increase of rainfall that occurred at this point was a boon for the drinking-water supply and the control of typhoid, but it was a worry in that the plan to flood Ladysmith was nearly workable, and this sort of natural assistance could be fatal if Buller did not hurry. Meanwhile, on the sixteenth, Buller opened his assault to the east of Colenso, attacking Hlangwane Hill—which he should long ago have taken and used as the anchor of *any* assault on the Tugela Line; but as usual, it took him three whole days to secure it. But he *did* take it, and for the first time "Sir Reverse" did not return to Chieveley after a battle. On the eighteenth he had also taken Monte Cristo Hill, the one with the best observation of the entire Pieter's Road to Ladysmith. British soldiers, Winston Churchill among them, could now actually *see* the small town which they had heretofore accepted was even there only on blind faith.

Below, the Boers were forced to evacuate Colenso and back up into the dreaded canyons behind it, fighting gamely as they awaited the Transvaal reinforcements coming by railroad from Pretoria. On the twenty-first, Buller's huge army forced its way across the Tugela on pontoon bridges northeast of Colenso and commenced operations to take a series of hills one by one—Horseshoe Hill, then Wynne Hill; then—on the twenty-third—the terrible battle for Inniskilling Hill which cost the lives of 450 Irish troops. This won, however, only three would remain: Railway Hill, Pieter's Hill, and the one last hill between Buller and Ladysmith: Umbulwana. And Umbulwana would be no problem, for the Boers there would desert it rather than have to fight White on the west side and Buller on the east.

Fighting ceased almost entirely on the twenty-fourth and twenty-fifth, for there were so many wounded of both sides left on the field that the two sides agreed to an "informal armistice" to collect them. In Ladysmith, there was dismay for three solid days that the pounding guns which had been heard for a week had suddenly stopped. Had Buller gone away yet another time? Then a heliograph was received that indicated action would recommence on the twenty-sixth, but still it did not, and there was no sun by which Buller could flash any hope to the town. Ironically, a supply train from the south had caught up with Buller this day, and red-blue-and-gold tins of chocolate from Queen Victoria were being distributed to every soldier. First things first. Or maybe Buller knew that this time he would get through, and he wanted to do it on February 27—Majuba Day—to thoroughly demoralize the Boers and erase that dreadful day from both Boer and British memory. The Battle of Majuba Hill was nineteen years before and had been fought on the day Maria De Jager was born. This birthday she was at sea off the west coast of France, two days out of Southampton.

February 27 was the most thunderous day of the entire Siege of Ladysmith. In a last desperate effort to retain their stronghold, or perhaps their pride, the Boer gun positions around Ladysmith began pounding the town more unmercifully than they ever had before, with Caesar's Camp and Wagon Hill receiving the worst of it. It was as if the Boers on Umbulwana and Lombards Kop could feel the heat of Buller on their backs now and planned to retreat *through* Ladysmith rather than around it. They could hear the thumping of Buller's pom-poms even more clearly than the town inhabitants could, probably could smell the awful lyddite drifting to them on the breeze if there was one, surely could read Buller's heliograph which flashed simply AM DOING WELL, perhaps could hear now the clash of sabers on Mauser barrels—the fighting had gotten this close—maybe knew (as the British within and without did) that Kimberley had been relieved more than a week ago and that, this very day, General Piet Cronje had surrendered his army to Lord Roberts at Paardeberg. By nightfall, Buller's army had only Pieter's Hill left to take before it could race across the plain toward Umbulwana and Ladysmith.

And the Boers fired at Ladysmith all night, not with heavy guns now but with blazing Mausers fired blindly into the town to hit whatever moving object strayed in their path. What the British inside did not yet understand was that the Boers' purpose was to fire off all their ammunition rather than have to surrender it or have it captured. So the town was awake all night.

At dawn on the twenty-eighth, Buller's artillery increased the orchestrated racket. His army fought all the Boers now—old men and women, young children, wives, burghers, whoever was in the trenches making one last-ditch effort to fire back, hoping that this mighty army which had failed at

Colenso and Spion Kop and Vaal Krantz—you name it, they had failed there—would fail yet one more time when all they had to do was descend the northern face of Pieter's Hill and charge for Umbulwana, which even now they could see being evacuated before them.

All morning long, the inhabitants of the town and garrison —sleep- and food-starved both now—watched to the south, knowing it was about to be over, glimpsing Boer wagons pulling away from Umbulwana and Lombards Kop and Gun Hill and Long Hill, Pepworth Hill and Surprise Hill and Telegraph Ridge and Rifleman's Ridge—the entire circle which had roped them in for 120 relentless days—dragging their Creusot Long Toms and ammunition carriages behind them. Those citizens who could ran wildly about the town, carrying news of desertions of Boer positions on the entire circumference to those too weak to do anything but sit and listen with tears in their eyes. Shortly after noon, Buller heliographed what everyone already knew: ENEMY FULLY DEFEATED—AM SENDING CAVALRY IN PURSUIT. An hour later British horsemen could be seen charging along the Colenso–Newcastle Road, five miles to the east, through the rough bush country toward Joubert's headquarters, which had already fled its position below Modder Spruit Siding.

But the town seemed not to feel itself free until Buller's force had *come to* it rather than rushed by it. And at four they saw the cloud of dust gathering size along the main Colenso road to the south of Umbulwana, coming straight at them, closer than the Intombi Camp now and never slowing. And they could see only one horseman, waving a Union Jack above him as high as his right arm could hold it, flapping straight back in the backwash of his speeding mount, its farther reaches disappearing into the smoky upheaval of the thousand horses' hooves pounding the iron-hard dirt of the road behind him.

22 THE LETTER

Now, seventy-five years and some four months afterward, Ann Macgregor adjusted herself to a more comfortable position against the rock at the lakeside where she and Jason Glass had so often, she so curiously and he so cynically, discussed Roberts Menzies before. She looked up from the final sheets Glass had written, saw Duncan skinny-dipping in the lake in the now-bright early afternoon sunshine. She looked long at him, not to make sure he was safe, but to assure herself that he existed. The very fact that he did assured her that his great-great-grandfather had. And Duncan was there in the water, splashing a shriveled sheepdog he called Charlie because a curiously ambivalent Boer girl had spirited his great-grandfather, only a small baby then, through an eight-thousand-mile journey from Ladysmith to Johannesburg, to Lourenço Marques, to Durban, to Cape Town, to Southampton, to London, and to Glasgow. And five years after all that, she had sent him to Kyle of Lochalsh station, but this time in a dog crate instead of against her bosom. The past causes us, so why should we not have to recognize it and, if we can, understand what it is trying to tell us?

Ann heard the front door of Glass's cottage slam closed a quarter of a mile behind her. She turned to see him walking slowly away from the house toward where she sat; then she looked in the other direction to scan only briefly the ruined house in which Maria De Jager, survivor of the guns of the Boer War, had been cannoned to death by the grown man she had rescued as a child, gunned down as the *coup de grâce* of a drunken holiday prank. Glass had closed this section of his story of Roberts Menzies with an extended passage from Roberts' diary dated March 3 and 4, 1900, the last he was to write in Ladysmith. He was summarizing the previous three days:

As I watched from the shattered clock tower atop my hospital on the 28th, the roads seemed covered by insects, actually Boers in flight. The drifts were choked with wagons. On Umbulwana,

De Jager's commando had not fled as yet, for they had their Long Tom still firing in the other direction now, against Buller's column, seeking to do what damage they could before it was inevitably done to them.

Later we saw the cloud of dust coming up from Intombi, a crowd of breakaway soldiers who had already liberated the hospital and now were to do the same for us. And I could see horsemen from our own defensive perimeter riding out with equal speed to meet them. All stopped momentarily, saluted each other about a mile south of the town; then they turned back toward Ladysmith and thundered on, not even pausing at the Klip but rather plunging their horses down the steep embankment on the south side, spraying through the water, then vaulting up the other bank into town. Here this vanguard of relief lost its identity as it was absorbed by our own soldiers and civilians. And it pushed up High Street, past the Anglican church, the crowd and the soldiers yelling and howling like wild animals, the Zulus and kaffirs dancing deliriously in the streets, the children clapping their hands and jumping to tap the ankles and spurs of their liberators. People cried and laughed together, waving both to Colonel Gough, the first officer in, and to General White, who had joined him on horseback at the river's edge. Finally White dismounted just below me on the Town Hall steps and stood on the top one to quell the crowd. But it kept cheering, thrice for Buller, then thrice for White, then thrice for Gough, whose name they did not, most of them, even know. I descended from the tower as quickly as my cane would take me so that I could be in position to hear White when the crowd finally allowed him to speak.

From sickness and from emotion he could hardly muster the words when his opportunity came. "Thank God we kept the flag flying. It cut me to the heart to reduce your rations as I did. I promise you, though, that I'll never do it again." The crowd cheered him ecstatically. In the building beside the Town Hall, the gaol, several Boer prisoners watched from a window without expression.

Later that evening White gave a small celebratory dinner at his quarters on Convent Hill. As I wandered the happy streets late that night—looking up at a sky filled tonight only with stars and not with searchlights and shellfire—I felt oddly detached from it all. As I had feared, my own sense of purpose has almost dissolved with the siege. I saw Winston Churchill walking along in front of Harvey Greenacre's store with Colonel Dundonald; he looked me straight in the face, smiled patriotically, but did not recall me from our train ride together more than three months ago. I went back to my quarters in the Town Hall and tried to sleep.

The next day a series of events occurred which must have been seen or heard or both over a seventy-five-mile radius. Once their train was loaded, the Boers moved across the bridge over Modder Spruit, stopped, and discharged one man, and he returned to the bridge and blew it up. The explosion stunned Ladysmith for several minutes, almost as if, through lack of serious attention, we had been laid siege to again. Then there were more explosions, and several other doctors and I rode north out of town to determine if our services were necessary. There before us was an enormous bonfire, set by the Boers to destroy all the equipment and ammunition that they could not flee with. Shells burst in the flames for hours, sending a column of fire and smoke into the air several hundred feet above the veld. It was black smoke by daylight, a demonic geyser of sparks and flame by night, and spread the heavy smell of gunpowder over the town itself.

On March 3rd, with all the citizens lining the High Street to greet them, Buller's entire army made its ceremonial entrance into Ladysmith. The parade ended with a speech by Mayor Farquhar in which he graciously thanked Buller for his efforts in reaching us, then lengthily thanked White for the protection he and his men had afforded us for the last four months. But White was too weak to reply, merely smiled a wry smile and waved feeble acceptance to the mayor and to the townspeople.

Sunday, 4 March 1900. I am to leave Ladysmith with the first batch of sick and wounded for Pietermaritzburg. General White, who has fallen more gravely ill with fever, has requested me personally and allowed me to incorporate my own remaining eighty-nine Dundee patients in the unit. We are to travel to Colenso in Buller's ambulances, cross the Tugela there, then board trains where the rail line is again intact at Chieveley. We should be at Martizburg tomorrow.

But my initial happiness and gratification at having again been chosen by White to be his attending physician—and my relief that my patients will at last leave here—are terribly muted at this moment. I bade a tearful goodbye to my nurses and to

Major Donegan last evening. Major Donegan, as he grasped my hand before all the nurses and patients on the ward, smiled and uttered aloud the standard formalities and thanks and then whispered three sentences before turning to thank the nurses himself: "You have been singled out to go first for a purpose, you know. Mrs. Doveton is in Pietermaritzburg. Be careful, Menzies." He gripped my hand more tightly, looked in my eye for several more seconds, told me silently he did not care how the medicine had come, and thanked me, also silently, for that service as well as my official ones. I will be careful, Major, my eyes, not my words, replied.

Glass moved quietly up behind her, though she knew he was there and so was not startled. He kicked off his shoes and sat down against the rock beside her. She leaned over and kissed him once, said nothing, then returned to her position, gazing toward and almost through the swimming Duncan and Charlie. Glass could see she had finished reading his manuscript, said nothing, waited for her to comment first. After five minutes, she did.

"Jason," she said with a hopelessly resigned sigh, "what does all this mean? Rather, what are we to think, in summary, about Roberts Menzies?"

"Ann, I think the word that has already gotten me into biographical trouble once—or apparently is about to—is *summary*. I have come to the conclusion you can't summarize about anyone. Roberts was a daring, patient, courageous, self-sacrificing doctor who should have received the George Cross; and he was a dastardly, scurrilous traitor and manipulator of other people who should have been hanged—still better, shot on sight." Now Glass sighed. "I have been hoping Roberts would be a despicable animal who could be held up as an example of what human conduct should never be, and Farquhar was hoping that he could be made to be superhuman, an ideal to which every man should aspire. Just like Annie Daly, I suppose. But I have decided that neither category exists: only humans exist. So what would the true story of either Roberts or Annie show—just more of the same? What I'd be saying in either case to a reader is 'Look, reader, here is still another moral photocopy of you and me—altruistic at one moment, devilishly selfish the next.' And all for what reason?"

"There's the trouble for me, Jason. The reason is clear after what I have read here. We are selfish to get whatever we feel we need and deserve in this life, whatever the cost to others."

"So why be altruistic, then, even for a moment?"

"To look ourselves in the eye, to think better of ourselves, to be able to endure ourselves."

Glass did not answer. He supposed he had come to that conclusion already himself. "And yet . . . and yet . . . don't some of 'us'—not me, maybe you—have higher standards for looking ourselves in the eye than others? Some people I know smile right back at themselves easily; others never can. Take Roberts. He had a soft life here. There was never any real reason to set foot in a place like South Africa to begin with. So why did he? He could have blackmailed the troop commander in Dundee into just getting him and his wife out of there, then could easily have left Ladysmith before the Siege, been back at the Castle Menzies enjoying life within a month. Yet he got a hundred and one patients out in twenty ox-driven ambulances, then saved ninety percent of them despite the fact that even previously healthy people survived at a far lower rate. Why? And then there's the lovely other side of Roberts. Why that, too? Two thousand soldiers died in the various efforts to relieve Ladysmith. So Roberts' total impact amounts to zero."

"At least he responded—you gave those words to Louis Botha in your writing. And what was Louis Botha's effort worth?"

"Well, we could on the one hand say that a descendant of Botha's—who currently is head of the South African Government—has benefited from his ancestor's efforts. South Africa is once again free of British rule; but it is subjecting its citizens, black and white, to the very things the British Empire, at least, knew were wrong long before the Boer War ever started! Jesus Christ!"

She had no better answer to this than he did, so she changed the subject. "So, now, Jason, have you looked in those pages of Maria's diary? You have the whole thing now, though I can't say that what you'll read there is about to lessen the complications any."

"I haven't looked yet, though I see your editing instinct has set about saving me some windy reading. Where do I start?"

"Here," she said with full certainty as she removed the top two translation sheets and pointed to a red-marked section on the third. "She arrived in Glasgow on the third of March, just about the time it seems that Roberts was packing to leave Ladysmith with General White. She took a flat in a building owned by the mother of a medical-school chum of Roberts—hence the address she was given on Gallowgate. She waited through the month of March for word of Roberts, of his return—had in fact circled the date of fourth April on her calendar as the likely date of his arrival. You see, she had given him as many days to show up in Glasgow as it had taken her. Finally, on twelfth April, she had her landlady's son, a practicing physician in Paisley, make official inquiries into the medical units that had been dispersed from Ladysmith. Hence, the entry for the sixteenth." She tapped the sheet with the tip of a red pen she had taken from her breast pocket, and Glass read the entry semiaudibly:

Monday, 16 April 1900. They have, it has turned out, found out what Bob had done at Ladysmith, but not all of it. They know he was in league with the Boer people in some way, that he received medical supplies from them, and that he must have paid them with something. They do not know what, but they have got Bob in the military prison at Durban and will send him home to be tried for treason. The witness against him is a kaffir, one of the wretches who were collecting many rand for carrying medicine in from the spruit cache. Several of his patients have asked to testify in his behalf, as has another doctor who served with him; but the tone of the War Office correspondence, Dr. Fletcher says, is very hostile. When I asked what his punishment could be, Dr. Fletcher said they could kill him. Which is what the Boer people would do.

Nothing else was written on this page—this stark factual information was all there was, though Ann pointed to several brief underlinings on ensuing ones which attested to a growing panic that she would be left alone, stranded in industrial rather than agricultural poverty. No entry contained any reference to what might be called "love" for Roberts—concern over his well-being, yes, anger at what was being done to him, fear that the inevitable might already have been carried out, but never love. Somewhere in the month of April she had gotten a job tending the produce table at a local street market, and this was how she was managing to feed herself, Bruce, and her unborn child; but there seemed, according to Ann, to be no references to Bruce or how he was being cared for.

The next entry Ann had circled in red came five or six pages later:

Wednesday, 9 May 1900. Bob is free. He has escaped from prison. I know he shall soon be home. His letter was posted from Johannesburg on 19th April, and it took only three weeks for it to get here. He should be here any day.

"Which is a very sad entry indeed," Ann remarked as Glass studied Krige's words on the page. "She clearly did not understand at this point that anyone writing from Johannesburg just weeks before it was to surrender to the British was unlikely to be able to return unimpeded to England. How do you suppose he escaped?"

Glass was silent for a moment. "I would presume that Botha had something to do with it. I just got the impression from Roberts' Ladysmith pages that some sort of *Blutsbrüderschaft* had developed between them. Look what they had done for each other, after all! Churchill had escaped from a Boer prison in Pretoria without help, but that prison was a school building. The British in Durban would have done things right. He would have needed help."

"It could have been Botha, Jason, though Durban would have been a long way behind British lines to slip in an operative for that sole purpose. And Botha himself we know to have been in Johannesburg and Pretoria at this period, for he was the commander through the final days of defense there."

"Who, then?"

"Donegan."

"A possibility, yes." Glass reflected for a moment. "But given the fact that Roberts turned up in Johannesburg at a time when Joburg was a dangerous place to be, I presume that Boers had something to do with it. Plus the fact that we find them all guerrilla-fighting together later. What's the next passage?"

She moistened her thumb and went several more sheets down in the pile: "This one." She tapped it rather more firmly this time.

Friday, 18 May 1900. A man who has bought tomatoes from me for the past three weeks turned up at my door this evening carrying a medallion and a card I could not read. He said he was from the Special Investigations Section of Scotland Yard.

It turns out that the way I received my letter from Bob so quickly is that it was censored at Cape Town and hand-carried all the way to my postbox. They seemed to think I knew where Bob was, would try to write him at a specified address in Johannesburg, where they could seize him once the city itself has fallen to Lord Roberts' army. And they have read all the post I had laid out on Mrs. Fletcher's table, thinking I would write to Bob. But I cannot write to him, and the only post I had laid out was applications for other employment, which, surely, have never been delivered or, if they have been, have been stamped as from the wife of a traitor to the Crown. I must leave here, for Mrs. Fletcher has been allowing them to look at my things, perhaps search my room. I must get somewhere where they cannot find me, or else Bob may never come to me in safety.

"You know," mused Glass, "this entry is more interesting for what it doesn't say than what it does. May seventeenth was the date on which Mafeking was relieved—the last of the three besieged towns. According to the research I've done, it was the first signal Britain had of the end of the Boer War, though we know how false a signal it turned out to be. Perhaps Maria disregards news of the event because she knows how tenacious her people will be about quitting, or perhaps it's that she has come to her senses and knows 'Bob' dare not come home, even after the war ended."

"The latter, I am sure, Jason. But now, look at this one." She flipped through the pages on Glass's lap until she came to the translation of the May 31 entry:

Thursday, 31 May 1900. Johannesburg, they say, has fallen today. It is hard to imagine Joburg "falling," for it was so infested with Uitlanders and moneygrubbers that it never even stood. I am sure all Lord Roberts had to do was walk with his men down Commissioner Street with all the fashionable British people, in their long dresses and straw hats, collecting near Payne Brothers and the jewelry store to stay away from the niggers who would surely be using the pavement further down the street for the first time in their miserable lives. Bob is safe so far, and they will not even look for him in Joburg because I have got a letter from him, which certainly they have read, which came from Pretoria. But that will fall too, and fall will be the proper word this time, and the Orange Free State has already fallen, so where next can he go? I must find a way to tell him where.

Ann had a triumphant look on her face as she flipped more sheets. "Now, Jason, this Boer girl, who at the age of nineteen has done so much, is not likely to remain helpless for long. Read this, now."

Wednesday, 6 June 1900. Pretoria was lost yesterday and Kruger will try, the papers say, to run the government from a railway car at Machododorp. The papers do not count the war won, however, for there are too many uncontrolled commandos loose on the veld. The British Government fears guerrilla tactics now. Lord Chamberlain claims Roberts and Kitchener and Buller can handle that, but I doubt he knows much about that of which he speaks. But what of Bob? He cannot come home to Scotland, and I cannot go home to the Transvaal. We must seek a neutral land, a land in which I am not a Boer and he is not a British subject. That will have to be America. But not yet. Bob will have to get out first and that will take time. I have not heard from him except twice and then he was in Johannesburg, and now he dare not be, and later in Pretoria, where he dare not be either. I hope he does not write to me and tell me where he is, for then he will be telling them too without even knowing it. I must guess where he will be.

"And did she guess?" Glass asked when he completed this entry.

"She made quite a good stab. The next day, assuming him to be a man without a country and a man with a dogged professional devotion, she decided that he would most likely have joined the neutral Red Cross operations east of Pretoria, where the war had now shifted. Not a bad assumption, do you think, Jason?"

"Not bad at all, frankly. So, without making me read all this just now, how did she handle it?"

Now she looked up at the lake and paused. "Duncan, stay away from that side, dearest; you'll get bogged in the undergrowth. Swim to the other side, that's a good chap." Duncan swam away from where he had been surface-diving on the "wrong" side of the lake. "Now, here is what happened, Jason." She had a good yarn to spin, knew Jason would be an expert listener, and prepared to tell it as well as she could. She sat up straight, leaving Glass in his slouched position. "She went to the Red Cross office in Glasgow and learned that an orphanage in Paisley was recruiting personnel to go to South Africa to see to the needs of Boer children orphaned by the war. Already the altruistic side of British imperialism was beginning to rear its guilty head, you see. They planned to set up two bases of operation: one at Bloemfontein, the other at Pretoria—the two capitals of the annexed republics. From there they would operate in the field as necessary. She wrote Roberts a letter—addressed, of course, to Bob Menzy—and asked that it be taken with the Pretoria contingent and held until they crossed paths with a Red Cross doctor by that name."

"Even that there would be such a Red Cross doctor was a long presupposition."

"Right you are, Jason, but you've already admired her inductive powers. Now let me continue, will you?" She did resent interruptions, as much as all good storytellers do. "Now, her diary for ninth June is fairly clear on what the contents of the letter were. She suggested that they both, by their own routes, head for America and join there in New York. She would not, however, leave until she received word from Roberts that he had agreed to the idea and was making positive efforts to go there himself. She would hoard whatever money she could to book passage when the time came."

"And how was *Roberts* supposed to get money? I doubt he was carrying much by this time."

"He was to steal it, more or less."

"How, Ann, does one 'more or less' steal?"

"By taking something that does not belong to the people who have it. Now let me tell! The De Jagers came from a place to the northeast of Pretoria called Tuinplaas. As each Boer commando was organized the previous October, the departing families would remove all the valuables from their homes and bury them somewhere about the garden, wherever they felt the British, the Uitlanders, or just plain freebooters were least likely to look. Now I have a big surprise for you, Jason. The De Jagers practiced the accepted Boer custom of digging a very deep hole, say eight feet down, and placing most of their most treasured items in a metal box. Then they would fill the hole in with, say, two more feet of earth, then bury a second box with only a few things in it! This way, anyone discovering the location of the hole would take only the top box, assuming that two candlesticks and three gilt-framed pictures of the family ancestors would be all there was! In the case of the De Jagers, not wishing to even lose the top box, they covered the whole thing in, mounded it off, and marked it with a gravestone that they switched from somewhere else in their family plot! Ever hear of this being done before, my dear?"

"Holy Jesus Christ! So the excavator of the empty graves was Maria—I mean the graves we opened along Loch Killilan! Goddamn! So it was *she* who never buried Roberts there in the first place, buried her diary instead, then buried herself—except it was really the grave of her sheepdog, Botha—on top of him. And even marked the grave with the proper year of Roberts' death and, by guess, with the proper year of her own. Damn! But why?"

"That, I suspect, will turn up later. Let me tell you the rest of this first." She squinted back toward the lake into the bright sunshine and waved Duncan away from the weeds toward which he was again straying. "She told Roberts to journey to Tuinplaas, to dig up the treasures—making sure to get down deep enough to get them all—and then to sell them for the fare to America. She was quite explicit as to what was legally hers and what had been earmarked for her dowry; told Roberts, or 'Bob,' to take these first *but*—ever the pragmatist—to take anything else that would bring enough for him to make it to New York."

"But what if the letter fell into the wrong hands and someone else got there first? What if it were just opened by a nosy voyeur —the sort who can't stand the sight of a sealed envelope and *must* know what's inside even if it's none of his business?"

Ann was laughing happily. "Jason, let's assume she was simply smarter than you or I, or at least that you and I refuse to give her credit for how crafty she was. She listed no fewer than twenty different hiding places, which, at eight feet down apiece, would require one hundred and sixty feet of digging—over twenty-six fathoms! They would have had to import a crew from the Rand. But she did not want Roberts to have to go through all that; so after each hiding place, she inscribed an epithet. After the first location, under a bluegum tree to the front of the house, she wrote KITCHENER YES; after the second, behind some jacaranda bushes to the rear, she wrote KRUGER YES; after the third, next to the cow barn, she wrote BULLER YES; after—"

"After the grave of her great-grandfather she wrote BOTHA YES!" Glass was grinning broadly.

"Most definitely YES!" Glass could not understand why they were consumed with glee at this, but they were, and they were hugging each other and rolling on the ground and laughing, they were so happy. "Come, come, Jason, enough time for this later. Now let me tell you how Roberts got the letter."

"He actually *got* it?" He sat up and dusted dry grass from the front of his sweater.

"He did indeed, though not the way she intended. The letter reached Pretoria with the orphanage group in mid-July and was placed with the Red Cross unit that was to follow the British advance toward Komati Poort, on the eastern border of the Transvaal with Portuguese East Africa. This was confirmed by the simple mailing of a Red Cross nurse-recruitment notice that Maria had addressed to herself in Paisley and had asked the orphanage group to mail to her as a signal that the letter had been set on the course she requested. It was postmarked Sunday, fifteen July 1900. In late August, Roberts turned up with a Red Cross unit that was following Buller's advance into the extreme eastern Transvaal, though the nurse who identified him was not in possession of the letter. She did, though, do the three things she was supposed to: she posted another nurse-recruitment letter to Maria dated twenty-five August 1900 from a field hospital outside Lydenburg which was treating mainly Boer rather than British casualties; notified the group's headquarters in Pretoria to send the letter forward to Lydenburg with the next entourage of supplies and personnel; and told Bob Menzy that there was a letter from Glasgow in search of him. Maria was able to receive all this information uncensored because she was now a patient, and later an outpatient, in a Paisley hospital after the birth of her son, Piet, on September sixth.

"September sixth was also the day General Buller captured Lydenburg, and it was apparently on the fifth that Roberts, having been recognized by a British officer he was treating as being the escaped prisoner-doctor of Ladysmith, fled the area—without ever having received the letter he awaited. It was apparently ready for delivery, according to what Maria had been told, after the dust of battle had cleared on the seventh. The letter later traveled, with this same nurse, as far east as Komati Poort, which the British occupied on the twenty-fifth of September.

"Sometime during the remainder of 1900, the nurse who had

the letter was reassigned with her unit, which moved out through Lourenço Marques and by ship to Port Elizabeth and then inland to the British hospital at Bloemfontein. Here she returned the letter to the other headquarters of the orphanage group, and this group notified Maria through the Red Cross in Paisley that the connection had been entirely missed at Lydenburg but that the letter was now at Bloemfontein. More than four hundred miles from where Bob Menzy had last been seen! The date when Maria attests to having learned this was eight January 1901."

Finally Glass could not restrain comment, though the expectant look on his face had warned her that interruption was coming. "So—four months! She had assumed for four months that Roberts had heard of her plan, was seeking safety so he could communicate with her (would surely react positively to her plan, she must have felt), only to find out that he was still in ignorance! And she with year-old and four-month-old babies now, closer together than the Creator in His wisdom ever expected a woman to have two separate children, still stranded in Glasgow at the height of the cold, damp never-sunshine of winter, stashing away what pitiful money she could, only to find out that as yet she could not use it. The babies crying, her mail being censored, her future dependent on the goodwill and the memories of Red Cross nurses and Screamer Do-Gooders six thousand miles away!" He shook his head in pity and disgust.

"The next time Roberts turned up that Maria was to find out about was in June of 1901. A Red Cross unit had followed the British column northward out of Bloemfontein. This was the group that was to build the blockhouse lines from Bloemfontein into the Transvaal. In the section between"—here she flipped through several pages of the translation to get the detail correct —"between Kroonstad and Ventersberg in the Orange Free State—though now it was called the Orange River Colony, at least by the English—an English doctor brought in a wagonful of sick Boer women and children in search of various medicines that he could not obtain. He asked one of the nurses whether they had come from Pretoria and was disappointed to hear that she had been sent up from Bloemfontein instead. He mentioned having missed a letter that the units from Pretoria were to have delivered to him in the eastern Transvaal. Though the nurse to whom he had spoken knew nothing of it, a woman representing the International Orphans Society *had* heard of it and said she would see to its being brought up the next time, in about a week, that she was rotated back to Bloemfontein with the orphans she had so far gathered.

"Then, on August sixth, a Monday, he got it, though definitely the hard way. Roberts and the band of guerrillas he was operating with had been confined for some time to an area in the southern Free State called the Brandwater Basin. I can show it to you on a map. They were getting progressively more depleted as the blockhouse and barbed-wire lines extended farther and farther. Some, however, got away into the hills, Roberts among them, and he was trying to find the Red Cross units he assumed would be along the British lines working between Heilbron and Wolvehoek. He had a number of wounded for whom he was seeking treatment and, surely, wanted to ask yet again whether the letter had passed that way. The blockhouse line at this point had extended farther than he had expected, however, and he found he could not skirt it as he had hoped but rather would have to cross it to get to the Red Cross unit, which, to his dismay, turned out to be on the other side. So they located the most widely spaced blockhouses—a mile was the best one could hope for, apparently—and waited for nightfall on the fifth of August. Vigilance in the blockhouses was known by the Boers to often be less than alert—the soldiers in them were so bored that they slept, smoked, talked, gambled, often to the exclusion of scanning the veld as they were supposed to. At night, this was doubly the case. But the British used armored trains equipped with searchlights to patrol all the blockhouse lines along a railway, and one of these happened along while Roberts and the commando he was with were cutting the wires. They thought they had been spotted as they fled back across the veld, but apparently they had not, though they did have to lie face down on the earth for nearly an hour until the scanning beam of the search light finally got out of range. Then they went back to snipping the wires again.

"Then a fluke accident occurred. The barbed-wire lines apparently had one strand of wire that contained tins filled with pebbles which would rattle if anyone tampered with the wire. The Boers knew this, of course, so the first thing they always did was locate that strand and then have men hold the tins in the palms of their hands so they would not rattle. Roberts later attested to having the wires entirely severed, in fact to having five patients on litters already carried through, when rifle fire erupted about two miles to the north."

"Another commando going through another place?"

"Perhaps, but unlikely. Stories abound, I have read, of wild animals getting caught in the barbed wire in the dark, of rattling the tins, then of having the bored, perhaps frightened men in the two nearest blockhouses begin firing wildly into the night."

"Which could easily trigger the other blockhouses down the line to start the same thing, I'll bet."

"Precisely—which is apparently what happened on the night of the fifth. Roberts' group, which had operated so carefully, suddenly found itself in a hail of crossfire, fire into the night at no particularly visible target. At any rate, Roberts was wounded, as best Maria could determine by the reports she got, in the upper thigh or groin, and several others with him were also wounded. About a half-hour after it started, the firing finally stopped—it usually took a long string of telephoning from one blockhouse to the next to quiet such things down—and the healthier men in the commando dragged the litters and newly wounded away from the rail line to positions behind kopjes where the searchlights could not find them when the trains passed through. After sunrise on the sixth, they proceeded to the Red Cross field hospital. Roberts was operated on to remove the shell. While he was still under anesthesia, a nurse recognized his name—despite the fact that the Boer who brought him in had spelled it 'Bob Mentje'—and the letter, at long last, was given to him when he awoke."

"So it took a year, but it had gotten there. Incredible!"

"Fourteen months, to be precise, Jason. That letter must have journeyed a full ten thousand miles by the time it reached him. And now he replied. The IOS woman who delivered the letter to him gave him a nurse-recruitment brochure and told him to pen a brief reply among its printed lines, so the communication Maria received three weeks later simply said: 'After the bitter end has come, yes. There. You and Bruce and Peter'—spelled P-e-t-e-r, not P-i-e-t—'will come when I write.'

"Red Cross units are neutral, of course, but stories were rampant at that time of the British laying for discharged Boers so they could round them up before they got back out on the veld. Which is why, I suppose, that according to Maria's entry for the nineteenth of September, Roberts and the other wounded from his commando slipped out during the night a full week before they were due to be released. An IOS member communicated all of this to Maria in a bold letter dated the twentieth of August, and this—as far as I can tell—is the end of that liaison between Maria and the orphan group in South Africa. Maria's entry for the nineteenth of September—Duncan! *Duncan!*"

She was suddenly shrieking at the top of her lungs, leaping up from the rock even as she did so. When he first spun his own eyes toward the lake, Glass did not see Duncan, but then he did —back at the right side, where he had been told twice not to go —his head lunging momentarily above the water to gasp and cry and spurt, then going back under as a result of the counter-thrust of his desperate upward leaps. He was some fifty feet out from the shore on which they had been sitting, and Ann was sprinting down to the water's edge, kicking off her shoes and blouse and jeans as she ran. She ran out into the water until she was knee deep, then dived headlong, pushing as far out as her legs would propel her. For several seconds Glass could see only her panties and bra beneath the water, and Duncan not at all, but then both surfaced as they got closer together. Glass stripped off his own clothing, lunged into the water the same way Ann had, and began swimming as hard as he could toward the trapped boy. He was a stronger swimmer than Ann and was saving breath by not calling out as he swam and so reached him at the same time she did.

This was virtually the same spot where Duncan had hidden the bag of Maria De Jager's bones several weeks before, but it was deeper now because of the amount of rainfall that had found its way into the lake and the rivulet through The Gap which fed it. Duncan had entangled his left leg in a thicket of subsurface growth which, had he stood still, probably would not have pulled him down far enough to submerge his nose; but with his continued frightened leaping, he was spending more time below than above, dragging in great gulps of water each time he disappeared.

Finally they freed him, and Glass carried him over his shoulder back to the shore, hanging his head far down his own back in an advance attempt to try to have the water flow from his stomach. He laid the boy's nude body on the grassy slope of the bank, face down, head lower than the feet, and then Ann took over, straddling his body and lifting him by the midsection until his buttocks made contact with the front of her white bikini underpants and then lowering him back to the ground. When she had all the water out of him she felt she could get, she spun him over on his back and lay on top of him, looking for all the world like his lover in the final stages of undress, her open mouth joined to his, panting and breathing regularly into it, pressing her chest into his abdomen as she did so to force the air she had just breathed into him back out again.

Soon the boy's purple face began to lose its eerie color, and he started to breathe on his own. She knelt and sat back on her heels, breathing harder and less regularly now. They had brought yet another Menzies back to life.

Part Five
CONSEQUENCES

23 THE ROAD TO ST. LOUIS AND THE RIVER AWAY

YET TO WHATEVER EXTENT JASON GLASS was responsible for the preservation of Duncan's young life, within four months he would be equally responsible for the loss, apparently by cold-blooded murder, of the life of another Menzies: Aunt Elizabeth.

In many ways the months of July through October were very eventful for Jason Glass, but in others they were very isolated, lonely, ineffectual ones. While he dabbled in (perhaps more properly, explored) the past, the present seemed to charge forward despite (perhaps more properly, *to* spite) him. And so when the murder occurred, he had the sense of having let the present drift unimpeded toward a dangerous end while he tried to pretend he could reshape the direction of the past simply by discovering and trying to understand it.

By the time the murder occurred in late October, he had not seen Ann in nearly four months, had become very lonely for her, had decided his life in the present had not much meaning when she was not playing an active role in it. He felt sure that he loved her, though he could not understand why, when he had her within his reach, he had not reached out for her. In the days before she left for her project in Australia, they had dug and delved more and more through Maria's diary, trying to make it jibe with what little was left to them of Roberts'. They visited the castle several times to explain their findings to Farquhar, each time, oddly, to have him accept the "truth" as he heard it only to reject that same "truth" on the next occasion they visited with a new one. It was almost as if the longer he reflected on it the less he could handle it. And they took a motoring trip together for a few days—visited well-preserved castles at Perth and Braemar and ruined ones at Kildrummy and Tantallon, tried to peek at Balmoral but were run off by local police for blocking the highway, and stood on the amazingly tiny battlefield at Culloden Moor. They had enjoyed each other, had ruled the whole subject of Roberts Menzies out of their lives for four days to relax their minds and had almost abided by their rules, though they never quite could. They knew they loved each other and told each other so, yet at night they slept in separate beds in separate rooms—Glass knew that if he asked her to join him in his she would have, and Ann by now knew that she would have equal success with a request of her own. So it seemed as if this knowledge was what caused them not to make any attempt to prove it. Glass was not sure what was restraining him. Why Ann Macgregor held back, when she knew she could break his isolation just by initiating things herself, he did not know. Nor did he ask.

But then she went away, and he truly yearned for her, often wept when he went to bed at night. He hated himself for using the ever-ready Sybil to satisfy his needs, hated himself because she was a married woman, because she was Ann's sister, because she was like Margot, because he empathized, therefore, with Clyde, however boorish and drunk he was. Sybil had visited him after midnight the day he and Ann had saved Duncan, had wept earnestly about how poor a mother she had been and how thankful she was that he had been there—she never mentioned Ann—to do her duty for her. She had offered herself that night and he had taken her up on it. Clyde never made mention of Duncan's near-demise in any way. Once Ann had left, Sybil took to making frequent nighttime appearances, running up the dark Gap road in her nightgown, carrying it back rather than wearing it when she left. Once Clyde left a note tacked to his cottage door which threatened violence against Glass the next time it happened. It happened that night—the next three, in fact—but Clyde never made good his threat. Glass thought it might be wise to vacate the cottage, however, before the next year's Dunedin Games.

So Ann had been sent to Australia by her publisher to assist with a book on the involvement of Australian regiments in the Boer War—she was suddenly the best expert the publisher had on the subject—and by October had been in Sydney for fifteen long weeks.

Besides hiking and swimming with Duncan, fornicating with his mother, and performing the basic tasks of daily survival, Glass did little other than work. He rarely saw Henrietta. She was clearly avoiding him. He saw Farquhar only when he had to and always met the same reaction: today's information was good and interesting, but last time's had become unacceptable. Glass had, in fact, begun considering subsidy publication in case the whole thing was refused by both Farquhar and Farneswells at the end. He had even written his agent to look into the legalities of this.

The response he received in mid-September evaded the issue nicely—agents were as good as lawyers at doing that—but filled him in on the latest news from America.

Margot was becoming an item in her own right. She had switched partners during the summer, once Glass had turned over to her all the profits from *Gratuitous Glory*. Larry had enclosed some newspaper and magazine clippings about that. She had taken up living with a poet some ten years younger than herself outside Provincetown and had appeared with him, and been photographed, at the International Book Award ceremonies and also at the nude beach on Cape Cod. The latter picture, with Margot fully stripped, facing the camera, smiling, ignoring her cesarean scar, made its way into *Bare Celebrity* magazine.

Glass wrote her a letter, demanding to know where the children were and how they were being cared for. She did not answer, so he wrote again. She did not answer this time either, and he knew he would not hear from her until the profits from *The Legacy of Ladysmith* started to accrue.

And so the story as he had come to know it by the time he was prepared to interview Aunt Elizabeth, which he never did:

Sometime between the twentieth of August, 1901—that is, the date on which Roberts and several other wounded commando members slipped out of the Red Cross hospital—and mid-December, Roberts had become aligned with the most effective guerrilla commando of all, under General Christiaan De Wet. Glass always used the word *aligned*, for he could find little evidence in any of the remaining scattered pages of Roberts' diary that he was ever actually fighting. He seemed instead to be simply a doctor who looked after wounded guerrillas and, when they came upon them, sick and helpless women and children. It must have been rather late in this four-month period that Roberts joined De Wet, for the latter had been out of the Free State for a time trying to invade the British Cape Colony in order to make commando raids there. He had, however, been forced back into the Brandwater Basin triangle among the three towns of Bethlehem, Lindley, and Reitz in the Orange Free State. They had been fighting mainly evasive and defensive actions until that point. But at the time Roberts joined them, according to the diary, De Wet, Prinsloo, and several commandants were planning for renewed offensive action both against the British patrol columns that were scouring the veld for them and others of their kind and against the corps of engineers and soldiers erecting the ever-lengthier blockhouse lines. At a meeting in Blijdschap, near Reitz, in late November, De Wet announced he would take his force of seven hundred men against well-supplied detachments of British blockhouse builders to get food and clothing and horses—and, of course, to deprive the British of them as well.

Sometime during December, he decided upon the exposed and poorly defended but well-supplied head of the blockhouse line under construction from Harrismith to Bethlehem. By then it had reached Tweefontein Farm, about twenty miles to the east of Bethlehem. Roberts was definitely with the guerrillas at this point, for he records that it was the row of white tents around the kopje called Groenkop which most interested De Wet, the ones which housed vast stores of bully beef and rum. On the twenty-first of December, Roberts accompanied a scouting party which reconnoitered the back side of the kopje with the idea of climbing it and descending upon the British from above, rather than hammering at them from the open veld on the more sloping front side. For three straight days, Roberts wrote, the back side of the hill was without a single picket after sunset. There was a gully which cut through the steep cliffs and made a path to the top. There was likely to be much drinking going on on Christmas Eve; hence, De Wet planned an attack for the early hours of Christmas morning.

The burghers had managed to climb about halfway up the back of the hill when the lone sentry stationed at the top heard them. He called a halt, fired several warning shots, then sped away down toward his camp on the other side. The burghers stormed over the top and down the other side and soon were in complete command of the camp. They had shot no more than they felt they had to, though this number was sufficient. When things were in hand, De Wet—looking more like a banker than a guerrilla with his gold key chain, his neatly trimmed beard, and his briefcase—told the soldiers there would be no more shooting if resistance ceased. It did, whereupon the Boers took all the wagons of food, several horses, and the clothing off the soldiers' backs. They set fire to the weaponry and ammunition they had to leave behind and departed over the veld.

History records this as one of the greatest humiliations the Boers inflicted on the blockhouse system, but it was a Pyrrhic victory. Within six more weeks Kitchener had it completed to his satisfaction, especially in the guerrilla-infested Free State, where it hemmed in the veld like a large cattle pen. Yet somehow, if the letter from Mrs. Douglas was correct, and if it was Roberts of whom she was writing (There could hardly be any doubt of this), De Wet had escaped into the western Transvaal in early 1902, which would be equivalent to "escaping" from one pen into another. Several brief entries in Roberts' sparse diary for January show the commando in the Klerksdorp area, as Mrs. Douglas suggested; then, of course, there is the lengthier entry Glass had known about for some time dated Thursday, 16 January (when the commando burned a Boer farmhouse in which British officers were resting and where he speaks of the 40 women and 73 children they had with them in thirteen wagons). These people, according to an earlier entry for the thirteenth, had been acquired by the commando when they fled a stalled train on its way to the concentration camp near Bloemfontein.

But the British policy was now clear, and these 113 extra souls, many of them weak and unhealthy, were an extreme liability to the commando. The British were beginning to use columns to pin the commandos against the barbed-wire lines and there defeat them. Roberts and De Wet had more than one argument about this, the latter insisting these women and children were better off *in* the camps than driven relentlessly about the veld, the former warning him over and over of the terrible health conditions that would exist in such places. Perhaps De Wet's faith in the camps as protective devices for the women and children resulted mainly from false hope—his own wife had been placed in one at some earlier time. Finally Roberts won out by suggesting that if the 113 were dispersed to the camps, he would accompany them rather than the commando (which needed his services) and make his way back to it when and if he could.

The whole problem was settled, of course, by the grisly incident of the sixteenth: the entrapment of Roberts in the barbed-wire fences and his amputation of his left arm in lieu of being stripped alive by predatory vultures. Somehow, probably through the intervention of some of the Boer women whom the British soldiers once again rounded up and prepared for the shipment to Bloemfontein, Roberts was picked up from where he lay half-dead on the veld and sent there with them under the catchall label of "general undesirable." They had no other name to attach to him. On the nineteenth of January he was able to scrawl in his diary, with the wrong hand, "I will be half a surgeon." This was the first entry made in the hand Glass had earlier labeled "Non-Roberts."

Then, of course, came the infrequent pages he and Ann had already investigated: January 20, about the Bloemfontein camp and its difference from the Bloemfontein hospital and from civilization in general; February 12, the lament over Kitchener's progressively bagging commando after commando and Roberts' celebration of Smuts; and May 30, on his impending release and in which he says he will not go home. On May 31, the day the peace treaty was signed in Vereeniging between Botha and Kitchener, Roberts must have walked out the gate of the concentration camp—no one had ever discovered who he was, one-armed and one-eyed whereas the Roberts Menzies sought for treason was supposed to be in possession of two of each—and went, not home, but toward Tuinplaas and one of its ancestral graves, which, eight feet down, would yield what he needed for passage to America. *If* he got there before the De Jagers did.

On Gallowgate in Glasgow, Maria was three months beyond her twenty-first birthday when she recorded reading on June 1, 1902, a Sunday, of the final Boer surrender. Bruce Menzies was nearly two and a half; Piet, three months short of his second birthday. Her diary reflects patience still, but now her anticipation began to increase as she waited through the summer for word of Roberts. Then, in August, came the expected news, but not from Roberts—from her family. Pasted in her diary was the brief letter her mother wrote her, which Krige had translated as well:

Bob Menzy arrived here this week and told us where to find you. Not that we want to. We consider you a traitor, not only to your country and cause, but to your God and your family. We are a beaten people while you live softly in Glasgow. Your father died in the retreat from Ladysmith when some ammunition he was destroying exploded. Christiaan was killed at Co-

lenso, which I think you knew. Your brother fought for a time with De la Rey but was captured. He is at Tuinplaas with me now. Not that you would care. Your sisters and I spent the last year of the war in the concentration camp at Krugersdorp, which at least was better run than I have heard most were. At least we are alive. Tuinplaas was burnt to the ground by Kitchener.

Bob Menzy has told us that you wish him to bring you your possessions and your dowry. I gather you even told him where to find them. With the farmhouse burnt down, though, he would have had a difficult time knowing which family plot to excavate. But I can tell he would not have stolen anything. You would; he would not. He has agreed to help us rebuild—to the extent he <u>can</u> *help. I have not told him, but I will give him what belongs to you, but not your dowry, for you have never married.*

He is a good man, Maria, but the war has been even worse on him than on us. We have no country, but neither has he. And he has been badly wounded. He has lost his left arm and his right eye, which he covers with a patch. He walks very stooped over but seems otherwise strong. And he was wounded in the Brandwater Basin at another time and says he can father no more children. He tells me he already has two, one by you. It does not matter to me. But he lives with us in the tent the British have given us until we build another house. He will be the man of our family for a while.

She signed it simply "Mother," without love or affection.

Over the next several months, Maria's diary shifts from patience, to annoyance, to rage. She began writing to Roberts, first telling him to hurry, then reprimanding him for seeing to the welfare of one family while neglecting his own. None of his responses are recorded. Maria doubted that he even received some of her letters. Roberts seems to have stayed at Tuinplaas through the summer and left there finally in February of 1903, carrying with him enough of Maria's possessions to survive with but not enough to buy his way to America. But he started westward toward the Cape—the right direction, at least.

Then, in early April, Maria records receiving an envelope return-addressed to P. Cronje in Klerksdorp, roughly the same location at which Roberts had suffered the misfortunes that cost him his arm and his eye. The letter indicated that he had been recognized at the rail station there by the occupying British forces and had had to go underground. He found refuge in the home of Cronje, the famous trekboer general who had captured Leander Starr Jameson in the raid of '96, who had whipped the British at the big battle of Magersfontein in 1899, but who had inexplicably gotten himself trapped at Paardeberg Drift and meekly surrendered his army to Lord Roberts on February 27, 1900, one day before Ladysmith would be relieved on the eastern front. So this was the beginning of Roberts' alliance with Piet Cronje, who was just home from St. Helena, where he had been imprisoned for the duration of the war, sleeping, he claimed, in the same cell that Napoleon had occupied.

But Maria took hope at this, for apparently Roberts had told her in this same letter that Cronje had a scheme for getting both of them to America "after next summer." So Maria began to wait again, and save some more, though it is clear from her diary that she, living now in the Northern Hemisphere, had gotten her seasons mixed up. She took the end of summer to mean the end of *her* summer, the following September, five months away. Roberts had meant the end of the next South African summer, more like eleven months away. So she waited through that too. Bruce was now four, Piet eight months short of that.

In May, 1904, she received a letter from Roberts in America —not in New York City, where he was supposed to meet her, but in St. Louis, Missouri, which she had never heard of. There was to be a huge World's Fair there that summer to celebrate the one-hundredth anniversary of the Louisiana Purchase, which she had never heard of either, and he and Cronje had agreed—as a famous Boer general and a not-so-famous victim of the Siege of Ladysmith—to reenact the surrender of Paardeberg in a rodeo arena each day with several dozen Ozark hillbillies dressed in British uniforms and Boer slouch hats. Cronje was to have by far the bigger part, galloping around the corral-fence perimeter three or four times, leading his small commando hooting and hollering, he waving his Mauser over his head, they firing bird shot into the air. Then the red-coated hillbillies—no official seemed to understand that the British Army had worn khaki instead of red coats in the Boer War— would ride out and surround them and force them to throw down their arms. Then, in the only fully scripted moments of the charade, modeled entirely on written records and photographs of the surrender, Bob Menzy, playing the role of Lord Roberts, Field Marshal of Pretoria, would walk with ceremonial dignity into the arena and accept the famous old trekboer's gun and horse. This was done twice a day for the duration of the Fair. Cronje's plan for his money was to rebuild his farm—not for himself, for he was almost seventy, but for his great-grandchildren; Roberts' plan was to pay for Maria's and Bruce's and "Peter's" transatlantic transportation and overland rail fare—on the *Wabash Cannonball*, the same way he and Cronje had come—to Matoon, Illinois, a small town desperately in search of a doctor. With no other candidates, it had agreed to take this hunched-over, one-armed, one-eyed man, who must have looked eighty by this time but who was really only thirty-two. Maria agreed to this and in October, 1904, readied herself in Glasgow to come.

But just as one and one make two, two and two make four, so do four and four make eight. Shortly after the closing of the World's Fair, as Cronje was preparing to start back to South Africa (even though he had heard he was no longer wanted there because he had disgraced the Boer cause by reenacting the surrender at Paardeberg) and as Roberts was preparing to shift his belongings to Matoon, Illinois, the St. Louis City Police received a request from the British embassy in Washington to "arrest and detain" one Roberts Menzies, alias Bob Menzy, until extradition papers to Britain could be finalized. The first letter Maria received after this was dated Wednesday, November 2, 1904, five years to the day after Ladysmith had fallen under siege, and was written from the St. Louis City Jail, which had a return address of Thirteenth and Market Streets. Matoon, Illinois, he said, had been quick to disavow its association with him, and Roberts now had only one friend who could help him: Piet Cronje.

Cronje delayed his own departure and took up residence in a nearby flophouse on the St. Louis riverfront while he tried to seek legal help. What he found was little; what little there was was slow. Finally Roberts did it the easier way. He gave a jailer five hundred dollars, half of what he had apparently earned at the St. Louis Fair that summer, simply to leave a series of five doors unlocked for a series of five consecutive minutes. So as easily as he had been in and out of Ladysmith in search of medicine, he was out of the St. Louis jail: it had simply taken him two months to understand that where Boers traded in code-books and medical supplies, Americans traded in money and silence.

Since Roberts was something of an international celebrity in this insular Midwestern American city, Cronje strongly recommended that he—actually they, for Cronje was above all loyal to this man who had been loyal to him and his people—*not* depart to the east on the *Wabash Cannonball*, the way they had come. Rather they should leave by boat to the south, toward New Orleans, the closest seaport and the shortest route out of America. One can imagine Maria now, packed and awaiting instructions in Glasgow as she received successive letters from Cairo and Memphis—not the ones in Egypt but the river towns in Illinois and Tennessee which she had never heard of—and from a place called Hattiesburg, Mississippi. By the end of January, 1905, she knew they were in New Orleans after jumping, legally or clandestinely, on a series of barges and riverboats headed south. But she understood that New Orleans was a French-settled seaport and that boats went from there to New York or, at worst, from there to France, which she felt Roberts would assume would be the next-best place to meet her now that he was being sought in both England and America. And again she waited.

Then, on Tuesday, March 21, 1905, she received the letter with Roberts' final instructions. She could not believe its postmark—not so much its date as its place:

> I have a job and a place to live. I am very tired and only part of me is left, but I see only peace and quiet in the future now. I have enclosed three hundred pounds. Pay your expenses, settle your affairs, bundle Bruce and Peter against the damp spring, and join me here. I will love you, Maria.

It was dated February 28, 1905, the fifth anniversary of the relief of Ladysmith; and—to Maria's horror—so was it postmarked from there!

On Wednesday, March 22, 1905, though she is not precise about how she did it, she "*sent Bruce Menzies to his putrid family lands where, for all I care, they may bury him and perhaps will have to.*" She had bound him hand and foot and gagged him and placed him in a secondhand dog's shipping crate with only punctured air holes in it and shipped him, for two pounds, thirteen shillings, and fivepence, to the Castle Menzies—which luckily some railroader knew was near Kyle because Maria had no idea where it was—and was rid of him and, for many years, his father. But in less than fourteen years she and his father would meet again, and in a few more months after that so would she and Bruce—who would be less than nineteen then. But he would not have forgotten her—and on Saturday, June 20, 1925, freshly home from a day of festivities, he and his grandfather would take advantage of her flight from rising water at the height of the worst storm the district could even now recall and, with crashing thunder to cover their actions, would cannon her to death with a gun the ancient Menzies had been too petulant or cowardly to use on Culloden Moor but had shot for the hell of it for two centuries afterward—so why not at a useless forty-four-year-old interloping Boer widow?

And this was why Jason Glass asked Henrietta to set up a meeting for him with poor mad Aunt Elizabeth—actually Henrietta's mother, though she did not call her that; and this was why, probably, Aunt Elizabeth was shot "by an awfully large bullet" which passed through her body and into Loch Duich as she wandered, no doubt babbling to herself, about the water-encircled grounds of the Castle Menzies.

At roughly 9 P.M. on the twenty-sixth, Glass sat alone in the nearly deserted public bar of The Angus Bull, pulling thoughtfully on his second pint, trying to think of Roberts and his appearance next in the First World War, but thinking achingly of Ann instead. Then Charles Peebles walked in. The atmosphere outside was an unbroken cold drizzle, and Peebles had baguettes of moisture all over his dark blue pea coat and the blue stocking cap he was pulling backward off his head. He began addressing Glass even before he was halfway across the room.

"Jason," he called with his eyes innocently wide, "have yer heard what's the latest about them Menzies?"

Glass looked up, his eyes burning through the smoke of the room, wondering why Peebles was not sloshing a pint across it as he usually was. "Don't confuse me with more than I'm already confused by, Charles." He reached in his pocket and flipped the young man a fifty-pence piece. "Here, have one on me."

Peebles caught the coin but did not turn for the bar. "They've started to killing each other, they have. Aunt Elizabeth, the old woman who's been daft for more than twenty years? Somebody shot her through the stomach this afternoon!"

Glass's face was at first confused, then appalled. "I was supposed to meet with her next Saturday—to ask her some questions about when Roberts came back here after the war. I—"

"Well, yer won't be askin' her much now, will yer?"

"Who did it? Do they have a suspect?"

"Nobody in particular. The only one around was that old gatekeeper Fuckqueer pays to scare off intruders. They're questioning him pretty hard, I understand, but they haven't arrested him."

"Where was Farquhar?"

"Yes, now, there's the man I'd question if I was the constables. He'd fix her just for gettin' in his way. But he's been gone for two weeks."

"Gone where?"

"I don't know. Nobody seems to." Now he handed the fifty-pence piece back to Glass. "Anyhow, Mr. Glass, Henrietta asked me to fetch you up for her. She's stuck with the whole mucky thing, you see. I'll drive you to the castle in my lorry now, if you'd like."

When Glass and Peebles drove across the causeway, they parked behind three police cars, and for the first time found the castle gate unobstructed by either iron or the hunched old gatekeeper. Peebles had clearly never been on the premises before, but he followed closely behind Glass as the writer vaulted up the outer stairway two steps at a time. It was drizzling much harder now, so they did not wait for the butler to admit them. Glass went up a flight to the Banqueting Room, where the interviews were being conducted. Even as he awaited recognition, Glass could hear the unpleasant old man saying, as if for the fiftieth time, that he had *heard* the shot, and heard it very clearly, about four thirty that afternoon, but Aunt Elizabeth's body, he insisted, had been found, by him, diagonally across the small island from where the gatehouse was and so he had not *seen* the crime. Finally, Henrietta approached them, dry-eyed, courageous, but quite haggard.

"Henrietta, I am sorry about your mother. I can't be—"

"Thank you, Jason. Aunt Elizabeth had her three score and ten and a few more additional. She has not been able to appreciate much of the last score or the additional, I fear. She lost nothing she held dear, I assure you of that."

"Yes, but murder, Henrietta! Why should a helpless old woman be subjected to that? All the way over here I've felt it was because she was about to talk to me about the last years of Roberts' life."

"I suspect that as well, Jason. Though I cannot imagine who would be so upset by that prospect that he would have to resort to this. I have given it to the police as a possible motive, however." She turned now to signal a plainclothes policeman away from the interrogation of the gatekeeper. "Inspector Ross, this is Jason Glass, the American writer you asked to have me turn up."

Ross approached nodding, smiling as pleasantly as he could, hand extended. "Yes, we've met. Very good of you to come so quickly, sir; we'd great need of speaking with you."

"I am not a suspect, I hope." Glass did not see how he could be but was unsure what the answer would be.

"No, no, Mr. Glass. I am sure your whereabouts of this afternoon will require little documentation." Glass did not like the answer, knowing he had spent the entire day alone at his cottage writing. Not even Duncan had been by. "I wanted to see you because, in the absence of Mr. Farquhar Menzies, you would know most about the recent doings in the Menzies family. I thought perhaps your research might have turned up something that would be of value to us."

"Such as?"

"Such as, first of all, do you know where Mr. Farquhar Menzies is, by chance?"

"No. I did not even know he was gone from the district till an hour ago."

"When did you last see him?"

Glass ruminated on this for several seconds. "About three weeks ago. I visited him here in this room to show him the writing I had completed and to discuss some other matters with him."

"And what was his humor during that meeting?"

"Standard."

"Which means?"

"Which means, Inspector, hacked off about the last writing I had done for him but eager to see the next installment anyway. The way he always was on my visits."

"And what 'other matters' did you discuss with him that day? Anything that might have upset him?"

"Nothing that appeared to then, though, as I say, he always was upset about the last time the next time I saw him. So he could have gotten upset after I left. As I recall, that was the meeting at which I told him I would have to interview Aunt E— eh, the deceased to clarify some information about the years 1919 through 1925. Those were the years Roberts Menzies had returned to the Lochs after an absence of more than twenty."

"Did he seem to *not* want you to speak with her?"

"If so, he did not indicate it. I fully expected him to object before long, however, so I kept the actual date of it a secret." Now Glass saw where he was being led and so pulled up short. "I do not for a moment, however, feel he would have shot her to shut her up. He simply could have barred me from getting in."

Ross turned to Henrietta now. "Miss Menzies, I wonder if I might speak to Mr. Glass alone for a moment?"

Henrietta was about to object, but the look in Glass's eyes suggested that he would tell her anything she needed to know. She walked over to Peebles, who still stood by the door with his stocking cap in his hands, took him by the arm, and led him toward the kitchen for coffee and warmth. There was no fire alight in the room in which they spoke, and the air was dank.

"Mr. Glass, I do not at the moment suspect Mr. Menzies myself. My question would rather deal with the matter of whether or not anyone else was a party to your conversation."

"On that occasion, no one. Several months ago, my editor accompanied me on these visits, but she has been in Australia for almost four months. I was alone."

"But was he?"

Glass was annoyed. "Damn it, I told you it was just the two of us. Excuse my temper, but this whole Menzies family and the things they do—or have done to them—have about done me in. This is the last straw, as we say in America."

"Yes, we say it here, too." Ross laughed through his accent. "Could there have been anyone listening you could not see—as, say, through there?" He pointed upward along the wall, above the medallions and crests which colored the gray stone to the height of eight feet. There above them were the two slits in the wall that Ann had shown him the first night at the castle, no more than three inches high but about two feet long, with about two more feet horizontally between them.

"Well, possibly. I did not recall those. I don't know."

"Come with me. Mr. Glass, and I will show you what I mean." He led the way back out of the room, down the interior staircase, and out the main door into the rain, then all the way back down the outer steps. They were very slippery, so Glass held the handrail the entire way to the bottom, mowing the droplets of water off it as his hand slid downward. He dried his hand on his jacket when they got to the courtyard. Ross led the way out of the lights of the yard around to the south side of the castle, using his flashlight for guidance. Finally he came to another downward staircase, and started to descend it carefully. The only noises they could hear were the steady raindrops clicking against the lonely surface of the Loch and the irregular snapping of the castle electrical plant in the outbuilding to their rear.

The staircase went only about six steps down, at which point they entered a rusty iron door which, unexpectedly, did not squeak or groan as such doors were supposed to but rather opened as if it were well oiled and frequently used. Just inside this door was an awkwardly narrow staircase, so tight that it was hardly shoulder width, which ascended upward at an exhausting angle. Ross led the way, holding his flashlight tight against his hip, pointed downward to try to illuminate the steps for both himself and Glass. Glass presumed they must have done a full twenty twists upward without a landing to rest on before they came to another iron door. Ross pushed this open, and again it swung easily.

"Duck down, Mr. Glass. The ceiling in here is no more than five feet high. And stay close. The room is little more than that square as well." Again with only the flashlight to illuminate their movement, they both got inside this cryptlike compartment and squatted on their haunches. Then Ross snapped the light off. Within seconds, Glass was aware of two narrow slits of light which penetrated their confinement from in front of him. When his eyes focused through the glare, he could see the three uniformed policemen, the gatekeeper, and after that Henrietta and Peebles carrying coffee cups in the Banqueting Room below them. Glass estimated they were nine feet above the floor of the room.

"You see, Mr. Glass, someone could easily have been in here

on any occasion listening to your conversation with Farquhar Menzies. Perhaps that person would have been more upset about your forthcoming interview with the deceased than Mr. Menzies would have been."

"Yes, perhaps. But what makes you think *anyone* would have been in here? They could have been inside the clock case down there too."

Ross snapped his flashlight back on and pointed it at the floor. It was strewn about with at least three dozen cellophane wrappers. Glass picked one up and examined it in the light. It read: BULLY GOOD BEEF STICK, PACKAGED IN EDINBURGH BY DUMPHRIES AND SONS LTD. It was not by any means old.

"This is beef-jerky wrapping," he said. "You can buy these things in any pub. I have. They taste like crap."

"I tend to agree, but someone must like it. But you can't buy this brand in *any* pub—only in ones allied with Scottish and Newcastle Breweries. Such as the one several hundred yards back up the road."

"So what you're saying is"—Glass was conscious of his knees' and ankles' starting to hurt from his squatting position—"that someone, perhaps all along, has been stopping at that pub, getting himself some snacks, then sneaking up here to hear Farquhar and me go over my latest discoveries about Roberts? I hope he's either very short or in good physical shape, because we would usually talk for three hours or more. How would he get by that gatekeeper, though?—and you can discount the gatekeeper himself, for he can barely make it up the front steps, much less get all the way up here."

"Yes, I tend to discount the gatekeeper. But there is another way onto these grounds than through the gate."

"How?"

"By water—swimming or in a boat."

"And you think this person could have rowed up this afternoon and shot Aunt Elizabeth without even setting foot on the grounds?"

"No, not at all. She was shot from the other direction—toward the gate, not the open side toward the Loch. She was facing him, or her, when she was shot, and fell backward. We estimate she was fired at from at least fifty yards away—therefore by a *very* good marksman—with a gun that fired very big shells. The bullet—surely from a rifle of some sort—passed through her without an instant's retardation and, probably, traveled well on out into the Loch. It will be impossible to recover."

"Could she have been shot from above? From a window or the top of a wall?"

"No, she was shot from ground level—there was no trajectory to the wound. But in any event, Mr. Glass, I've asked you to come over here tonight and creep into this womb with me to ask your help with something."

"Gladly, but how much longer do we have to stay in here?"

Ross laughed. "Let's be on, then. But think about this, will you? The CID have now several Menzies-related incidents we are bothered about. If you have any thread that can sew these together for us, we'd appreciate your help."

Now Glass laughed. "I wish I had that thread, Sergeant. But I recall what your beads are, I think: the death by exposure of Farquhar's wife in 1970; the suicide of Annette Macgregor in '72; and now the murder of Aunt Elizabeth in '75."

"Precisely, but string on the others for us too, will you? Those empty graves we found last summer—we know *you* opened them, Mr. Glass, and we can tell there was not a human body to be found in them ever, but how did you know that? And next, a Dr. Hamilton Macgregor who died about five years ago, two days before Farquhar's wife—we tend to connect those two deaths but we don't know how, though we do have evidence of a good deal of suspect behavior in the final years of his life. And one new thing—to make a neat half-dozen to string together in a nice set."

"Which is?"

"The Macgregors' daughter."

"Sybil."

"No, your editor, Ann."

"What about her?"

"Where does she fit?" He stopped abruptly, and the amazed Glass could hear his knees crack as he rose to lead him back down the staircase from the unpleasant chamber in which they crouched. Then he turned back over his shoulder halfway down, and the shadow asked Glass: "And when do you think we can interview her?"

"She's in Australia. You're mad if you suspect her of—"

"No, Mr. Glass, I suspect her of nothing—at least, nothing

to do with this. But she knows enough about things in general to help more than her ongoing absence will allow her to—and enough to help you more than she is apparently bothering to."

24 THE MACGREGOR FAMILY TRADITIONS

ON THE FOLLOWING MORNING, Monday the twenty-seventh, Glass managed, with the cooperation of Farneswells' London office, to trace Ann in Sydney. While obviously shocked at the news of Aunt Elizabeth's murder, she required no prodding to realize the probable motive—or the clear present danger to Glass himself. She also recognized that Farquhar, as the instigator of this whole project, could be in jeopardy as well. She promised to return by the following day and make sure that Farquhar did as well. Glass could not but be curious about the second promise.

Shortly after Glass hung up, Ross called, wanting to know if he had found anything out. Glass said he felt that both Ann and Farquhar would turn up by the following evening, though at least one of them was coming a long distance. Ross said this was fine, that he would like to call at the castle about nine the next night and would request that as many of the family be present as possible. But what he had meant by "find out" was more the information Glass might have in his research which might, even in the wildest speculation, begin to string together the four deaths, the empty graves, and—he continued to insist—an as-yet-unidentified role for Ann Macgregor in the Menzies mysteries. Glass knew of two other deaths he would like to "string" on as well—Maria's, which he had solved, and Roberts', which he had not. He decided not to mention these for the time being, however.

And so he spent the rest of the afternoon on the one aspect of the project that seemed to have the largest, perhaps most available dimension. This was the suicide of Ann's mother in

1972, the death of her father in 1970, and the two-days-later death of Farquhar's wife, Catherine. He decided to try a source he had so far neglected, and by four o'clock was signing more copies of *Gratuitous Glory* for Mrs. Sciennes. He noticed they were not selling as well anymore. He fought his way through ten minutes' worth of questioning about the murder before he could get to the subject he wished to—though this interrogation had confirmed for him that Mrs. Sciennes sought and recorded the sort of random information (in America called gossip) that he needed.

"Mrs. Sciennes, what I came to speak with you about, if you can give me a few more minutes, was some points for my book on Roberts Menzies, some information I want to be sure I have straight."

"Yes, Mr. Glass—if as many people will read the book as read your last one, it would pay to have it accurate." He ignored both the implication and the conditional mood.

"Yes, yes, it would. Now, help me with that so I can sign some copies of the next one for you. My interest today is Dr. Macgregor. You knew him?"

It turned out, of course, that she had. Everyone would know the single doctor in the Lochs surrounding. Ham, as he was known, had opened his practice in 1937 or 1938, immediately upon completion of his medical degree at Edinburgh. Orphaned at a young age, he had in fact been taken in by Bruce Menzies so that he would not have to be reared at the orphanage in Paisley. He had, moreover, been steered into the medical profession by Bruce and old Dr. Scott, almost as if they were substituting him for the errant Roberts. According to Mrs. Sciennes, Scott had planned to retire as soon as Roberts returned from South Africa, but had instead practiced up until his dying day in 1922.

"So it was Scott rather than Bruce who coaxed Ham into medical school?"

"Neither did, I think. Bruce, as impending clan chief, took it upon himself to supply a doctor, yes. And Scott in his last years —he was ninety, after all—let young Ham help him with the simpler surgical procedures. No, I am almost sure it was Roberts who made a doctor of him."

"Roberts! He knew Roberts?"

"From what my father tells me he did. Although Bruce would never have condoned it probably, Ham frequently, especially in the warmer months, came over to The Gap to fish with Roberts. Roberts apparently told him Boer War stories and how he went about saving all those patients. All his special techniques and such."

"Not all of them, I'll bet." Glass noticed her quizzical look. "Skip it. A tasteless joke. How old would Hamilton Macgregor have been in 1925, when Roberts died?"

"Only about sixteen or so. Now he had no doctor to associate with, so he seems to have done some unofficial doctoring on his own—patching up and things until his 'patients' could get to Inverness or Fort William. Then at eighteen he went off to university, so except in summers, the Lochs were without a physician for a decade. In fact, it's a miracle that Ham even came back at all. He did so well in medical school that they wanted him to stay on and work in the research labs there. But Ham knew his loyalties and so set up a wee laboratory in the upper story of his house in Loch Killilan where he would work at night and well into the early morning hours."

"Which makes him, finally, a different sort of doctor from Scott or Roberts. He was not the clone the Menzies seemed to expect him to be."

"Perhaps not, Mr. Glass, but he always attributed his research interests to Roberts as well. He used to say that Roberts told him that you could run out of your medical knowledge about five minutes before a patient who could be saved ran out of life. Roberts, even in Ladysmith, was studying hard so that this would never happen to him and cause him to lose one of his patients that he moved from Dundee with him. Hamilton so admired Roberts' dedication to saving lives that tales started to get told about his own lifesaving—people liked to say that Ham could bring dead people back to life. There was one chap who seemed to have drowned, but Ham revived him. Another got his arm cut off in a grain-mill accident, and Ham brought him through shock when his mates thought he was dead. Ham had a great fear of his own death as well—not a fear of dying so much as a fear of dying before another doctor was ready to replace him."

"This explains, surely, his attachment to Owen Menzies."

"Exactly! But he overdid it. When the Second World War came along, Ham wanted Owen to sign up for the medical brigade. You see, Ham truly admired what Roberts had done during the Boer War, the heroism and all. He really regretted, I think, that he had never been to war himself to do the same."

"From what I have heard, however, there is a terrible irony here. Owen was not assigned to the medical corps, was he?"

She shook her head. "No, he was a common soldier. He was killed in the last year of the war, almost as soon as he got there. He bled to death on the battlefield before his mates could get him to the hospital station. Also, Mr. Glass, it is ironical that this was exactly the sort of death Ham had been training himself to prevent. You might have heard about his 'Sibyluma' project—some medicine he was working on to slow down the vital mechanisms to delay the dying process, I guess. I didn't understand it."

Glass had heard enough of this before, so he turned the conversation to Macgregor's wife's suicide. Mrs. Sciennes admitted that she knew less about this. "After her husband's death in 1970, she started to seek employment elsewhere. Since she had always worked in his surgery, she found that she hadn't got all the most recent certificates that she needed to be employed in the government hospitals. But with her training she felt she ought to have them without further study. It was when she was getting information together on her background that she suddenly became quite depressed. Very much so. Then there was a phone call from Glasgow one day about three years ago. Later her older daughter found her dead of sleeping pills or some such. You'd have to ask her the full details on that."

"Is she buried here? I heard she was not from this district."

"She is, Mr. Glass, unless those grave robbers last spring took her as well. No, she was an orphan from Paisley, but she *did* have some relatives in the Lochs. I'm not sure I know who, though, for none whatsoever showed up for her funeral. Just Ann and Duncan and I even bothered to."

"What was her maiden name?" Glass almost remembered, and almost remembered something else as well, was five seconds from assembling both.

"Wallace. Annette Wallace."

Glass reeled against a produce bin. "Holy good God! You bet she had relatives here!" Mrs. Sciennes merely gaped, somewhat disappointed that Glass knew something she did not. She resolved to ask him next time she saw him what it was. For now, he was running out the back door of the store, speeding on foot up the hill which led to the shortcut into The Gap.

Both Ann and Farquhar arrived late Tuesday evening, by coincidence on the very same train from Inverness. The meeting with Ross had been moved back until nine to accommodate them, though when Glass first saw Ann enter the Banqueting Room at the castle, she was very drawn, not just by a day's travel but, it seemed, from overwork, perhaps from worry as well. She smiled warmly at Jason, who waved to her across the room, but they could not speak beforehand because Ross was already under way. Farquhar entered a few minutes later, looking equally tired and, clearly in his case, bereaved at the loss of his mother.

Ross gestured toward a woman detective who accompanied him. "Miss Kribbs would like to interview each of you in a few minutes to determine your whereabouts on the afternoon of Sunday the twenty-sixth, so could you please be collecting your thoughts on that beforehand." There were eight others present —Farquhar, Henrietta, Clyde, Sybil, Ann, the bent gatekeeper, the butler, and Glass. "Of course, we have no reason to suspect anyone in particular as yet, but it would help if you could give us some indication of how we might verify your whereabouts on that occasion." Glass wondered if anyone else but he would come up short here. He hated the thought of disappointing Miss Kribbs, who had a gorgeous smile that she was fixing on him, in fact had a paperback copy of *Gratuitous Glory* protruding from the purse that rested on the floor beside the red velvet chair in which she sat.

"We will try to make this as painless as possible owing to the tragic circumstances," Ross continued, "but I should like to go over certain information to assure myself that everyone is in agreement as to its veracity. First, I should say that Mrs. Menzies' autopsy has shown that she died instantly from a bullet to the stomach. She was shot facing her assailant from a distance of approximately seventy meters. Since the bullet passed entirely through her body, and we have been unable to recover it, we are not sure what the weapon was; but it must have been a rifle or a long-range pistol that used an extremely large shell. The marksman either was a champion or had very precise sights or was extremely lucky."

At least they seem sure it wasn't a cannon this time, Glass thought and wanted to remark, but didn't.

"The shot was fired apparently from ground level on the east side of the grounds, near the gatehouse"—the gatekeeper squirmed at this but continued to look unpleasant in his usual way—"and the deceased was struck about thirty meters from the water's edge on the west side. A patron at The Sheepshead Inn on the promontory to the west heard the report—which apparently was terribly loud, as would befit a large-shelled gun—and looked up to see the deceased falling to the ground. He called the District Crime Squad immediately from the Inn, and Officer McCrorie discovered Mrs. Menzies dead when he arrived at six minutes after four. She wore a robe and a nightgown and nothing else."

"That was all she ever wore, Sergeant. There was nothing odd about that." Henrietta, as usual, wished to avoid those things she already knew.

"What we should like to determine first is her mental state. I have gathered from various people in the district that she was, shall we say, eh . . ."

"Somewhat senile," Farquhar filled in.

"Stark, raving mad," Henrietta corrected. Miss Kribbs noted both on her pad.

"And," Ross probed further, "she had been this way for . . ."

"Approximately twenty years or so," said Farquhar.

"Exactly twenty-five—since 1950." Henrietta and Farquhar had never been together in Glass's presence before, something he vowed to aim for in the future as well.

"And what was the cause of this change in her, eh, shall we say, loss of . . ."

Farquhar was wise enough not to respond, deferring with his open palm to his sister.

"A trip to her homeland."

"Her homeland?" Ross asked the question that Glass wanted to.

"South Africa. She came from Ladysmith, in Natal." Glass's mouth dropped, but of the others only Ann's did, and hers was too late and not far enough. "She came here after the First World War to marry my father."

"They had met somewhere before? In Europe or . . . ?"

"No. My grandfather—Roberts Menzies—spent 'some time'

in Ladysmith in the years before the war. She was the daughter of the mayor of Ladysmith at the time of the Boer War and in the years after. When my father, Bruce Menzies, sought to marry, for the purpose of siring Farquhar, over there"—she pointed as if Farquhar were a statue or a sack of trash—"his father wished him to have the most beautiful girl he had ever encountered. He sent for her. Bruce, though he agreed with his father on very few things, did match tastes in women. They married very shortly after she got here, in 1922."

"Yes, fine. Now, this trip—in 1950—back to South Africa. This was her first since she left to marry Mr. Bruce Menzies?"

"Yes."

"And what was it that caused her derangement?"

Henrietta's pause was too long this time, and Glass wondered what the British equivalent of the Fifth Amendment was. "No one knows."

"Not even the physician who treated her?"

"He may have, but he is dead now. It was Miss Macgregor's father."

"Might there still be records in his files, Miss Macgregor?"

"There may be," Ann said, the normal force and spirit of her voice badly depleted, "but it would be unethical for me to turn them over to you without the proper papers."

"Quite right. You shall have them if we require the records." Ross flipped a page in his own notebook. "Now to motives. Is there anyone who might have expressed any animosity toward this poor woman? An argument over money or inheritance, say?"

Farquhar waved this off. "In the Clan Menzies, Inspector, the chief controls all the wealth. I am the chief. No one stood to inherit anything from her."

"Insurance money?"

"She had none." Farquhar twisted in his chair. "She needed none. The Menzies are well taken care of by their own investments and do not have to rely on potluck deaths."

Ross scratched his chin—not because he itched, but to signify transition. "Surely there is no love motive or jealousy."

A ripple of low laughter went though the assembly, though Glass thought he saw the gatekeeper and the butler purposefully abstaining.

"What, then?"

Glass raised his hand, knowing that Ross expected him now

to tell what they had already discussed. "She was to meet with me next Saturday, the first, to give me some information—or try to, at least—on a book I am writing on her father-in-law, Roberts Menzies. I have often found information hard to come by, and perhaps someone wanted to stop her from speaking to me." Glass looked hard at Farquhar, but he knew Farquhar would have a clean alibi. He looked less hard, without intending to, at Henrietta.

"Well, that eliminates me as a suspect," Clyde burped, even now with a boozy laugh. "The more information she could've given Mr. Glass, and the faster she gave it, the better I would have liked it." He leaned forward toward Ross. "You see, Inspector, I know who done it, I do." He seemed to be imitating a Soho drunk. "It was Sybil. She's the only one I know of who wants Glass here to keep his rocks in the Lochs." He laughed at his poetry, and Sybil belted him across the mouth with the back of her hand. Ann stared at Jason.

"Come, come, now," Ross said with irritation. "All right, we shall discuss such matters individually. I would ask that each of you visits with Miss Kribbs to give her your whereabouts on last Sunday. Mr. Glass, might I speak with you first? Very good." Everyone but Henrietta had begun to rise from his or her chair when Ross voiced an afterthought. "Whom shall I name to receive the remains from the morgue in Ullapool?"

Henrietta gestured at Farquhar. "Let the Chief take care of it." She used the noun the way a cowboy might refer to any lone Indian.

"No, no. I will send instructions. She is to be taken to Ladysmith for burial according to her will." He was uneasy. "I will make contacts for someone to receive her on the other end."

Ross was perplexed. "This is irregular. Sir, perhaps your sister might accompany—"

"No, I won't." Henrietta was, as she always was, terribly firm.

"I will do it. I will accompany the body to South Africa." Ann was haggard from the exhaustion of her trip from Sydney, and now in the space of several hours was to be on her way back to the other hemisphere again.

Glass never knew whether his own words now were spoken from love or charity or sympathy or sheer opportunism. "I will go also. Farquhar, you will make the arrangements?" Farquhar nodded wearily and turned to Miss Kribbs to be the first to cover his movements on the twenty-sixth. Glass could see him pulling an envelope of airline ticket stubs from his inner coat pocket for the young woman to look at. Glass wondered what he might be able to pull from his own pocket.

Ross took him by the arm and escorted him to the far side of the large rock-walled room, below the spy slits above them. "Now, Mr. Glass, you recall my questions to you on Sunday. What have you found out?"

"About what?" There was so much he had been sent to "get" that Glass was really in the dark about Ross's meaning. He expected the wrong lead, however.

"About the Macgregor girl. Have you got anything more on her?"

Glass squinted at him, feeling his enthusiasm to have been wrongly aroused. "I have nothing *on* her, no. I don't think you'll have much luck yourself getting anything *on* her either."

Ross laughed to stem Glass's annoyance. "I'm sorry, Mr. Glass—I did not mean 'on' the way you suggest. I mean can you connect her with the Menzies more tightly than you used to?"

Glass's reply was a half-second too slow, and he knew it. "No."

Ross was still smiling. "You know, sir, I am known to be terribly slow among Royal Scottish Police detectives to point an accusing finger at a potential suspect. I don't like upsetting people just to see them sweat their way to innocence. But in return I demand certain things of the innocent whose upper lips and armpits I've allowed to remain dry."

"And that is?"

"Cooperation. Not withholding evidence. Now, Mr. Glass, I am quite sure in my heart that Miss Macgregor had nothing to do with the death of the deceased. But likewise am I sure that she holds pieces to a puzzle that I have been seeking for five years. Now, either you can tell me what you have learned about her in the last forty-eight hours—and I can see that you have learned *something*—or I can take her aside and begin making trial accusations."

Glass was angry now. "Can't you see she's tired? She probably hasn't been to bed in two days and has come all the way from Sydney today."

"Tired people are the best of all talkers."

Glass was disgusted. Glancing idly upward to survey his options, he noted the two slits. "Aren't you afraid of someone listening in on us, Inspector?" He pointed upward. "Someone might be chewing beef jerky a mile a minute up there right now."

Ross laughed heartily. "Why, of course. Come with me over to The Sheepshead Inn, and we shall do our business over a pint of bitter."

Glass shook his head. "I can't right now. I wanted to speak with Ann—Miss Macgregor." For some reason he backed off from seeming too friendly with her and instantly hated himself for it. "Besides, I haven't made my confession to Miss Kribbs as yet."

Ross took him by the arm and guided him toward the stairway. "A mere formality, Mr. Glass. I don't suspect you for a second. You can give it to her later." Suddenly Glass found himself in the chill, damp night air, heading for the unguarded gate with the electrical plant spatting away behind him.

Glass swirled his second mug of beer. He had drunk the first pint terribly fast. Ross had waited for the second one to return the conversation to Ann Macgregor. Now he did. They stood at the bar, the only two there this late Tuesday night, while all the other patrons sat in booths or at tables. The pub could stay open beyond the normal licensing hours for its in-house guests, among whom there numbered, this night, the police.

"I will tell you what I learned on the condition that you will let me be the one to relay it to her. I doubt that she knows this information, and she will be quite upset when she learns it."

"Of course." Anything was all right as long as he got it.

"In my research on the Menzies project I have gotten onto a diary of a Boer farm girl whom Roberts Menzies met"—Glass was careful with his verbs—"in South Africa. When his wife died of enteric fever, Roberts fell into a liaison with this Boer girl"—now he altered the timing—"and fathered a child upon her. He sent her away from the war zone in South Africa to have the baby, but he apparently deserted her and the child." What Roberts had really done was too incredible for summary, so he let "deserted" stand as a poor synonym. "This child, named Piet, grew to be a young man in Glasgow, and in 1918 left his mother to join a South African regiment in Germany. In one of the first passages I saw translated from this diary, it was clear that *two* women saw Piet off to war, not just his mother. The other was a girlfriend of not too long a duration, I expect, but long enough to get pregnant. In later passages, at least, Maria is giving her a good deal of money to help with expenses, and I could not think of any other reason why she would be doing so."

"She *had* money to give—a woman out of her own country, deserted by the father of her child?" As with all the rest of the Menzies story, it was difficult to intrude an outsider into it without having incredulity set in.

"She had, let's say, been saving for something that never eventuated. Yes, I gather from her diary—though it's a diary and not a bankbook—that she was not badly off at all by 1918. Anyway, she saw the girl through her pregnancy, even after Piet was killed sometime during the last month of the war—there's a gap in the diary that does not precisely date it. In December, 1918, a daughter was born to Piet's mistress—I can find no evidence that they got married, however hastily—and Maria paid the expenses to have the child put into an orphange in Paisley that she had had dealings with during the Boer War. That episode is too complicated to summarize.

"At any rate, the child was to be brought out of the orphanage to live with Maria and her husband—yes, Roberts—who had decided to come back to her after the war." "Decided to come back" was, in this case, a euphemism for "was allowed to come back": Roberts had been cited by the British, South African, and two other governments for medical valor on the battlefield during the entire war, though the South African medal had been awarded to a "Bob Menzy" and the English medal to a "Roberts Menzies."

"Let me just summarize a lot of complicated material by saying that first of all, Roberts met resistance enough around these parts to his returning; that second of all, he had a Boer wife who wasn't even legally a wife; that third of all, they were not likely to accept the bastard daughter of a bastard son of an illegitimate family and unwanted marriage."

"So the unwanted Boer wife, Mr. Glass," Ross summarized, "left money to do the job for her—with the Paisley people, I mean."

"More or less, though her diary shows until the end that she never gave up the hope of bringing the girl up here to the Lochs. But Maria was killed in the Big Storm of 1925"—again he lied (what if Ross read his book later?)—"when the child would have been only six. Roberts died about the same time too."

"And so ended the child's chances with the Menzies."

"Not so, it turns out, though at first I thought so. You see,

Aunt Elizabeth, the same whose death you are investigating, would have been the wife of the chief—Bruce—then. And I now find out that she had South African ties, though surely not Boer ones. She must have been part of one of the Scottish families who settled in South Africa in the 1800s, run off by the Clearances. Since there was, in 1925, theoretically no difference between British and Boers in South Africa any longer, Aunt Elizabeth took up the cause of bringing the orphaned granddaughter of her dead father-in-law and his dead Boer wife to the Lochs."

"But if what I know of Bruce is true, he resisted?"

"He forbade! But when Bruce went off to war in 1939, Aunt Elizabeth, operating entirely clandestinely, brought the girl's attention to a want ad for a nurse in the Lochs which had been running in the Glasgow papers for more than three years. The girl had completed nurse's training this same year and snapped up the job—first because she needed one, and second because she had been led to believe she had relatives in the Lochs, not knowing the relatives were an exclusive group who did not accept many outsiders. So she got here, went to work for Dr. Hamilton Macgregor, and in 1942, married him. Her name was Annette Wallace Macgregor, and the woman whose daughter Maria helped place in the orphanage in 1919 was simply called "the Wallis girl."

Ross's eyes opened wide across the top of his pint, which had stalled at his lips for the last sixty seconds. "That means . . . that means . . ."

"Yes. What it means is a lot of things. First that Ann Macgregor, whom for some reason you have targeted, is Piet De Jager's grandaughter and—"

"And Roberts Menzies' great-granddaughter!" He whistled loudly enough to attract others in the pub.

"But if you think about it, there's worse. That would mean that Sybil Menzies, also a great-granddaughter of Roberts, is married to Clyde Menzies, a great-grandson. They would be cousins."

"Then isn't their marriage illegal?" Ross seemed more confused than enlightened by what he had heard. "Mr. Glass, do they have children? Sybil and Clyde, I mean?"

"One: a son named Duncan, nine years old."

Ross sipped his beer carefully. "And . . . is he . . . ?"

"Yes. I'm afraid he is."

Miss Kribbs came in from the castle at this point. Ross put down some coins to buy her a drink, but gestured to her not to break his train of thought.

"So if we just held all this up to the light and looked at its reflections, we could probably explain Annette Macgregor's suicide, couldn't we, Mr. Glass?"

"I have already *held* it up to the light. Annette was raised a thoroughgoing Calvinist—at Maria's request probably, since that was the Boer faith—and Hamilton Macgregor was also, as Scottish people often are. They were sign-watchers, as we call their American counterparts in the northeastern United States. Being an orphan is evidence that God does not favor you. Failure to succeed in one's work, as Macgregor failed in his most critical experiments, is another. Having a daughter of low sexual morality is a third—but then, if you have reason to trace your lineage in order to fill out government forms for employment, and find out who exactly you are, and that in reality your loose-thighed daughter is incestuously married to the town drunk and has given birth to a retarded son . . ."

"That about ends the sign-watching, doesn't it? In different terms, we can get convictions on a lot less evidence than that" —now he acknowledged his assistant, who was sipping something Glass could not identify—"can't we, Miss Kribbs?"

Miss Kribbs, not having been party to the line of reasoning, could only reply with polite but meaningless agreement. She was holding her paperback of *Gratuitous Glory* poised. "Mr. Glass, I have been reading your book when I have some free moments"—Glass could see that she was about two-thirds of the way through it—"and I do like it so much. Annie Daly is such a wonderful person, a model of what we all should be. I can never be like that, I fear, but it is good to know such people have existed. I was wondering if . . . ?" She allowed the stunning smile and her large pecan-shaped brown eyes to speak the rest of the sentence for her. "My name is Felicia Kribbs; could you possibly . . . ?"

Glass agreed, though a streak of sarcasm suggested this might be torn out within the hour and sent on to Glasgow for handwriting analysis. Unable to restrain the tendency entirely, he wrote, with two pints of beer to encourage him, *"To Felicia Kribbs, in memory of our 'night' together. Your servant, Jason Glass."* She laughed happily when he returned it to her to read.

Ross yawned. "Well, I have some paperwork to do before

retiring. Good evening to you, Mr.Glass, and many thanks for your assistance. Keep me informed of your whereabouts, won't you? Felicia, don't forget to get Mr. Glass's, you know, statement." He waved, left the pub, and ascended the stairs.

Glass and Miss Kribbs sat down at a table together and ordered, by the time their interview ended, three more rounds of drinks. Only as the publican was beginning to turn out the lights did it dawn on Glass that at this hour, he would have no way back to The Gap besides his feet; that he would have to take a room at the inn for the night. And only as the lights were going out did Miss Kribbs, a chipper-chatterer who seemed an unlikely detective, remember to take out her pad and get his alibi. He said forthrightly that he had none and drunkenly said more than that.

"No, I was home all day and alone. I had enough unobserved time not only to murder Aunt Elizabeth but also to rob the bank in Ullapool and expose myself on the beach after that."

Miss Kribbs thought that awfully clever. "Well, perhaps you'll have something by morning. If you think of nothing, we can create something."

Glass's eyes cleared a bit. "Create something?"

She looked at him knowingly. "We cannot very well spend the night together and then have you trot off without a proper alibi, can we?"

"Spend the night together?"

She looked confused now. "Well, yes . . . what you wrote in the book and . . ."

He smiled. "Oh, Miss Kribbs, I was not propositioning you. It's just that I don't get questioned in a murder investigation every night. I—"

She was hurt. "Then, we shan't . . . ?"

He shook his head. "You are a lovely young lady. You really are." Now they had to rise and leave, for all the lights were out. He walked her to the door of her room on the second floor. "You are, after all, the police. The protector of good order. And remember Annie Daly. What would she do?" Glass was beginning to have new information on what she might.

"I do not sleep with a badge on," Miss Kribbs said as she put her arms around his neck and looked as mistily into his eyes as he did into hers, "and I am not Annie Daly. I've told you that."

She was terribly pretty, and Glass desired her. He kissed her once and rubbed the palms of his hands up and down her waist and hips. He could feel the outlines of her very abbreviated underpants, but fought off his temptation. He wished she were Ann. "No. Go in, now, like a good policewoman—all right?"

She changed her tack. The police seem to know what people are thinking even before they themselves know they were thinking it. "Do you know what Miss Macgregor's alibi was—for last Sunday?"

"Plane tickets which prove she was in Sydney then." The question did not seem as out of place as it should have.

"And do you know what Mr. Farquhar Menzies' alibi was?"

"I have no idea."

"Plane tickets which prove *he* was in Sydney then too." She did not smile, but rather looked deeply into his eyes in the dim sepia light of the hallway.

When he awoke in the morning, he wanted to cry, but Miss Kribbs was already sitting upright in bed, her sea nymph's breasts exposed above the sheet which covered her from the navel down, her pad propped on her upright knees, Glass's alibi all but completed.

25 *JASON GLASS IN LADYSMITH*

LADYSMITH. STANDING BEFORE THE TOWN HALL, its clock tower no longer visibly scarred by the Boer shell that had struck it on December 21, 1899, Glass had the same feeling he had had when he was taken as a child to the battlefield at Gettysburg after he had steeped himself in virtually every account he could find of the episode. Once again the past seemed entirely present: the booms of the Long Toms unbearably deafening, the disease in the air, the despair in the atmosphere, himself Roberts Menzies. They had paved the streets and lined them with parking meters, cars were parked where cavalry horses had been tied, neon signs had replaced board ones, the clock tower was whole again—but otherwise it was the same town that Glass had viewed in the photographs of Mournful Monday, save that he viewed it for the first time in color. The townspeople could not disguise that fact; perhaps had not wanted to.

During their journey to South Africa it had been difficult to determine who was more miserable and guarded, Jason or Ann. For himself, Glass could not pinpoint exactly what was bothering him, though the sudden absence of sexual attraction for Ann had to be at the center of it. It was not simply because she looked so haggard—and she did, terribly so—for a bit of rest once this latest episode was over would restore her beauty. Perhaps it was the same emotion he had felt when he found out that Annie Daly had been selling her body to advance her siblings' welfare; that Sybil would spread her legs for other men, him among them, almost in her husband's view; that Henrietta, almost as chaste as a nun, was vulnerable only to her lost brother or somebody—Glass again—who looked like him; that policewomen went to bed with suspects and helped them forge their alibis as reverse payment; and now that Ann, the untarnished and untarnishable, had been for at least two weeks in Sydney with Farquhar, committing, probably, another round of blissfully ignorant incest. He did not mention this to her, but it was turning him away from her and he knew it.

Yet why should it? He had himself had quite a few women after Margot left, and several more in the Lochs, Ann's roommate and her sister among them. Where did he get off passing judgment on Ann, even tacitly? He did not and knew it and so passed none. His next move undoubtedly would be to make a vow of chastity for the remainder of his life. Lots of people would have been better off if Roberts had done that, and lots would if he did also.

Ann's misery was hard to define as well. She was clearly exhausted. There was no sleeping car on the pokechug train from Kyle to Inverness which stopped at everything that even looked as if it might be a station, but he had insisted that she take a compartment on the next train to Glasgow, and had even gotten her into it an hour before the train departed while he supervised the transferral of the coffin. Then he had sat in the chair in her compartment, reading when he could by a slight crack in the window shade, holding her dark green dress across his lap so he would not wrinkle it. Though it was chilly outside, the compartment had been terribly hot, and she had kicked off the covers in her fitful sleep and lain prone and elongated as if dead before him. The smooth skin and tight muscles of her belly and thighs had been as beautiful as he remembered them, the soft shoulders which he used to pull the bra straps away from when he kissed them so that he could have them whole and uninterrupted, the outlines of her nipples through her sheer bra itself, the place where her bikini panties puffed up slightly at the bottom—these were all there before him; but he did not long for them as he once had. These seemed unreal now, a picture in a magazine to be looked at but the subject never to be possessed, the prospect of possession never even to be considered. When the slums of Glasgow began to appear in the window, he had shaken her shoulders slightly, and she had jumped up as if she had been fired from a catapult. After she got her bearings, she had pulled on her dress and panty hose and shoes, and had finished combing her hair just as the train rocked to a stop in Glasgow Central.

She had been awake but fairly quiet on the third train to Prestwick Airport, much the same for the hourlong flight to Heathrow. She had rarely if ever stirred on the all-night flight to Johannesburg. Her head had lain on his shoulder most of the night, but still he could not revive the interest in this woman—or even any woman—that he had always had and now no longer apparently wanted to have. Schopenhauerian pessimism, he felt, must be setting in. Carried to its logical conclusion, this philosophy held up celibacy and nonextension of the species as the best, indeed only, solution to the filthy complexities of nonteleological earthly existence. On the train to Ladysmith the next morning she had wept. Glass had not asked why. He knew only that had they never looked into the matter of Roberts Menzies, neither of them would have been here now, much less ever have met each other in the first place, and so would not be crying, she in actuality, he internally.

They had taken rooms in the Royal Hotel—she in 203, he in 204. There was no connecting door.

At dinnertime he had not awakened her but rather had eaten alone in the dining room, the same dining room in which Frank Rhodes and Leander Starr Jameson and their cronies had waited out the Siege with their cache of champagne until the Boers began to shell it.

He had debated groggily with himself on the trip down whether or not he would seek oral testimony of people who had known Roberts Menzies. He now resolved to; but it was a full sixty years since Roberts had left Ladysmith for the First World War, and he knew he would have to be directed to English-speaking people in their seventies and eighties to help him out, ones whose memories were still sharp and intact. He decided to risk inquiry from a pleasant-looking woman of about fifty who was behind the main desk when he emerged from dinner.

"Excuse me," he said, after tinkling the desk bell slightly to turn her away from the mail slots she was working on. "My name is Jason Glass. I am a writer, and I am doing some research for a biography of a man who spent a good portion of his life here just after the turn of the century—up till the First World War. I was wondering if you might put me on"—he was not sure this was a correct idiom—"to some elderly citizens who might have recollections of Ladysmith then." He hoped she spoke English.

She did. "Yes, Mr. Glass, we know something here of who you are." She pointed to a rack of paperback books to the right of the main desk. *Gratuitous Glory* was prominently displayed on the top row all the way across. "The afternoon clerk told me you were here, but I did not at first think it was the author Jason Glass—though surely not many people have so fragile a name as that." She smiled in a motherly way.

Glass flushed. How long would it take the correct information about Annie Daly to reach South Africa? he wondered.

"Thank you. You see, I am looking to find someone who knew a doctor who practiced here, a Scotsman who worked without a left arm or a right eye. He would have—"

"Dr. Bob Menzy?"

"Yes! You have heard of him. Do you know anyone who knew him?"

"*I* knew him, Mr. Glass. Quite well, in fact."

Glass frowned hard at her. How many one-armed, one-eyed doctors could there have been in such an off-the-track place as Ladysmith? This woman would have to have been born a good ten years after Roberts left, probably after he died as well. The woman was uncomfortable under his speechless gaze.

"But how could that be? He died in Scotland in 1925!"

She laughed, with apologetic haughtiness. "Well, I am sorry, Mr. Glass. The Dr. Bob Menzy I knew treated me for a general run of things from constipation to allergies until the time I married. It was about that time he retired."

Glass was still scowling, could not wipe the scowl from his face no matter how hard he tried. "What year did you marry?"

"Nineteen forty-nine."

Glass blew through his cheeks. "Shit!" The woman scowled back now. "Did this man walk with a stooped-over posture?"

"And a cane to prop him up. Yes, it is certainly the same man. I was born in 1927, and he delivered me in my parents' parlor when my mother went into premature labor."

Glass calculated years, squinting into his memory for Henrietta's genealogy. "In 1949 he would have been . . . seventy-seven. Was this man that old?"

"At least that old, Mr. Glass. He looked seventy-seven in my earliest recollections of him, more like ninety-seven in my later ones. He always had steady hands . . . hand, I should say, however.

"And you say he retired?"

"Was forced to, actually. You see, the government ordered him to stop treating both white and nonwhite—one or the other, but not both. He was, however, a legend—to himself as well as the town, I expect—for he had saved all color of lives during the Siege at the turn of the century, from all variety of maladies. He liked to hear himself say that he could not afford to be a specialist in either race then, so he was not about to start being one now."

"And he left the area after he retired?"

"Just a few miles. He took up residence at the Pretorius farm about halfway down the road toward Colenso. The farmer apparently had some connection with Dr. Bob back in earlier times—was probably, in fact, Dr. Bob's best friend in the whole district. They drank and hunted together until their deaths, I'm told."

"When did they die?" Finally this can be nailed down, Glass thought.

"They died in an automobile crash, together, in the summer of 1950—January or February, I think. Rumor had it they were both drinking fairly heavily at a small reunion of those still alive who had fallen under siege—fiftieth anniversary of their relief, I think. They drove home in a pickup truck from an outdoor cookery atop Bulwana. The road down the side is very treacherous—too much so for two feeble old men with their minds and eyes out of synchronization from liquor."

"They were killed instantly?"

"No, I don't think so. They were both brought by ambulance to the Ladysmith hospital. I can't recall which died first, though both passed on within the week. You could find that information on file at the Town Hall in the morning if you require it."

"Yes. Yes, I *do* require it. Thank you. Thank you very much, madam." Glass was weary but strangely exhilarated as he climbed the stairs to 204 for an early retirement. In 203, he could hear Ann breathing steadily through the old wooden door. Tomorrow was Saturday, and the records office would be open only from nine until noon. On Sunday everything would be closed, but South African farm families named Pretorius could be counted upon to stay home and rest for the day. On Monday, Aunt Elizabeth would be buried by the few still-living Farquhars, most of whom probably had had little idea that she even existed. And on Tuesday he and Ann would start the long trek back to Scotland. Before he left, however, one coffin would be in the ground, and the lid, Glass felt, would firmly be nailed down on another once and for all. This done, Glass could finish his work and be back in America if not by Thanksgiving, at least by Christmas.

The English-speaking clerk in the Town Hall had not come to work this Saturday morning, so Glass and Ann, who seemed greatly recovered by now, physically if not emotionally, had to fight their way through the language barrier with the Afrikaans-speaking girl who substituted. They were able to string together words they had become familiar with in Maria's diary to convey what they sought. As the girl and Ann conversed, Glass could not help being struck by the similarity between the clerk's general features and what Glass had heretofore thought was a slight Germanic cast to Ann's otherwise delicate British facial structure. He wondered if she noticed it as well.

Finally, the death certificate, written in both languages, was produced—listing the deceased in English as Roberts Menzies, in Afrikaans as Bob Menzy. DATE OF BIRTH: April 17, 1872. DATE OF DEATH: March 5, 1950. CAUSE OF DEATH: Injuries received in an automobile accident on Bulwana Road, Tuesday, February 28, 1950. AGE AT DEATH: 77 years, 10 ½ months. OCCUPATION: Physician. CITIZENSHIP STATUS: Noncitizen. CITIZEN OF: (left blank). ATTENDING PHYSICIAN: Henrik Voort." After

Voort's name was the name of someone else "also in attendance," but it was an unreadable prescription-label scrawl with an M.D. after it printed in by another hand.

When they emerged from the Town Hall, Ann sat down on the front steps—right in the middle, not off to either side—so suddenly that Glass assumed she had suffered a relapse into her previous day's exhaustion. Rather than pain, however, the look on her face was that of smirking irony.

"You know, Jason, when I was four I distinctly recall a time when my father and mother shipped Sybil and me off to live at the castle with Aunt Catherine while they went off to a medical conference in Washington. We loved the castle so much for those two weeks that we wished they would stay in Washington longer so we could remain there for additional time. But they came back on schedule, though they hadn't been to Washington."

"Where had they been?" Glass could not have cared less, was being polite to urge her up off the steps—probably the first person to loiter squarely in the center since General White had thanked his siege garrison for their patience.

"That second signature on the death certificate."

"Yes." More impatience.

She understood his embarrassment and reached up her hand for help in rising. "It was my father's."

Glass was no longer flabbergasted by anything, so acted as if her father had had a practice across High Street from the Town Hall all along. "So four came, not three—Elizabeth, Farquhar, Henrietta, and your father?" He chuckled for lack of any other reaction.

"Well, five if my mother came as well."

"No, she was probably in Korea that year."

"Doing what?"

"I don't know. But they had a war begin there in that year. You'd have to have somebody from the Lochs available to make sure it got started right." He pulled her forward by the hand. "Let's get lunch. It's hot out here."

The current eldest Pretorius was roughly the same age his grandfather—the one with whom Roberts Menzies, or Bob Menzy, at least, had chummed around—would have been twenty-five years earlier, so it was difficult for Glass, and seemingly for Ann as well, to understand at times that they were speaking to that man's son and not to Roberts' friend himself. Perhaps, too, they became further disoriented by the fact that this was only the first male—and only the second person of either sex—who had actually *known* Roberts Menzies and could talk coherently about him.

The Pretorius farm was apparently a prosperous one which dealt in both dairy products and beef. The farmhouse was a product of this century, for the original house, as they were quick to find out, had been dynamited by the British in 1901. This was the standard treatment for all families who were either Boers or Boer sympathizers and might be hiding arms or guerrillas. The Pretorius family had done both.

"Some of De Wet's men would slip out of the Free State," old Pretorius said that Sunday afternoon over glasses of chilled rum in his parlor, "to see what families like ours just inside Natal had managed to accumulate in the way of ammunition or clothing or food stores. They would return to the war zone with these, and sometime later, when they had given us enough time to hoard more, they would return. Whenever Kitchener drove them into the corner of the Brandwater Basin nearest us, they would come here."

"You are old enough to recall that?" Glass asked. He had noticed that Pretorius was more responsive to him than to Ann because he lacked a British accent. He would have liked to tell the old fellow that he was speaking to Bob Menzy's great-granddaughter, but since that would have been even more of a shock to Ann than to Pretorius, he abstained.

Pretorius waved the question away with a kindly smile. "I was only five at the time, but war is a terrible thing. Five is old enough to remember. The soldiers came by and gave us five minutes to get together what we could and leave the house. I don't think they gave us that long, for my father and I were going back for another load of clothing when we saw two sappers finish digging the holes for the dynamite and engineers plant the explosives. I was ahead of him approaching the house, and suddenly I felt him grab me under the arms, spin me around, and half-carry me in the other direction. He had a game leg from a wound he'd received during the attack on Caesar's Camp at the Siege, so we could not entirely get out of the way. The house blew up while our backs were turned to it, and he threw himself on top of me for the duration of the initial blasts; then we watched, both of us crying, and all we could see was a billowing column of black smoke and a pile of tin and boards where our house had been. Then we took what consolation we could from the whole affair. We backed up further to where the forest starts"—he pointed out a window toward what looked in the distance to be a grove of tall pines—"for we knew that all the things we had stored in the cellar had not blown yet. The British soldiers sneaked back cautiously and were well within range when the place erupted no fewer than seven more times."

"You had ammunition on hand?"

Pretorius laughed triumphantly. "We had everything—cartridges, Mauser shells, guns, dynamite, cannon shells, and even lyddite. My word, did the place make noise and smell! Several of the soldiers fell wounded from dumdum bullets which had not even had to be fired from a gun to find their marks."

"Dr. Bob Menzy, Mr. Pretorius: how well did you know him?"

"I first recall meeting him sometime during my adolescent years. He had settled here some years after the Siege. He had been a member of the besieged in Ladysmith during the war, and for some reason he chose not to go home. He practiced medicine in Ladysmith for nine or ten years before the Great War. How he did it, I'll never know. He had a kaffir man who assisted him, and while he stayed away from extremely complicated procedures, he did, despite his lack of an arm, deliver babies, pull teeth, and sew up lacerations with considerable dispatch. He would visit us here occasionally; my father and he had become close friends over the years. They could get pretty drunk on occasion, I recollect, but he also helped my father add indoor plumbing and electrical wiring to this very house in the years after we rebuilt."

"So he stayed here until the next war started?"

"Yes. In 1914 he had to weather a crisis here that probably caused him not to return for more than ten more years once he left. General Christiaan De Wet, perhaps you know, had become disaffected with Louis Botha's government in Pretoria and was attempting to raise a guerrilla band to resist the ongoing British–Boer alliance of the day. Since Bob Menzy had performed bravely for De Wet's guerrillas in an earlier time, De Wet sought him again, his one arm and one eye notwithstanding. Bob was put in a difficult spot. First, he had clearly come to love the peace and calm of life here, was not addicted to war, as poor De Wet seemed to have grown, and was a supporter of

Botha, whose eye could not be turned. Yet when the Great War began in 1914, he seemed to respond to Botha's call for his medical skills with the South African regiments in Europe, not so much to go to war (which he would not have had to do, since he was over forty by this time) as to escape his still strong but potentially treasonous love for De Wet. He was forced off to war by a conflict of heart and conscience, you might say."

Glass looked across the room at Ann and could see the pain in her face. No matter where Roberts tried to set himself down, or when he tried to do it, he was inevitably chased off or left pulled on the rack between two conflicting loyalties which, in balance, were almost equally strong.

"My research has uncovered that he was decorated by both the South African and the British governments for valor in action throughout the war."

"Apparently, yes. But as I say, he did not return here when the war in Europe was over. At the end my father got word that he had gone back to Scotland, where he had come from. He was nearing fifty. Although Father believed him to have been sexually impotent due to an old war wound, he must have got married when he got there. I know when he returned here in 1924, he was planning to bring a wife and a child with him the following year."

Glass muttered "Annette Wallace" under his breath almost too loudly. Ann had heard something, but he could tell she was not sure what he had said, had raised her eyebrows as if to request that he repeat it. Glass did not.

"You say 1924? I had information that indicated it was 1925."

"The wife and child were to come then, but Bob Menzy was here by Christmas of 1924. Here, I can show you." He walked slowly across the room to a standing cabinet, opened it with a key that was already protruding from its keyhole, and selected a dark brown leather-bound album of photographs.

And so, six months into his project, Jason Glass finally viewed a picture of the man he had been writing about and investigating. Pretorius opened the book to the family Christmas portrait, dated with white ink "1924," and laid the book in Glass's lap. Ann crossed the room herself to peer at it over his shoulder. There must have been thirty people in the photograph, ranging from small babies to old men and women. The Pretorius who had been Bob Menzy's friend stood behind his parents at the center of the picture, and the current Pretorius, a man then something short of thirty, pointed himself out standing at the right side of the gathering, his arm around a robust, very Dutch-looking woman of roughly the same vintage. There was only one face that was not Germanic, and this one wore a black patch over its right eye.

In 1924, Roberts Menzies would have been fifty-two. He looked twenty years more than that, just as the woman at the hotel desk had claimed he would. His hair was entirely white, which set off the stark black patch strikingly; his skin—though the picture was not in color—looked as if it might be harshly ruddy, perhaps even leathery. While it could not be seen because of a person who sat in front of him, Glass could tell he was supporting himself on a cane, his shoulders hunched pronouncedly forward as a result. His face did not smile, as almost all the others did—rather, his single good eye seemed locked on the single good eye of the camera lens, as if to speak to it or to peer truth out of it as if it had lied to him a moment before. If Roberts Menzies had been a short man to begin with—five feet seven or eight was his reputed height—the use of the cane reduced him to something just over five feet. While the others were dressed in their best dark Sunday suits and white dresses, Roberts wore an open-necked shirt of a light color—perhaps khaki—and like-colored trousers. In his single hand, slightly in front of the cane, he held a broad slouch hat with its brim pinned to the right side, causing him to resemble a guerrilla leader who had arrived at a church picnic to gather a commando. And yet he was *not* pathetic in the slightest, seeming to suggest, as he pinioned the camera eye with his own, that he was ready for what would come next even though he had no idea what it would be.

What it would be, of course, would be the death of his "wife."

"Why is it that his wife and the child did not come with him in 1924?" Glass asked after they had put away the album and settled back to freshly refilled glasses of rum.

"I did not know all the details, of course, Mr. Glass. He was my father's friend and merely an acquaintance of mine. It must have been a last-minute decision for him to leave Scotland in the first place—there was some family trouble there, I seem to recall—and I gather the child was not living with them at the time. His wife—who, by the way, was a South African woman, not a British one—was to collect the child, settle their affairs, and follow him at the end of their winter. In the fall of 1925—our fall, their spring—he received a letter from his father saying that the woman was dying, that she would be unable to travel."

"Around April?"

"Approximately. Then in the early winter he got word of her death. There was no mention that I recall of the child—perhaps Bob's wife never collected it. I don't even know if it was male or female."

"It was female," Glass mused offhandedly, and again Ann's face twisted in confusion. "To the best of your knowledge, Mr. Pretorius, did the death of his wife end any relations Roberts—Bob Menzy—carried on with his family in Scotland?"

"Yes and no." Pretorius seemed to wince a bit as he entered into this aspect of the story. "When he heard of his wife's death, he telephoned her family, who lived somewhere north of Pretoria—just a mother, a sister, and a brother, both married—about having the body returned to them for burial. They said they would like to bury her in the family plot at . . . at . . ."

"Tuinplaas?"

"Yes, I think that might have been what it was. But they had no money for the transport. So Bob borrowed the money from the Farquhar family, a prominent English family in Ladysmith, and sent it to his father with instructions to ship the body to Tuinplaas."

"And I am quite sure it never arrived."

"Correct! It never did! How did you know?"

"A hunch." This was not good enough. "I've looked a lot into the mentality of Menzies of late. I know how they think. So that ended it?"

"Almost, but not quite. You see, there was one other connection between people hereabout and people in Scotland. In the early twenties, probably the most beautiful English girl in this district left to go to Scotland to marry Bob's son. The daughter of Mayor Farquhar. Her name, I believe, was Ellen."

"No, it was Elizabeth." Glass paused a moment. "Perhaps I did not mention that research on this book is only my secondary reason for being in South Africa, Mr. Pretorius. My primary one is the return here for burial tomorrow of the body of Elizabeth Farquhar. She died last Sunday of . . ." He reached to invent a cause.

"Gunshot wounds." Ann had plainly done with any form of deception at this point.

"No!" Pretorius seemed to well up with tears. "She was *murdered*?"

"Apparently," said Glass, with some annoyance at Ann, "though no one has been caught or accused."

Old Pretorius took a few moments to calm himself. "Now, there, Mr. Glass, is a tragic story from beginning to end. She was one of Bob's first patients when he came back here around 1905. She was dying with a fever and Dr. Bob brought her back to health. There had been great friendship between him and her father during the Siege; I gather they had a bit of a falling-out after it was lifted—over something inconsequential, undoubtedly—but this cemented the relationship until Mr. Farquhar died in 1940. Dr. Bob watched her grow up, and she became almost a daughter to him. He took her on picnics, taught her to be his left arm in simpler medical procedures that he did not require his kaffir for. They even took trips to Durban once a year to buy her a new dress and hat, which Bob always paid for. And it was always the frilliest, most feminine thing that the styles recommended that year. They would leave on the earliest train on a spring morning and return on the latest one. Whatever Elizabeth had worn away in the morning returned in a box that night because her new dress was already on her, as was the hat. Dr. Bob especially loved her long blond hair, and word was about that he and only he was allowed to cut it for her. She was quite broken up when he left for the war when she was in her early teens. I recall I went through a period of jealousy myself—she was the finest-looking girl around, and I think I resented that she chose to spend her time in the company of a badly wrecked man in his forties rather than around girls her own age where boys her own age could have access to her.

"I am not sure if she corresponded with him during the war or after, but I know that Bob had selected her in his own mind to be the wife of a son I did not even know he had, named Bruce—correct?"

"Yes."

"When he sent for her, both she and her father trusted Dr. Bob so implicitly that she was dispatched supposedly for a visit to Scotland, but both knew it would be to live there. She married and bore him several children."

"Three—two sons and a daughter."

"Yes. Well, it was a mistake nonetheless. Apparently she had sided with Bob in whatever the dispute was that caused Bob finally to leave Scotland and return again to South Africa in 1924. I really think Elizabeth would have come with him, except she was pregnant with her first child. During the thirties, Dr. Bob told my father that she was seeking to divorce her husband and return here—but Bruce would not grant the divorce. Dr. Bob and her father even paid for solicitors on each end, here and in Scotland, to try to do something to assist her, and after several years they managed to persuade her husband to release her."

"They did?" Ann was struck by this point. "Yet I know for a fact that no divorce occurred."

"Correct, for her husband would not give up his two sons—the older would inherit the family lands, of course, and the next he just seemed to have some special affection for. So all Elizabeth would have been allowed to leave with would have been Bruce's unwanted daughter."

"Henrietta," both Glass and Ann said softly but not without awe, looking each other straight in the eye as they formed the name.

"So she stayed, though her letters both to her father and to Dr. Bob indicated that she was miserable. Her husband seemed to have some sort of score to settle with the world that made him impossible to live with. Dr. Bob would never elaborate what this was, nor would Elizabeth in her letters. Gloriously, however, the husband decided to enlist in the Second World War, perhaps to settle it there by gunning down Nazi soldiers, but instead got himself gunned down. Old Mayor Farquhar was dead by then, of course, but Elizabeth wrote Dr. Bob an unapologetic letter saying she had not a single pang of sorrow over his son's death. I'm not sure Dr. Bob cared much by that point either."

"She lost a son of her own to the war the following year, you know."

"Yes, I did know, though till this moment that had slipped my mind."

"Did she make any attempt to return here then?"

"Not initially. When Dr. Bob died in 1950, however, she accompanied her remaining son and daughter to try to be with him before he died in the hospital here. And she did make it, barely. She spoke to him before he passed away, I'm told. I think she loved him more than any other person in her life, her children included. I saw her in town one day—she was nearly fifty by then, but she was still beautiful, and the blond hair still stood out about the gray. The only close relative she had in Ladysmith by that time was her mother, who was very old and sick. Now—and this I am not entirely sure about—she did decide to remain here with her mother at least for the time. The old woman would only live until 1952, as it turned out, and the word was about town that Elizabeth was to move in with her rather than return to Scotland with her son and daughter."

"But she did *not* stay, did she?"

"No! At the last minute she changed her mind and almost disappeared without ceremony. No one particularly understood it."

"Mr. Pretorius, I know a detail such as this is very taxing to the memory, but do you recall anyone else arriving with Elizabeth and her two children that year—when Bob Menzy died?"

It turned out not to be taxing at all. "Yes, certainly. They brought a doctor and a nurse with them. Quite irritated old Dr. Voort as well, for they seemed to imply—perhaps just by their presence—that South African medicine was still in the hands of Zulu witch doctors. Voort had studied medicine in France and America, though ironically, he had no large practice here until Bob retired in the late forties. So this was the second slap that the old gentleman received at the hands of this Scottish family. Is it Menzy or Menzies, by the way?"

"It's both, I guess, especially for the member of it you know. Can you describe the circumstances of Bob's death?"

"The one thing my father and Dr. Bob loved to do together, Mr. Glass, was drink. Drink anything. Rum, beer, wine, whisky. They both worked hard at their very different callings until the sun went down each day, but four or five nights a week Dr. Bob would be driven down here by his kaffir. They would pour the black fellow a third of what they had and leave him to sit in the truck and drink it while they consumed theirs in the garden in the warm weather, the parlor in the cold. They cared not in the least who else was around to hear them as they told over and over again the old Siege and commando stories, changing them a bit each time to make them a bit different from the last and so better and more interesting, cursing like madmen the more liquor they got inside them. They would laugh uproariously as well. Whenever they finished what they had, and there was more some nights than others, for it depended on what they could lay hold of, Bob would go out to the truck and shake the drunk kaffir awake and they would weave their way back along the empty road to Ladysmith. Lucky it was that it was empty, too, for the kaffir was not an expert driver even when he was sober. A good medical assistant, however, I'm told.

"The date on which my father and Dr. Bob had the accident that cost them their lives was the twenty-eighth of February, 1950. For many years after the Siege, the residents of Ladysmith would celebrate the day of the relief each year with a party at the Town Hall. The main attenders were those old enough to have been involved, but others came as well. As the older people died off, however, the party became less regular—it was held only once during the Second World War, and only once after that. So my father and Dr. Bob had the idea to celebrate the fiftieth anniversary by gathering together not only the remaining British citizens who were invested but also all the local Boers who were part of the Siege force and have the party atop Bulwana Mountain, which was the anchor of the Boer perimeter during the Siege. Most who came were of Boer stock—there were more of us still around the area, naturally—but some English joined in as well. At fifty-three, I was just about the youngest one there. Some of the people could barely stand up, but the party was a rousing success. Everyone was totally drunk, and we nearly had several brushfires in trying to get our meat cooked.

"Now, the big event was to be the firing of an old war cannon that the Van Dreegnans had dragged home with them in 1902 and that my father and Dr. Bob had the idea of hauling to the top of Bulwana for the festivities."

Glass looked at Ann and she gazed back at him steadily. A Menzies would always be a Menzies even if he called himself Menzy instead.

"So once nightfall came, the artillery experts from the war began popping away at the fallow land on the Springman farm —which was acceptable because Springman himself was lending a hand. They were creating a tremendous racket, having a jolly time, drunk out of their minds from too much consumed on too hot a day. What no one knew was that some local adolescents, perhaps incensed at not being invited to the gay times themselves, had unearthed a howitzer from where it had been buried by the fleeing Boers along the veld—there are known to be a number of such guns about—and had moved it to Lombards Kop. They had no particular ammunition, of course, but they managed to get their hands on a small supply of gunpowder and a few rocks of suitable size for muzzle loading. Around ten o'clock that night, they parked a car at the base of the kop and pointed it toward Bulwana and began flashing a coded message with the headlights. It was an obscene expletive, of course, though only Bob Menzy knew enough code to read it. He was good with codes, it seems." In literary terms, this irony was dramatic rather than pure—he seemed not to know the truth of what he was saying.

"Then the gun on Lombards Kop commenced firing; it could not reach the top of Bulwana or even get close, but we could hear whatever they were firing falling into the trees down below. All the while this obscene message continued to flash from the car lights. Some of the Bulwana party were considerably irked by this—they did not know till later who was doing it—and some just had ideas for a different sort of fun. So the pom-pom was fired three successive times toward Lombards Kop; this was out of range for an old pom-pom too, but one of the three shells did strike a vehicle on the road at the base, and suddenly much screaming and crying erupted and the headlights went dead. Now either my father or Dr. Bob realized what had happened and called off the firing, and Bob and my father and the kaffir driver jumped into the pickup truck and sped down the road to attend to the injured. There is actually little more to say. The kaffir was more drunk than either of the two old men he had with him, if that be possible, lost control of the truck on the descent, and rolled it over, killing himself and mortally injuring my father and Dr. Bob. My father died two days later of spinal damage—he was seventy-five—and Dr. Bob died several days after that still in shock from the crash. He must have been . . ."

"Seventy-seven, almost seventy-eight." Glass shook his head in exasperation as the younger Pretorius woman summoned them in Afrikaans for dinner. "How can a man survive the Siege, guerrilla warfare, amputations, dismemberments, homelessness, loss of spouse and children, and who knows what else —vultures and gunfire to boot—and then get knocked off by a drunk driver trying to rush to the aid of a pack of teenaged hoodlums?" And even worse, Glass reflected, was the fact that these young toughs must have been flashing their GET FUCKED, OLD FARTS or whatever South African youth considered appropriate and effective from the exact spot at which Roberts had last seen Catherine, alive or ever, when he and Maria De Jager had released her diseased body to the Boer wagon driver. Everyone had gone into the dining room, but Glass held old Pretorius back for a moment. "What exactly were the two doctors in disagreement about in the last days of Bob Menzy's life?"

"Last day only, for that was the day the Scottish doctor arrived. He seemed to be claiming that not enough attempt had been made to delay Bob's death so that he could be moved to the hospital at Dundee, which was better equipped. He was even angry when Dr. Voort signed the death certificate; so, to hear Voort tell it, Voort just stormed into the records office and told them that as far as he was concerned, Bob Menzy was not 'officially' dead until the Scottish doctor got around to thinking so also and signing the death certificate himself. I don't know if he ever bothered or not—I suppose then he would have had to."

"Yes, I've seen it. He signed it, though he left his M.D. off and somebody else had to fill that in." Glass followed Pretorius into the dining room and prepared to consume a meal which smelled with the essence of a veld fire just after manuring.

At eleven that evening, both Glass and Ann sat in the bar at the Royal Hotel, with full glasses of beer before them which they could not muster the intestinal stability to consume. The woman clerk from the front desk suddenly slipped in and handed Glass a telegram. It was from Inspector Ross: MR. F. MENZIES BADLY WOUNDED BY GUNSHOT IN SHOULDER. CLAIMS ACCIDENTALLY SELF-INFLICTED. PROBABLY NOT. RETURN ASAP. YOU MAY BE IN DANGER. ROSS. It had been wired from Glasgow and received at Ladysmith.

On Monday, the third of November, Ann and Glass, the whole Pretorius family, and what scatterings of Farquhar relatives there were saw the body of Elizabeth Farquhar Menzies, beloved daughter of the late Mayor James Farquhar and Mary Dodd, wife of the late Bruce Menzies, mother of Farquhar, Owen (deceased), and Henrietta Menzies, laid to rest beside her father in the Anglican churchyard at the south side of Ladysmith, within a short block of the Klip River at the drift through which Winston Churchill and Major Gough had splashed the day they liberated Ladysmith more than seventy-five years before. And Ann and Glass took note of the other stones as well. One read: JAMES FARQUHAR, 1863–1940, MAYOR OF LADYSMITH AT THE TIME OF THE GREAT SIEGE, 2 November 1899–28 FEB-

RUARY 1900. Another gravestone read: MARY DODD FARQUHAR, 1870–1901, THE LORD GAVE HER A DAUGHTER BUT DEMANDED HER PRESENCE WITH HIM IN RECOMPENSE. Then the newly opened ground above which a sharply chiseled stone already stood: ELIZABETH FARQUHAR MENZIES, 1901–1975, SHE LEFT US FOR THE SORROWS OF THIS EARTHLY LIFE BUT HAS RETURNED TO US FOR THE JOYS OF ETERNITY. And then, on an old grave, an older stone: DR. BOB MENZY, 1872–1950, TAKEN BY HIS CREATOR TO ETERNAL LIFE AFTER LONG DAYS OF DOING HIS WILL ON EARTH. And one last grave, next to Roberts', which they had not expected; CATHERINE CLYDE MENZIES, 1875–1900, DEAD OF THE SIEGE. THE WORLD IS POORER FOR HER EARLY REMOVAL. THIS STONE PLACED BY HER HUSBAND ON THE 25TH ANNIVERSARY OF HER PASSING, 2 JANUARY 1925. MAY SHE THANK GOD FOR HIS WISDOM AND FOREKNOWLEDGE.

26 *THE EXPULSION*

THE RELATIONSHIP OF A SINGLE HUMAN LIFE to the course of history demanded, insofar as Jason Glass was concerned, a clever metaphor to characterize it. Yet he had never been able to turn out an apt one—and, he felt, no other author had either. Many had been tried: looms, gyres, spiderwebs, dominoes, threshing machines, rippling pools. But none quite explained it. There was something of the whirlpool or downward spiral about it, something of a cycling wheel, of interlocking gear wheels, of a spool. His mind reeled with possibilities this rainy mid-November Sunday afternoon as he drove with Inspector Ross and Farquhar from the hospital in Ullapool to the castle some thirty miles away on narrow, one-car-at-a-time roadways. Whether one knew it or not, he was always caught in a cycle of events caused by someone before his time. And this cycle, like a whirlpool, could suck him under if he allowed himself to look too closely into the center of it.

He could not, therefore, claim that all this mess was Cecil Rhodes's fault, that because he had lusted for wealth and empire he had started the Boer War and so ensnared Roberts Menzies and Maria De Jager in his cycle; and that because of this, Farquhar, Ann, Sybil, Duncan, Clyde, Henrietta, Jason Glass, and old Peebles had had their own lives sewn into the same irrevocable pattern as well. Yes, Rhodes had thrown a South African war into Roberts' path, but Roberts had chosen, by either reaction or response, to pursue the course he had—as had Maria, as had Bruce, as had Farquhar, and all the others, with the exception of poor Duncan, who was too young and too ill equipped to ever, probably, *choose* much of anything. It was reaction and response. Bruce perhaps had reacted—he had resented the dog crate, hated his father for not coming home, and so lashed out with instinctive rejection and punishment against both of them. He mistook the terms of his life as he was born into it for the power of moral responsibility he himself had and all men have within those terms. Henrietta's seemed a reverse reaction, but still a reaction: because life is this way, I will choose not to participate by living actively.

The reason Annie Daly and Roberts Menzies were, then, worthy of Jason Glass's time, an inkmaker's ink, a tree's pulpwood, a publisher's investment, and a reader's precious eyesight was that they had *responded*, whereas most of us react; by responding they did not dub themselves per se moral or immoral, only *active* against the course of events rather than passive in allowing it to proceed unchallenged.

Such reflections put Jason Glass to sleep in the backseat of Ross's car while the detective and Farquhar rehashed the events of two Sundays before in the front. When he was awake, he heard a conversation that was clearly, by this point, a replay of one the two must have had several times already in the Ullapool hospital.

"Once more, now, Menzies, to make sure I have it straight, give me the course of events on Sunday the second in which you were wounded in the shoulder."

"Damn it, Ross," the florid-faced clan chief said from beneath the blanket which covered him to the nose against the dank chill air that poured through the slightly open windows, "you are trying to trip me. I was not wounded—I wounded myself. The first is passive, the second is active. I feared a threat against my life, so I took one of the handguns from my collection and readied it. It fired on me because the trigger guard was corroded and did not hold as securely as I had expected. I know almost nothing of guns—I was a prime target for such an accident."

"Yes, good, I recall that now. And then you said it happened in the Billeting Room, in the head chair at the table?"

"Yes."

"Good. And now what were the answers to these two other questions? You know, why no gun in your collection was found which fired so large a shell as the one which passed through your shoulder? And why no shell was found and no mark on the ceiling? I just need those answers once more."

"Ross, you know I have given you no answers for those, so how can I give you them 'once more'? The shot was at such close range, I suppose, that it did more damage than it would have normally. Where it went I don't know—I heard it ricocheting off the walls and ceiling not less than a half-dozen times. The entire room is lined with stone, bricks, and mortar. Bullets don't stop quickly in such a place. It could have wound up in the fireplace, for all I know. You've smelled the gun—it was fired once, you've agreed on that."

Ross wound the car off the road into a passing place so an oncoming vehicle could get by, waved to the other driver, and proceeded. "The gun we checked was fired, yes, had your fingerprints on the trigger, yes, and turned up no bullet, yes. But that is *not* the gun that wounded you, nor was it fired in the Billeting Room, for it gives off a lot of powder and there is no trace whatsoever of gunpowder in that room. Nor of blood."

Farquhar was tired, disgusted, chilled, and still in some pain. "Offer a better theory, then."

"I've two, as I have told you several times, Menzies. One is that you tried to do yourself in and mucked it up. The other is that you know exactly who killed your mother, that this same person is now in pursuit of you, but that you owe this person some loyalty which will not allow you to turn him in. Now be a good chap and tell me which one it is."

Menzies responded with silence. Glass pitied the man at this moment almost as much as he disliked him for putting him, Glass, through this whole ordeal, for perhaps dabbling in Ann's affections, for being an egomaniac, and most of all, for being a Menzies. The man was depressed, trapped by a conception of the past that bore no relation to reality, wounded, hounded now by both an assailant and a protector.

Ross's theory, which he had voiced on each of the four occasions when he had met Glass at The Angus Bull in the past two weeks, was that someone had allowed, perhaps even wanted, the project to take shape for a while, but now it was going too far. Aunt Elizabeth, no matter how mad or senile, had had stray pieces of information which a researcher as good as Glass was proving to be, at least on this project, could ultimately string together. She had had to go. Farquhar had been a valid target because he was the motivation behind the whole information-gathering process, no matter how much he wished to censor or rearrange the truths that had been uncovered. The story was just not panning out, and even Farquhar was apparently unable to get it not so much "right" as "good."

The killer, however, was not a professional bloodletter, Ross felt. Aunt Elizabeth had had to go first to eliminate an urgent danger. Had Farquhar called off the project, sent Glass home, and accompanied his mother's body to Ladysmith as a good son should have, the bloodshed would have ended. But he had not called it off, had let the dreaded Glass go in his place to Ladysmith and there uncover still more unwanted information, and had allowed him to return to bang away ever more relentlessly at his calumniating typewriter. Word was all over Loch Killilan that Glass had been unhappy from the start, would love to collect what he was due on the project, quit it, and go home to America. There his last book was crumbling on bookstore racks, his wife was becoming more recognizable to the public by her pubic hair than by her face or voice, and his children were consigned, permanently it seemed, to some unidentified Western state with unknown people. Kill Farquhar, and Glass goes home, the gunman—or gunperson—had decided. Ross frankly advised early departure.

Glass could think of a number of writers he knew in America who would readily accept a flat fee to knock the manuscript into shape for Menzies, a fee that would probably not have to be paid when the triggerman fixed Glass's replacement before payday. In his more bitter moments, Glass decided to find the best scholar-vulture currently at work on the Annie Daly material—perhaps Feldman—and send the Menzies offer to him—not to get him off Annie Daly, but to get him killed. So why did he stay?

There were, he felt, three reasons, though he preferred to admit to only one, at most two, of them. First, he did not like to leave things uncompleted—even his pitiful novels he had finished just to say he had not been a quitter. Second, he wanted to "know"—knowing the full story of Roberts Menzies was like waiting for the end of a mystery. One cannot just say to the book "I don't care whodunit" and slap it shut.

The third reason was Ann. He hated her for staying away so long, for probably having Farquhar in her bed, for accepting so easily the fact that he was crushed and wished to be apart from her. He had not seen her in nearly two weeks, though he had heard that she had visited Farquhar several times in the hospital. He wanted her to deny everything so he could love her cleanly again. He could not love her openly as long as it was as dirty, as sordid as it all was; but he would accept lies and never check them, just as he had never checked the lies in the Annie Daly story because she was *his* relative and he did not want to know them either. If he could not love Ann openly, he loved her clandestinely and, still, loved her terribly.

They reached the castle and Ross drove across the causeway, which was slippery with a film of ice. Glass held Farquhar under his good shoulder while Ross guided him by the waist and led him through the gateman's gate, up the outer staircase, and into the care of a nurse whom Henrietta had in waiting. She and the butler took control of Farquhar, and Ross and Glass departed without entering.

"Now, Glass," Ross said overcheerily after they had reentered the unmarked police car, "let me buy you a beer at The Sheepshead over there." He pointed to the inn on the promontory, which was hardly visible through the fog off the Loch. He rubbed his red hands together and blew into them, also overenthusiastically.

"I'd love to, Inspector," Glass said longingly, "but it's after hours. The place'll be locked till seven."

Ross smiled as he turned over his shoulder to back the vehicle back over the causeway to the highway. "No, it won't—at least, not to us. You see, I've a warrant that allows me to use the premises for the afternoon. Drinks are included, for we'll be residents for the next two hours."

"What's the use you'll be claiming to make of it? Besides getting drunk at midafternoon rather than early or late, I mean?"

Ross turned onto the highway and drove slowly toward the inn. "Three Sundays ago there was a murder committed here which was witnessed from the pub window. Two Sundays ago there was a wounding no one saw. Last Sunday, there was no crime, but a person was seen loitering in the outer grounds whom no one recognized. We are going to see what happens *this* Sunday."

Ross's scheme had something to be said for it in theory but not in actuality, and he seemed quickly to know that. There was simply too much cold fog this afternoon for someone with criminal intentions. As the detective and the writer sat inside the fire-heated pub room of The Sheepshead, their table pushed up against the large window which viewed the Loch, there were great stretches of time when they could barely see it or the castle at all. Wisps of coagulating moisture blew thickly through the roughly three-hundred-yard space that separated the inn from the island, and at the best of times they could only make out the square outline of the castle's main building. Rarely was it even as much as an outline. Ross drank his beer disconsolately—he was sure this would have been the day on which he bagged something, even had two police cars stationed around the other side of the closest mountain with which he was in radio contact. Glass drank his own beer patiently; having little else to do, he did not mind peering idly out the window, pretending to look as hard as Ross was looking, which was intently. Since they said little to each other, Glass made mental calculations as to when he could go home to America.

As far as he was concerned, he knew the whole story by now of Roberts Menzies. The last missing section had been filled in by old Peebles the previous Wednesday night when Glass, on another hunch he should have pursued before, invited him out to drink at The Angus Bull on a particularly rainy night. Because Peebles had been so forthcoming, and because the things he said that it was possible to verify had stood up, Glass felt he had only another two weeks of writing to go, then another week of polishing the text. With nothing else to do, he could spend the entire day on it every day. This would allow him to take the manuscript to Farneswells in London in early December, whereupon he would agree to remain in town for two weeks while their "editor" went over it. He would then depart for home and attempt to spend Christmas with his daughters—he already had Larry trying to find out where exactly they were and if they could be brought to Boston for the holidays. At that point, though he did not tell Larry, he would decide whether or not he would return them.

The conversation with Peebles which had allowed him to begin planning his immediate future had been promising from the first sip of beer. Glass did not know what the old fellow's capacity was and so tried to pace him so that he would not "fuzz out" before what he knew could be divulged. Yet he also wanted him to have enough so that he would not withhold anything. Glass reflected at the time how often he had used the pacing of liquor on this project to loosen tongues yet keep them steady; he had not used liquor on anyone in the Annie Daly research, and obviously now he should have. Yet he could not imagine that Peebles, given his hate for the Menzies, planned to censor himself. Glass would have to watch out for excesses instead. He had inquired first about Roberts' return from the war in 1919.

"It was, yer see, Mr. Glass, doomed from the start. It was to be a war between the men Menzies and the women Menzies for the next half-dozen years. And since the men Menzies was real Menzies and the women Menzies was distaff Menzies, the winners were appointed from the start. Old Angus had fairly well come to hope that he'd never lay eyes on Roberts again. Yer see, he had been terrible crushed when Roberts stayed away after the South African war—a man who loses his oldest son after he's spent a lifetime getting him ready does feel empty."

Glass could see Peebles' analogy: they had both lost their sons, for different reasons.

"Angus spent almost ten years fretting about it before he decided, somewhere around 1910 or 1912, that even though he was over sixty, he still had time to build a replacement son in Bruce, his grandson who had no mother or father. So that's the way he done 'er. He taught Bruce everything about the land, the investments, the holdings, the operation of the clan that he had already been through once with Roberts, except that Roberts always was more interested in doctoring than chiefing in the first place.

"Now, Margaret—that was Angus' wife, Roberts' mother—she didn't get it fit together quite so neatly. She'd been searching for Roberts from the day the African war got itself over with. It took her a couple of years to locate him, but folks are pretty sure she finally did. But the word got around the Lochs that Roberts had got himself in some kind of trouble during the war

—the African one, that is—and wasn't allowed to come home. Some said it would be the gallows for him if he ever showed up. So he didn't, and Bruce got his place. And when the Great War come along, Angus pulled every last cord in the belfry to keep Bruce from having to go to war—probably figured he wouldn't come home for one reason or another either, and Angus was seventy now and knew he had no more time to work up another son. Nor even a boy child to work up into one either. So he didn't let him go—not that Bruce was looking to."

"Yet Bruce *did* go to the next war—in 1939, when he was forty and wouldn't have had to! And he allowed *his* oldest son to go when he became eighteen."

"Whoa, Mr. Glass. For a famous author you have a fact or two wrong and a conclusion or two you forgot to draw. First, Bruce did not *let* Owen go to war, because Bruce was killed in '43 and Owen went in '44. Bruce didn't know nothing about all that. And besides, Owen weren't the oldest anyway. Farquhar was, and Farquhar hid his arse from a battlefield just as clean as Bruce did in the Great War. Now, then. Why did Bruce skip the first war and go to the second? Easy. Those of us who did go, who were jacking around Loch Killilan and Loch Alsh on splints and crutches, flipping our medals and flapping our gums for years afterwards, we made a bad comparison. Clan chiefs are supposed to lead into battle, not sit home and ask what happened from anybody that's lucky enough to get back. You might of heard, Mr. Glass, that the Menzies have pulled up short in such matters a number of times?"

Glass nodded. "Menzies chiefs seem to do their duty against that fake Viking ship each June on the Isle of Skye."

Peebles grinned. "Well, you've drawed more than I thought, I expect. So you see, when Roberts come home, lookin' like he not only been in his share o' wars—which he had—but sportin' noticeable vacancies about his body to prove it, in case you fergot, not to mention enough medals on his chest and inside velveteen boxes to make a coat of armor out of—medals from the Queen, from the South African Government, from the Americans and the French and the Red Cross and even one from the Canadian Air Force—Bruce looked like a piss-poor chief, a position he was nicking off his father anyway. It wasn't his father he hated so much as his father's medals and wounds and all the things his father had to have and to do to get them that he resented."

"So there was open warfare from the start?"

"You can wager on that, you can. Even *before* the start. In the early part of 1919, Margaret got a letter from Roberts in Glasgow saying that his problems from the African war had been solved, that he had been allowed to reenter the country and would get his standing back—how a few years of history do change everything, don't they, Mr. Glass?—and that he was due to be decorated in the big victory parade in London in March. He said he had a wife that he hadn't seen in nineteen years but that he had found in Edinburgh or Glasgow or someplace, and he was coming home that spring."

From this point in Peebles' narrative, Glass had the luxury of two sources of information: the man to whom he was listening and the sporadic diary entries made by Maria De Jager that covered the period. Glass unobtrusively slipped his note pad onto the pub table, watched the corner of it soak up spilled beer in an instant, and made abbreviated notes about those points which jibed between the two versions, those which seemed substantially if not entirely the same, and those which contradicted each other. Most of what Peebles had to say about the parade in London, for example, was fairly much the same.

"I recall it was an especial warm day when we left here for the trip to London. Several of my mates and I were going to march with our regiments—we was just enough recovered to be able to do it, just enough still banged up to work the crowd's sympathies—and Margaret Menzies went to meet her son for the first time in over twenty years."

"Bruce and Angus didn't go?"

"No, sir! Not a bit of it for them. Well, we all marched and got drunk and kissed whatever women we could find about the streets looking to be kissed—we had all done all this once before, the day we got off the boat back in December, but now we did it some more. Probably our real reason for going all the way down there in the first place. The trip back up to the Lochs on the train was not as happy, though."

"Margaret's fault, right?" He knew this from Maria's account.

"Correct. You can hardly blame her, though. Somewhere she must have heard that Roberts was not all in one piece, but seeing it was different. I was struck myself, though I didn't cry all the way back as she did. He was terrible wrecked, Mr. Glass. No arm on his left side, no eye on his right. White hair that made him look like somebody who had nicked off from a pensioners' home rather than a big medical war hero. He walked with a cane and stooped way over." Here Peebles got up from the table to demonstrate: a man who was somewhat stooped himself, he went further forward to emphasize Roberts' posture. "And he, by the calendar anyway, not even fifty-year yet. His mother asked him to tell how he lost his arm and his eye, but he never would that I know. Said he couldn't stand up straight because of poor diet at Ladysmith that gave him spine curve. He really was a sight, looking like almost a joke with all those medals dangling off his front, like it was those that was tilting him frontways and not spine curve. And the wife didn't help Margaret any."

"She had lost a son by Roberts in the war. Did you know that?"

Peebles looked at Glass through the smoke of The Angus Bull as if he were mad. "Know it? She never let anybody forget it, including Roberts. She was a big bruiser of a woman, not only tall, about six feet, but heavy, thick, fat—about three hundred pounds I'd bet. You'd of needed three of Roberts to balance a beam she was on the other side of. And she had a loud voice and a thick German accent that was making everybody in our carriage on the train pretty angry, seeing as how we had heard the last Kraut we wanted to for a while and this one was doing nothing but crying and bitching at Roberts."

Glass, of course, had found no reference to this in Maria's diary. "What was she on him for, for God's sake?"

"Seemed that their son—Peter, I think his name was—had died in the same field hospital that Roberts was assigned to, maybe even in the same operating room, maybe even on the next table, maybe on *his* table! She seemed to think Roberts should have knowed by radar or something that his own son he'd never even seen was around needing to be saved. Picture this little doll-sized man, toting a chestful of gold and bronze and silver medals from five or six different countries, being drummed on by a woman three times his size for something he couldn't have done nothing about."

Glass could picture it. "Yes, very ironic." He laughed with some bitterness as he pictured Margot in command of *Gratuitous Glory* and all its proceeds at this very moment.

Now Peebles laughed. "Not as ironic as something else, when you think about it. Since Roberts only had one arm, he always had with him a colored South African man to serve as his left arm during surgery in the war. A year later, when he spoke of bringing the man to the Lochs from South Africa and opening a surgery here—old Dr. Scott was on his last legs, you see—his wife wouldn't have a "nigger" in the district, much less in her home, which is where the surgery was going to be. You know, the house by the lake in The Gap. So you see, she blamed him for not saving Peter, but she would not, if she knew about it, have let Roberts' black arm help his white arm in saving him anyway." Peebles' old face curled in such a way as to condemn not only Maria but a large part of the human race as well.

"Did Roberts ever practice medicine in the five or six years he spent here after the war, Mr. Peebles—in any way?"

"Not at first, mind you, but later he did a bit." Glass waved the pub girl to bring two more beers. This was going well, and it was time to refuel Peebles. "For a year or so, he gave up the idea of bringing the colored man to Scotland and must have decided he could not doctor without him. For about the same amount of time he probably thought he would be the clan chief when his father died, so perhaps he got hisself ready for that, not knowing the war that was being fought around him. It was his mother and his wife, who had begun to knock off some stone to get ready to be the wife of the clan chief, who fought on one side against his father and his son on the other. Angus was over seventy and was looking to pass on the control and had in fact planned to do so on Bruce's twenty-first birthday, except that his father had returned by then to muddy up the issue."

"And Roberts was not in this fight?"

Peebles shook his head. "Not that I know of. The chiefship was something he figured would just fall on him by bloodline—I don't think he even wanted it, but he had got pretty good at dealing with what he didn't want, I expect. On the one side he wanted to be a doctor; on the other he wanted to write something about his years in the African war. When he could not have his colored man, he took up writing. His wife and mother would be slugging it out with Bruce and Angus at the castle, while Roberts sat with a typewriter on a table out behind his little house by the lake pecking out his memories with one finger on one hand. Besides, the real trouble did not start until 1922."

Glass could not but be curious as to what had become of these typed memoirs. He had never heard them mentioned. "Nineteen twenty-two is the year in which Roberts imported a wife for Bruce; correct?"

"Correct, and if that was all he imported, things might have turned around, for Bruce fell in love with this South African girl the moment he saw her. This was Aunt Elizabeth, you know, and she was the most beautiful woman I have ever seen around here—blond, blue eyes, the eyes always smiling even if the lips sometimes didn't, slender, graceful. There wasn't a young man among us in the district, no matter what our class, that didn't yearn just to see her about. She had known Roberts for some years in South Africa when she was growing up, and Roberts must have wanted her for his only son from the start. She loved Roberts very much, and for a time Bruce liked his father better just because she did."

"So the villain now would be Angus alone?"

"No, even Angus settled down when Roberts seemed to have no desire for power and when he produced such a fine specimen of womanhood for his grandson. No, the villain, if that's what you want to call her, was Roberts' wife, and before two more years were up she had got him driven out of the district for good."

He sipped at his beer while he searched for the proper order of detail. "Several things happened at this same time, Mr. Glass, which upset her pretty much, word had it. First, here was a beautiful English-speaking South African twenty years younger, who Roberts cared for more than he did her, even if just in a fatherly way. Roberts' wife, as I said, was a loud giant of a woman—a painful difference. Second, Roberts' wife still wanted her husband to have his rightful role in the clan, even if he didn't care himself; and now she knew this woman would likely be the most important woman about instead of her. So any good that Margaret and Elizabeth could now do for Roberts was being harmed by his wife's behavior. And third, the one thing Margaret had learned and Elizabeth knew in the first place was that Roberts was a doctor in his soul, that he was even less than the half of Roberts Menzies that was left if he could not be that—so they got him what he needed to be one. Which was . . ."

Glass could guess, even though there was no mention of this in Maria's diary. "Which was the kaffir man from Ladysmith!"

"Yes, sir—or the 'nigger,' as Maria called him. They—Margaret and Elizbeth, I mean—brought him up as a 'gift,' you might say, for Roberts' birthday. In the spring of 1923, I think it was, just a few months after Dr. Scott died. The four of them went to Kyle station to collect the man one day, though Roberts and his wife did not know what was coming in and were sent to wait at the baggage window while the two ladies slipped the black man off the train further down the platform and popped him out to the car while Roberts' back was turned. Then they led Roberts himself to the car, except his wife came too, and showed him his black left hand, and Roberts hugged him and they danced a jig together in the carpark. Both men cried for happiness. But it did not last for long."

"Wait, let me guess. Less than five minutes. Maria would not ride in the same car with him and so they had to send someone back to fetch her."

Pebbles looked at Glass oddly. "Half-right, sir. She would not ride with him, so someone had to come back to fetch the black man *and* Roberts. This was probably the beginning of the end. She would, of course, not allow the man to live in their house at the lake, and as I have already told you, she would not even let Roberts establish a surgery in the house if the man was to assist—as of course he had to. So Roberts defied her again. He—"

"He came to you to see about buying your interest in the stone house across the road." Glass knew this was correct, even though he had only just guessed it. *None* of this was in Maria's diary—only self-pitying records of abuse she suffered at the hands of Bruce, Angus, and, surprisingly, Elizabeth. She cited Margaret alone as an ally. "He told you that if you would accept payment for the improvements you had already made (which he did not have to do, since the Menzies owned it and he could have just taken it), he would use that part for a surgery and allow you to convert the rest of the house to your own interests. Am I right?"

"Just about entirely. Since he did not have the ability to refurbish the building for himself, however, he asked me to do the labor on the surgery end in exchange for the rest of the building. Which I agreed to, though I knew it would be two or three years before I would have the money to rebuild my own end of the house. Which, as it turns out, I was never allowed to do once Roberts left. But I did finish the surgery for him, for that end of the house—the one which today has the hole in it from the lightning—was pretty far along from my work of three years before. So the black man lived in a canvas tent by the lakeside that summer and would slip up now and again to help me drive nails or saw wood, though every time Roberts saw him doing that he made him quit for fear he would hurt his hands and be useless in the surgery. But some nights Roberts could not stop him, for we could hear across the roadway his wife's German voice cursing him in two different languages, never even breaking her sound to draw a breath, it seemed, for two full hours. At which point she would always finally stop and probably fall asleep—she drank a lot, it was said, and perhaps had put herself out that way—but Roberts would never be seen again that day. Maybe he was slipping something into the drinks to make them work faster on her.

"So by the end of the summer, after Roberts himself had done the wiring of the place, the surgery was open. The black man was assisting as he had done for many years before that, living in the surgery and sleeping on a cot at night. Since Roberts was the only doctor south of Ullapool or west of Fort William in those days, his practice was very successful for about a year. He set aside two days a week for those who had to come long distances over narrow roads so that no one would be sent away without help. It took less time than you would think for people to become used to two different-colored hands working on them at the same time, the black man's eyes steering the one-eyed man's hand, the white man's schooling telling the black man what to look for. If they had been here longer, they would this day be a legend; as it is, that part of Roberts' life, like so much of the rest of it, is unknown to any but those of us still alive who were treated by him, and even most of those seem to have forgotten."

Now as Glass sat in the otherwise-vacant taproom of The Sheepshead, peering out toward the fog-shrouded Castle Menzies, he reflected back on Peebles' description of Roberts' last days in Loch Killilan in 1924, painting mental pictures of what had haunted him for the four days since he had heard it.

Maria had become more abrasive by the week. So Bruce and Angus had finally, even blatantly, come to Roberts to ask that she be disposed of, be sent back to South Africa, where she belonged, to start there, if she needed to, an internal war among the Boers rather than the one she kept afire among the Menzies. But Roberts had sent her away from her home once, left her alone for nineteen years, and would not do it again no matter how much he wanted to. He was that "moral," at least by now. And he endured her screaming, her accusations, her multilingual cursing, her insults that he was in every way only half a man, in limb, in eye, in groin, and in courage to demand of his father and son what was rightfully his—no, *theirs*. But he would not. So she got a lawyer—three of them—to work on the matter, promising a hefty fee when Angus and Margaret died (which would not be long now) and their vast wealth was left to their son—Roberts—instead of to the grandson to whom Angus was, illegally, planning to bequeath it. Twice the matter was reviewed by the Highland courts, and the second time they ruled in Maria's favor.

Open warfare now broke out. Roberts was denied access to the castle, and all Menzies were forbidden by Angus to make contact with Roberts. This was dangerous for one Menzies in particular—Elizabeth.

Early in 1924 Elizabeth had become pregnant with her first child. What Roberts had known since he first became her physician when she was five or six was that her hips were too slender for a safe natural childbirth. When he became her physician again in 1922—the girl's body now a woman's, the child he had loved now the wife of his child, the woman so sexually appealing as she lay nude before him on the examining table (though he had lost his sexuality the very year in which she had been born)—now he confirmed that he had been correct and told her early in her pregnancy that she could not deliver naturally. So she had planned on and accepted the fact of a cesarean section all along—except that now, seven or eight months into her pregnancy, she would not be allowed contact with the one man who could do it. Nor would Bruce, in his bitter anger at his father and his father's wife, even accept the verdict. He had even by this point hired a midwife to perform the delivery. As November approached, as Maria continued her legal machinations and Bruce exacted his revenge, Roberts and Elizabeth, who had loved each other in many ways and places for twenty years, fretted ten miles apart from each other, the doctor knowing she would die, the patient knowing it also because she had utter faith in the doctor who had warned her.

And so an incredible deal was struck. Angus, ill and in his own final year, suggested that Bruce allow Roberts to perform the cesarean section on his young wife on the condition that Roberts then leave the district forever and take Maria De Jager with him. To which Roberts agreed instantly, but Maria did not. But time was short—they were within days of the child's birth that November—and Maria was still resisting, still consorting with the lawyers to secure her wealth and her position *before* Angus died. So Roberts agreed to the further dimensions of Bruce's scheme. On the night of Wednesday, November 19, 1924, Roberts would see to it that his wife was heavily drugged. After Bruce had confirmed this, he would allow Roberts access to the Castle Menzies to perform the cesarean section on his wife. Bruce would have Maria removed from the cottage in The Gap, placed in a car, driven to the castle, and from there—once Roberts had done with Elizabeth and her child—driven with him and the kaffir to Kyle of Lochalsh to await the early train to Inverness. To this Roberts had agreed in his urgent need to save Elizabeth.

And in the early hours of the twentieth, he and his kaffir cut into the soft white flesh of the beautiful Elizabeth Farquhar's abdomen and pulled from her belly the boy child who was to be named Farquhar. Then they sewed her together—Roberts inserting the needle and the kaffir pulling it tight as he had been taught—and pronounced Elizabeth vital and out of danger. The boy had cried loudly at the first slap of his inverted buttocks.

Within minutes they were escorted from the castle to the large touring car and driven, by Bruce himself to make sure they left, to the station in Kyle—except that Maria was not there in the car. She had been sent ahead, still drugged, on the night train to Inverness, which Roberts did not know was a freight train and not a passenger train, and been transferred to another train to Glasgow despite the fact that Roberts and the kaffir man were ticketed for Edinburgh. And in Glasgow the freight handlers had been frightened almost out of their wits at Central Station because wooden coffins were not to have live bodies in them, were not to have two small holes drilled in them so that, in someone's single act of charity, the live body could breathe at least a bit. And when they pried the lid off in the baggage room, when those who could not stand it had been escorted out to the main terminal, she was released, her fingers almost shredded of skin because she had tried for hours to claw her way out. And they removed her gag and lifted the dead carcass of a dog from across her belly where it pinned her down. Glass did not know if she had cried in fear or cursed in anger. But whatever she did, when she recovered she had her hands bandaged in the Red Cross office, took her purse, which Bruce had filled with a hundred pounds, consigned the coffin with the dog's body still in it to the baggage car, and bought a ticket not to London and Southampton, where Roberts and the kaffir were headed, but to Inverness and Kyle, where she went back to her cottage and her lawyers. And seven months later, on Saturday, June 20, 1925, she was cannoned to death by her father-in-law and his grandson.

And now Ross thought he saw something in the fog. It had lifted for a moment, enough that they could see the full length of the grounds all the way to the wall at the most distant end. It was a human figure—perhaps a boy—moving slowly along the base of the castle wall, crouching low as if to avoid being seen through the basement windows, carrying a long, slender object vertically in front of him as he moved. Then, as quickly as he had been revealed, he disappeared behind a thick curtain of moisture. Both Glass and Ross had seen him—it had not been an illusion.

Ross was quickly on the radio. "Move up quickly. Two men come directly across the causeway in the car, two others on foot through the water at the base. We've spotted someone easing along the south wall, surely covering his approach, perhaps armed with a rifle. Proceed with caution. I'll move in from the west." He snapped off the device without waiting for a response.

Ross and Glass dashed out the front door of the inn, pounced into the unmarked car, and gravel-sprayed through the carpark, entering the road through a wooden guardrail which Ross had not seen in the fog. He moved as quickly as he could down the highway, but it was too foggy to do more than crawl. He cursed under his breath, knowing in advance that the fog would spoil his efforts. When they reached the turnoff for the causeway they could see the taillights of the other vehicle already moving along it toward the castle. Ross parked his own car at the end of the bridge, then jumped out and scrambled down the embankment to the edge of the Loch with Glass close behind him. Ahead of them they could hear the other two police officers sloshing through the water at low tide. Finally all six men came together, two on the causeway above, four directly below at the center of the middle arch. They could see only one another's outlines.

"We saw him too, Inspector, as we were rolling along the highway. The mist lifted for a moment as he was turning the back corner in this direction." The man was puffing. "But we've traced all the way back along it and there's no sign of him. We thought we heard shooting, but it turned out to be that noise from the electrical plant that we've fallen for before."

"Did he see you?"

"Yes, sir, he must have. We had the headlamps on and the blues flashing. If we could see him for a second, he could see us for longer than that. It's low tide. I expect he's cut out wide of the island back along the road to the east." He pointed in the direction instinct told him was east, though all he pointed at was swirling clouds of mist which deadened his voice as he called into it.

"Damn it all." Ross was frustrated. He had given up a Sunday afternoon for a near miss. He gave his instructions even though he seemed to know how futile they were. "All right, then, prowl back along the road to the east. See if you see anything of him. Wail your siren if you do. Do you think he's armed?"

"Quite sure of it, sir," said one of the two men above on the bridge, who now were almost out of sight as well. "Looked like a rifle with a very long barrel."

"Well, take care, then, for you're not. On with it, now." The four officers clacked and splashed back toward their cars while Ross and Glass continued to stand calf-deep in the Loch water. "Come along, Mr. Glass. Let's just assure ourselves that everyone's okay inside; then I'll take you home." They slogged out on the highway side and crossed the causeway at a slow trot, grasping for firm footing against the ice film. Glass's pants, socks, and shoes were frigidly wet. "Hope you've got a swill of brandy or two when we get there."

Glass assured him he did in fact have more than one or two.

27 PATRICIA AND ELIZABETH, ANNIE AND ANN

FARNESWELLS HAD BALKED AT GLASS'S bringing the manuscript to London for review—perhaps they did not want to pay his expenses there for two weeks, or perhaps they just knew that final approval had to come from Farquhar Menzies, and he was in the Lochs and not in London. So they had told him to stay put, that they would send "someone" to go over the manuscript with him and to intermediate with the clan chief over disputed points. He regretted his own snotty letter in response, in which, while agreeing to their desires, he had ordered that the "someone" be someone else. He hoped that they were not as petty as he and that they had not listened to him.

It was at six o'clock on the evening of Saturday, the sixth of December, that Glass found himself peering down the tracks into the snow-swirling darkness at the Kyle station. He had left Sybil's car idling in the carpark to keep it warm inside, but now the train was late, delayed somewhere back along the line in one of the small Loch villages in which it was compelled to stop despite the fact that it rarely had anything or anyone to accept or discharge there. So he returned to the car, shut it off, and went into the tiny coffee shop which served little more than what its title advertised. He bought a cup and sat down at a dirty table in the corner to continue polishing his prose style. The light was bad and he found himself squinting at the heavily edited pages before him, the sleet-snow clicking against the window beside his ear without cessation.

The full manuscript had been done for nearly two weeks, and he was now in his third trip back through it, rearranging parts in fairly insignificant ways, rebuilding sentences, replacing words, most of all documenting in endnotes the sources of each piece of information he had. RMD and MDJD were symbols he used for the two diaries he had worked from, though he had decided to use little of what Maria had written after 1919 because it seemed, in retrospect, mostly camouflages and lies. For example, the entry for November 20, 1924, simply read *"Botha* [the dog] *died today while I was in Glasgow attending to some business*"—ironic understatement in its classic form. He also had symbols for the various types of official military documents he had used, and others for the key interlocutors who had put him onto various dimensions of the Menzies tale: Mrs. Douglas, who knew of his self-amputation; Peebles, who knew at least Roberts' side of his five to six years back in the Lochs; Mrs. Sciennes, who knew of legendary matters such as the Great Storm and factual matters such as the doings of Dr. Hamilton and his family and his surgery; old Pretorius and the hotel clerk —he had written to Ladysmith and been given her name—who had told him of Roberts' final years and death there. But he had two other abbreviations which he was careful to employ as well: JGX and JGC, which meant Jason Glass by Experience and Jason Glass by Conclusion. In the first category came the discussion of the Menzies and their Culloden cannon in 1975, in the second the same matter as it might have occurred in 1925. Glass warned his readers to evaluate all things the endnotes labeled "JGC" very carefully.

And so, by this night of December 6, 1975, he had, as far as he could determine, only one point untied, and the book could certainly stand without it: who killed Aunt Elizabeth—she had become a very tragically sympathetic figure in the Menzies story —and why exactly did that person do it? As he had mentioned to Ross several days earlier, the quickest way to solve all that would be to get the book published immediately so the American professor named Feldman, operating now with Margot to shred the Annie Daly myth, could get to Scotland and turn up the information for his next scholarly article. When Ross mentioned the unlikelihood of Feldman's coming for so small a detail in the book, Glass ruefully remarked that he *would* come to go for the jugular vein of the whole book itself; and only when he found out how tightly researched this one was would he have to content himself with so minor, though not unsensational, a matter as writing the postscript.

Then the train arrived. Glass could see its Cyclopean beam coning the snow in front of it long before the engine ever pulled its pitiful string of four nearly empty carriages up to the Kyle platform. And when the guard put the box at the base of the last car's door and wiggled it into the gathering snow so it would not slip, Glass knew that Farneswells had misbehaved, had disobeyed him and sent him the person he desperately had wanted them to. Ann was more beautiful than he remembered, her blond hair almost neatly combed draping down upon the shoulders of her red coat and black velvet collar, her blue eyes smiling in anticipation even if her mouth was being more cautious, her cheeks red from the cold wind that blew stingingly in from Skye. He stood by the door of the greasy coffee shop, did not approach her. She saw him immediately, then walked cautiously across the wet platform, her eyes always on his, not knowing what to do in greeting.

But then two seconds disappeared without record and he was kissing her and she him, both of them crying freely and smearing their tears across each other's cheeks and creating a scene rarely seen at Kyle because few ever came back who had stayed away long enough to be so missed. And so he took her small bag up from where she had dropped it beside her ankle, and he guided her around the station rather than back through it, her head tucked tightly under his chin the whole way as she continued to cry tears that were entirely happy. There was something about the rhythm of her shoulders which said there was no sadness in this, that whatever had gone wrong in the past would now be used to guide the future rather than pollute and punish it, that they had both—with a month to reflect in individual isolation—gotten a perspective they had so far lacked and were prepared now to do what they had demanded of Roberts and all those in his wake: to respond rather than, as they had done, react. When they reached the car they still said nothing, continuing to kiss each other with soft violence for another ten minutes before Glass realized how cold it was and turned on the engine to bring some heat. They finally started out for The Gap fifteen miles off, but were advised by a policeman that the road, a treacherous one which skirted a steep cliff above Loch Killilan, was totally iced over. He told them they should, if they could, find accommodations in Kyle for the night.

There was no hotel in Kyle, so they simply went up to the doors of houses arm in arm, inquiring if they might get bed and breakfast for the night. The second woman they went to knew of someone who during the summer months "did B and B"; she directed them there, and they signed in as Mr. and Mrs. J. Glass. When the woman who admitted them pulled a copy of *Gratuitous Glory* from her apron pocket and asked him to sign it for her, he knew she had disregarded what she must have known from the start was a lie. There had been a story in *Buck-*

ingham Magazine that month on Margot Glass, and he could see from her magazine rack that she subscribed to and read it.

They undressed each other, not quickly, but tenderly, seeming to trade garments one by one, and found they were each wearing seven and came out even at the end. And they made love, which did not take very long the first time but was longer and happier the next two. As they embraced and interlocked their bodies, Glass could not understand, nor probably could she, what retrospectively unimportant facts or abstractions or petulances or timeworn customs had been allowed for so long to deprive them of the single purpose toward which the order of nature and even the order of history seemed to have aimed them. And what better evidence has man yet uncovered than nature and history as to what, in their murky depths, might be the order of God?

When they awoke at four in the morning, they had to block each other's recriminations: Ann for Farquhar; Glass for Sybil and Policewoman Kribbs and Henrietta and how many others he could not count. Ann tearfully admitted that she had once planned to submit the placebo version for publication simply because Farquhar was a Menzies. His cynicism for once repressed, Glass could not help pressing to know in what such "duties" were grounded.

"It is rather impossible to say, you know. It did not take the revelation of Mother's bloodlines to establish an incestuous connection between my family and the Menzies. We have been committing at least figurative incest with them for generations. My father—who, believe me, Jason, was a good man who never acted except with the best of motives—had almost no identity beyond the Menzies. They brought him up, they paid for his education, they established a role for him in the Lochs, they gave him for a time the son he never had, then gave him instead a son-in-law. And now you have found out that they gave him a wife as well by recruiting my mother to the Lochs. Without the Menzies there would have been no Hamilton Macgregor as he had come to know himself, and without him there would have been no me as I know myself. And it was not just duty on his part, it was love. As a boy he must have loved Roberts and wanted to be a doctor even half as good as he was with twice the physical equipment. He loved Farquhar and Owen and Henrietta; even loved Clyde just because he was a Menzies and, as such, did not get the further examination he otherwise might have had and should have.

"But he died a broken man, Jason. He had lost Owen and blamed himself inexplicably for the battlefield shortcomings of his profession that allowed Owen to bleed to death when he shouldn't have. He was crushed when Duncan, his hope for the next generation of Menzies, was born retarded. If I had to guess, I would bet he even researched its causes and knew at some point what you have recently found out. But incest would not have shocked him either, for he saw it as I see it—blood connections would have been by that point superfluous."

"Does that account for his dash to Ladysmith in 1950?"

"It has to. Roberts was his lost mentor over and above just being a Menzies. He would have done anything to save him to make up for the opportunity he had not had to save Owen. And he failed again, except that this time it was worse because he had actually been there during Roberts' last hours. I recall as a little girl thinking that a medical conference in Washington must be a very sad thing for all the moroseness he demonstrated after he returned—not from Washington but, as it turns out, from Ladysmith. And you know something else, Jason? He took much of the blame for what happened psychologically to Aunt Elizabeth as well. He said over and over again that she had lost her mind through some failure of his. I had always assumed it was a medical failure, but I suppose it was rather a tactical one instead."

"You mean his carting her down there to see Roberts on his deathbed? That seems strained to me, Ann. We all witness death, we grieve, and we go on. Yes, it was her father-in-law, but by this point I should think that she would be willing to let a seventy-seven-year-old man who, pardon the expression, had led one hell of a tough life, that she would be happy to see him finally pass away peacefully and rest from his wars, his maimings, his rejections and persecutions. All right, she was a little girl he took on the train to Durban to buy dresses and bonnets and she had tried to return the favor by standing with him against her husband and even against his strong-willed wife. So she would have cried to see him dying and then dead, Ann. She would *not* have gone crazy, not the woman I have heard her characterized as being."

"I am not justifying my father's feelings, Jason. I'm just telling you of them. Had he lived two days longer than he did, he would have blamed himself for Farquhar's wife's death by exposure as well, for telling her something or other on his deathbed that made her act irrationally. Don't ask me to explain it all, Jason, or blame me for it. I am just telling you how he was."

Glass was silent for a moment. There was a piece still missing somewhere. He thought he was done with this project, but he wasn't. The killer of Aunt Elizabeth was a matter of postscript, perhaps, but this wasn't. The last piece lay with Hamilton Macgregor, dead more than five years now, and it was a piece that Ann either had or didn't have. What had Macgregor told Farquhar's wife that might have caused her death? He began to fear in his stomach that Ann *did* know but would not tell.

"So you see, Jason, I was supposed to accept Farquhar's proposals, which he's made for three years now, to be his second wife, to fill the role of first lady of the clan. But I did not—I have failed in all the most crucial aspects of my duty and loyalty that my father succeeded in even as he felt he was failing."

"So you slept with him." He had intended that to be a polite question, but it had come out a flatly ironic statement instead.

"Yes, but not very many times, Jason. Never, in fact, while you have been in the Lochs; and he turned up in Sydney without my expecting him. Jason, you know him only as an employer who at first tried to get you to compromise your principles. He is a man of great emotion. The depth of shame he feels for his family's machinations in the past is beyond my comprehension and would be beyond yours as well if you knew him better. He knew much of Roberts' suffering before you arrived, was aware that Roberts had saved both him and his mother from his father's foolish hatreds and schemes of vengeance, had known perhaps that Roberts represented both the best of the Menzies and the worst. What your writing began to teach him is that Roberts was good beyond what he had imagined or known, but also was in many ways worse than he had suspected as well. He has said over and over to me, Jason, how unfair it is that all Roberts' good intentions and sufferings had to be balanced on a scale which held several momentary mistakes, no matter how ultimately consequential, on the other side. Roberts tried to do better than that, had done better in ways that no none even knew about. Farquhar wanted, out of his love for his family, but especially for Roberts, who had saved his mother, to have you tell only the good things, not find more bad ones as well. And he had never even *known* Roberts."

"I did not make the truth what it is."

"Nor did he."

For the first time, perhaps, Glass was able to include Farquhar Menzies on an ever-lengthening list of human beings—everyone was on it by now except Margot—who had not sought the terms within which they had been required to live. The Truth is the Truth—there is nothing anyone can do about it other than accept it. Glass could feel Ann breathing steadily in his arms, asleep again. "I only wish," he said slightly aloud, "that there was not one more piece of the Truth we will have to learn—and I don't mean who killed Aunt Elizabeth, either."

When they finally arrived at the cottage the next afternoon, a bleak and snowy Sunday, Ann proceeded on to get her things from Henrietta's while Glass faced up to three letters which had arrived after he had left for the station the previous day. One was from Margot, another from an unfamiliar party in Montana, and a third from his agent in New York. He decided to encounter them in that order, the masochist in him insisting that he endure the worst before allowing himself anything that might be pleasurable.

Dear Jason,

I want you to talk to Larry for me. The money for the British royalties on GG just came in. It was $50,000 total of which he took 20%—$10,000—instead of 10%. He screwed me out of $5,000, but in case you don't feel too bad about that, he actually screwed your daughters, for that was the $5,000 I was going to send to the West to see to their welfare. They need Christmas presents, and boarding-school tuition is due right after the first. I can't expect people who are almost perfect strangers to keep footing these bills forever. So please tell Larry to cough it up and send it to me—or you cough it up and I will make sure they get it.

My New York lawyer told me that I can get a divorce from you for desertion after two full years of your being away, but my Boston lawyer says he can wangle it for me after one year if you don't accidentally show up. So don't, will you?

I've sold the house, which didn't bring much. $40,000, but I had to give 7% of that to the realtors—$2,800—and another $600 to my Boston lawyer to get me out of a claim by the new owners that the dump turned out to have termites in the roof beam and would probably collapse within the next two years even if they exterminate right now. I got back most of the $600, though, by holding a garage sale. Just about everything went—all the furniture, most of the kids' clothes, some of yours, the lawn mower, my old sewing machine (I'm not as into sewing as I used to be). I thought you'd like to know that I held back the silverware your parents gave us. I kind of like it, and it just didn't seem right to sell that at a garage sale. Anyway the garage sale brought $589, so I only came up $11 short on the reputed termites.

I guess you heard by now that Annie Daly was a whore. Too bad, but lucky nobody found out sooner.

Well, that's about it, Jason. I hope you will get on Larry and tell him to stop shafting your daughters. I'm not living with anybody at the moment, so I don't have any male muscle to help me out right now, except the lawyers, and they don't think they can nail Larry—which means there's not enough in it for them and they won't bother. One guy in Providence wrote me and said he would try it for 50% commission on the take, but that wouldn't leave much for the girls. This woman who went in with me on the Truro beach house thinks you ought to change agents before you actually sell this book on the Crimean War, or we might get shafted out of more. How soon will you sell that?

Jason Glass was in a cold sweat by the time he tore open the second letter. Given the information in the last one, he decided Larry's should be second.

Dear Jason,

I have seen you through a lot while we were waiting for you to make it big in this game, and now that you have, I hate to drop you off my hook. But I cannot afford to represent you if everything I make on it goes into legal fees and secretarial time to fight off Margot. You know damn well, Jason, that I get 10% on domestic sales and 20% on foreign ones, so would you please tell her that and get her off my back? Some lawyer in Providence wrote to say that he feels he can nail me for $5,000 on the British GG sales, of which he stands to get half. He offered to drop the case for a straight cash payment of $1,500, though I finally got him down to $1,000. I have been in contact with Farneswells and have tightened the screws down on the Ladysmith book so I can't get nailed again, but I'll have to drop you if I keep having to prove that what's mine is really mine.

At first I thought we were going to have trouble unloading

the Ladysmith book in America or anywhere else, but there's been a big break and it'll go for top dollar. This guy Feldman and his graduate student barked up the wrong tree because, you see, they were not allowed direct access to the Phalon & Son records. So they had to have some minimum-wage secretary go through the old records in her spare time and they set her looking for an "Annie Daley," misspelling the last name and forgetting to tell her that her official first name, as you mentioned only twice early in GG, was Bridgit, which she hated and never used. So not only did they miss the Bridgit Daly they wanted, but they then set out after one of the eleven Annie Daleys they eventually managed to locate in New York in the 1880s. They figured the one who had seven brothers and sisters and was also a whore who died a ways down the line of VD—this was the one they decided looked most like yours and so took it. Seems they wanted to get their findings into print while GG was still on the paperback best-seller list. But they flopped and now won't make it into print at all.

You've got somebody in England to thank for this, Jason. Somebody connected with or working through Farneswells in London sent someone through New York on his way to Australia to subpoena Phalon's records under the pretense of investigating publishing fraud. They didn't look at the records for ten minutes before they found Bridgit Daly at work every day for the full three years she was supposed to have been. After that, the whole Feldman case collapsed. Annie Daly lives!

But so does Margot Glass. If she turns up dead, Jason, I won't say anything if you won't.

Best,
Larry

P.S. It's the eleventh month of the year. Do you know where your children are?

The utter joy Glass felt over Larry's letter diminished sharply as he turned to the letter from Montana. It was return-addressed MONTANA CHRISTIAN ACADEMY, 1200 NORTH 30TH STREET, BILLINGS, MONT. 59101.

Dear Mr. Glass:

We have been attempting to find you for some two months now, and were able to do so only with the help of your publishers.

We have had your daughters, Patricia and Elizabeth, as resident students of ours for the past six months. They first came here to participate in our summer remedial program in English and mathematics, though it seemed to us at the time that the level of these courses was somewhat too low for their abilities. Then they stayed on for our midsummer Bible classes, which were not supposed to be remedial in any way, though here they could have used some brushing up. They both failed rather badly, as evidenced by the fact that they never did grasp the correct number of apostles, the concept of virgin birth, or even what Jesus Christ had come here to earth to accomplish. It took us a full week to convince them that Jesus Christ was not a personal friend of their mother's whom she frequently called on the phone—which seem to be the only occasions on which they could recall hearing His name. They finished the summer with us as well in our riding and rodeo program. Patricia has become a rather effective barrel racer. Elizabeth did not seem to enjoy riding but is not ineffective with a lariat.

Their regular studies through the fall have been adequate, but, Mr. Glass, we are concerned for them. They seem to have no contacts beyond the school grounds. They are the only students to stay on during holidays and term breaks and have just today informed me that they will be here over Christmas. While it was their mother who enrolled them here, we have been unable to get a response from her to our pleas for help in this matter.

The tuition was paid through the first of October, and has not been paid since. But this is not our first concern, for we are a Christian and not a capitalistic operation. We think, Mr. Glass, they do not belong here. While I would not call them godless girls, the concept of a deity has little relevance to them. They need parental guidance, perhaps yours as opposed to their mother's. They are falling under evil influences. To wit: We have one rather incorrigible boy here who is kept on because his father is a minister whose congregation in Boise contributes rather heavily to our school. When the boy learned that Mrs. Glass had appeared unclothed in a national magazine, he defied your daughters to pose for such pictures for his own camera. They did.

We will, of course, not turn them out, Mr. Glass, but they need help of a different sort than we can give them. We would appreciate your earliest reply on this matter and, if possible, $978 to cover their last two months' expenses.

Yours in Christ,
Ernestina Bagshaw,
Headmistress

Jason Glass did not even take the time to be infuriated or exasperated at this one. Rather, he telephoned Sybil and asked that Duncan be sent up sometime within the next hour, which would be about two earlier than the boy normally appeared at Glass's cottage for their traditional Sunday evening suppers and whatever man talk a glum writer and a retarded boy could make together. Then he phoned an airline hot-line number, located a flight that took the polar route from Seattle to London and flights that connected with that one from Billings to Seattle on the front end and from London to Prestwick on the back end. He set the departure date for Sunday, the twenty-first of December, which would have them arrive at Prestwick in the early afternoon of Monday, the twenty-second. Then he called Sybil back and asked if he could borrow her car to go to Kyle on that day, found Sybil no longer home but got Clyde in her place, and was told that he could borrow it but would find a bomb rigged to the ignition switch if Glass didn't keep his own pants zippered and Sybil's up. Glass promised. Then he sat down at his typewriter and wrote a short letter to Ernestina Bagshaw enclosing a check for a thousand dollars (written on Farquhar's account) and asking that Patricia and Elizabeth be delivered to the Billings airport on the morning of the twenty-first. Then he remembered passports and almost undid all the instructions and reservations but then didn't undo them and noted on his calender for the next day to call the American consulate in Edinburgh for help. Then he wrote a one-sentence letter to Margot in Truro telling her he had placed himself in charge of the girls and hoped, with her in another country, he could teach them common decency so they would not pose nude for twelve-year-old perverts with cameras. And he sealed both letters, attached special-handling postage to them, and—when Duncan arrived in his pony cart—gave the boy the coins of his choice to trot them through the snow to the post office at Loch Killilan. When the boy had departed, Glass fell exhausted into the overstuffed armchair and went to sleep.

But something was still missing, something which had cost a respected doctor his optimism, a lovely woman her sanity and her beauty and eventually her life, another woman hers as well. And Glass was haunted by the fact that his own and Farquhar's and perhaps even Ann's might still be in jeopardy also. As Glass and Ann worked from eight until five at the kitchen table each day, editing and polishing the story of Roberts Menzies with only a short break at noontime to eat lunch and make love, this missing detail gnawed at him and continued to even at night when they tried to relax at The Angus Bull with Charles Peebles or Mrs. Sciennes or Henrietta or even, at times, Clyde—whoever wandered in and sat down with them. No matter when or where, it continued to pound at him. Not because he feared he would never find it out, but because he knew he would. He had found out everything else, so this was not likely to remain undetected even if he wanted it to—which he did.

He tried to fight his mind away from it on the sixteenth, a Tuesday, when he and Ann took a day trip to Inverness to buy Christmas presents for Duncan and Patricia and Elizabeth, but he could not. Ann picked out an entire line of clothing for girls ten and twelve, while Glass went through sporting equipment and coin collections in search of something Duncan could use and enjoy. And still he thought about it as they ate dinner at the Station Hotel and took the late train back to Kyle.

On the seventeenth, together with Duncan, they climbed up a steep wall at the top of The Gap above Henrietta's house and cut down three small pines to be Christmas trees for the three occupied houses in The Gap. On this day, Glass had managed to keep his mind free of Menzies reflections until they dragged the last pine past the two houses that faced each other on the Gap road—the one still whole in which Roberts and Maria had lived for five years, the one badly shattered in which Roberts and the kaffir had had their surgery and in which Maria De Jager had been destroyed by her father-in-law and her stepson—and again he began thinking.

On the eighteenth, Glass's cottage was jammed by more people than it could accommodate but all were happy and no one minded. For the first time since the Dunedin Games, every living Menzies was in one place—Farquhar, Henrietta, Clyde, Sybil, Duncan—and now Ann, who was ultimately a Menzies as well—and five Peebles, two Sciennes, Ross and his wife, the postman and his, the minister from the Scottish Rite church, various drinking cronies whose names Glass hardly knew but whom he had invited anyway, plus at least ten others whom Glass had never laid eyes on but who had been invited by others. Which made the number about three dozen, and most of those by midnight were happily drunk. Glass waited until he felt Farquhar was alcoholically receptive, then mentioned that he would be by the next day with the final manuscript of *The Legacy of Ladysmith.* Farquhar agreed too readily to have fully understood the import of what he had been told. He waved assurance with his sling-encased arm and turned back to his mug of beer and his gesticulations with Clyde and old Peebles.

The party broke up after one, and Jason and Ann were in bed by two. But Glass could not sleep, and he knew this would be the night it would happen to him.

When he was a child there had been a particular piece of movie film he liked his father to run on his home projector. It showed young Jason Glass, a stubby-legged lad of about five, flailing a shish kebab skewer loaded with meat and vegetables at his sister during a Fourth of July seashore barbecue. In the midst of his fun, all the food suddenly shot off the end of it and spewed into the air, staining relatives' shirts and pants and smearing his Aunt Evelyn's eyeglasses. For which, still on camera, young Jason Glass got a swat on the backside that made his lower lip curl and his eyes flood with tears which were quickly on his cheeks. What a slightly older Jason Glass had liked about this film was to see it run in reverse—himself crying up his cheeks and drying, his lower lip going from half-mast to immediate smile, all the stains leaping from the clothing as in television commercials, all the food which was currently airborne finding its way in the exactly proper order back onto the skewer, and the people who had turned to gawk suddenly back and smiling the way they had been, talking to one another in reverse, except that the film was silent.

Research is such a reversal of film so that somewhere, you hope, everything falls into its proper place in the only order it could ever have had. And you who researched presumed that at least you who had reversed the film would be able to finish smiling.

But now the missing factor presented itself to Jason Glass's mind, the one they had overlooked—or at least, he had—all along, and it was too appalling to think about. But suddenly everything was back on the skewer in the only possible order. And no one would smile, because now the past, and the present it had produced, was more horrible than anyone had imagined. He heard Ann sleeping soundly beside him, and at first his heart just pounded, but then his mind and soul were consumed with bitterness and hatred, and he leaped from the bed and reacted.

28 *THE SIBYL'S CAVE*

He ran down the narrow winding staircase, hitting his head as he frequently did in lunging off the bottom step into the hallway that led to the sitting room. He cursed. Rummaging through party debris, he found the phone book and fingered his way to the name of Peebles, tearing each earlier page in the alphabet as he discarded it. He found the number he wanted, misdialed once, hung up before it rang, dialed it again.

"Hello, Charles," he said, his voice trembling with hurry and anticipation. "This is Jason Glass. Look, I'm sorry to wake you." He tore through the Inverness newspaper as he spoke, ripping that as well in seeking the page he wanted, cursing silently the fact that there had to be pages he didn't. "But I need your help."

The groggy voice on the other end, probably just out of a stuporous sleep induced by plenty of beer and eggnog, tried to comprehend such a phone call at three thirty in the morning. Ann had by now come downstairs and was still wrapping herself in a robe against the chill of the unheated room which Glass, in his pajamas, apparently was not aware of. Like Peebles, she did not know what to make of this.

"The best time to get there is"—he scanned the column in the paper—"is four thirty-five. Can you get right over here?" Pause. "No, no, trust me. It can't wait. Bring your pickup truck and make sure you've got a shovel and a pick in it. Wear heavy boots. And . . . Charles . . . do you own a gun?" Pause. "You don't have something smaller? A handgun?" Pause. "All right, then, that will have to do." Another, longer pause. "I'll explain when you get here." He knew if he explained now, Peebles would never come. "Don't worry, I'll take the risks. You'll be safe." He hung up before the young man could object further.

He spun back through the room and was surprised to see Ann gaping at him, clutching her robe tightly to her neck as Glass unbuttoned his pajama top. "Look, Ann, damn it, you knew all along. Call Ross. His number's penciled into the front cover of the phone book. Tell him to get to the castle right now. We've got to be there at four thirty." He sped by her back up the stairs, stripping himself naked as he went. He ripped through his drawers, pulling out underwear and donning it as he groped through another drawer for socks, which he pulled free of one another with his free hand and teeth. He heard Ann hanging up the phone downstairs after having done as she was told. She returned to the bedroom.

"Jason, what is this all about?"

"Ann, you know damn well what it's about. Is Ross coming?"

"Yes, he said he'd be there at the end of the causeway, but he'd like to know what you have in mind. Why can't this wait till daylight?"

"It could. But then I'd have to wait another twelve hours, and I'm not up to that anymore." He pulled on his shirt and an old pair of pants and began kicking through the closet for a pair of high rubber Wellingtons he had bought in Inverness the week before.

She tried to grasp him around the shoulders, but he pushed her roughly aside. "Jason, I don't understand. Really I don't. Please tell me." He cursed under his breath while he pulled on the boots and said nothing more. "I'm coming with you if you won't tell me, then," she said, more angrily now. She pulled her nightgown over her head, and now she was unaware of the cold as well as she snatched a pair of panties from her drawer and pulled them on, then a pair of jeans and a sweatshirt and, seeing Glass's feet, a pair of boots that resembled his. Her heart was pounding as fast as his was, though her fear was of the unknown whereas his was, now, of the known.

"You told me he had failed, Ann," Glass nearly wailed now. "But he didn't, did he?"

"Who?" She was clearly in ignorance of what he was up to, and he relished that.

"Your father. The honorable Hamilton Macgregor, M.D., Esquire, and all that. Friend to the people as long as you accepted his friendship on his terms and didn't ask questions."

"What do you mean? He did not fail. He was a good man. Everyone thought so. No one would call him a failure." She was hurt and now chased him down the steps.

"You told me yourself he had failed, but you were lying to cover up the shitty bottom of this mess." He noticed a forgotten cigarette case on the coffee table, picked it up, and instinctively slipped it into his shirt pocket.

"*I* told you?"

"Not in his nose-wiping and wound-patching and his stethoscoping. In his research. You knew what he did, and that's why you quit the profession! You couldn't bear to think about it, could you?"

"Goddamn it, Jason, I don't know what you are talking about. The only research he ever failed at was his Sibyluma scheme, and . . . yes . . . in that he failed."

Glass leaned against the front door, peering out for Peebles' headlights. "How did he fail? Describe the failure to me. What was he working on—mice and rabbits?"

"And rats. They were approved lab animals. It's done everywhere—Edinburgh, the Sorbonne, Johns Hopkins. It's accepted prac—"

"I don't give a damn about the rodents. But what happened when he injected the stuff into them? Did it slow the vital organs and signs and whatever he needed slowed?"

"Yes."

"Then you lied when you said he failed—I knew it! You're trying to convince yourself that he did."

"He *did* fail. Jason, there are hundreds of drugs around which do exactly what they are supposed to do but which have side effects which make them useless. This one had two such—"

"Like he couldn't get the little bunny whose ass he shot it into to hop at regular speed ever again."

"Well, yes. And—"

"Nor think as fast again?" Glass was baiting her, loving it because now he hated her for not having told him. But she *had* told him once, he recalled, so now he hated her because he had not understood it.

"Well, actually, there was brain damage in some of the animals. They—"

"Oh, lovely, Ann. Retarded rabbits, hopping in slow motion, mistaking garden hoses for vegetation. So what did he do with these poor creatures he had ruined for life?"

Ann was angry at the insinuations. "Jason, don't talk like an amateur! You know nothing of medicine. When medical experiments are completed, the animal is put out of its misery. It's *always* done that way, not—"

"And was that your job? Clubbing the little rascals on the head with a shovel?" She started to cry now, and that had been his goal. "Sibyluma! Ha! It was *not* renamed after your sister, was it? It wasn't *that* Sybil at all, right?" He could see the headlights winding up the snow-covered road from the bottom of The Gap, so he threw on his heaviest coat and went outside. She followed, zipping her pea coat as she came. "You're not coming. Get back inside."

"I am, Jason," she insisted. "I don't know what this is about, but if my father is to be—" He slapped her across the mouth, and she bled instantly from her lower lip. When Peebles pulled the truck to a halt after turning it around, she tried to wrench open the door and get in first, but he pulled her backwards, and she fell on her back in the snow. He pounced in next to Peebles, who stared in amazement.

"Pull out fast, Charles. I don't want her in on this." Peebles tried to oblige, not sure he wanted to be in on it himself, but in his rearview mirror he could see that Ann had already thrust herself into the bed of the truck. Glass ordered him to forget her and drive as fast as he could for the castle.

Peebles did drive as fast as he could, but the roadway was covered with two inches of gummy snow, in which his wheels had to turn five or six times to accomplish the results of one normal rotation. Several times they skidded toward the steep embankment above Loch Killilan; other times they fishtailed badly on the roadway, once did a full spin. Peebles and Glass were breathing hard, the former from his driving, the latter in anticipation of what he knew now was about to come. They passed only one other driver in the entire ten-mile distance, and this turned out to be Ross, who was taking it more carefully. Glass shouted out the window to him to hurry as they overtook him.

Ross pulled into the carpark about three minutes after Peebles' truck and found the three people waiting impatiently for him: a burly man with a shovel, a medium-sized man with a hunting rifle, and a tall girl with a pick. Glass was waving to him insistently to run from his car; but Ross, the professional, took his time. No one seemed to have a flashlight, so he unhooked his from beneath the dashboard of his car. When he shined it on them, he noticed the Macgregor girl was bleeding from her lower lip. He whispered a confused greeting to the three, but noted that Glass was making no attempt to conceal his voice.

"Are you armed, Inspector?" Who was in charge here?

"No." He felt Glass thrust the hunting rifle in his hands.

"You know what to do with that better than I do," Glass said, and he took the flashlight in its place. Then, incredibly, Glass reached into the driver's window of the truck and began beating a staccato rhythm on the horn. Though its sound was somewhat diminished by the Loch mist and the still-falling snow, it was loud enough, and soon a light went on in the upper reaches of the castle. They could see the square profile of Farquhar Menzies appear and begin cranking the window open. Glass signaled him with the light.

"Menzies, it's Glass, and Ross is with me. Get down here . . . and *hurry*."

"Glass, blast it. What is this? Are you mad? Or drunk, Glass —which is it?"

"Neither one, Menzies," Glass yelled up at him in the thick wet night air. "The kind of stuff you people do for fun is enough to sober anybody up. Now get down here . . . and bring the keys."

"Which keys?" To Ann's ear and to Ross's the tone of this response was wrong. It was a question Farquhar did not have to ask because they could tell he already knew the answer.

"Quit frigging around, Menzies. You know which keys. It's getting late. Stop stalling." He shined the flashlight beam upward and struck Menzies in the face. It was a frightened face.

"I don't have them."

"Bullshit!" The expletive echoed in the mist, so shrilly had Glass yelled it. He seemed crazed to all who heard him. "Get down here, damn it. You're going to do the talking then. And hurry up—it's almost a quarter to five."

Ross took over. "I command you, Mr. Menzies, in the name of the Crown, to get down here this instant."

It was ten more minutes before he arrived. At which point Glass, still with the light, set out in front and led the four behind him downward into the Loch. It had passed low tide at four thirty-five and was rising toward their ankles already. Ross and Menzies had not worn boots and felt the freezing water in their shoes.

"Glass, I beg of you, let this alone. I will admit anything you want. Let's leave it till tomorrow afternoon, when we can handle it more safely." Menzies sounded as if he were crying in the darkness as they sloshed along below the causeway, bypassing the first arch, and then the second, but stopping at the third.

"Don't worry, Menzies. I'll not die of fright the way your wife did—nor will these people. They don't have the prospect she did of having to know the truth and then live with it. Isn't that what killed her, Farquhar?"

"She died of exposure."

"Medically, yes, Farquhar. But what was a sane woman doing walking around in the middle of winter in a nightgown and a robe? Aren't you cold, Farquhar?—I am. Her curiosity got too much, didn't it? So she checked the tide table and came out here and looked for herself, wearing slippers or maybe even barefoot in this ice pond, and then found she did not have enough nerve left to make her legs operate and get her back. Or maybe she just didn't want to get back, did she? She didn't want to wind up mad the way your mother did."

He could hear Menzies whimpering freely as they ducked under the last arch and Glass shined his light on a severely rusted steel door which was already beginning to be resubmerged beneath the rising waters. An aluminum padlock of more recent vintage than the door bolted it shut to the stone walls of the causeway. Glass demanded the keys.

"I tell you I don't have them. They're left with the gatekeeper in case of . . . We can get in through the back passage, but I caution you that—"

Glass interrupted the excuses by snatching the shovel from Peebles' hands and clanging it a half-dozen times full force against the rusty door, slivers of corroded metal dropping off it into the water with each contact. He shrieked, "Open up, damn it!" several times as he did so. No one responded, so he tossed the shovel back at Peebles and jerked the pick away from Ann and began hacking one-handed at the lock, nearly hitting her on the first downstroke as he did so. Ross snatched at his arm to restrain him.

"Glass, come now." He took the flashlight from his hand and shined it in such a way that they could study each other's faces in the rank darkness. Condensation dropped off the ceiling of the stone archway above them, running down their faces like tears. The water was over their ankles by now. "Yes, Glass, I have figured out what you are thinking. And I think you are right." The expression on Glass's face seemed one of gratitude. He did not speak. "Now, we must proceed with caution, musn't we?" In the light he could see some of the tension go out of the writer as the muscles in his shoulders relaxed and he allowed them to drop. At which point Ross ordered everyone behind him, handed the flashlight back to Glass, then raised the hunting rifle and aimed one shot at the lock. The blast echoed piercingly under the causeway, and the lock shattered and vanished into the black water. Ross opened his palm toward Peebles, and the young man handed him another shell, which the detective loaded into the empty chamber of the rifle.

Glass more calmly now hooked the point of the pick inside the door hasp and levered it against the stone wall to force it open against the rising water. When he had it far enough, Peebles slipped the shovel head inside the crack to hold it there, and then all of the intruders except Menzies used their collective strength to pull it wide enough to permit access. Farquhar stood behind them, hoping probably that it could not be done; but when he had seen that their desire was too great to be denied, he spoke.

"It would have been safer to go by the rear staircase, which you ought to have known about, Ross. Let me go first. Let me do the talking. There is great danger, I warn you."

Everyone was inclined to grant the request. Menzies took the light from Glass and shined it down a short passageway. Water flowed freely along the floor through the door, which had been left open. It was calf-deep and telltale as they shuffled through it. As the passageway bent to the right, Menzies put his hand on a wall switch and flipped it carefully. Ross cocked his gun as the room before them illuminated itself.

What they saw so stunned them that all but Menzies forgot his caution. They entered the room and stood abreast of each other, like an army marching forward with fixed bayonets—except that all they had was one hunting rifle, and only Peebles among them was the right age or sex to be a soldier.

The room was approximately twenty feet square. Three walls were stone as the passage had been, but the fourth was covered to its full height and distance by an enormous photograph which Jason Glass, at least, had seen many times before in his research. It was the picture of Ladysmith on Mournful Monday, October 30, 1899, the street before the Town Hall jammed with horses and mules and oxen, with soldiers mounted in the center and others on foot on the pavement before the shops, with kaffirs staring at the confusion behind them, with dust swirling in the air above the activity, nearly obliterating Harvey Greenacre's store and the Town Hall and the trees and the electric poles and Convent Hill behind them. It was life-sized, the horses as huge as real cavalry horses, the kaffirs as small as real kaffirs. It was a street on which Jason Glass himself had stood nearly three-quarters of a century later and on which he was now standing almost as it had been then. And the room itself was a litter of strewn tables. On one were bound leather volumes, the top one entitled *Intestinal Surgery*; on another were medals with their ribbons attached, not neatly displayed but in a heap, as if someone did not care about them or chose one randomly each day to wear and tossed it back there at night. On another were guns—large and small—pistols and rifles, some apparently in one piece but others disassembled. Strewn on the floor and, because of the open door, floating up with the water level were pieces of khaki clothing—shirts, pants, a jacket, even an inverted pith helmet of an older shape. And on the table nearest the opposite wall, with a desk chair behind it, were scattered books and papers. The books were green, paper-covered, yellowing with age, pages hanging loosely from them, and Glass knew instantly, despite his amazement, what green books they were. And the papers he knew too, without even crossing to inspect them—they were the three hundred photocopied sheets that Glass had progressively turned over to Farquhar Menzies for his approval, understanding only now why they had seemed acceptable on the day they were delivered but not so several days later. In the room beyond this one was the interminable electrical snapping which gave light and heat and convenience to most in the castle but gave, even more, a sense of purpose to one.

And now the lights went out, and in the total blackness they heard the voice. It was shrill, nearly hysterical.

"Welcome, Mr. Glass." Glass felt himself pale in the darkness. The voice was sexless, it was pitched so high. "I knew you would be along. Your curiosity could not control itself even once, could it?" The voice was getting closer now, and angrier. They could hear the person breathing hard as he or she sloshed through the water on the floor, assuming a position no one could be sure of. Glass could hear Peebles to his left gasp helplessly, Farquhar to his right still crying, Ross beyond him cock the rifle again. Ann made no sound whatsoever, as if she finally understood what Glass had thought she had already known an hour earlier.

The screeching voice resumed through a metallic rattling sound now. "Do you close the door when you defecate, Mr. Glass, or do you do it where people can watch you? Do you spend your whole life doing it, Mr. Glass, or just a few minutes each day? Do people peek in on you to enjoy you so exposed?" The combination of snarl and shriek was almost unbearable to the ear and to the soul. "You did not do well enough, Glass. Don't people deserve better than miserable efforts like this one? Don't people live too long to have it all amount to only this?" And now they knew where the voice was, for they heard a sheaf of papers spew violently into the air and then cascade into the water on the floor. Glass felt Farquhar move forward beside him.

"Please, please, I tried to tell him the way it should have been—"

His words were cut short by the most savage gunshot blast that Glass had ever heard. An orange ball of light flared up from the far wall behind the desk, illuminating for only an instant the dwarflike figure who fired it, and Glass heard Farquhar gag violently and splash forward to the floor. And Ann screamed and identified where she was, and then the lights went on brilliantly and the gun fired again and she spun violently to her right and crashed headlong into the table of books, then off the end and face down into the water.

And then Ross could see his target and aimed at it, but Peebles and Glass did not see him take aim and both lunged across the room and then across the desk. But the dwarf stepped sidewise as it loaded its Mauser with its teeth, and Peebles missed with his lunge entirely. But Glass caught it full force around the shoulders, forcing the muzzle of the gun to the ceiling, and the gun discharged again and the bullet ricocheted. And then Ross's bullet missed because the dwarf had moved and his shot hit the wall behind where it had stood. But Jason Glass had the dwarf around the shoulders as if embracing it, less than three inches between their faces, and he could see the grimacing mouth and sunken cheeks and the long white hair which hung below its shoulders and the single good eye and the gaping socket of the bad one where there was nothing but tissue and veins and nerves which no longer served any purpose and had not for almost seventy-four years. And the thrust of his forward movement carried the dwarf back into the picture, and there its ribs and its skull seemed to shatter from the dual impact and its knees collapsed. And Roberts Menzies, still locked to Jason Glass, embracing him in return now, slithered down the photograph and they both went under the water. And Jason Glass pulled himself up on his knees and, choking badly, crying, reached weakly back to extract his adversary and caught him by his single arm and pulled him to the surface; but by then he was a sack of crushed bones, bones that had lasted a hundred and three years, twenty-five more than they should have. So he thrust him under the water again and held him there until the translucent blue vein in his neck ceased to pulsate.

29 *THE LEGACY OF LADYSMITH*

THE DIFFERENCE BETWEEN THE PAST and the future, Jason decided as he fastened the neck button of his pea coat, is that the past must be accepted while the future can be shaped. But before it can be shaped, it must first be imagined. And even if it is imagined in impossible ways, the imagination has a reality of its own which can transcend—for a time, anyway—the dictates of necessity. He had to believe that.

Duncan was walking on the thick ice of the Gap lake, his stocking cap pulled so far down that little of his face showed above his turned-up collar. One end of his scarf was tight to his nose, but the other end trailed down his back almost to the ground. His pant legs were tucked into his boots, though his boots flapped their unstrapped buckles about like bells. Charlie was imitating an iceboat, racing up a head of steam, then digging his paws in all of a sudden and careening sidewise and backward until his momentum stopped. In a sense, Glass could not help envying their eternal innocence.

It was so cold that the funeral that morning was conducted swiftly. Farquhar and Roberts were laid to rest, side by side, in the small clan cemetery at the extreme west side of the island in Loch Duich, next to Catherine; Owen; Bruce; Angus; Angus' wife, Margaret; and all those who had come before them and so given them life. Then the small group had dispersed—there had only been Jason, Henrietta, Sybil, Clyde, and Duncan—each to his or her own shelter and own thoughts. Shortly after lunch Duncan had come by with Charlie, almost as if he knew that Jason needed not to be alone. And so they had walked along the lake, even though the temperature was only twenty degrees and the winds were strong and peppered with sleet. Jason had had no hat, so before long his hair was white, his face leathery from the cold. He hardly felt it.

He fought off the sense of finality that emerged from what had happened three days before. There was now simply nothing left to know; so the project which had not only given him identity but also affirmed his worth to himself and others was now, simply, *done*. A terribly powerful word. He thought of the rock across the lake beneath two inches of snow: M.D.J. IS DONE. And surely she was, at least in body. Hardly in spirit, however. Maybe with Roberts' death that would finally die as well.

He—Jason—was alive. He was not yet *done*, though he had no idea what his next move should be. He supposed he should rewrite the last chapter of *The Legacy of Ladysmith*, but that would take less than a day. He had no money—his own was tied up, and his benefactor was dead. He had no home, though he did have shelter. He had no friends, save a simple young boy who gave him love and companionship but little else. Henrietta was preparing to leave the district for good, and Clyde and Sybil were speaking of divorce, the only issue being who would take (not get) Duncan. No one seemed inclined to speak to Jason, the general feeling being that whatever the truth was, it would have been better off left unknown. It was almost as if they blamed him for the truth's having turned out to be as it was. Yet he held nothing against them.

Duncan was throwing snowballs at Charlie now, and Charlie was managing to dodge into the path of every one of them as he made motions to do just the opposite. He began barking in irritation. When Duncan stopped, however, Charlie lost his *raison d'être* and openly began to bait his master to resume his harassment. Duncan did, and Charlie began barking again. The wind blew so loudly that sometimes his barks were entirely obscured. As Glass crunched along the snow-impacted ground he almost wished that someone would at least fire a shot at him so that he would have some purpose return to his life, even if that was only to escape an adversary. Life, all life, was simply too complete. Everything made sense, at least logically. That is not the state most human beings prefer to attain, no matter how relentlessly they seek it.

Al Mentosi, his friend in St. Louis who had sent him the information about Bob Menzy's role in the World's Fair shoot-'em-up, had remarked to him once that even good fiction did not tie things up so firmly. Readers wanted, he said, a "point of intrigue" at the end at which they could imagine the future for themselves, shape the destiny of the characters to that which they wished them to have. In a sense, he said, every moment in all our lives was such a "point of intrigue," for who knew what the next one would bring? We could let Fate hand it to us, as a novelist hands his characters their individual ends, or we could imagine the future and so at least try to shape it—until we die, anyway.

Jason crunched on, occasionally lifting his head into the wind to see the steady stream of white smoke lifting from his cottage chimney. He thought of the last bottle of Scotch he still had left and of the warm chocolate he would make for Duncan and of the warm fire that Charlie would curl up in front of, so closely that they would have to put their feet on his back to keep them near it.

Jason tried to imagine his future from the point of view of what was apparently a terminal moment. But only apparently. He would find his way home, somehow. He would get some money from his book about the Menzies. Farneswells, in fact, owed him an advance which, because of Farquhar's subvention, he had never even bothered to ask for. He would find his daughters, even though he knew that Margot had gotten them out of the Montana Christian Academy before they could fly to Scotland as he had planned. He would find them. And he would have another idea for another book, and so he would—someday not far ahead—have a purpose again.

And Ann was not dead—yet. She could still live. The doctors in Edinburgh had said "critical," not "terminal." She had a one-in-five chance of making it. Those were not bad odds. And even if her left arm *would* be permanently paralyzed, *he* still had two; and three between them would be enough to care for three children—one arm apiece for Patricia and Elizabeth and Duncan—at least until they had another one or two to have to share them with. One in five was pretty good. It could have been one in ten.

Jason could imagine, from his point of intrigue, a morning in the following July—it would have to be that far away, he had been told—in which a young South African man named Paul Krige would bring a bottle of champagne to Waverley Station in Edinburgh to see them off. They would try to pop the cork quietly so that the station guards would not challenge them; then they would help Ann pour hers as she held the glass in her good hand. And they might sneak little sips to the three kids just so they would feel included. And he could imagine them having to drink it quickly so they could make the northbound train, which would take three hours to get to Inverness because it insisted on stopping at every place along the line.

He could imagine them arriving late in Inverness so that they would have to run to catch the next one, the one that would take yet another two hours to thread its way through the summer green of Achnasheen and Glencarron and Strathcarron and finally to the south of Loch Killilan rather than to the north simply because Angus Menzies had willed it to in 1871 and had underscored his will with the great Culloden cannon. And he could imagine them, all five of them, detraining there and being picked up by Henrietta, who had not gone away after all. And with the children riding in the bed of her pickup, they would pass the ferry for Skye, where Bruce and Angus Menzies had brought the cannon across at the height of the Great Storm of 1925, and the house where Jason and Ann had first made love more than fifty years later.

He could imagine them passing the Castle Menzies, a National Trust monument by then, where in 1924 Roberts Menzies and the kaffir man had delivered Farquhar Menzies while the dreaded Maria De Jager was being sealed, drugged, in a coffin for shipment on a freight train to Glasgow. And where, again more than fifty years later, this same Roberts Menzies would kill this same Farquhar Menzies to whom he had given life and do it with a German Mauser. And where Jason Glass would kill Roberts Menzies.

As he came within a hundred yards of his cottage door, Duncan and Charlie beside him now, he could imagine that next July, when there would be no snow on the road: he could imagine them—he even put Charlie in the truck bed now—passing the small churchyard in which Duncan had uncovered two empty graves and a diary which was really the truest clue of all to the past and to the future that the past had produced and allowed. They would pass the ruined house, which by then would no longer be ruined, which would be greatly restored and even about to be inhabited, the house in which Roberts had had his surgery and in which his second wife had sought refuge from a storm and had been killed by a cannonball rather than the lightning bolt she had feared.

He could imagine all these things, but he did not want to imagine too much. He did not want to sap the future of its intrigue. Perhaps he would write another book—he would see what the reviews of *The Legacy of Ladysmith* told him and respond accordingly. Perhaps Ann would continue with Farneswells if they allowed her to work mainly from the Lochs, or perhaps she would not even then. Perhaps she would decide to practice medicine after surviving the one-in-five odds and staying seven months in the hospital to recover. A high possibility, Glass thought. A doctor did not need both arms, necessarily. Perhaps they would go to America instead, if Jason's book produced enough money. But perhaps they would not.

As he unlocked the cottage door, he pushed Duncan and Charlie through quickly so that the warmth of the room would not escape. Charlie shook off his coat in front of the fire, steam hissing from it as the snow on his back struck the embers. Jason helped Duncan off with his boots.

He knew, once this one-in-five business was behind them, that they would respond rather than react, and act upon what they knew now that they hadn't known before because they had not then lived enough years yet to be able to know it. They would be happy with their successes and tolerant of their failures, modest about their attainments and honest about their shortcomings, would live their lives as fully and courageously as they were able to and die when their time came.

But not before.